EUGENIA DMITRIEVA
VASILY MAHANENKO

THE RENEGADES

*Books are the lives
we don't have
time to live,*

Vasily Mahanenko

THE BARD FROM BARLIONA
BOOK 1

MAGIC DOME BOOKS

The Renegades
The Bard from Barliona, Book # 1
Copyright © E. Dmitrieva, V. Mahanenko 2018
Cover Art © Timur Kvasov 2018
Translator © Boris Smirnov 2018
Published by Magic Dome Books, 2018
All Rights Reserved
ISBN: 978-80-88295-25-9

TABLE OF CONTENTS:

CHAPTER ONE

TOAD ROUSED US AT THE UNHOLY HOUR of eleven in the morning. We had played a corporate gig the night before and judging by the guys' faces, which looked like chewed up blotter, their impressions of the event hadn't yet settled in their long-haired skulls. Toad is Steve Michaels, our producer and manager. He earned his nickname through his savage gluttony and doughy, eternally-unhappy expression. Toad loomed over us with the demeanor of a disappointed parent.

"What the hell?" asked Beast, our bassist. His legal name was Edilberto, but his nickname did him more justice: Beast was as wild and unhinged in everyday life as he was on stage. Even I kept my distance when he was in a bad mood. At the moment, however, Beast spoke for all of us.

"The early bird gets the worm," Toad brandished a didactic finger.

Our manager liked to quote various popular proverbs and bits of folk wisdom. Either he thought it made him seem more respectable or he simply didn't have any thoughts of his own.

"Uh-huh. And the mangy old bird working the nightshift has already gotten an earlier worm," I countered.

Why was my leg still asleep? Why did my back ache so? Because it's better to sleep in a bed than splayed across the tattered armchair of a squalid hotel room. It was all thanks to Toad. He had again decided to save some money and get one room for all five of us. On the one hand, the price of a single room was clearly too much as it was and no one wanted to pay the extra money for another one. On the other hand, everyone had long since grown sick and tired of these teenage sleepovers. The guys had gallantly offered me the only bed in the room, but it stank so bad of cheap fabric softener that after I passed, only Beast risked sleeping in it. Judging by his gloomy mug and incessant scratching, he was already regretting that decision.

"Don't be a wise gal," Toad turned on me with gusto. "Instead of lounging around with these whisky-dicks, you could go down to the salon and make yourself look presentable. Don't forget that I'm the one who has to sell your mug."

"I'd rather you didn't," I objected. "I'd rather not be sold at all, not by the piece and not by the bulk."

"Ah, what sucker'd buy you anyway?" Toad swatted the air ruefully. "If you grew some tits, at least the paying public'd have something to look at. Hell, I'd even pay for the job." A note of hope sounded in Toad's voice as he broached one of his well-worn topics—and was promptly told to go to a well-known and well-studied address.

"What are you bugging her for, you toad?" Yuri intervened. Yuri Charsky was our unofficial leader, guitar soloist, backup vocalist as well as the *vox populi* on budgetary and everyday matters. He was also our champion booze swiller.

Like a spider's paw, Yuri's gaunt, tattooed arm appeared from the sleeping bag that enclosed its master and—judging by a muted clink—this morning's hair of the dog that bit master last night. The paw drew aside a corner of the sleeping bag, exposing Yuri's battered physique to the world.

"You spend too much time reading teen mags, Michaels." Yuri got up and brushed past Toad on his way to the mirror. "What a wreck..." He made a revolted grimace at his reflection. "We're rockers, Michaels, a dying breed. When it comes to the quickly fading epoch of true rock n' roll, you could say we're the last of the Mohicans. And here you are—part of the problem. All you seem to want is less lyrics and more cleavage. So let's figure it out once and for all: What do you want? Rock or striptease?"

"Why not both?" Toad churled. Happily though, this concluded any further discussion of surgically augmenting the band's creative journey, for the time being at least.

"All right," Charsky plunked down beside my

armchair and gave Toad an unkind glance. "Next item. What the feck did you wake us up so early for? Last night we toiled at that corporate thing until two and then went quaffing. And you won't let us sleep it off. Aren't you afraid of burning us out? Or do you have the replacements all lined up? Unless you've brought us some gig, there won't be any work today. I've got such a rattle in my head, you can hear it in the street. Hey Beast—wake Hal there, or he'll sleep through the entire band meeting!"

"I'm awake," the drummer objected without opening his eyes. "Why beat a dead snare? Yuri's right, Toad. Just give us the scratch and leave us alone so we can recover. Personally, I don't see myself rising before lunch."

"Money's all you lot think about." The very idea of paying someone sent a sharp pain coursing through Toad's heart, liver and kidneys. "But when it comes to thinking how you can earn it...Here I am, buzzing like a bee, wheeling and dealing, trying to come up with some lucrative gig for you..." Michaels swatted the air ruefully once again.

"Uh-huh, that's right," Charsky nodded frenetically. "You're a busy bee and we're a flea circus run amok. Speak your mind and all, but don't get carried away, aight? You make moola off us like Stromboli did off his puppets so don't act like some beneficent patron schooling his prodigal children."

To be fair, Yuri was exaggerating here. The

album we'd cut on budget studio time was selling poorly (to put it mildly) and even then only really among our band's local tribe of followers. Most of our income was trickling in from live performances at corporate gigs, weddings and other well-funded events. Naturally the well-funded revelers couldn't give a fig for our art. However, there was a deficit of live music in our part of the boondocks and everyone wants to get their rocks off to a tune. And so we'd migrate from Fidel Kennedy's birthday celebration to the wedding reception of one Anahit Agajanian, then rush over to the IPO for Horns&Hooves.com. Most of our work was as a cover band. We played old hits that had long since become social patrimony and seen their copyright lapse. But our own songs were popular with our crowds as well. Though, to be honest, we played them in the second set when the listening public had had its drinks and couldn't care less what to listen or dance to. We made up for the selling out by playing small, local concerts, but these only generated enough scratch to pay for gas, a street burger and a modest after-party—meanwhile, hunger came by each day.

Effectively, if we hadn't come across Michaels— who really was a wheeler and dealer—we wouldn't have even as much as we did. As frequently happens with musicians, we weren't very good at combining our art with business. We lacked the business acumen, the ROI synergy, the silvered tongue, and as a result Michaels became our dubious savior. And we were the same for him. In our age of growing unemployment, a former employee of a cultural center couldn't count on finding a full-time position with his skillset. With us he'd acquired a collective of four varying musical dispositions and begun spinning like a top, procuring work for us and percentages for himself. That's how we lived—without any particular affection for one another but with a clear understanding of mutual necessity. After all, the most upsetting thing was that we were good. It was just that proper TV and radio marketing was so expensive that our hopes of becoming independent individuals were melting away every passing day.

"We've earned our keep and then some," Charsky went on meanwhile. "Be so kind and toss the scratch on the table and stop acting like you're getting mugged."

This fiery speech was slightly ruined by Hal's smacking yawn and a deafening snore from Straus— our keyboard player and the last member of our band. Odd. I could swear that at the beginning of the conversation Straus was awake...

"Oh all right, what are you getting worked up for?" Toad began to backpedal. "I've come here with a once-in-a-lifetime offer. A chance to lock in an audience of millions for the next album."

These words woke everyone in the room in an instant. Even Straus—jabbed awake by Beast's elbow—sat up and began whirling his head, acting attentive.

"Well, get on with it," I prompted when the dramatic pause had lingered too long.

"Do you know where most of the youth who listen to rock hang out?" Michaels went on building suspense.

"Will you cut out your charades?" Beast, whose hangover had him in a fine, foul mood, banged the table. Everyone jumped, from Toad to Straus who finally woke up. "What'd you come up with, you toad?"

Michaels screwed up his face, but he'd grown accustomed to Beast's outbursts.

"In Barliona, my impatient friend. Just like the billions of our fellow citizens."

"In the game? What of it?"

"Why they're your target audience. What do you lot sing about? Epic battles, swords, magic, heroes, kings, warriors...All of that's in there, in Barliona. People play the game in pursuit of medieval romance."

"Okay, we get the idea," Yuri agreed. "What do you propose? You want songs about Barliona?"

"Precisely!" Toad grinned. "Just look at Nubar and the hits they have: 'Ballad of the Three Orcs and the Gnome' and 'Mommy's Little Griefer.' Or those other guys, what do you call them...Oh, right! Tarantula Progeny and their 'In the Name of Yalininka.' The devil knows what it all's about but the kids listen to it! Those bands hang out at the top of the charts for weeks at a time."

"As you yourself just pointed out, we'd be far from the first to write songs about games. What's the novelty?"

"You said yourself that you're talent," Michaels reminded. "Record a couple hits and people will talk about you. And we won't have to dump money on TV and radio campaigns."

"Well, I mean, I'm not against it," Straus spoke up. "I play Barliona myself. Never had any problems with it."

"Aren't you a gamer, Kierá?" Charsky turned to me.

He'd mangled my name the first day we met, stressing the last syllable and thereby creating my nickname.

"I'm more partial to the old school," I reminded him just in case. "Board games, classic singleplayer RPGs, casual free to play MMOs. I wouldn't know what to do in Barliona. And with the money I make, I couldn't afford an account or a legit capsule. But if you want to cover my, uh, marketing expenses—I'm all for it."

"Well what? It's not a bad idea," Beast agreed. "A chance to take a big leap."

Hal merely nodded mutely, as always agreeing with the majority opinion.

"Makes sense," Charsky concluded. "On the

one hand, no one feels like selling out, but on the other...It's the same crap we already write songs about. So instead of our abstract kingdom, we'll have..." He glanced over at Straus who was the most experienced gamer among us. "Malabar. Or Kartoss. Yeah, Kartoss is even cooler. Sounds more brutal. Don't they have like werewolves and zombies there?"

"Hey Michaels," I spoke up, "how are we going to eat while we're in game? It'll be a while until we get settled in and write something. Not to mention dealing with band practice and our social lives."

Here, I exaggerated—I didn't have any social life to speak off but it'd be a sin to pass up on the chance to squeeze the tight-wadded Toad when the chance presented itself.

"Uh-huh. And you'll have to buy us VR capsules," Straus pointed out. "And pay for our accounts. They're not exactly cheap."

The entire band nodded in unison.

"All right, I'll think of something. Maybe find some sponsors. Barliona's a global brand after all so it's worth the investment. As for now I want you lot to take some cold showers and deal with your business. Once we get the capsules, you'll be emerging only for band practice. Come on now my little chicken-hawks, left right left right..." Toad began to clap his hands the way he liked to do whenever he wanted to rally us.

"Are you daft?" Charsky rushed to deflate him. "What language do I need to tell you in that we're not doing a thing today?"

Michaels looked over our faces closely and waved his hand in resignation.

"Ah the hell with you artsy types..." He rummaged in his pocket and produced our pay. "Just don't go blowing it on spikes and Doc Martens."

"We're not punks, in case you haven't noticed," Charsky reminded.

* * *

As per tradition, band practice was held in the old garage that belonged to Straus' parents. Compared to us, Straus had been born with a silver spoon in his mouth, yet he never abandoned our band and would always contribute some scratch at the moment we needed it most. In return, we never gave him grief for his privileged origins. Today, instead of practice, we were doing our monthly planning. Shiny new gaming capsules—which Toad had acquired who knows how or where—were already installed in our apartments. Michaels teared up as he paid for our gaming accounts. All that was left was to figure out what we were actually going to do.

"I ain't deleting my main, don't even think of asking me to," Straus announced. "So we'll have to play for Kartoss. I transferred my character there last week."

"In that case, you should tell us what races to

choose and where to start," Charsky offered.

"I'm partial to goblins," Straus said—ignored the immediate gibes of 'bro, you're a goblin as it is'—and continued, "so it's better if you start with that race. The closer together you spawn, the easier it'll be to level up."

"Hang on," I spoke up, sensing that this thing was getting away from us. "Why are we doing this? To gain new experiences and new inspiration. But how are we going to gain anything new if we keep staring at our own ugly mugs? I see you guys out here all week as it is. And if we go in together, then we'll see all the same stuff and have the same thoughts et cetera. Nah. I suggest that we choose different races, get into the atmosphere of the place, level up a bit and only meet up later. We can share what's going on at our band practice and generate ideas based on it."

"Kierá's got a point," Charsky agreed. He opened a guide on the races of Barliona. "Goblins are taken, so let's choose from the other options."

Beast immediately grabbed a red orc, while Yuri settled on a drow. Hal couldn't make up his mind between taurens and trolls. In the end, he flipped a coin and got the former—a horned Kartossian minotaur.

"I like biotas," I announced, looking at the race of humanoid plants.

"That's a bit hardcore," said Straus, checking the guide.

"So I'll be a hardcore biota. If I can't handle it, I can always delete my character and roll a new one. The song inspiration's what's important and I'll keep that either way."

"Well, whatever you think's best," Charsky shrugged. "Since we seem to have figured things out, let's head home and enter the game."

CHAPTER TWO

M Y OLD BEATER—my former capsule, which had seen better days—had been shoved into the far corner to make space for the new, shiny, glinting model. I could hardly turn around in my room now, but I wasn't about to get rid of 'that heap,' as the Barliona technicians had referred to it. Call it what you like, but it's mine.

It took over six hours to set up the new system and adjust it to my psychosomatic metrics. I spent the time studying the guides and tutorials for new players. In principle, the basics were all pretty standard: HP and MP for health and mana, an array of character stats, and a leveling system based on gaining experience in the form of XP. Anyone who's played an RPG before would understand it intuitively. As for the nuances...Well, I could always consult the guides during the game. Plus I'm not so interested in the details. I'm playing this game to gather material, not to reach its top ranks.

Welcome to Barliona! Please set your sensory perception level.

Warning! We have not received permission to disable your pain filter.

Warning! We have not received permission to disable your pleasure filter.

Owing to the lack of permission, your minimum possible sensory filter setting is 70%.

They're a bit nuts here in Barliona—it's pure bureaucracy here. Okay, well, I'll just set my sensory filter to 90% and we'll see what the deal is later.

Choose initial settings.

Choose a faction to play for.

Selection made. Your faction is the Dark Empire of Kartoss.

Choose your race.

Biota. A race of humanoid plants. These creatures' odd appearance had really struck a chord with me. I'll check out the starting location, take a dip in a new culture, and if I don't like it, I'll make myself a new character.

You have chosen the biota race.

At the moment, it is daytime in Barliona. If you create a character during daytime, it will become a solar biota. If you wish to create a lunar biota, please await the coming of night.

Ho-hum. The game hasn't even started yet and I better RTFM. Turns out that the time of a biota's creation determines not just her type but her stats too. At least the race's stats were in the official game guide. Let's see now. What's a lunar biota all about?

Racial bonus to Intellect: +100%. Stat point cost: +4 for 1.

Racial penalty to Strength: -75%. Stat point cost: +1 for 3.

Racial penalty to Constitution: -50%. Stat point cost: +1 for 2.

Racial bonus to Agility: +25%. Stat point cost: +4 for 3.

Racial weakness: Cold sensitivity (+10% damage from ice).

Racial weakness: Fire sensitivity (+10% damage from fire).

Racial trait: Your character must drink water at least once every twelve hours to avoid the Desiccated status effect (+300% Stamina cost per action, -50% to MP regeneration).

Racial trait: Any drink that does not do damage, instantly restores Stamina completely and grants +100% to MP regeneration for 10 seconds.

Racial trait: Any bonuses from alchemical elixirs and potions are doubled. Biota do not consume solid food and receive no bonuses from it. There are numerous drinks that grant random effects to biota.

Racial trait: +100% to all damage types dealt by the character when fighting in natural terrain.

Racial trait: Due to their intimate bond with the natural world, biota are negatively affected by urban locations or other locations that are too different from their natural habitat. The strength of the Unnatural status effect depends on the type of location and the duration spent in it.

Racial trait: Immunity to herbal (and some other) poisons.

Racial trait: Most predators do not perceive the biota as prey and do not attack them.

Racial trait: Night vision. The biota's magical nature enables them to see even in utter darkness.

Racial ability: Natural camouflage. When in a natural environment, like a forest, biota gain the stealth movement ability.

Racial trait: Many of the other races do not trust biota.

Solar biota received a greater bonus to Agility and a smaller one to Intellect than lunar ones. I prefer spellcasting so I guess I'll have to wait until night falls. I suppose I'll spend the time reading up on this topic.

According to the game fora, the biota were introduced less than a month ago along with the last major update. Their home was in the borderlands of the Kartoss Empire. Though it wasn't clear where exactly. Maps of biota locations weren't publicly available and when I saw the asking price for a map of Kartoss, I began to consider a career in cartography. They sure do seem to be making hay in Barliona.

Walkthroughs and specialized guides for biota were likewise prohibitively expensive. Half the search results led to public versions full of incomprehensible gibberish, while the rest led to paywalls. What's there to pay for? What's so secret that I can't discover it after a few weeks of playing? A quest list full of 'go there and slaughter ten deer for dinner?' Nah. Human greed knows no limits. Stranger still was the utter absence of any videos about the biota starting locations. Was this paid content too?

The system notified me that night had come and I finally got back to creating my character.

You have chosen the biota race.

At the moment, it is nighttime in Barliona. If you create a character during nighttime, it will become a lunar biota. If you wish to create a solar biota, please await the coming of day.

Race selection confirmed.

Gender: female.

Do you wish to apply your real appearance to the character or create a custom appearance?

I paused for a moment and then chose the former option. I'm no beauty among beauties, but I've gotten pretty used to my face over the last 24 years and am perfectly happy with it.

The facial scan ended and a strange-looking creature appeared in the preview window. My avatar resembled a plant as much as a person. And its face resembled mine and someone entirely different too. At closer inspection, the green skin was an epidermis of cellulose—the superficial layer covering the stalks of a plant as I recalled from my botany courses. The system offered me a broad palette of colors to choose from, ranging from black to milk-white. I spent ten minutes turning my alter ego into a tomato, an eggplant, a rose, but in the end settled on the green option with whimsical little blue veins coursing through it.

The face too went through a series of transmutations. The system had recreated my general features, but the details were left up to me. As such, my eyebrows could be simple thick growths of the epidermis, thin lines of bark, petals, moss, lichen and a bunch of other options I'm at pains to describe. I suppose I don't remember my botany lectures that well.

I chose the small blue petals because they bore the closest resemblance to my ordinary brows from afar. The biota's eyes were larger than human ones. The irises were enormous and filled almost the entire pupil, which could be variously-colored too depending on what I wanted. The biota's ears were slightly pointed and consisted of leaves or flower petals. Hair was an entirely different story. It could be a bunch of twigs sticking out every which way like horns, it could be petals of various lengths and varieties, it could be stalks with leaves and even a topiaried bush.

I'm ashamed to admit that I spent no less than two hours fiddling with the various options and details. I swear I've spent more of my life playing around in character editors than watching make up tutorials and preening myself in front of a mirror. The result was well worth it though. My blue-green clone really stood out. Large, oblong flower petals covered me to my shoulders like a bird's plumage. I looked like an unholy combination of a tropical parrot, a liana, and the Original Sin. One of those unexpected love triangles.

"A creative salad," I concluded, lovingly examining the plant I'd created. "I guess it's time to experience the life of a vegetable!"

Attention! You may choose your character class if you like. Do you wish to do so now or will you make your selection later?

Yeah I wanna do it now! It's go bard or go home! This class was launched with the last update and there weren't any guides for it, if you didn't count random rants and observations to be found on the fora. Music was my life and I wasn't about to part with it, even in Barliona.

Your character is a bard.
Please enter a name.

A name...I paused to think. Well, it sure as hell isn't going to be my meatspace name. I need to come up with something symbolic. A musical name for a musical bard. One that has a ring to it. One that's memorable. Dispelling the sudden urge to have a laugh and name my character 'Franzlizst,' I went through the other options until Heinrich Heine's verses about an ancient legend floated up to my consciousness. Yup. That was it!

Your name is Lorelei the Captivating.
Subject scan complete.
Synchronization of player and character physiology in process...Physiology synchronized.
Starting location selected.
Character generation in progress...

The first thing I saw was a cocoon of a pleasant lavender color. A complete cocoon without a single seam or opening. And how am I supposed to get out of it?

Blinking in puzzlement, I reached out my hand and touched my prison's wall. Smooth and cool to the touch, it reminded me of something very familiar that

I couldn't place. Try as I could, I couldn't remember it and, meanwhile, the walls around me began to part, at first in the top of the cocoon and gradually lower and lower, so that a minute later I found myself in the center of a giant flower. Similar cocoons—some open and some still closed bulbs—grew around me. But I forgot about this unusual sight as soon as I saw the tree. And I mean, the Tree! A giant, colossal Tree, one of whose branches supported the bouquet I'd found myself in.

The giant's silhouette mesmerized as its myriad flowers glowed fluorescent against the background of a night sky. A forest version of Las Vegas, minus the deafening roar of the city. A wondrous fairy-tale giant in the midst of a no-less-fairy-tale night. A night filled with sounds that were both quiet and unusual. An owl hooted nearby, interrupting the singsong of the other birds. Cicadas were chirring happily, drowning out the already barely audible snatches of someone's conversation. There was neither the howling of security systems, nor the burble of advertising, nor the hiss of cars.

It was only too bad that I barely sensed any smells. In fact, I sensed very little at all. My sensory filter setting had a numbing effect on my body. I still felt touch, but the sensation was blunted.

This wasn't very pleasant on the whole, but I soon forgot about it all as I looked down. Even the darkness couldn't save me: Thanks to my night vision racial trait, I could see the entire length of the enormous distance that separated me from the ground. My mouth went dry and my head began to spin treacherously. I've been afraid of heights since childhood and even the certain knowledge that a fall here would result in a mere 12-hour rest from the game didn't do much to calm me (when you died in Barliona, you'd be ejected to meatspace and have to wait 12 hours before respawning again).

I quickly glanced away from the terrifying landscape and only now noticed the NPC biota standing beside my flower. From the petals on her head to the strange appearance of her floral dress, she was decked in shades of pale pink and red. Framed by the glowing shoots of the local flora, the NPC looked as regal as a garden queen.

"Lunar greetings to you, oh sister," the stranger smiled amicably, revealing a milk-white film in her mouth that was barely different than teeth.

Unwittingly I felt around my own teeth with my tongue and discovered a similar cellulose film there. Oh that's right—we can't eat anything. We can only drink. I guess the developers added this film as a reminder to the players.

"Erm...." I mumbled thoughtfully in reply. I still couldn't keep myself from glancing at the precipice beside me. What a start to my bard career—the eloquence was just pouring forth. If things keep on this way, I had better wait until they introduce a mime class.

I tried to focus on the NPC to stop thinking about the immense height separating me from the ground. At the same time, the thought that I should've chosen a dwarf as my race popped into my head. A dwarf wouldn't as much as clamber up a horse, much less a giant tree.

"Don't worry," said the imitator, noticing my discomfort. "Your Twilight Dream has ended and you shall now leave the Branch as a free citizen. The Tree never bore free citizens in former times, but lately many things have changed. In your Dream you beheld the world through the eyes of your brothers and sisters, but this knowledge is fragmentary and incomplete. I will help you gain your bearings and teach you everything you must know. My name is Amaryllis," the NPC introduced herself. "What is the name that came to you in your Dream? What is your name?"

"Lorelei."

"An unusual name."

Uh-huh. Right. And Amaryllis is so usual. Although...Maybe in the vegetable world it's as common as John, Li, Ivan, Mohamed...?

"Free citizens frequently dream unusual names before they wake," the NPC went on. "Come with me. We'll find you some proper integuments."

Great idea, I thought, following the biota—at the moment my 'integuments' could be only described as 'what the tree grew me in.' The typical loincloth of these kinds of games was in this case clusters of flowers in the proper locations. Moreover, I wasn't even really wearing this loincloth—it was growing out of me. I wonder what takes place in the local bordello? Do the petals simply vanish or do they kind of recede?

While I was contemplating the particulars of the local adult entertainment industry, Amaryllis confidently led me along the branch. Its width kept me from considering the long fall and the abrupt deceleration at the ground at the bottom, but my mind could not abandon the topic of falling. I wonder if anyone ever died right after creating their character?

To avoid looking over the edge, I began to look around, examining the neighboring branches. Most of them had bulbs like the one I started the game on— and here and there, I could see their petals opening to usher a new resident into Barliona. To my surprise, there were a lot more players than NPCs.

At the base of the grand branch—where it met the Tree's trunk—we found a spacious room full of mannequins wearing various clothes. Holy Spaghetti! I'd never have the imagination to design so many outfits with floral motifs, much less make them as pretty as these were. The NPC passed through this entire fashion show and stopped at some shelves full of green stacks.

"Here you go. An ordinary integument. Surely

in time you will find something more to your taste."

Items acquired:

Ordinary leaf pants. Durability 60. Physical damage resistance: 2. Item class: Common. Minimum level: 1. This item cannot be traded.

Ordinary leaf doublet. Durability 60. Physical damage resistance: 2. Item class: Common. Minimum level: 1. This item cannot be traded.

The set also included an ordinary jerkin and matching boots, no different in stats and requirements. Thanking the NPC, I dressed and immediately felt more confident. It doesn't do to go strolling around a city in your underwear, even if the city's just a virtual fantasy.

As soon as we left the 'dressing room,' Amaryllis stepped onto a giant leaf, which resembled a boat bobbing in the air and stared at me expectantly. A scene from the ancient movie *Honey I Shrunk the Kids* flashed through my mind. I felt like a tiny person about to climb aboard an immense bug and be carried away. Well, why not? Using this clumsy bit of escapism to trick my mind, I stepped aboard the leaf transport with the face of a brave explorer. The leaf rocked treacherously underfoot and I plunked down onto my rear entirely un-heroically. The loud guffaw of a player named Beastkiller the

Enlightened sounded from a nearby leaf.

"Relax! No one dies during the tutorial," he announced in an expert's tone and calmly followed his personal NPC guide onto a similar leaf-boat. I noted with some envy that the leaf didn't so much as sway beneath Beastkiller's weight.

Then the leaf I was sitting on drifted away from the branch and began to descend magically and smoothly like an elevator. I didn't risk getting up. Despite the barely-concealed laughter in Amaryllis' eyes, she didn't go so far as to make a comment. Either this was due to a sense of tact instilled in her by the developers or perhaps sitting while traveling in the leaf was a permissible manner of traveling after all.

Here and there, similar 'leaf elevators' were carrying players and NPCs among the Tree's branches. And it should be mentioned that they weren't quite following pre-planned, direct routes between their points of departure and destination, but rather traveling in the most whimsical trajectories that allowed the players to enjoy the work and attention to detail the developers had invested in this game location. The immense city-tree was worth seeing. I immediately recalled another classic flick called *Avatar*. Perhaps the designers had decided that everything that was new was merely the forgotten old and so recreated the landscape of Pandora in Barliona.

The gigantic tree glowed softly with its fluorescent leaves and flowers, painting the night with its neon colors. Various buildings grew from the immense, broad branches, each of which could accommodate my entire neighborhood back in meatspace. And I do mean *grew*: The buildings' walls and roofs were formed either from growths of bark or from sturdy, thick leaves. The entire infrastructure turned out to be vegetative as well: Armchairs formed from toadstools invited the player to rest, flower fountains burbled happily, vine-ladders wound from branch to branch...

The forest surrounding the Tree looked pretty unusual too: Trees you could encounter in real life grew among fantastical creations, giant ferns and flowers of impossible sizes. There was something of Lewis Carroll's tales in this strange juxtaposition. I definitely wouldn't be shocked to encounter a caterpillar with a hookah in these parts.

Tearing myself away from my observations, I finally remembered that I had wanted to record a video of this and turned on my recording—but here a notification popped up before me:

Attention! Video recording in this location is available only once the player has achieved Esteem status with the Biota.

Right. Looks like this is in reference to

reputation. According to the beginner's guide, reputation in Barliona works in several stages: from a neutral relationship to friendship, respect, esteem and finally exaltation. In the other direction, this progression looked as follows: neutral, mistrust, dislike, hostility and hatred. By default, my reputation with my native faction was at friendship status and it didn't seem like reaching esteem would be too difficult. On the other hand, now it's clear why there aren't any videos of this location on the fora.

"How do you know how to get around this place?" I couldn't keep from asking as we flew past another branch. To my untrained eye, they were similar and all their multi-level intertwining seemed entirely impenetrable.

"Oh this is not as complicated as it seems at first glance," Amaryllis calmed me. "The branches grow from the Tree's trunk at several levels, and each branch serves its own purpose. We departed from the Branch of Slumber. This is where the bulbs bearing your sleeping brothers and sisters grow. Right now, we are passing the Branch of the Craftsmen. This is where the enchanters, artists, smiths, sculptors, alchemist and others study. That there is the Branch of Vocation. This is where the Woke receive assistance in finding their Way and get to know it. You will encounter Coleus there. He will tell you about the Bard's vocation."

Hearing about the bard instructor, I perked up

and stopped staring mindlessly around me. I'll have time enough to enjoy the landscape later. For the moment, I am eager to get to know the class I chose. And yet the sightseeing tour went on so I decided to spend it with a purpose.

"Where did the Tree come from?"

"One of the Creator's sons, the bright Eversquetor, created us and the pircs to fight the monsters that his brother Harrashess had flooded the Hidden Lands with. Eversquetor planted the Tree in the center of the Hidden Lands and the biota grew from its flowers. For many centuries we fought alongside the pircs against the monsters of Harrashess until we eradicated almost all of them. However, not long ago a new evil appeared in our lands. Only this wasn't the dark spawn of Harrashess but something else. A blight that afflicts the creations of Eversquetor and corrupts them."

All right, this is getting interesting. Clearly an intro to some quest.

"Why are these lands called hidden?"

"They were not so once long ago but the other races of Barliona began to invade our territory, burning and cutting us, boring mineshafts in our mountains. They were destroying our homes and so we allied with the pircs and destroyed the uninvited guests. Then our mages and druids created the Arras, which concealed our lands from our hostile neighbors. Since that time, many races view us with suspicion and even hostility."

Well that's unpleasant. As I understand it, with a bad rep, I'll have to struggle for every quest I get. On the other hand, I'm surrounded by an immense unexplored forest which should have enough quests for many months to come.

"Only the people of the forest can guide one through the Arras," Amaryllis went on, and here suddenly her voice filled with menace. "But I must warn you: If you bring a foreigner here without having obtained permission from the First, he shall be killed and you shall forever be banished from the Hidden Forest."

Message for the player: If you lead another player or NPC through the Arras into the Hidden Forest, without receiving permission from the First, your reputation with the Biota and Pircs will fall to Hatred status.

Uh-huh. So I better look for a party from among my own kind. Either these biota or the pircs.

"And who is the First?"

"You didn't see her in your Twilight Dream?" the NPC asked surprised. "The First had been our fearless leader since the biota first appeared in Barliona. Hers was the first bulb to bloom and her life as well as the lives of the Ten became the basis for the Twilight Dream that all the subsequent generations of biota have seen."

At these words, dim images began to appear in my mind like...yes...like the snatches of a dream.

A beautiful biota with pale-green skin and lilac petals in her hair, and behind her another nine biota. One after the other, visions of battles flashed past my eyes in which the armies of two races led by the First and her black-furred beast fought against first terrifying monsters and later the sentient races of Barliona.

The visions dissolved but something told me that if I concentrated, I would be able to 'recall' further fragments of my Twilight Dream. Not a bad topic for a song. Or even an album name. Several tales collected under the title *Twilight Dreams*. I'll have to bring it up with the rest of the band.

"Tell me who the pircs are," I asked once I'd finished mentally divvying up the royalties from the non-existent album.

"Eversquetor created the pircs in the image of predatory animals and sentient creatures, taking the best from both species. The majority of sentients consider them monstrous in appearance and savage in behavior. Before the Arras was put in place, some of them even tried to hunt the pircs, but the pircs quickly showed them who was the predator and who was the prey."

"So should I be cautious around them?" I asked just in case.

Historical allies is naturally a good thing, but perhaps the two races had drifted apart over the intervening centuries? I wouldn't want to become a vegetable side.

"No, Lorelei. The pircs have always been our trusted allies."

But of course. If the pircs are predators, I doubt they have much interest in two-legged salads like biota.

"Do the pircs live here on the Tree too?"

"No, they live in the mountains. A network of natural caves called the Lair serves as their home. The forest is their hunting grounds."

New class ability unlocked: Bardic Lore.

Bards are the collectors and guardians of legends and tales of yore. They are renowned for their ability to listen to others and discover grains of ancient wisdom in their speech. Bardic Lore allows the bard to uncover extra information in her conversations with NPCs, the chance to identify an item without assistance, to learn an item's hidden properties as well as other information about Barliona.

Skill increase:

+10% to Bardic Lore

Oh wow! That's like one of the main bardic abilities in the ancient AD&D rulesets—which are rightfully considered the ancestors of today's virtual RPGs. Normally, this is information that the DM would tell you. Wonder what happens here in Barliona? Will I be blinded by a tooltip or will it just kind of slink into my vision? Either way, this is freaking cool! I'll finish this tutorial, find myself some buddies and we'll sally forth like the adventurers of yore, a merry band to slay some goblins...No. Not goblins. You'd have to be Tolkien to write anything epic about a battle with some goblins. Better, monsters—right—monsters corrupted by some mysterious evil. The lyrics were already streaming into my head.

Amaryllis drew me out of my reverie. It turns out that we had already reached the branch we needed and the NPC was waiting for me to leave the 'leafevator.'

"Are you sprouting roots in there?" she shared a bit of the local, vegetable wit. "Coleus awaits you."

That's right. The bard instructor. But uh how can he already be waiting for me if I was only born a few minutes ago...Ho-hum. Or was I hatched? Ripened? Gemmated? Fell out of a tree? Spawned? That's the one! I hurried after Amaryllis. Only an utter newb would skip a tutorial.

CHAPTER THREE

WE WERE STROLLING along a broad street running the length of the branch which was filled with all kinds of obstacle courses and training facilities. The air hummed with arrows hurtling at targets. Spells snapped, crackled and popped overhead. The breeze rustled the leaves, carrying the jingle of test tubes and alembics. Biota warriors? With the race penalty to strength? I couldn't believe it. And still it was as plain as the nose on my face—or in the given case, the bit of lettuce—that we were on the branch designated for class training.

The facility for training bards was a...circus. We had walked up to a tranquil, shallow creek (though, what the hell is a creek doing on a tree?) and here a bridge had been constructed... crafted... grown... well, it was there, the bridge: two wooden beams with something resembling a cobweb stretched taut between them, the way netting is arranged on ships sometimes—all of it ending at the arched entrance of a circus tent. The circus tent itself was a giant lilac bulb, which for some reason reminded me of a jellyfish.

I set foot on the cobweb bridge with a deal of caution, but it turned out to be quite solid, bending barely noticeably under my foot. I stepped into the circus tent. And what a circus it was. A geometric pattern of various dots and circles—forming a snowflake or a flower—ornamented the floor of the arena. Three sets of bleachers radiated from the arena, facing a smattering of training dummies, solitary like cacti.

About thirty players were hanging around the tent, looking quite preoccupied. I selected several and checked their properties. All of them had unassigned classes. I guess they'd shown up to get to know the newly-introduced class.

"Buncha' crap," muttered a player named Green Pea.

He fumbled with a lute in his hands, strumming it carelessly. The lute produced heartrending shrieks and several seconds of this aural hell culminated in a half-transparent, rainbow-colored arrow that went flying at a training dummy. I have no idea how much damage the arrow dealt, but the awful noise that preceded it just about killed me.

"Clowns..." Pea went on. "And no damage to speak off. A class fit for autists."

Having voice this verdict, the player marched for the exit. Yup. An inspiring beginning.

An NPC biota stood in the center of the circus,

surrounded by players. His dark-blue epidermis stood out against his scarlet-red hair of leaves and similarly-colored veins along his body. Several sprouting stalks created the effect of whiskers beneath an eggplant nose.

"This is Coleus, your instructor," said Amaryllis. "He will tell you about your class and explain what you should do next. If you need me, Coleus will tell you where to find me. Or speak to any guard. They'll set you in the right direction. Good luck, Lorelei."

"Thanks for your help!" I replied automatically and almost bouncing from impatience, hurried toward my class instructor. He was just explaining to the players clumped around him how to use a spellbook. Following his directions, I opened the one I had. Two spells, as I understood it, was the accepted standard in Barliona.

Magic Missile: Using performance, you shoot a Magic Missile (magic damage) at your enemy. The damage done depends on your Intellect stat. Time to cast: 4 seconds. Cost: Character Level × 4 MP. Damage: Intellect × 3. Range: 20 meters.

Song of Healing: Your performance heals the chosen target for the duration of your performance. HP healed depends on your Intellect stat. This spell is channeled. Cost: Character Level

× 3 MP per second. Healing rate: Intellect × 2 HP per second.

"What's this performance thing?" asked a player named 'Dill the Pickled.' The recurrent humor in the players' choice of names was a bit dull of course, but I suppose it could be overlooked given the features of the biota race.

"A spectacle. Any spectacle you wish the audience to experience," Coleus explained. "You could play an instrument, sing, dance, do a gymnastics routine...I had a student who juggled various items."

I could see it now: A raid. Muscles rippling, bones groaning, the tank takes a resounding blow from the hulking boss. He staggers. A bead of sweat streams down the healer's face as he recites healing incantations. Thunder and lightning erupt from the mage's fingers. The hunter draws and releases arrow after arrow at his target...While off to the side, a humanoid bush is juggling some colored balls. Spectacle indeed!

Judging by the giggling players, everyone else imagined something similar.

"So what's up? Do we have to know how to play something?" asked someone named Prune the Desiccated.

Mmm...yeah...My name's really going to stand out around here.

"Strictly speaking, you can cast spells without

having mastery of some skill," Coleus replied with evident disapproval in his voice, "but who'd want to listen to it?"

"Who cares, if the dps is good?" Prune waved dismissively.

"By the way, on the topic of dps," spoke up Dill. "Why's it so low? I get that we get a bonus to Intellect and all that, but I'd hardly call it a multiplier. Mages and necromancers get 4x from Intellect! Even those bumbling shamans get 3x!"

The gathered players rabbled their approval.

"Being a bard is vocation, a calling," Coleus cut off the rabble coldly. "If you wish to wield the power of the mages, go speak with instructor Verbena."

"You know what? That's the first bit of good advice I've heard from you," said Dill. He, Prune and several other players huffed out of the tent.

"Are the rest of you sure you've come to the right place?" The biota inquired in a weary tone.

The four of us who remained, nodded our heads.

"In that case, let's learn how to cast magic. Open your spellbooks and touch the Magic Missile entry."

I followed these simple instructions and the inscription for the spell stuck to my hand.

"Now clench the spell in your fist or merely close your fingers over it—however you prefer—and place it in your active spells."

Do you wish to add Magic Missile to your active spells?

Uh-huh. I do.

Magic Missile has been added to your active spells. To cast the spell, choose a target that you wish to attack, mentally activate the spell, and perform any performance for four seconds.
Active spell slots remaining: 7 of 8.

"Was everyone successful?" Coleus asked, examining the players clenching the air with their fists.

The group mooed something resembling an answer and I guess our lack of enthusiasm finished off the instructor completely because he waved at the rack of musical instruments behind him and sat down on a bench with a despondent expression on his face.

But my eyes lingered on the rack he'd indicated. I instantly fixed on the lute when another player named Pickle grabbed the instrument by the neck—causing it to utter a pitiful whimper—and snatched it off the rack. I almost got upset before I noticed something strange: The lute remained on the rack, while its copy was now in the hands of Pickle. Perhaps my puzzlement was so evident on my face that another player with a mohawk of gray-green leaves on his head butted in to explain:

"Each player gets his own copy of the instrument. There's enough for everyone."

He was one of those who had completed the spellcasting training by the time I showed up. And as he spoke, he placed the same lute on the rack, causing it to vanish without a trace. He reached for the oboe next—though judging by his face, in his mind, anything from oboe to French horn could simply be called a 'pipe.'

"What do you play?" I inquired, jumping at the chance to strike up a conversation with a fellow player. Like all the others, Agave the Green had not chosen his class yet.

"That's the problem. Nothing," Agave confessed and looked doubtfully at the oboe in his hands. "But I still want to try playing as a bard."

"I feel you," I replied. I picked up the lute and immediately almost dropped it on the floor.

The cause of this was Agave who had blown into the oboe with all his might. The poor instrument uttered a revolting sound like a tomcat who'd had his tail trodden on just as he was serenading his cat girlfriend. If you take into consideration the creative endeavors of the other players trying out their instruments...I couldn't help imagine being the NPC instructor and having to listen to this cacophony day after day. Judging by his sour face, it wasn't a fun time. I'd even say it was hellishly awful.

Sympathizing with the poor fellow, I finally read the notification that had appeared some moments earlier.

Item acquired: Common Lute. Two-handed item. Durability: Unbreakable. Description: Used by bards for performance. Item class: Common.

Attention! You cannot remove this item from the training area.

And that's it? No bonuses? By the Pasta and the Sauce...

Readjusting the lute in my hands, I strummed an arpeggio, checking its sound. Look at that. It's in tune! Targeting a training dummy, I activated the Magic Missile spell in my mind and began to play the first thing that came to me—a tune called 'Goldentown.' Four seconds later, a shimmering rainbow arrow flew from my strings, striking the motionless dummy without any issues.

8 damage done. (Magic Missile Damage ÷ 1 (Target Level ÷ Character Level)) × 2 (Natural Environment damage bonus).

Skill increase:

+10% to Intellect. Total: 10%.

What's this then? A short dive into the guides revealed that depending on what I did, I could boost one or several of my stats. For example, casting spells boosted my Intellect. When the boost reached 100% it would permanently increase my Intellect stat and reset to 0%. I wonder whether I'll need the boost to reach 400% when it comes to increasing Constitution. I'll need to check. And anyway it would do to examine all my stats. So what do I have right now?

I've got 3 in Constitution, which means I have 30 HP. My Intellect is at 2 and that grants me 20 MP. Everything else is at 1.

It's odd how few stats there are in this game. There's neither wisdom, charisma nor luck. And I was especially fond of the last two, since they made the game unpredictable and interesting. But I guess I have to work with what I have. I returned to the guide to study what it had to say about the main stats.

My main stat was Intellect. This determined the magic damage I would do as well as my mana pool and the rate at which my mana regenerated. At first glance, I didn't really need Strength and Agility, but Constitution determined my life pool and the rate at which I spent and regenerated Stamina. It follows that Stamina is like an analog for action points. Almost everything costs Stamina, from running to playing the lute. This is no good. I'll need to come up with some alternative way for leveling up Constitution. But that's for later. Now, I need to estimate what kind of combat potential I have.

A few brute calculations brought me to a

disheartening conclusion: In the best of circumstances, I might be able to handle a mob of my level, after which I'd have to wait for my mana and life to recover. Yeah. This bard class is definitely a bit underpowered. I'll have to find a party and figure out a way to gain at least one level in the city. Then dump everything in Intellect and try to kill mobs before they reach me. Or first grind Intellect and Constitution by some alternative means and only then wander outside of the secure area.

An ear-shattering bang right beside me caused me to jump where I stood. I was seized with the sudden urge to crawl under one of the benches. At the same time, a five-minute long disorientation debuff, indicated that Barliona had some undocumented features. The spellbook said nothing at all about disorientation. Strictly speaking, this thought only occurred to me once the debuff had expired and my thoughts stopped wandering all over the place.

The source of the hellish clamor was Pickle, who'd swapped his lute for a timpani. Even though it wasn't very large in Barliona, a mere thirty centimeters in diameter, the noise the drum made was much louder than I expected. On top of this, Pickle was hammering the poor instrument with such violence that I could only assume he'd imagined the timpani to be some mortal enemy standing in his way.

At this point, two of the remaining players cursed colorfully, declared the whole thing a dolt circus and left the tent. I noticed that the instruments in their hands went up in smoke as they stepped out. By this point, our ranks had thinned significantly: More than half of the original players had left the training ground—I suppose to seek better deals from the other class instructors.

Meanwhile, the effect produced from his beating of the drum left such an impression on Pickle that he immediately decided to repeat his fortissimo. But barely had he brandished the mallets above his head when a captivating strain from a clarinet filled the tent and a shimmering blue sphere appeared around him. It took me five seconds to realize that the sound wasn't coming from the timpani. It was Coleus who was playing the clarinet and, it seemed that his spell blocked any sound coming from Pickle. Interesting. So it follows that a bard can be disarmed with a counterspell.

Pickle to his credit noticed the sphere too. Leaving the timpani alone, he tried to step out of it, but the magical shimmering moved with him. Pickle's lips began to move mutely but what he was saying remained a mystery. I bet there's plenty of girls out there that'd pay good money for a spell like that...

"I'll be a monkey's uncle...Wish I had one of those for my mother-in-law," said a voice behind my back.

"What, does she drive you nuts?" Someone else inquired sympathetically.

"Nah—she just sits at home all day, doesn't have anyone to chat with, so in the evening she starts calling," the unfortunate husband explained his sorrow. "I mean, she's a worldly old bat and all, but you just can't shut her up when she gets rolling."

"Ah, well, that's still not the end of the world..." rattled a third voice and here the discussion of family matters drew to a close.

Pickle, meanwhile, realized the cause of the spell he'd been cursed with. He made a show of placing the timpani on the floor, at which point it simply vanished. Coleus put away his clarinet and simultaneously the sphere around Pickle vanished too.

"What the hell?" the player asked outraged.

"Music," Coleus replied in a mentorly tone, "is not noise. A bard must first know what he wishes to achieve with his performance. For instance, if there were a pirc, an elf or a drow nearby—your performance would have required the intervention of a healer. Those creatures cannot bear loud and strident sounds. Despite its seeming simplicity and allure, the way of the bard has its disadvantages. One peril is unexpectedly finding yourself turned into a scratching post. A pleasant idea, don't you think?" He looked around his silent audience.

"Please be cautious around irritated nobles and rich people," the instructor went on enumerating the perils we faced on our journey to fame. "Rogues, pirates, and warlike tribes. Every one of them may thank you from the bottoms of their hearts—or to the contrary, send your spirit to the Gray Lands. So don't tempt fate unnecessarily."

"In other words if you don't know how to play an instrument, choosing a bard is pointless," Pickle summarized.

"Let's put it this way: I doubt anyone will find you very valuable," Coleus restated.

"What a dumb class for a bunch of dumb nerds," Pickle rendered his verdict and proudly stepped out of the tent.

The rest of the stragglers followed his example and a sacred silence descended on the tent. Finally, I could practice in peace.

My fingers touched the strings and the lute's clear notes swept across the tent. Not bad the acoustics in this place. You could easily play a concert here. But that's still a ways away. For now, what do I have to do for today?

A song of healing. I drag the spell to the active spells, activate it, play and enjoy the results. The spell poured into the training dummy and my Intellect grew by 10%...Okay. And if I want to heal myself? Same thing. No problem. What about Coleus?

Having exhausted my mana and raised my Intellect bar by 50%, I grew bored. The paltry arsenal of spells had been learned and there was nothing else to do. Is this it? All of the bard babble ends with this nonsense? 'Now you are ready, my young Padawan, go crush some mobs...?' Seems a bit dull. I was expecting more. I should ask my teacher whether he's not perhaps wasting his time.

"Say, Coleus, what's next?" I asked, sitting down beside the bard. Looking at him, I didn't want to be overly formal or shower him with compliments. He smelled of dusty roads, voyages and bonfires. "So I mastered a couple spells but so what? Surely the point of the bard lies elsewhere. We travel the world, collect tales and share them with others. We're wanderers, seekers of adventure—not mages with guitars and trumpets."

The biota's face filled with the expression of a teacher pleased by his student's progress.

"I am happy that someone understands this. For a bard, knowing how to tell a tale is much more important than weaving some spells together. If you really want to become a true bard, prove that you can captivate an audience. Travelers frequently have to travel lightly, earning their bread in city squares, taverns and even palace functions. If you manage to earn twenty silver pieces before dawn—by playing in front of an audience—come back to me to continue your education."

I grinned unwillingly. This was pretty much the way Ash, my music teacher, had taught me how to play. Thanks to his method, I had no stage-fright whatsoever.

Quest chain available: *A Bard's Calling*.

***A Bard's Calling*. Step 1: Earn at least 20 silver pieces with your performance. Quest type: Class-based. Reward: +30 XP, +10 Reputation with the Biota, and a Bard's Bag. Deadline for completing the quest: Before dawn. Penalty for declining the quest: 30 days until the quest chain can be restarted.**

Hah! Easy as pie! And it was only once I'd accepted the quest that I recalled a small but important detail.

"It'll be my pleasure, but what am I supposed to play if this lute vanishes as soon as I leave the tent?"

"Head over to Pirus the Luthier and tell him that I sent you. You can choose whatever instrument you like. Only make sure to choose wisely. If you want to change it, you'll have to pay the luthier the full price of the instrument and his work isn't cheap."

It wasn't that simple to find the luthier. I didn't feel like wasting time on finding Amaryllis first, so I asked the first NPC I came across. The biota happily explained that I need to reach the Branch of the Craftsmen and it took me another few moments to realize that there was a small problem here too: I had no idea how to use the leafevators. I didn't want to appear dumb chasing after the polite NPC who had helped me, so struggling against my vertigo at the sight of the ground far below me, I stepped onto one of the leaves docked beside the branch. The vertigo was too much and I was forced to take a seat and think what to do. Amaryllis hadn't uttered any code phrases during our first ride and I could see no operating lever, so I had to try something else.

It occurred to me that the tech employed in Barliona delved fairly deeply into the human mind. This was how the system determined when someone was telling the truth or lying—or could, for instance, find someone an attractive imitator in the local bordello. How did I know all this? The debates and protests about this issue had been broadcast across our entire planet. Human rights activists complained about the invasion of privacy and claimed this was a violation of human rights, while the Barliona Corporation claimed that its employees could not access the system and you could just as well accuse lie detectors of the same violations. On the whole there was a big ruckus, but afterward everything went quiet quickly. The players saw the advantages quickly and did not object to the mental scanning that made the game more interesting. It was now my turn to check out the new tech.

Getting a bit more comfortable in the leaf, I squashed my desire to adopt the lotus pose and do some meditation—especially since it wasn't like I could contort myself into a lotus pose if I wanted it— and focused as clearly as possible on my desire to reach the Branch of the Craftsmen. To my astonishment the leaf moved and smoothly drifted toward one of the branches.

Achievement unlocked: 'Flying Vessel Level 1' (19 flights in transport leaves remaining until next level).

Achievement reward: +1% to transport leaf movement speed.

You can see the list of achievements in the character settings.

I bet it's a real thrill to be taken on a whimsical tour of the Tree when you really need to get somewhere. I hadn't grown tired of the landscape yet, though, and savored the view the entire way.

Master Pirus looked like a luthier from a movie about some ancient violin—he was gaunt, sinewy and he moved quickly around his workshop examining everything with engaged, glinting eyes. When it came to me, the look he gave me was full of unconcealed doubt. I could understand him—when a tree is full of wandering biota with extremely dubious manners, it makes sense to regard every new face with suspicion.

"Choose whatever you like from the rack," he pointed in the direction of a rack beside the entrance, stocked with the most basic instruments. "My students' work."

Oh sure. Render to Caesar the things that are

Caesar's, but render to a janitor the things that are a janitor's. Casting a longing glance in the direction of a grandiose rack upholstered in ermine and proudly displaying instruments that just by their appearance alone would cause any musician to salivate, I looked over at the assortment offered to me.

"This one," I didn't bother tarrying with my selection and pointed at the lute closest to me. I mean, it didn't have any cracks, the action looked decent, so it would do as a start. Either way it would be better than what I'd started with—my first performance irl had been on a devastated acoustic with a pencil for a saddle.

Item acquired: Student's Lute. Two-handed item. Durability: Unbreakable. Description: Used by bards for performance. Item class: Common. -25% to casting time for Bard Spells when equipped by a bard.

Attention! This item cannot be traded.

Ah! A faster casting speed! So it's not that basic of a lute after all. I should pump Pirus for info on how I could get one of his own instruments, though something tells me that I'd need more reputation and a whole lot more gold than I have. Plus I got this countdown timer ticking. Dawn's coming and I need to get on with my first quest!

The square in the Market Branch was bristling

with flower-tents among which vendors and customers milled buying and selling. An enormous orchid grew in the very center, serving the function of a fountain. Various biota would go up to it, scoop up its water and drink thirstily. What a healthy ecological set up. If they tried this in my city, they'd wither up in an instant.

An unusual spectacle dispelled my ruminations on the fate of my planet: A pirc had appeared among my tribesmen. A furry, snow-white giant named 'Spiteful Chip' walked along the square, grimly examining the biota around him as if he was choosing a side for his entree. He was wearing green pants and a hooded jerkin, boots that laced up to his knees, and mittens with cuffs on his hands (or would paws be more correct here?). A bandoleer girded his chest and a rucksack hung from his back. Yet perhaps the most curious element of this creature's outfit was his hat. It resembled a bycocket—that is, Robin Hood's hat— that bore a bob and a feather from a bird I was not familiar with. It was truly a silly bit of clothing for such a terrible monster.

The pirc, like the other players of whom there were many here, roved busily between the various market stalls, trying to sell something and at the same time examining the NPCs' wares. Every once in a while, players would approach the giant, ask him something, receive a curt reply and walk away quickly. I couldn't hear what was said—the pirc was too far away—but I figured that the players were trying to recruit him to be a tank in their party. Judging by Chip's face—such offers had long since begun to grate on him.

"Have they lost the plot here the lot of them?" exclaimed a biota necromancer named Prickly Sloe beside me. Not a bad name, by the way, especially in view of the branches sticking out of his head. I could not say the same for his companion—Girasol the Majestic. Where this person had encountered a majestic artichoke remained a mystery to me.

"Check this out—the local bank branch isn't affiliated to the one in the capital. In fact, it's not affiliated with any other bank at all. My guildbros have sent me a bunch of stuff—bags, gold, equipment and whatnot—I have the password and everything, and I can't withdraw any of it! And it's the same deal with the mail. I can send you a letter, but when it comes to the world at large—forget it! The auction is local too. It's all pircs and biotas. I can't even buy gold for real cash. When they say biota is hardcore, they're like really serious about it."

"Well, that's the way hardcore should be," Girasol replied. "With stats like that, they'll have to carry us in their arms! Once we get out of newbspace, we'll pump Con and avoid all these penalties. I'll level up, sink everything into Int and then I'll heal like a demon or an angel...a demonic angel!"

At this point the two players walked out of

earshot. So there's no link to the outside world here. Makes sense. This way you can't get presents from higher-level friends, or buy high-level gear or potions for meatspace cash. All the better for me—I won't feel inadequate among the populace.

The pirc meanwhile stopped at a nearby stall. As I looked on, my old acquaintance, Pickle, approached the giant and slapped Chip familiarly on the small of his back, since he couldn't reach his shoulder due to the height difference.

"What's up bro? Catch my invite, you can tank for me, I'll be your dps—we'll pwn everyone."

When I was a child, I would spend time at my grandmother's house where I really liked messing with the cat. A large, fluffy, calico. And when the cat got angry, she'd press her ears to her head just like this pirc just did. Unlike my grandmother, Pickle didn't have a cat. Or brains or a sense of self-preservation—otherwise he wouldn't buddy up to three-meter-tall Chip.

"So what do you say? You coming, fluffy?" And my acquaintance playfully punched the pirc in the belly.

This was the last straw.

"Hold this," Chip shoved his halberd into the hands of a stunned passerby. The pirc's voice fit his appearance—a low growling bombast which rolled across the square like an avalanche. It seemed that Pickle began to figure out that his life was about to take a turn for the worse, but the only thing he managed to do was shut his mouth. That was it. The pirc grabbed him by the waist, lifted him and hurled him into the fountain, roaring: "Three pointer!"

Pickle traced a pretty arc waving his extremities and plunked in the water with a splash.

"And the Chicago Bulls have reached the finals!" the pirc barked triumphantly, taking his halberd.

The passersby scattered, casting fearful glances at the bellowing pirc and the sputtering and spitting Pickle. The poor fellow tumbled over the edge of the fountain and wadded away into one of the alleys adjoining the square. He clearly didn't want to continue tempting fate.

"Should've done that earlier," the pirc growled to no one in particular and looked around as if looking for another basketball. To his surprise, the new basketball turned out to be Pickle again—coming back in the company of a town guard. And I should mention that the guard was quite the sight: His body was clad in bark with a tough layer of leaves, forming something like scale mail.

"This one! He attacked me!" Pickle pointed at the pirc. "Attacking a player is a PK felony!"

The guard launched into his script, projecting a replay of Pickle approaching the pirc and slapping him on his back.

"You landed the first blow," the guard rendered

his verdict and closed the projection. "You may go," he told the pirc.

Pretty simple justice system here. One, two, and that's it.

"Hey! Why'd you cut my reputation?" Pickle cried, but the guard wasn't listening to him. The pirc, on the other hand, scowled happily and asked,

"Yo, ikebana, you got a sharpie?"

Stumped by such an odd question, Pickle merely shook his head.

"No, why? What's an ikebana?"

"The Japanese art of flower arrangement. I need a sharpie because I like to show my work when I do my math," Chip explained, leaning forward and bringing his ice-blue eyes with their slitted irises right up to Pickle's.

"Math?" Pickle gaped.

"I was going to divide you by zero," the pirc explained, jerking up his lip and demonstrating a row of glittering teeth, sharp even to the eye.

At first Pickle started back reflexively. But then, I guess he remembered that he was dealing with a mere virtual avatar of a creature that didn't actually exist—as well as that he was in the middle of a city whose guard wouldn't permit the killing of a player— as well as that even if it came to that, he was still at level one and had nothing to lose but a few hours of waiting.

"You're getting way ahead of yourself," he

replied proudly, turned and made a show of waddling off with his chest stuck out—that is, without giving the pirc a chance to get the last word in.

"What a child," the pirc remarked and deciding that this dispute had been resolved, began looking around in search of whatever it was he needed.

If at my first sight of the pirc I had begun to fantasize about him joining my party as a tank, then now I definitely thought better of inviting Chip to do quests with me. It seems that he'd chosen his epithet accurately—he really was spiteful. What if he'd off me somewhere for the sake of a few XP or coppers? And in general, I came here to do my quest chain, not to find party members. Time to get to work.

Looking around surreptitiously, I plucked a small cup-shaped flower from one of the buildings and began to look for a good spot to perform: one that was busy enough with foot traffic and spacious enough to allow people to stop and listen. The side of the fountain that Pickle had taken a swim in looked great, but the noise of the water would overwhelm the music. On the other hand, the auction dais (or rather the enormous broad stump used for this purpose) seemed perfect. The auction crier looked bored to tears. I guess the low-level players didn't have any rare goods, or money to buy them with, so there were no objections to my taking over the area as a stage.

Placing the flower I'd picked in a conspicuous place—where the audience could render unto me their silver pieces—I clambered up on the stump, switched the lute from my back to my chest and ran my fingers along the strings to check its tuning...But, uh, what am I going to sing? All that was coming was a song from a children's show... '*Everyday when you're walking down the street, everybody that you meet / Has an original point of view / And I say HEY! / What a wonderful kind of day / Where you can learn to work and play / And get along with each other...*' But something told me that theme songs to children's shows wouldn't find a welcome reception among the biota, much less since there weren't really children around here. Plus it was night so...

Back at the training tent, an old lute composition had occurred to me. It had been composed a long time ago, but remained popular enough. A wonderful song about a fairy-tale golden city seemed to fit this location perfectly.

My fingers danced along the strings, I inhaled deeply and realized that I was as anxious as I had been during my first performance. But the melody that came out, scattered my fear like a spring rain, and carried me and my listeners away to a different world. The auctioneer perked up, placed his papers aside and began to listen to me closely. Incidental passersby began stopping, caught by the harmony, and even the grim-faced guards softened a little. Only the pirc looked up at the first chords, then grimaced like he'd gotten a whiff of vinegar and stepped away.

But I didn't have time for him anyway. In these kinds of moments I had no time for the rest of the world.

The applause when the song ended suggested that the NPCs were quite happy with my level of play. Otherwise, I could as well forget a career as a bard in this game.

Several coins clinked in my flower cup, while a series of notifications popped up before me:

+1 Reputation with the Biota. Current status: Friendly. You are 2999 points away from the status of Respect.

Oh, so it follows that we start at friendly status with our own faction? How nice. And the fact that I could level up my reputation with this kind of performance is nicer still! Of course, it would take me a while to perform three thousand songs...And that's not even taking into account that my stamina fades as I perform...

Experience gained: +1 XP. Points remaining until next level: 99.
Skill increase:
+1% to Agility. Total: 1%.

Cute. I can level up by singing. A hundred more songs and I'll get +1 to Agility. I wonder if I have to play a song or whether a few verses will do? I should experiment.

Quest updated: *A Bard's Calling.* **Step 1: 2 silver and 34 copper coins earned.**

Achievement unlocked: 'Busker Level 1' (30 silver pieces until next level).

Achievement reward: +1% to money earned busking.

You can look at the list of achievements in the character settings.

Well that's quite a serious achievement. Something to be proud of, what can you say?

Attention! A new stat has become available to your character: Panhandling. Panhandling increases your chance of earning donations and increases the amount received as well. At a certain level, you can beg NPCs to receive unique quests or items.

Do you accept? Attention! You will not be able to remove an accepted stat!

I'd never think of such a thing! It's a cool stat. The devs seem to be having fun with us. I don't mind earning some cash as a bard here and there but I'm not about to start begging full time.

"Excuse me," someone's polite voice distracted me.

Bowing my head, I encountered the pirc and jerked from surprise. Chip stood right before my stage, the edge of his halberd dangerously close to my toes.

"Do you know anything other than the busker's standard repertoire? It's just that I have a band of buskers camping out under my window and every morning for the last two months I've been getting up to songs about golden towns with gates of glass."

Will you look at this jerk...Is it my fault that everyone's beaten this horse to death? Although, two months really is too much to hear this ditty. All right, I'll sing him another song if that's what he wants. Several options (mostly concerning werewolves) flashed through my mind, but then I looked at the two-legged beast before me and for some reason began singing something else entirely.

The drawn-out melody spilled across the square, filling its occupants' hearts with sadness and homesickness. Alongside the song's wandering hero, my listeners traveled endless dusty roads, dreaming of a home bathed in sunlight. Even the pirc froze, forgetting his desire to toss me into the fountain. Not that I cared anymore. The lovely, unjustly-forgotten song absorbed me and I dissolved in it. Neither the game, nor the biota, nor the pirc were around me any longer. I was the hero of the story. Cursed and drawn by fate, I was the wanderer who wandered among ruins and tombs. The tormented earth groaned beneath my steps and I dreamed of a city at the edge of the very sun, where faith, hope and love awaited me.

A portion of the players had stopped scurrying between the merchants' tents and drew nearer to listen to the little-known rock classic, and once the last chord had rung their applause brought me back to the game.

Standing nearby, Chip wriggled his little pink nose and rendered his verdict:

"Not bad. You have an excellent voice. I'd happily hear you underneath my window every morning," he said and placed—and I mean 'placed' instead of 'tossed'—a coin in my flower cup. My quest update indicated that the coin was a silver one. It's not much, but at my level, it's a good sum. I was now the proud owner of almost seven silver coins. Prosperity, here I come!

It took me a half hour and five songs to earn my twenty coins. As soon as the quest was complete, a new system notification popped up:

New class ability unlocked: 'Master of string instruments.' Bonus to spells cast with string instruments.

Ah! Now this I understand. Taking a bow to my audience, I hopped off the stump, grabbed my flower cup and was hurrying back to Coleus when I noticed my stamina level. Holy meatballs! It was down to 16! Yeah. I definitely won't be able to perform an entire concert like this. Biota use liquids to restore their stamina, so I guess I can expect to do a lot of drinking in this game—in the best bardic traditions of course. It's just that I couldn't see a pub nearby and the only source of water was the same fountain that Pickle had recently bathed in. I had neither a mug nor a flask, so I had to drink the old fashioned way: bowing down to the water and sipping from my palm. At least my stamina was restored immediately. Okay then. I will have to get myself a flask at the first possible opportunity. Quenching my thirst, I noticed the same ornament at the bottom of the fountain that I had seen in the circus tent arena. I suppose it's like a local logo or something.

But I wasn't nearly as much interested in ethnography as I was in my skills. It wasn't difficult to find an unoccupied leafevator and as it carried me back to the bard tent, I studied my spellbook.

Magic Missile: Using performance, you shoot a Magic Missile (magic damage) at your enemy. The damage done depends on your Intellect stat. Time to cast: 3 seconds. Cost of attack: Character Level × 4 MP. Damage: Intellect × 3. Range: 20 meters.

Okay. Looks like this spell has grown stronger.

Checking my hunch, I opened up the game guide. Yes, that's right. The damage formula is now similar to that of other hybrid classes—like shamans and druids. So the bards weren't left out in the cold after all. I guess a certain someone simply lacked the patience to complete the quest chain and unlock the additional class abilities. This spell paled in comparison to what the mages and necromancers could cook up, but those guys were pure casters anyway. High dps was their bread and butter.

I wonder what my healing powers are?

Song of Healing: Heal target for the duration of your performance. HP healed depends on your Intellect stat. This spell is channeled. Cost: (Level × 2) MP per second. Healing rate: (Intellect × 2) HP per second.

Yup. Here the mana cost has decreased and conversely the opportunity to level up has increased. The only strange thing is that the speed buff from the new lute doesn't seem to factor in, but perhaps the devs simply rounded instead of splitting decimals. The hell with it. It works as it is. I'd like to imagine that I'll get another bonus by the end of the quest chain.

My leaf docked at the branch I needed and I happily marched to the tent. Several newbies had wandered in while I was gone and were now torturing Coleus's instruments and nerves. I wonder if this poor fellow has some kind of deputy. Does he have to spend all day and night in this aural hell? Do NPCs even sleep in Barliona? I should sit down and read up on the game a bit more. But I can do that later. Right now I need to complete my quest and continue the chain.

"My first honorarium," I bragged, handing Coleus the flower with the clinking coins.

The bard happily used this opportunity to escape the tent and we stepped out on the street. I wonder why he doesn't simply kick out the hapless musicians, declaring them unsuited for the profession? Does his script lock him in?

"You handled that quickly, a good beginning," Coleus praised me as soon as we stepped out into fresh air. He poured the coins into his palm, jingled them pensively and then held them out to me.

"Take these. They're yours. Buy yourself something."

20 silver and 14 copper coins received.

"This bag will help you in your travels," Coleus went on, offering me a plain rucksack. "It doesn't look like much, but it has room for all your instruments and songs."

Item acquired: Bard's Bag (20 slots). Durability: Unbreakable. Attention! You may only

store items (including songs) used for performance in this bag.

Cool! All I have to do is figure out what songs are supposed to be in Barliona. I wonder if there's something about this on the fora? Or am I going to have to pay?

"I'm ready for more complex instruments," I hinted transparently to my instructor.

He hummed enigmatically, rubbed his beard of twigs and nodded.

"We're about to find out. A Bard's Calling isn't to entertain the rabble, but to heal the spirit, to awaken courage and love within it, and to grant warmth and succor, and instil true joy and light sorrow. If you prove that you have mastered this art— a number of difficult quests you cannot handle yet— then you will study with me for two months. And only afterwards will you receive another attempt."

Quest available: *A Bard's Calling*. Step 2: Demonstrate that your performance can awaken courage and love, grant warmth and succor, instil joy and light sorrow.

Quest type: Class-based. Reward: +120 XP, +100 Reputation with the Biota, +5 gold, songs from Coleus' songbook. No time limit. Penalty for declining the quest: 60 days until the quest chain can be reset.

Eh. That's the entire description? And how am I supposed to do all this? All right. If I can't figure out myself, I can always ask someone. There's got to be some high-level bards around here who've done this quest chain before.

"How will you know when I accomplish all of this?" I asked just in case.

"Trust me, I'll know," the NPC's face took on such a sly expression that I suspected some trick. But there was nothing else to do but accept the quest.

"Before I leave...I have several questions."

"Ask away," Coleus nodded, glancing at the tent which buzzed with chaotic discord.

"Can I learn to wield some weapon? A lute is great of course, but once my mana runs out, what am I going to do?"

"Every five levels you will receive training points which you can use to learn other classes' skills. You can use them to hone your skills using weapons."

Look at that! This means that Barliona has preserved the ancient tradition of treating the bard as a universal class. I'll need to figure out exactly what the deal here is.

"So I can study to be a full-fledged hunter then?"

"I doubt you'll become a full-fledged hunter," Coleus was quick to check my enthusiasm. "The hunters' instructor will offer you one of the starting skills to choose from. At level ten you'll receive another training point and you'll be able to choose from the hunters' second tier skills, or for example from the first tier mage skills. In other words, either you follow a single skill tree from another class (yet still lag behind dedicated hunters) or you take a little from everywhere but end up with pretty basic spells and skills. In addition to this, their efficacy will be decreased to 70% and you won't be able to learn specialized class skills. You can learn the standard spells of necromancers, but you won't be able to learn spells available to demonologists."

In other words, the skills are more basic and their efficacy is truncated. What's the point then? I asked the last question out loud.

"You can amass a unique assortment of skills and spells that is custom-tailored to you. You can acquire additional healing abilities or learn how to shoot a bow or learn the art of stealing. It's up to you."

"Is that all to say that it's best to develop within one class?"

"Depends on the individual. You can choose some class as an auxiliary, go through the class initiation and receive access to the stronger skills of that class, as well as a wider selection of skills and an increase in their efficacy. But in that case you'll be closing off other classes to yourself—their instructors will refuse to help you."

"So that means I can become a bard-hunter?"

"Yes—this specialization is called a Wild Bard."

"What are the other combinations?" I wondered.

"There are very many. I doubt even I've heard of all of them. But I could list the main ones."

Having received the nod of confirmation, Coleus went on:

"There's the aforementioned Wild Bard—a child of nature. Her songs are tied to nature, she is capable of taming beasts, she is a good shot with the bow and is close to the hunters' fraternity. The bard that follows the way of the druids can use her performance to pacify animals and call them to her aid; she can speak with plants and animals too. If you wish to dedicate your life to the service of one of the gods of Barliona and follow the way of the priests, you will become a Divine Bard. As a rule Divine Bards are adept healers, famed for their psalms which strengthen the party they travel with, but here everything depends on the given patron deity. Their opposites are the Singers of Death, who wield the spells of necromancers. Their songs can bring death, destruction, ruin and illness, weakening their foes. A Scaldic Bard is a courageous warrior who inspires himself and his companions with songs and verses. A bard who studies the art of wielding daggers and short swords with rogues becomes a Singer of the Edge. If she studies deceit, stealth and thievery, she becomes a Spy. There are bards who have become the

Voice of the Elements. There are others called Dark Minstrels, Acrobats, Jesters...I don't know all of them, but you can try and learn about them in the library."

My eyes went wide from the plethora of options. It follows that the devs had collected just about all of the diversity available to the bard class, turning the different variants into individual specializations. All I had to do was reach my fifth level and figure out which way I would grow from there. And I really did need to stop by the local library. What if I find a good description of the various directions there?

"Say, Coleus," I asked the last question I had. "And if I want to remain a simple bard? Borrowing certain skills, but without merging with any other class?"

"Then you will be able to choose your own way within our class, but you and I shall discuss that only when I see something special in you."

"And what is that?"

"I'll tell you when it happens," Coleus replied enigmatically and, clearly indicating that our conversation had ended, headed back to his tent.

CHAPTER FOUR

INSPIRED, AND AT THE SAME TIME A BIT PUZZLED, I wandered from the bards' tent considering what I should do. I couldn't keep my mind on Coleus' quest. My thoughts circled around the class specialization and that something 'special' that I had to accomplish in order to delve further into the bard class. Some special quest? An item? A secondary characteristic or several carefully chosen secondary characteristics? Most likely the latter. If only I knew what to choose and how...It was pointless to rely on the guides, so the library was my only hope. And yet, I really didn't feel like riffling through dusty parchments. I wanted to take a stroll, to look around and take in the beauties of this place. So that I could tell the boys about this location at our next practice. Tomorrow morning I'll go see Amaryllis to get the info she promised about increasing reputation. I'll eke out some newb quest and go hunt some bunnies or some other dangerous monsters. And why not? Maybe biota are like carrots to them—a delicacy—and our biota race struggles for survival battling their merciless teeth.

But all that tomorrow. Right now I'll go for that walk. Only I seem to be lacking something...

The Market Branch bustled with activity: Players darted between the vendors' stalls, the bank and less frequently the auction. NPCs praised their goods, talked with each other or simply stood around not doing anything. My eye was drawn to Prickly Sloe, the necromancer I'd met earlier, who was now doing something odd. Paying utterly no attention to the looks he was getting, he was going around with a wicker basket full of gorgeous flower garlands, decorating the vendors' stalls. The vendors didn't object, so I doubt this was entirely Sloe's initiative. The conclusion was that he'd come up with some quest.

"Hey! I'm not getting in your way, am I?" I greeted the necromancer, approaching him.

He glanced at me suspiciously and muttered a reply:

"Hi. What'd you need?"

Why is everyone so touchy here anyway? First that Chip, now this Sloe...

"Nothing much. I simply wanted to ask about this quest you're doing."

"I'm helping decorate the city for the coming First Bulbs Festival, whatever that means. It's like they don't have enough flowers here as it is."

I was forced to agree. In my opinion, the Tree didn't need further decoration, but I guess the devs had decided to give players a chance to level up and earn some gold with this kind of activity. Considering that Sloe was the only one doing this, I suppose the majority of players preferred slightly more interesting quests.

"And who can I speak to about getting such a quest?" I asked just in case. What if it'll come in handy?

"Talk to the NPC who met you when you hatched," Sloe advised.

It just so happened that right then a party of players was passing us, consisting of a necromancer, a mage, a hunter and a priest. Noticing what Sloe was doing, they began to giggle and point at him.

"Look at that! He's doing a social quest, the moron!"

"Clean my boots! You'll get some rep!"

"Come level up with us, you ninny!"

Prickly Sloe twitched a muscle but didn't reply, focusing on the garland he was arranging. I could see now why he'd responded so defensively when I approached him.

"Thanks," I thanked him sincerely, trying to dispel the impression left by the stupid players, who had lost interest and headed off on their business. "I guess I'll help arrange the festival too."

"Uh-huh," Sloe barked ambiguously and here our conversation drew to an end.

My review of the market wares ended up being

brief and informative. Practically everything on offer exceeded my paltry budget. Even the most modest bags cost at least one gold, to say nothing of prettier or more elaborate versions.

The one silver lining was that there were plenty of vessels for water on sale and the cheapest one cost exactly 20 silver. Having examined all the options I noticed that there was a difference between flasks, bottles and other containers—and that was their volume. My basic one was enough for four gulps and then I'd have to find a source of water to refill it.

The most expensive, meanwhile, despite its similar size contained as much as a hundred gulps, which meant I could restore stamina a hundred times with it as well as increase my mana recovery rate. On the other hand, that one cost five hundred gold. An amount I couldn't imagine at the moment.

The sky was beginning to lighten and—at a whim—I went looking for a good vantage point. The edge of the branch opened up on a stunning view of the surroundings: An endless, it seemed, forest rolled in waves of treetops up onto a mountain range, from behind which the sun was rising. It turns out that when it rises from behind a mountain the dawn looks different.

The mountain range occluded the purple dawn and so the sky was gradually losing its darker colors, paling and then filling with bright gold rays as the sun peeked from the jagged peaks.

The desire to leave the Tree and see what was going on around us, as well as test myself in battle, flared up somewhere in the pit of my stomach. As a friend of mine used to say: "Sometimes the boot up your ass is the piston that drives you onward." Either way, I found a leafevator and sitting down as per habit, thought about how I needed to descend to the Tree's roots. And as the leaf obediently carried me downward and toward new adventures, I took my lute in hand and imagined my heroic victory over some rabid squirrel or roly-poly or whatever mobs had been prepared for us newbies. I had it all calculated. I'd slay one or two mobs, get some XP, check out the combat system and maybe even find some cool loot.

The leaf landed in the middle of a peculiar forest which looked like no forest I'd ever seen before. Impossible trees wound with vines chockfull of stunning flowers...birds singing...

Damage taken. -32 HP (Blighted Lynx bite: 40) - (Physical resistance: 8) HP Remaining: 0 / 30.

Attention! We recommend you disable damage detail in combat settings.

Attention! Respawn Penalty: -30% XP. Current XP: 24 / 76.

The Barliona launch screen appeared before me with a large inscription announcing:

You have died. You may enter Barliona again in 12 hours.

And before my eyes the 12 changed to a cheeky 11:59:59 and began counting down.

"Oh sure," I muttered to myself realizing what had happened. It looks like I'd miscalculated.

Checking the logs didn't teach me anything I didn't know, but it did occur to me that in addition to the damage detail I should disable every other notification as well. Agility bonus percentages, points to Intellect et cetera, made for some pretty dull reading. Luckily the abundant interface settings allowed me to keep only notifications about new actions that cause my stats to grow, as well as notifications of when my stats reached integer milestones.

I clambered out of my cocoon, stretched my limbs and body and plodded off to the kitchen. My basic autocook fixed me a cup of coffee and I dug up some chocolate candy from my pantry. Having provisioned myself in this manner, I set out to adventure in the toxic climes of the Barliona fora.

Searching for 'biota' led me to an unbelievable amount of reference information and other noise all mixed in with various ads for paid guides. Sipping my coffee I rephrased my search query to 'biota combat low level' and a couple other phrases that added up to 'what the hell?' I should mention that the first results were way more informative, even if it was way harder to read them. Briefly put, players who played biota were emotionally asking the Barliona admins why this race's starting location was chockfull of aggressive monsters. And not only aggressive ones but also ones that were no less than Level 5. And the only response from the admins was a reminder that biota are a hardcore race and are hard to play—but not impossible. The players were advised to stop screwing around and team up. And this was mixed in with glaring links to the already-familiar paid guides as well as random users bragging about solo leveling with pure aggroed mobs—in response to which, such users were called trolls and told to go to places dark, gloomy and uninhabited. In general, just like any other community hubs, the Barliona fora were paragons of harmony and understanding.

Three hours spent studying the guide allowed me to come to grips with the main game professions and choose a suitable one. While I was at it, I checked out the pirc race—our closest neighbors and allies.

Racial reputation penalty: Most races regard pircs with distrust. -50% to reputation growth.

Racial bonus to Strength: +50%. Stat point cost: +2 for 1.

Racial bonus to Constitution: +50%. Stat point cost: +2 for 1.

Racial bonus to Agility: +25%. Stat point cost: +4

for 3.

Racial penalty to Intellect: -50%. Stat point cost: +1 for 4.

Racial trait: Resistance to cold. -10% damage from ice.

Racial trait: Resistance to magic. -10% damage from magic. This trait has no effect on fire sensitivity and is added to the race's cold resistance. This trait likewise weakens incoming healing, auras and other beneficial magic.

Racial weakness: Fire sensitivity. +10% damage from fire.

Racial trait: Gluttony. The pircs must consume raw or cooked meat no less than once a day. Otherwise they receive the Hungry status effect (-50% to Strength).

Racial ability: Silent step. When in a natural environment, like a forest, pircs gain the stealth movement ability.

Racial ability: Magic defense. Temporary immunity to magic (10 seconds. Cooldown: 30 minutes).

Racial trait: Savage mien. Most other races of Barliona consider the pircs savage in appearance. -10 Attractiveness with NPCs.

Racial trait: Large predator. Many animals are afraid of the pircs.

A curious race indeed. As I understand it,

reputation and attractiveness determines whether an NPC will issue you a quest or not, as well as how much they'll charge you for their wares or whatever else. And the poor pircs have to break a sweat to earn the trust and pity of these same NPCs. At least they don't die from a mere breeze like the biota do. The logical thing to do is go visit the pircs and join one of their parties. Judging by their penalties to Intellect, the furballs could use some casters and healers. I'll need to locate Chip and ask him how he managed to reach the Tree without drawing aggro from the mobs infesting the woods.

The words I was reading began to resemble series of garbled symbols, hinting that I should take a break. There was no practice scheduled today and I didn't have any orders from my freelancing gig, so I decided to go out and take a walk.

The real world greeted me with evening dusk and the feeling that I had traveled in time. I had watched the sunrise but a short while ago in Barliona and here I was back at sundown in real life. Although it wasn't like I could see it: The city's impenetrable rows of high-rises merely allowed me to bask in the glory of some pink-tinted clouds, which for an urban dweller is as nice as it gets in terms of nature.

My neighborhood was a quiet one. My neighbors, whom I knew by face if not by name, nodded to me politely. Children chased after a canine imitator. The adults stared into their visors. A real living pigeon sipped water from a puddle. An ordinary evening to an ordinary day. I put on my headphones and wandered aimlessly along my preferred route (where my legs take me) enjoying the music and not thinking of anything in particular.

At an intersection, a screen on a building was broadcasting the news: A huge helicopter was launching rockets at invisible enemies from its stubby wings. Soldiers in power armor led a column of prisoners who cast around, looking at their captors fearfully. I couldn't hear anything but it was clear that this was footage from the ongoing African conflict.

That's the way people are—we can always find some reason to go to war. On our little planet, even despite our universal government, there was always conflict. Either someone didn't like someone else, or some spiritual prophet would appear who'd claim to know the one true way to salvation, or simply (and typically) someone didn't split the money they had earned. More frequently than not, it all ended with a visit from the cops, though sometimes, like now, our brave army would rally all the king's horses and all the king's men to restore order. Of course, there were still some pseudo-sovereign states remaining like the ancient Christiana and Sealand, but they were independent strictly formally-speaking. Who's going to start a war over some tiny piece of land? So the microstates continued to exist, minting coins and printing money for the tourists. As for Africa...There was always a coup happening there. Someone was getting deposed or reinstated. Typically, all that was really going on was yet another warlord trying to shove his way to the trough. It was the same story year in and year out: As soon as Somalia calmed down, Sudan flared up. When Sudan calmed down, it'd be Libya's turn. On top of all this, a year ago— maybe for a change of pace—a riot broke out on the moon. The miners were unhappy with their salaries and their living conditions. It didn't get much further than some yelling and rabbling: Someone in the lunar administration was fired, someone else was brought up on charges and everyone calmed down.

A building's wall bloomed into a holographic ad for Barliona, interrupting the news footage from Africa. A vivid ad that ended with the words: "*Feel* the world you love!" This was followed by the address of the nearest support center. I brought up the city's map on my visor and looked up directions to the center. It was less than thirty minutes from me and open 24/7 so I headed that way without giving it more thought.

The branch building was stylized to resemble a small castle—it even had towers with embrasures. I bet it was the recreation of some famous in-game location but it wasn't one I was familiar with. It's not a bad marketing ploy: You're walking along a street when—bam!—you come upon a castle...or a tavern...or a fortress. Or even one of the biota buildings. And then you get your décor, your marketing and your service center all in one place.

A smiling girl stood at the administrator's desk. She met me as warmly as if I were one of the company's directors. When she learned the purpose of my visit, she offered me some green tea and a comfortable sofa to rest on while I familiarized myself with the substance of the testing waiver. I didn't refuse and began to carefully study the document. I could only make out several points from the impenetrable legalese: I would grant the Corporation access to my medical history, I would acknowledge that the testing could cause me pain and I would waive my right to complain about it.

"Tell me, why is the testing necessary if I want to remove the sensory filter for pleasurable or neutral sensory content? What is the danger of being able to touch a table or feel the texture of bark under my fingers?"

"The problem is that neutral and pleasurable sensory contents are practically indistinguishable. Some people like the taste of chocolate; others find it uninteresting. As a result we group these categories together. At the same time, pleasurable sensations could cause complications. If you have an addictive personality, then the complete removal of sensory filters is not advisable. Players with heart issues should not be exposed to sudden jolts and therefore should not lower their filter settings either."

"If you have heart problems, I'd imagine that an attack by a PKer is much more shocking than, say, the scent of summer grass."

"The difference is liability. The Corporation is not liable if you are attacked by another player, but if you have a heart attack as a result of being exposed to sensory content that is too intense for you, we could bear liability."

It's like anywhere else: You sign the papers and undergo the testing, while they look out for themselves and make sure they're safe. And once they're safe, they couldn't care if the world burned down. It's no longer their problem.

The testing itself was pretty simple, although a bit tedious. I was placed in a capsule, connected to a virtual lab and then subjected to various sensations. The pleasurable and neutral ones were turned on at full blast, but the painful ones would be ramped up bit by bit. It wasn't very pleasant, but I was curious what level I could handle. My threshold turned out to be 60%, after which my pride gave in and I cried uncle. Nope. I wouldn't choose that setting for anything. I wonder if there are masochists out there who drop their sensory filters below 80%? For my own self I decided: 90% was my personal limit. That's 10% worth of sensory content that would let me know what side I was being smacked from and do so quickly enough without turning the game into a torture chamber.

On the way home, I dictated a few new ideas and verses into my visor and, upon reaching my crib, collapsed in my bed to slumber with a clean conscience. We had a brainstorming session scheduled for the next morning—on the topic of our new album.

But in actual fact, this turned into an exchange of stories and impressions accompanied by a few beers. Still, the conversation stimulated my imagination and I spent three hours with my guitar synth, trying to recreate the fledging melody. Again and again I got the impression that something was lacking and, deciding that I was at a dead end, I climbed back into my VR capsule.

CHAPTER FIVE

Welcome to Barliona!

You may set your sensory filter preferences.

I DISABLED THE FILTER for pleasurable and neutral sensory content entirely and trimmed the filter for pain down to 90%. Heroically overcoming torments in a game is a pointless waste of time.

The launch screen indicated that my time in the Gray Lands had expired and I pushed the enter button.

The stars that had welcomed me during my first instants in Barliona were shimmering in the sky now too. It was night once more in the game—yet this time, it felt real. Saturated with the scent of flowers, the air intoxicated. The warm breeze stroked my skin and everything I touched caused a sensation that was indistinguishable from real life. I suppose I looked pretty funny: A humanoid plant twirling its head in shock, touching the giant bouquets next to it and even the bark under its feet.

The local cemetery where I respawned

reminded me of the Branch of Slumber. The same gigantic flowers, though most of the bulbs here were open like in some strange loge. Various vague images flashed through my mind, reminding me of snatches of dreams. A funeral procession comes to a halt...The body is placed carefully in one of the flower bulbs...Its petals close and everything grows gray...

Attention! You have used Bardic Lore to recover lost information about the Branch of Oblivion.

So that's how that works for biota—a stylized vision from the Twilight Dream. I wonder how they do it for the other races? A voice whispering in your ear? A hallucination? New memories or a simple system notification? I'll have to ask someone when I get the chance.

I examined the black bulbs closer. So these are like tombs for biota. There must be thousands of these, given the centuries of the race's existence. Perhaps Amaryllis could explain what's happening? I need to go see her anyway. Before descending from the Tree, I need to gain several levels using the local quests. I'll help get the festival ready.

Here in the Branch of Oblivion I also noticed the geometric ornament that resembled a snowflake or flower. I'll need to remember to ask someone— maybe I'll level up my Bardic Lore in the process.

I found Amaryllis at the Branch of Vocation, at the druidic training grounds. She was speaking to another NPC. Nodding a hello, Amaryllis gestured that I should wait and returned to her conversation. Yeah. This isn't your grandmother's *Ultima* where as soon as a player appeared the NPCs dropped everything to speak to him. Barliona was much more realistic in these matters.

Having nothing to occupy myself with, I began to examine the player druids. To my surprise, everyone here was at Level 1. Curious. Leaving the training area, I walked down the branch checking out the players I came across. Almost everyone was at Level 1. Where are the higher-level players? Did they die out or something? Or do most players delete their biota once they've slaked their curiosity and go on to choose another race?

"Did you want something, sister?" Amaryllis interrupted my thoughts. While I was wandering around, she had time to end her conversation and come find me on my promenade along the Branch.

"Eh? Yes..." My thoughts remained stubbornly circling the low-level players and it took me several seconds to recall what I had wanted from the NPC. "I met one of my brothers here—he was decorating the Tree for the First Bulbs Festival. Can I help with the preparations? I'd just like to do something helpful."

"But of course, Lorelei! The more helpers we have the prettier our Tree will be during the festival.

The palace square has to be clean, but we just don't have the flowerpower. Wash it until it shines and I'll give you a lovely bag as a gift."

Quest available: *Festive Preparations*.
Description: Wash the palace square within the next 24 hours. Quest type: Annual scenario. Reward for completion: Lovely Bag (20 slots), +40 XP, +50 Reputation with the Biota, +10 silver coins. Penalty for failure: -50 Reputation with the Biota.

Mmm...yeah. Not quite the quest I was expecting, but taking into account the aggressive monsters camped out at the foot of the Tree, I'll need to eke out all the XP I can.

"I'll be happy to help out with the preparations!" I said, accepting the quest and swiping away a notification that I had received the items I needed to do it. I'll see what they are later. At the moment, I've accumulated a bunch of questions.

"Who're these First Bulbs that we're celebrating with the festival?"

"This is the day when the Tree bloomed with its first ten bulbs, bringing our leader into the world."

"And the other bulbs?"

"The first biota and her fellow nine, whose bulbs opened next, convened our Council. Nigella the Druid is the First. She is the one who speaks for the biota to the Guardian and the Tree. In the Council her vote is deciding. Salvio the Warrior is the Second. Our commander-in-chief, he has spent his life battling other sentients. He can be brusque and even cruel but these are precisely the qualities our allies, the pircs, prize in him. It's thanks to the Second's iron will that we put a halt to the invasions of the other sentients. Fresia the Paladin is the Third. Another hero of the biota, her sword is guided by Our Forest Father—Sylvyn. The Third is equally a master of the blade and divine magic and her words are always carefully-weighed and wise. Ageratum the High Priest is the Fourth. He speaks the word of Sylvyn. Ageratum is the most influential member of the Council, after the First. The Fifth is Portulac the High Mage, fallen in battle with the red orcs many centuries ago. The Heart of the Sixth, Astilba, his betrothed, is to this day filled with mourning for her fallen mage. Her sorrow is so great that the most powerful necromancers have spent centuries searching for a way to bring her love back to life. Her judgments, which were always just earlier, are now blighted by her hate towards other races. Eben is the Seventh. He is our spymaster. Thanks to him we know what takes place in the world beyond the Arras. Cunning and elusive, Eben can find a way out of the most complicated situation. Enotera the Hunter is the Eighth. Her judgments are as true as her arrows' flight. Monarda the Harbinger is the Ninth. She is one who speaks with the Spirits of the Higher and Lower Worlds. She has always been guided by her spirit, not her mind, and her counsel is therefore especially valuable. A yawning void has formed in the Council after the passing of the Harbinger. But among all the members of the Council, it is the Tenth, Cypro, who should be most interesting to you. He is the bard who first sang on the day of the First Bulbs. He is the chronicler of our people's history, capable of reminding us of past mistakes so we don't repeat them, as well as to cheer us up with tales of feats, instilling our hearts with faith and true strength."

In the next instant, a whirlwind of visions from the Twilight Dream descended upon me.

I found myself standing in a bulb, my heart skipping a beat as a world I could only dream of unfurled itself before me. An enormous forest, its peaks breaking against a magnificent mountain range in the distance. My forest. I can feel each one if its trees, its every living creature. A moment of complete oneness with the earth that Sylvyn entrusted to me. Born of a fleeting union of the sun and the moon, I stand in the viscous twilight, melding day and night, basking in the power of the two heavenly bodies. The first biota witnessing the setting sun.

The dream faded out, replaced by a series of others: One after another, illuminated by the sun and the moon, the other biota emerged from their bulbs. The future Council of my race. After these scenes of their births, came the scenes of deaths. A long sequence of battles in which the biota fought shoulder to shoulder with the mighty pircs against the treacherous invaders: the orcs, the trolls, the drow, the undead...Countless battles.

The forest alight, the flames' reflections glinting in my eyes. Ground wet with the blood of the various races: the red of the pircs, the green of the biota, the boiling rust of the red orcs. The hot air sears my body but I move stubbornly forward to the orders of the Fifth. We fall on the flank of a horde of red orcs, inch by inch cutting our way forward to unite with our main force. I can see Portulac fall, slayed by the poleaxe of the orc chieftain. Exhausted by the interminable battle, the high mage can no longer resist. Astilba does not witness it—she feels his demise and rage distorts her face. Blinded by her loss, the great necromancer, the Sixth in the Council, opens a portal to the demon world. The ranks of nightmarish creature rush from the portal and smash into the orc ranks, turning their unexpected counterattack and routing the invaders. For a moment I freeze from horror, seeing the red orc chieftain dragged to one of the demonic portals as Astilba laughs maniacally: What is the price that the Sixth shall pay for such assistance?

A new battle. Fires from the enemy camp stretched into the horizon. The allied armies of eight races striving to destroy the Great Forest and its denizens. Kneeling, Ageratum begs Sylvyn to come to the aid of his children and a blessing descends on the biota army, paltry in comparison to that of their opponents. Monarda flies overhead in a deep trance. At her bidding, the Spirits summon a thick fog that covers the forest and the enemy camp. The terrifying face of the Seventh looms amid the darkness. The spymaster seems to appear from nowhere, holding a terrible trophy in his hand. It is the bloodied head of the drow queen. Seven assassin adepts appear behind Eben, his students, a crowned head in each one's hand.

Nigella leads a huge pack of predators from the Great Forest. The beasts heed her call to defend their habitat and in a silent sprint fall onto the enemy who are exhausted from the long march and blinded by the sudden fog. The Second barks terse orders and at his command, fire, ice, lightning and everything else the biota mages can cast explodes around the enemy. The terror in the leaderless, enemy camp reaches its peak when fallen comrades suddenly rise from the bloodstained earth, grab their arms and wield them against the former friends. Like the Sixth's, the undead eyes are empty and black.

The Second orders a retreat and the predators step back and fall in line with the pircs. Their time is still to come. Meanwhile the thunder of a terrible and grim march rumbles over the field of battle and to its cadence, figures march to the enemy camp as if woven from the fog into one cloth. A phantom army. Cypro, the great bard, has summoned the fallen heroes of lore to help in the fight. Biota and pirc heroes whose memories he has kept alive in his songs. Their spirits heed the call of the Tenth and return from the Gray Lands to fight for their people one more time.

By the time the officers in the enemy's camp have finally taken command of their forces, their host has shrunk by a quarter—and yet still it is enormous. Now the first warriors manage to break through the phantoms and undead—only to be felled by the arrows of the Eighth and her marksmen. And when the arrows have abated and the piles of bodies are tall enough to conceal an entire grove, the pircs enter the fray. Those of the enemy who managed to break through the forest army meet their death at the steel and claws of the beastly warriors.

The cruel battle lasts all night, the next day and the next night. I think that I'm about to collapse from exhaustion, but as soon as a bit of my magic is recovered, I turn once again to pour fire onto the enemy.

A great portion of the enemy army has been annihilated, but there are still too many of them and our forces begin to falter and wane. It is then that Monarda makes the greatest sacrifice to her Spirits. She gives her life and in return receives a spell of unprecedented power. The Supreme Spirits of the

Earth cleave the ground beneath the enemy and plunge them into a precipice that will be henceforth called the Stone Maw. We have withstood them. We have turned them back.

The setting changes once again: In a regal hall, the Sixth argues bitterly with the First, enjoining her not to trust the foreigners who've tried to destroy the forest multiple times. The Second supports Astilba, counseling her to accept the offers of a new faction and with it forever end the threat of invasion. The Seventh objects, pointing out that the sentients have changed and the new faction will be no less dangerous than their former foes. A shaggy pirc with coal-black fur, bares his fangs and growls that he is not afraid of anyone in this world, but the Kartoss races must pay for the crimes of the past. Ageratum shakes his head, saying that Sylvyn won't forgive an alliance with a faction that is an enemy to nature itself, one that wishes to see both light and dark destroyed. The Council votes in favor of an alliance with the Nameless Dark Lord of Kartoss. The Sixth screams something wrathfully but the vision fades.

It took me a moment to realize I was standing next to Amaryllis. The vision was so real, so lifelike, that it took me a bit to come to my senses and collect my thoughts.

Attention! You have recovered lost information about the biota through Bardic Lore.

Still under the spell of the vision I'd had, I swiped away the system text. That was awesome! Easily worthy of a long, beautiful ballad. I'll need to find out more about it. At the moment, most of these visions were lost on me, but the locals will surely be able to explain all these legends in detail. At least Amaryllis. She, by the way, had remained patiently waiting for me to complete my conversation. Curious this local etiquette—is she waiting for the vision to end or is this just a feature of the NPCs tasked with introducing new players to the game?

"I...In my Twilight Dream, I saw the appearance of the Ten. Some of them left their bulbs as solar biota and others as lunar and only the First's bulb bloomed at dusk. Did this affect her somehow?"

The NPC's face expressed surprise and elation.

"This is a great rarity and a significant honor—to see the First in your sleep and all Ten to boot. To witness the day of the First Bulb with your own eyes...You are very lucky, Lorelei. I'm sure this is because you have budded as a bard, the collector and keeper of history, legends and lore."

Hmm, that's interesting. Is this just more boilerplate or a bonus for bards?

"It is true," Amaryllis went on, "that the First is special in that both the sun and the moon are her patrons. As a result she combines the best characteristics of the solar and lunar biota within her. They say that when her time comes, the moon and the sun shall join in the sky and the Creator shall bless the bulb that will grant us our new ruler."

Now here's something I can get behind. A good system. No elections, no power struggles. Kings and queens growing in a vegetable patch, waiting for the right time to sprout. Although, stop. Why wouldn't there be struggle? What'd I see just now?

"I also saw the Council argue about a new alliance, but I didn't really understand what was going on."

When I was rolling my character, I clearly indicated that I wanted to be aligned with Kartoss. Yet it turned out that the biota were an independent and closed faction. A bit odd, that.

Amaryllis' face grew grim at my words. Had I said too much?

"We always knew that one grown in a bulb may see this in her dreams. Let's go—I will bring you to someone who can tell you the meaning of what you saw."

Following Amaryllis to the local eco-friendly means of transportation, I couldn't help but wonder who this dream-interpreter could be. Some local oracle? Or do the mages fulfil this purpose? Maybe, just like in *Avatar*, I'll be hooked up to the Tree and it'll reveal to me some immense truth?

Amaryllis didn't answer my questions and we spent our journey to the Tree's higher branches in silence. The creature I encountered once we'd entered one of the buildings was neither mage nor oracle. The epidermis of the biota sitting at his desk was black like cooled embers and his yellow fibers turned his face into the terrifying mask of a predator. The branches sticking straight up from his head in lieu of his hair completed the picture. The Seventh. A master assassin and one of the first biota to appear in the world.

"Please accept my highest esteem, oh Seventh," Amaryllis bowed and I hurried to mimic her genuflection. I couldn't help but recall the bloodied drow head in the grim biota's hands.

"It is a great honor for me to see one of the first of my people," I uttered my greetings respectfully.

"Yes, I am one of the first biota to behold the Barliona heavens," the Seventh agreed majestically. "I have been alive for a very long time, do you know this?"

"Yes, oh Seventh," I replied deferentially.

"In that case try and imagine how tired am I of hearing these endless platitudes and get to the business at hand," he said, screwing his mouth into a smirk. "What has taken place, Amaryllis?"

"What you were worried would happen, Eben," she replied enigmatically as I stood staring at the Council member at a loss.

"And what did she see?" the Seventh said grimly.

"The schism," Amaryllis said and Eben's face

grew even dourer—just as Amaryllis' had done when I first told her.

Can someone please explain what I've done wrong?

As if reading my mind, the Seventh sighed and turned his full scary face to me:

"I am sure that the reason for this is that you are a bard. Your lot always sees and knows more than everyone else. Our race's particular feature makes it very difficult to keep everything a secret. Any moment of your life may be seen by one of our kin who is still in the Twilight Dream. As a result, we try not to keep secrets from one another. Life's much simpler that way. We live in accord and agreement. At least this is the way it was until recently."

The chair squealed as it slid back. Eben stood up and began pacing back and forth.

"Not long ago a shaman named Geranika managed to assassinate the two major leaders of our continent. The Emperor of Malabar and the Dark Lord of Kartoss fell and the world began to change drastically. Free Citizens began to appear in the Dark Empire, and later even here, emerging from our bulbs. Geranika drove two cursed daggers in the imperial thrones and if no one finds a way to extract the defiled items, the Empires will lose their new emperors as well. Despite this mortal peril, the new Nameless Dark Lord of Kartoss is concerned for the future of the peoples in his empire. Without wasting time, of which he does not have much, he sent messengers to all the races living in the Kartossian borderlands that are not part of its empire. He offered us an alliance. The Dark Lord has no doubts that the renegade shaman Geranika will not stop at what he has achieved, and thus offers that we and the pircs forget our ancient enmity with Kartoss and join its empire. It seems he was right too because Geranika himself approached us offering an alliance. This shaman wields a tremendous power, a part of which he is willing to share with his allies. Geranika offered us the chance to exact revenge against our old foes. He spoke convincingly and his gifts are generous, but many of us have traveled beyond the Arras over the last few years to study the other peoples. Some have changed for the better, some have remained as they were, but one thing is evident: Despite our former disagreements, we do not want to destroy them. It turned out that not everyone shared this opinion. The Sixth, the Second and Kodiak—one of the pirc chieftains—argued before the Joint Biota and Pirc Council to accept Geranika's offer. An unparalleled power, a long-awaited chance for revenge, the bounties of new lands—all of this fogged our reasoning, but the majority in the Council voted in favor of the alliance with Kartoss. The Sixth and her faction refused to accept the Council's decision and a schism took place—as a result, the renegades abandoned the Tree."

The Seventh cast me a dusky look and went on with a sigh:

"We hoped that our friends would cool off and change their minds, but soon after they departed, terrifying changes began to take place. An alien blight appeared in the forest. Some of the animals began to change and attack us. Parts of the forest changed entirely, vegetation and all. We have not found a way to restore them and are therefore forced to destroy them to keep the rest of the forest safe. If you decide to descend from the Tree, you should be very careful. The Hidden Forest is dangerous even for us now. If you find a way to kill a dozen of the blighted beasts, you shall be rewarded."

Quest available: *Slaughter of the Blighted Beasts*. **Description: The forest around the Tree is flooded with blighted creatures which have been altered by some unknown magic. Help save the forest—kill 12 blighted beasts. Quest type: Common. Reward: +100 Reputation with the Biota, +200 XP, +5 gold. Penalty for failing/refusing the quest: None.**

"I will do everything I can to save the forest," I assured the Seventh, accepting the quest. "What do I do if I find the source of the blight or a way to heal the defiled creatures?"

"Then you shall become a hero, bard." The

smile on Eben's face resembled a terrible scowl. "If you do that which neither the Council nor the mightiest druids of our race could accomplish, you shall receive a worthy reward indeed."

Quest available: *Source of the Blight*. Description: A blight is spreading through the Hidden Forest, changing everything that lives. Find the source of the blight and/or a way to heal the blighted creatures. Quest type: Rare scenario. Reward: +1000 Reputation with the Biota, +1000 XP, +200 gold for accomplishing either objective. If you accomplish both objectives, you will also receive an extra +500 Reputation with the Biota and a scaling item from the Biota Council. Penalty for failing/refusing the quest: None.

"I will try to find the source of the blight, oh Seventh," I announced triumphantly, regretting that I couldn't go riffle through the guides this instant to find out what a scaling item is.

"Perhaps, Lorelei, perhaps," judging by his voice, Eben didn't share my optimism. "But at the moment, I'm more worried about something else. We are keeping the schism that has afflicted our Council a secret for the moment, as well as our coming alliance with Kartoss. We are doing this in order to prevent any panic among the populace. At the First Bulbs Festival, the Council will announce the embassy's arrival and the Council's ratification of the alliance. When our people see with their own eyes that the other sentients have changed, they shall accept the idea of an alliance. Besides, I am afraid that the Sixth and her adherents might come up with a provocation to imperil any future negotiations. This is precisely why it is vital to keep the embassy's arrival a secret. Do you understand how serious the situation is, Lorelei?"

"I understand, oh Seventh."

"Then give me your word that you won't tell anyone what you saw in your Twilight Dream about the schism in the Council or what you heard from me."

"I swear this will remain a secret between you and me."

Your reputation with the Biota has increased by 50 points. Current status: Friendly. You are 2944 points away from the status of Respect.

Attention! You have been charged with a responsibility: You may not use any means of communication to tell anyone about the schism in the Council, the departure of the Sixth and her adherents or the arrival of the Kartossian delegation and the coming negotiations. Penalty for violating your promise: -1000 Reputation with the Biota and a variable punishment from the

Seventh.

And that's it? Where's the reward for staying quiet? Where's the invitation to the negotiations? What happened to one good turn deserves another? But okay. Let the drowning biota rescue himself.

"Since I've accidentally become a part of this affair, perhaps I can be of assistance by getting things ready for the arrival of the Kartossian messengers?"

"You can discuss this with Amaryllis, Lorelei. This is not within the scope of my cares," the spymaster replied. "It's time you go."

I bowed politely and followed Amaryllis out.

"You have chosen difficult times to behold the stars, Lorelei," the NPC smiled wistfully. "As for preparing for the meeting with the messengers, the preparations are already under way. Only, everyone thinks that they're preparing for the First Bulbs Festival. If you take care of a simpler quest, I'll consider what else you could do."

"Help me with one more question. In my dream I saw the Tenth among the Council, but I didn't see his demise. Did something happen to him?"

"Cypro journeyed beyond the Arras almost five hundred years ago. He has not returned since. Many biota see his travels in their dreams and we hope that the Tenth still wanders along the countless roads of Barliona."

Well, crap. So the head Bard isn't even in the

Hidden Forest? This means I can't rely on this source of class wisdom.

"Last question. Several times I've noticed an ornament that consists of intersecting circles," I traced a vague semblance of the pattern in the air. "Does it mean something or is it simply decorative?"

"This is Cypro's personal sigil," the NPC smiled. "No one knows why he painted them, but if you meet the Tenth you should absolutely ask him about it."

Quest available: *The Mysterious Sigil.* Description: For reasons known only to him, the Tenth left his sigil in various locations around the Tree. No one knows whether this is a jest, a prank or a hint for inquisitive minds. Perhaps you are the one who will discover the answer to this mystery? Quest type: Rare. Reward: Variable. Penalty for failing/refusing the quest: None.

A class-based quest from someone other than the bard instructor? Curious. I'll need to look for any patterns in the sigils' locations. I accepted the quest, opened my journal and couldn't help but smile: What an assortment of quests—everything from global politics to custodial duties. Nothing to be done. I'll need to do the basic quests first to get something a little more interesting.

CHAPTER SIX

I T WAS NOT THE HEROIC ENDEAVOR I had envisioned when I fantasized about my future adventures in Barliona. In my mind, I had imagined journeys to distant climes, libations in taverns, webs of intrigue, sweeping battles and encounters with monsters and dragons—and here I was about to wash some floors. Although, what's so surprising? I'm basically no one here. My name means nothing and at Level 1, I doubt I'd even be a worthy snack for a dragon. So all in all this quest was a fitting one. I could naturally object that this isn't a task for a player—that manual labor should be left to the NPCs—and yet it's not like anyone was forcing me to do this. And the extra XP, reputation and cash wouldn't hurt right now either. This being an RPG, even this modest quest chain could easily lead me to some high-level meeting—even if only as a servant. At least I'd get to see the servants of the Dark Lord of Kartoss if not the Dark Lord himself. The way the players on the fora talk about it, seeing the rulers with one's own virtual eyes is a rare occurrence that one shouldn't pass up.

Having used this reasoning to pacify my pride, I made my way to the enormous spiral staircase that led to the palace. The spacious plaza before this staircase had been entrusted to me—to clean. Well they wouldn't just let any old biota clean something as important as the palace square. Even here, there was a progression to observe. First wash the square, then the staircase, then the royal balcony, then the royal toilets...Hmm. I'm getting carried away.

Like every other architectural detail I'd encountered, the staircase was vegetative in nature. A vine that grew spiraling around the trunk and fleshy leaves that served as stairs. Another vine, a bit thinner, served as the rail and banister. Both the staircase and the square around it were quite dusty and tarnished, as if the level designer had tried to skimp on the flowers for this location.

"Enough labor from here until sundown," I muttered an old proverb, examining the work ahead of me.

It wouldn't be such a big deal if I could imagine how I was going to actually clean all this. I was used to having imitators clean the house. Right this instant, my own cleaning imitators were setting my apartment in order on the other side of the virtual barrier. All this feels slightly karmic actually: The imitator is cleaning my place and I'm cleaning the imitators' place.

Along with the quest, I'd received a bucket, a

rag and this like T-shaped stick that I had no idea what to do with. Could I use it to pick fruits in the orchard? At least the bucket part is clear enough— that's for holding the water to do the cleaning with. Why hadn't any book I'd read ever discussed this topic? All they'd ever mention was something like 'she scoured the floor with a wet rag and muttered profanities at the passersby.' All right. If it's scour and mutter, I can scour and mutter.

I wandered over to the nearest creek, still beset by the problem of how a creek could run down a tree. The only hypothesis I had was 'high-proof magic'— which happened to be Straus' favorite explanation for anything he didn't understand. At least there was a surprise waiting for me at the creek: yet another sigil of the Tenth on the bark at the edge of the water.

Quest updated: *The Mysterious Sigil* **(1 of 36 sigils located).**

I guess the ones I'd found earlier didn't count then? Well, that wouldn't be difficult to remedy. I'll wrap up this social quest and swing by the other sigils. I filled the bucket with water and dragged it to the square with a little difficulty. My stamina dropped by 30 points. Sucks to be weak. After some consideration, I dumped the water onto the incredibly disgusting wooden surface that reminded me more of imitation parquet than bark. Then I tossed the rag into the puddle I'd made. Okay. Now the scouring. Scratching my head, I stepped onto the rag and began to drag it back and forth. The puddle spread out but nothing seemed cleaner. I'm doing something wrong, aren't I?

From over my head, I heard a monotonous grumbling that slowly arranged itself into the melody of the theme song to one of my favorite sci-fi shows. Looking up, I beheld the rear of a pirc, covered in taut green pants. A slit in the seat of the pants allowed his clipped tail out into the air where it jiggled to the rhythm of the song. Every thirty seconds or so, the singing gave way to the sounds of a wet rag splashing against a wet floor—instantly telling me what Chip was up to. The same thing I was. Only his take on the act of cleaning was much simpler than mine: Chip brandished the T-shaped stick in his hands having draped the rag across its crossbar. In two swift motions he cleaned a step and moved on to the next one. Just like that. One-two, one-two and the surface was clean and the singing pirc stepped down. And another observation: After every two steps, the furball rinsed and squeezed out the rag. I'm no Sherlock Holmes or anything—I can't just adduce the profession of some random person, but I can say with a great deal of certainty that Chip the player had washed a floor or two irl before. Maybe he was some insane janitor? I'd encountered these hardened roleplayers before. Grown adults who maintained their role even at home: cooked food in ancient crockery, sewed their own clothes and, well generally lost their minds in their particular way. There was nothing bad about it of course, mere idiosyncrasy really.

"Ba-ba-bam," Chip was clearly in an excellent mood. No, there's definitely something wrong with him. Who in their right mind enjoys this kind of tedium? This guy's having a ball!

"This is heavenly..." Chip rinsed the rag and finally deigned to notice me.

"Greetings fellow culture warrior! He bellowed joyfully and saluted me with the wet rag. "What? Have you too been enjoined to put the place in order?"

"Looks like it," I replied without an inkling of the pirc's enthusiasm. Kicking the rag one more time, I sighed and glanced over at Chip, trying to see how he handles the mysterious T-shaped stick. Look at that. A complex tool which must be integrated with the cleaning medium in order to complete the quest. A puzzle.

"I'm just recalling my youth," the pirc shared.

In the name of the Pasta and the Sauce, what a grin this fellow had. I wonder how much time the model artists had to spend in the zoo to recreate this phiz?

"Long before I was issued my rifle, I was issued a mop. The first day of the academy actually," Chip shook the stick with its rag. Perhaps how I felt about his enthusiasm could be read on my face because the pirc examined me carefully, then the puddle at my feet and not so much asked as summarized: "I gather that the mop, the rag and the bucket are not your friends, my dear."

"I'd sing a strange song about how diamonds are a girl's best friends, but I generally consider friendship with inanimate objects a form of sociopathy," I replied with dignity. "I can see this isn't the first time you've undertaken this type of quest?"

"Any respectable airman has no choice but be proficient at waltzing with the mop," he replied eagerly. "Pursuant to which, I propose we unionize and effect an evolutionary breakthrough in this impasse by means of a simple division of labor."

This last bit was so incomprehensible and unlike the way the pirc had spoken back at the Market Branch that I found myself at a loss for what to say. Seeing Chip now, I wouldn't dream of concluding that he was irritable or combative.

"What is this division of which you speak?" I asked suspiciously.

"Elementary, my dear Dr. Watson," the pirc extended a claw and punctured the air with it for emphasis. He nodded at my bucket and current stair. "You can stay here and play me a song (only not about that Goldentown, I beg you) and I'll waltz around with my trusty little moppet..." Chip stroked his object of affection and made his cutest face, which on a pirc looked utterly terrifying.

"And what will I owe you in return?" After my experience with the paid guides I had begun to suspect that even the flies in Barliona wouldn't buzz for free.

"Nothing." It seemed like my question had caught Chip off guard. "It's just one of those symbiotic things: I get a morale boost and you get a clean palace square. One good turn for another, in other words."

Encountering this kind of generosity in a trivial quest would be odd any day of the week, but encountering it from this pirc was beyond the pale. And yet it would be silly to refuse help, while offering nothing in return would have been dishonorable.

"Let's form a party in that case. I'll share the quest with you and once we complete it, we'll receive the reward," I offered a little uncertainly, mentally prepared to turn and run at any moment. After all, I could still remember what happened to Pickle when he offered something similar.

"What is this party thing?" the pirc howled. "Does anyone here know how to speak normally? Healing, tanking, aggroing...Why doesn't this game come with a dictionary?"

So that's what was driving him insane! Chip was a newbie gamer and gaming argot, with its rich history of a hundred years, may as well have been Greek to him. Well, that's easy to fix.

"Let me explain..."

The crash-course on gaming slang didn't take very long. I showed Chip how to accept an invitation, create a party and add players to it. I showed him how he could share quests from his quest journal and also covered the structure of a party and the basic roles that players performed in it.

My new companion listened attentively, periodically asking questions or clarifying the meaning of this or that bit of gaming slang. By the end of our improvised instruction, he understood the various requirements and challenges fairly well.

"Well? Shall we begin?" he asked once the lesson ended. He stood up from the stair he'd been sitting on and waved his arms.

With a pirc in my party, the work became more fun. Initially, I really did perform a few songs in 3/4 time, but after that, my knowledge of waltzes ran out and I turned to a different repertoire.

Warm beer and cold women, I just don't fit in...

The pirc kept time fairly well, twirling around (or as he put it, waltzing) with his mop at a breathtaking speed. He hadn't paused once the entire time, interrupting his scrubbing only to change the water in his bucket. Meanwhile, I belted out tunes on my lute with perfect bliss until a system notification distracted me. I was used to playing as various drunkbodies crawled up on my stage or when the crowd hurled various presents my way. We didn't miss a beat even the time some ancient punks set some ancient seats on fire—and yet the notification that appeared was much too unexpected. I reflexively began to read the text, and the lute went silent in my hands. Chip twirled his ear with surprise and looked at me quizzically.

"Has something happened?"

"Sorry," I muttered and peered into the notification. "It looks like I'm being offered some new bard stat. Let me read the description, figure it out and then we'll go on."

The pirc nodded and got back to work while I re-read the notification.

Attention! A new stat has become available to your character: Fame.

Your mastery as a performer has been honed by years of practice and now bears fruit: Your audience is more receptive to your songs and the spells you cast grow more effective as a result. If an NPC enjoys your performance, he will receive the 'Impressed' status effect. This increases your Attractiveness with that NPC by an amount equivalent to your Fame trait. The status effect lasts (Fame × 3) minutes. Once the 'Impressed' status expires, your Attractiveness with this NPC increases by 25% of your Fame. The frequency of this permanent bonus to Attractiveness is

calculated individually for each NPC. The permanent increase can only take place once a day. If an NPC does not like your performance, this effect may be reversed.

Do you accept? Attention! You will not be able to remove an adopted stat!

What an interesting stat. If you choose the right song, you'll be loved. If you choose the wrong one, you'll be banished to the forest. Nice role-playing touch. Well at least, I'll get a chance at being famous in virtual reality. I'll be a celebrity among the NPCs on this side of the Arras.

You have adopted a new stat: Fame (Currently: 1).

I couldn't wait to experiment with my new stat, but my partner was making a show of his suffering at the absence of accompanying music, so I had to wait a bit.

"*Et voila!*" Chip announced ten minutes later, having finished cleaning the last bit of the square and saluting me with his mop and the rag draped over it, like a Roman legionnaire with his aquila.

"Listen, where'd you learn to handle a mop like that?" I ventured a question.

"Why, at the academy of course," the pirc smiled. "I was on duty frequently, and then later, in my third year, they made me PS. And before that, Gomer, my best bud who's in Angola at the moment, and I would constantly get disciplinary action for some nonsense."

I sincerely tried to digest what I had just heard but failed pitifully.

"For me, what you just said is the same Greek as 'kek, my death knight alt can tank a raid better than your pal main.'"

"Sorry," Chip scratched his chin. "By academy I meant the Federal Military Aviation Academy. I'm a helicopter pilot. When I first entered, I'd be doing custodial duties. And PS means platoon sergeant. Simply put, I'm a run-of-the-mill grunt—just one that's got a big rotor overhead that keeps him hovering in the air."

"You're pretty well-read for a grunt," I said, not believing him. "You speak well, but the words you use are atypical..."

Chip burst out laughing in response, snorting happily and slapping his hips. Then he pointed to his head and made a daft face:

"I use it to eat!" And once he'd done giggling at his own joke he explained: "Meaning, all I use my head for is eating. But don't worry—I promise to stop using weird words and try and communicate using simple sentences." He giggled again.

His reaction forced me to blush. I deserved it too. He'd basically just pointed out to me that my earlier statement effectively added up to "I thought you army people were dumb jarheads, incapable of putting two words together." Not very diplomatic of me...

"Sorry, it's simply that I've only encountered different military jargon until now."

Strictly speaking my experience with servicemen came down to arguing with a retired warrant officer who was in charge of security at the cultural center where we'd play local gigs. And it should be said that basically anything the warrant officer said could've been substituted with 'bow-wow' without losing an ounce of sense. His lexicon had nothing to do with that of Chip.

"Well, sure, the army is the army. They'll teach you to drink and cause a mess," the tailed beast nodded eagerly, clearly relishing my confusion. "By the way, your name is excellent! The last thing I expected to find here is a lover of poetry," Chip raised his chin and declaimed:

"I think that the waves will devour
Both boat and man, by and by,
And that, with her dulcet-voiced power
Was done by the Lorelei."

He fell silent and added:

"And it is therefore inadvisable to allow you to sing in a boat. Wet fur has a chilling effect on my skin."

That was unexpected. I had figured that there was a chance that someone might remember the old legend of Lorelei, but hearing Heine's verses recited...Most of my acquaintances don't even know who that is. They'd most likely imagine it's some small-time actor.

"Does everyone in the army learn poetry or are you a special case?"

"Many do," the pirc took of his hat, carefully adjusted the pompom with the feather, smoothened the fields and replaced the hat on his head. "It helps us relax. Well, and it's entertaining, especially if the translator is decent. I tried to read Kipling the other day—my niece sent me a 'new translation'—well, that particular translator shouldn't even be allowed to translate limericks."

"Sounds like your brothers in arms would make good competition for me in my freelance gig," I hummed and waved my hand in the direction of the nearest leaf. "Time to go complete the quest."

"Agreed," the pirc nodded. "Let's hear what new wisdom the salad wishes to bestow upon us. Maybe we'll get something useful to do. By the way, what's your freelance gig?"

"I'm in a band. I play guitar and sing," I admitted. "But for a while now, I've been earning money as a freelance writer. I manage my clients' correspondence and write letters for them. Typically of a romantic nature. Especially verses, confessions, and other such purple nonsense. Few people read books anymore and being able to compose an intelligible letter—one that can charm a girl's heart is, uh, well a rarity. And I've encountered so many romantic lines and verses in songs that I can write this kind of Pabulum with my left foot while dozing on the couch. And I get paid for it too. Not much, but in our age of unemployment, it's something. If everyone was as well-read as you, I'd be screwed."

"Well the truth is that there are plenty of well-read people," Chip didn't agree. "Even among civilians. But you've given me an idea about what to do when I retire. Maybe I'll start composing letters for people as well. The important thing is to not confuse them with lampoons."

"There's plenty of demand for lampoons too," I reassured my potential competitor. "The heartbroken ladies commission them by the truckload, so you won't starve, don't worry. I even have a steady client for this line of work. Judging by the volume, she has an entire herd of jerks. I can't imagine where she finds them."

"Same place as my ex," Chip smiled crookedly and fell silent.

I didn't wish to delve into his personal life and this topic of conversation petered out between us.

The leafevator accepted our weight and drifted off on its picturesque route—shamelessly wasting the time we paid for to be in-game.

"The slang here is cute," Chip was the first to break the silence. "Some kind of hybrid of specific terms with everyday expressions."

"It's been several decades in the making, starting back during the board game days, where we'd use dice to roll for outcomes. There were many different gaming communities back then and some terms came from other languages as well as from other games. If you add to this the fact that gamers come from all strata of society, each with their own vocabulary and the blending that took place year after year—and you get gaming slang. VR is a curious place where a billionaire may chat with an ordinary kid. Everyone's subject to the game."

"I doubt a billionaire would waste his time or money here," Chip mused. "Those people like to keep track of their finances. I take it, this isn't your first time in Barliona?"

"No, it is. But I've been playing games since childhood." I said and added, "I don't agree with you about the billionaires. Money in Barliona is converted to legal tender at the government level, so there's some serious funds in this game. The leet guilds..." Noting the unhappy twitch in the pirc's ear, I corrected myself, "The best guilds give real-life corporations a run for their money, in terms of income. And their leaders are millionaires. If you see a guild leader from among the top dozen guilds, you can be sure that that's a billionaire."

"No way," Chip didn't believe me. "Are you saying that you can earn money by playing here? So why doesn't everyone get rich and log out?"

"In theory, yes, you can get rich. You get money for doing quests and then you can cash out irl—uh, I mean in real life. It's just that the subscription as well as your costs in-game and all the various paid services will consume all your income. Here you have to buy a purse, there you have to buy a new weapon, a horse, a snack at the tavern or resources for leveling up in your profession. The outcome is that at best you break even but end up making enough to pay the subscription. Many players invest money from reality in the game to ensure that their gameplay is comfortable. That's why I never played Barliona before. I couldn't even afford the monthly sub."

"And now you can?" Chip asked and immediately waved a paw apologetically: "Sorry. Not my business."

"Don't stress it. I decided to gain new experiences in search of inspiration. Someone gave me a few months of playtime as a gift."

The leaf stopped at the Branch of Vocation and I buttonholed the nearest NPC who informed me that he'd seen Amaryllis at the druidic training ground.

"How is it different from an ordinary training ground? And why would druids even need a training ground—aren't they like pacifist gardeners?" Chip wondered aloud.

"There's no such thing as pacifist players in games like this one. Even the holiest of healers can cast a nightmare debuff on you. As I understand it, training grounds are there for all classes in order to develop their skills and practice casting their spells. Rogues use them to level their agility, stealing and whatever else. Bards blast targets with their instruments in their tent. And druids work on their own skillset. As I understand it, they're not pacifist gardeners here, but simply forest mages with their own particular spells. Haven't you chosen a class yet? Try and play as a druid if you haven't. By the way," I remembered a question I wanted to clarify, "how do you change classes? Are all of them available to you or is there some ladder?"

"The spellbook has the starting skills of all the classes but they're not active. I go to an instructor—or whatever they're called—from a class that I want to study. He activates the skill of his class, I figure out what I need to do with it and then test it out. Something like that."

"And who are you at the moment?"

"A warrior. Actually, one of the reasons I came here was to check out the witches and whatnot. Pircs don't do well with magic. Although they do brew a mean ale," Chip added and squinted with pleasure.

Amaryllis handed over the promised reward and sent us onto our next quest—now we had to polish the same old palace square with some wax. The surprising thing to me was that she made no objection about the increase in the number of the party. So I could share a quest with a hundred players and everyone would get the same reward? Interesting...

"Wait a few minutes." I stopped Chip who was headed back to the leaf. "I want to test the new trait."

I quickly summarized the Fame trait to the pirc and he stepped aside with his ears perked and ready to listen. I picked out a biota headed in our direction and began to play an ancient heartrending romance from the 19th century. The NPC stopped to listen and once the song ended received the 'Impressed' buff. My Attractiveness with her was precisely 21. Not wishing to relinquish my hold on my audience, I performed another song in the same vein and by the end, had three listeners. Once I concluded, the buff timer for the first NPC reset and the newcomers received the buff for the first time. My Attractiveness with the first biota stayed at 21. This meant that I wouldn't be able to farm Attractiveness with a long concert. Too bad. On the other hand, I learned that the status effect only appears once the song ends. By the way, on the topic of ending...

I ended my next song in the middle and looked closely at the NPCs' properties. The buff did not reset. In other words, cutting corners didn't do the trick. What about this way?

I recited a short poem from a kids' book. It was brief but complete and I performed it to the end. However, the NPCs did not find this convincing. They looked around disappointed and went off on their business. I managed to check the properties of each one. 'Disappointed' and a -1 to Attractiveness, which had now returned to the baseline of 20. And what if I play something infinite like 'A billion bottles of beer on the wall?'

"They don't seem to value such classics," Chip sympathized when I gave up at the 999,999,985th bottle of beer. "Are you going to carry on with your experiments or shall we get on with our our MCD?"

"MCD?" I echoed, puzzled.

"Maintenance and cleaning day," the pirc explained. "The day of the week designated for putting things in order, maintaining equipment and resolving other custodial issues."

"Yeah, sure," I couldn't help compare our quest with Chip's military characterization. I suppose it *was* an MCD. "Let's go do this quest. I'll carry on my trials some other time."

"How did you reach the Tree anyway?" I asked Chip several minutes later as we huffed polishing the floor. If it weren't for the experienced pirc, I'd never even figure out what to do. "It's teeming with aggressive monsters, you can't walk or ride through it."

"Escort duty..." Chip cracked a cruel smile and

explained: "I got assigned to escort a caravan. There are these caravans here that travel regularly between the pircs and biota. If you wait for it to appear, you can travel protected by the guard—unless you're that guard. And if you help them, you gain experience along the way too. The only drawback is everyone keeps begging you to 'tank.' What a dreamy, magical forest, huh? They give you a stick and a rag—why not just give us a mop? The penalty for careless performance of duty is two days in the brig and a diet of water and bread," he exclaimed. "All right, I've had enough of this crap. Let's get on with it. Otherwise we'll be here until the carrots come home."

"Erm..." It's not that I particularly enjoyed a detour into history but I did want to complete the quest. "What about the quest?"

"The quest must be completed," the pirc flourished a claw. "Only we'll make it more logical, quicker and funner. Do you have a knife?" With these words, Chip drew his handaxe and began to quickly whittle the piece of wax, scattering the shreds around the square.

"No, my only weapon's this lute," I said, watching my partner work with wonder. I didn't even want to imagine what he had in mind.

When he finished crumbling the wax, he threw the rag onto the floor, spread it out and ordered:

"Squat down like a street bum and give me your hands."

"I'm a little scared," I confessed, sensing something bad coming, but I did as he asked. 'Yolo, so whatev' as the ancients used to say.

Chip turned his back to me, grabbed my hands and began to drag me like one of those rickshaws that carry tourists around the historical parts of Ho Chi Minh City. I couldn't gauge the speed exactly, but I'd estimate the pirc was about as fast as a sleigh dog.

"Buy the ticket ride the ride!" he hollered happily. "Don't I make a good pony?"

I have no idea where Chip learned this method of polishing floors but it worked. In a mere five minutes, a notification appeared announcing that we had completed the quest and we had a good laugh.

"That's it...Whoa there, pony!"

"Whee-eee," Chip whinnied obediently and stopped in place.

"We can go complete the quest," I got to my feet. One nice thing about VR is your limbs don't fall asleep from squatting in an awkward pose. "At this pace, you and I will scour the entire tree, receive exalted status and become council members in one day. I suppose they'll put of us in charge of cleaning. I wonder, do they have a ministry of health here?"

"If they don't, we'll make sure to introduce one," Chip nodded decisively. "We're already responsible for at least two innovations in these parts, so why not arrange a third? Healthcare, housing administration, public transport..." Just then, a leafevator full of passengers drifted across the pirc's ken causing him to sigh bitterly: "Never mind. I think they've figured out the last bit."

"I propose we make use of it. By the way, how did you end up in Barliona?" I inquired when our leaf began to carry us from branch to branch. "You're unfamiliar with gaming slang, so you're not a gamer."

As if distracted, the pirc hesitated a few moments, examining the landscape rushing past us.

"Just kind of..." Chip pulled off one glove and snatched a flower off a branch with his paw whose finger pads resembled little pillows.

"I'm experiencing a long spell of R&R at the moment." The pirc crushed his catch in his claws and inhaled the aroma. "Rest and relaxation, that is. I'll be spending the majority of my time between four walls for the next three months. So a friend of mine suggested I try this out. He started himself recently—to make his furlough go by faster. He told me that, unless I get too involved, I could knock back and relax here."

It was clear that Chip didn't wish to elaborate on this issue, so I didn't bother inquiring further. Who knows what happened to him? Maybe he'd been suspended or something and now he's rotting from boredom in some FSM-forsaken place. Maybe he has health issues or maybe there's something else. People enter Barliona to get away from reality too. It wouldn't do to pry into someone's personal life.

"Why'd you choose the name you did?" I asked another question that had occupied me.

"That's the name of the cat in my wing," the pirc grinned. "A massive furry ruffian. He's as shameless as a warrant officer weeks from retirement. We got his name from a movie character. There's this ancient movie about a toy soldier with an embedded AI that comes off the assembly line and starts to wipe out everyone who gets in his way. Our kitty's the same—from the moment he got there, he's been shredding the rats and other critters into fur and feathers. He's dug up gophers, pulled agoutis out of tree trunks and rassled snakes. The bastard even put away our logistics officer's pet chinchilla."

This became the first of a series of war stories. The time flew by unnoticed. I found another sigil of the Tenth and after two further cleaning and polishing quests, I received my long-desired second level—as well as a simple cape with a leaf-shaped buckle.

"Cool," I said once the glow around me faded and the wave of pleasure receded. "Do you think that if you reach a new level somewhere in enemy territory at night—the enemy will be able to see the glow?"

"Well if they do, at least you'll have announced your arrival to everyone present," the pirc replied and laughed happily. "You'll lead the hit parade!"

"You have a point. A bard sneaking around in stealth when I have to play music to cast spells—is a bunch of nonsense."

The thought of stealth jogged a lever in my head.

"Listen, there's an idea!"

"For a fancy, vanity suicide?" the pirc asked puzzled. "You haven't been reading Hagakure too much have you?"

"I'm not talking about that," I waved him away, delicately omitting the fact that I'd never read that book (or author?). "I came down from the tree yesterday and one of the local critters ate me instantly. I kept thinking about how to level up around here. I mean, even if I fight alongside a tank, I'll get slain before he can step over to help me. Just now I remembered that biota can hide in the forest. This means that if we go together and I'll start out camouflaged, the predator will attack you first and then I'll pop out of hiding and pile the spells on him."

It wasn't a bad idea, but...Well, there were several buts. Like for instance that there could be more than one predator. And that my singing could draw more aggro. The local fauna could detect biota despite our racial trait.

"But if that doesn't work, we'll have twelve hours until our next respawn ahead of us," I admitted openly.

"Let's do it." My companion nodded without any further thought.

"For safety's sake we should invite someone else to our party. I can heal or I can do damage, but I can't do both at once."

Chip grew pensive and began scratching his head.

"I don't have any candidates," he finally admitted. "But I'm only for it."

"With a pirc in our party, we shouldn't have trouble finding someone," I reassured him. "But while we're still in town, we should resolve the question of our professions. Have you committed to anything?"

"Uh-huh," he nodded. "Back when I was joining the academy. I've remained true ever since then," Chip made a grim face and saluted with his paw.

"I'm talking about your gaming specialty, you old jarhead!" I snorted. "A sculptor, an artist, a smith, some kind of herbalist...I've counted about fifty various professions so far on the fora."

"Why I'm a man—uh, cat—uh, pirc of many talents," the furball quipped. "I can paint so well that the final result will end up among the sculptures of Michelangelo in the Louvre or Hopper's paintings in the Art Institute. You just point me at my model and don't think too hard." Chip crossed his eyes and licked a bit of straw from his nose. "But speaking seriously...I actually haven't thought about this."

"Strictly speaking, you can study whatever you like. The only limitation is that your first chosen profession becomes your main one. Any other one can't be developed further than ten points above base. It's therefore better to think a little before choosing the first one. I've decided to become a Cartographer."

"Topography?" The pirc thought for a bit and then swatted the air with resolve. "Let's double down! I'm not bad at sketching plats and I know how to read a map."

"Plats? What's that?"

"Roughly speaking, a sketch of an area," the pirc explained. "You draw the most conspicuous landmarks like a river bend or a tall hill or something like that."

"Thank Pasta, it's not that complicated here. All you have to do is recall what you've seen and your hand automatically draws the map. You don't need a lot of brains to do it and even an inept topographer like me can become a cartographer."

The pirc scowled happily and rubbed his paws.

"We'll start a cartography company!" he announced. "We'll rake in the money with shovels. The only thing we have to do is find some aircraft with a nice combat radius. Any ideas?"

"There are flying creatures that you can ride, like griffins," I recalled my earlier research. "But something tells me it's not that simple. Otherwise anyone who felt like it would make maps and they wouldn't be worth a thing. I read that some of the rarer ones get sold for hundreds of thousands of gold. They're not world maps—rather maps of localities."

"How much?" the pirc wheezed, his eyes popping. "Right, we'll need a blimp or something like that as soon as possible. We're going to be billionaires, you and I!"

"Uh-huh. Just remember that the cheapest griffin costs a million gold."

"Why my *Mayhap* costs less!" Chip objected. "Have they lost their minds, charging such prices?!"

"I mean, that's the entire idea underpinning the game—they're trying to squeeze as much money as they can out of us," I decided to let the pirc in on the worst-kept secret of Barliona. "What's a Mayhap?"

"Not 'what,' but 'who,'" Chip corrected me. "She's my chopper. My beauty..." he said with sincere gentleness and some odd, sorrow in his voice.

"Well I'm not sure that a griffin is harder to get than a chopper, but either way they aren't cheap. To be honest, I have trouble imagining why someone would sink so much money into the game. But whatever—let's go see the Cartographer. Scrooge's heaps of gold didn't earn themselves."

CHAPTER SEVEN

THE CHIEF CRITERION for choosing cartography as my main profession wasn't some virtual mountain of gold on the horizon but rather the hole in my pocket out in grim reality. Mining was out of the question since it required leaving the secure area and spending hours among the angry mobs looking for resources and extracting them. And a crafting profession like blacksmithing didn't fit owing to the lack of resources and money for acquiring them. As a result, cartography was the simplest option. Leveling up in this profession didn't require a lot of investment and according to the fora, drawing maps was pretty easy. Additionally, the profession's bonus to Intellect was worth keeping in mind as well as the opportunity it afforded to solve Cypro's riddle. One way or another, I'll have to scour my immediate surroundings to level up and that means I'll find and mark all the sigils on my map. Then I'll be able to find patterns in them and solve Cypro's riddle. And I had no doubt that this was a riddle. Otherwise, why make this a class-based quest and link it with the top bard of the race?

As I assumed, the cartography instructor was on the Branch of the Craftsmen. I had to admit that the Tree was conveniently designed—everything was simple and intuitive.

"Have you decided to learn how to make maps?" asked the old Cartographer with a wrinkled face of bark. More than anything, he reminded me of a short ent from Tolkien's classic. "An admirable choice, young lady! Bards wander the world like tumbleweeds. You will find cartography invaluable in your travels."

I nodded enthusiastically, demonstrating that this was precisely the logic that had led me to cartography and therefore to this instructor. Chip sighed and scratched noisily behind my back. We paid 20 silver each to study the profession and received a cartography set in return. The little case contained parchment and ink for drawing maps.

"Oh, I see that you've chosen cartography as your main profession!" the cartographer exclaimed happily when the blue glow of education had faded around us. "I am flattered! Most of our people prefer to live closed, quiet lives, never straying beyond the Arras. As a result, cartography is not in demand. The biota and pircs know the hidden lands without any maps and do not leave their boundaries. I'm ashamed to admit it but I hardly have anything to offer for sale..."

The old man sighed and indicated his paltry

wares: a map of the Hidden Forest, maps of the Tree and the Lair, the pirc city, and several maps of the territories abutting the Arras, which by his own admission featured more whitespace than corroborated information. On top of all this, due to recent events, parts of the Forest had changed and some of the maps were out of date. And yet, despite all this, the maps cost quite a penny: from one hundred to three thousand gold. Considering that my budget—which had grown after I completed my quest—barely withstood the expenditure of 20 silver on studying my new profession, I could forget acquiring one of these maps for a long time. I'm better off wandering around the Tree and drawing my own.

Hmm...drawing my own map...

"And what if my companion and I create our own maps during our travels, ones you don't have, and bring them to you to add to your stock?"

"Oh that would be wonderful indeed! If you, young lady, and your fellow traveler manage to bring me proper maps of the lands beyond the Arras, I shall reward you handsomely! I will pay gold for general maps; for rare exemplars with details, I shall allow you to make a copy of my prize jewel—an entirely unique map which contains an encrypted guide to an ancient treasure."

Quest available: *Maps for the Cartographer*. Description: The old cartographer is sad because...

Quest type: Rare. Reward: Variable. Penalty for failing/refusing the quest: None.

I just about began to drool. When I leave my starting location, I'll be sure to chart every step I take. Then when I come back, I'll make bank. All that was left was to chart some unexplored territory and get my hands on that treasure map!

"I will be happy to help you!" I promised, accepting the quest.

"Why lose time?" the pirc suddenly spoke up. "We were about to descend from the Tree anyway. We can make corrections to the maps as we journey. The only problem is that we don't have a map to correct. If you gave us one, we would have something to work with."

The cartographer grew pensive: On the one hand the offer was reasonable and arguing with a terrible beast didn't seem appealing, yet on the other hand, giving up a map for free was out of the question. I had to give Chip his due—he'd really put the issue in its proper terms.

"If I start handing out maps to anyone who shows up, I'll be left penniless," the cartographer's response suggested that greed had won out. I had to intervene urgently.

"You don't have to hand them out for nothing," I began to prod the vendor. "You can simply lend us a map temporarily and you'll get it back with more details."

"And what if you use the map but don't do the work?" The cartographer objected for appearance sake, though I could see that he was ready to give in.

"Then you can charge us for renting the map," Chip offered.

The old man hesitated, calculating something.

"If you don't return the map in one month— improved by at least five percent—you shall pay me half its value: 150 gold. I will pay you twenty gold for each percent of accuracy above the nominal 5%. And if you improve the map by more than 20%, you will receive a special reward."

"Thirty-five gold, not twenty," Chip began to haggle. "We have to take into account transportation costs, food, as well as a surcharge for complexity and pressure. Additionally, charting in dangerous territory will incur a threefold charge. And note that I'm omitting rations and daily allowances here."

"I don't quite understand what it is you're talking about, my clawed friend, but my conditions stand—twenty gold and no more. I am taking a risk as it is—you could simply copy the map and pay me half its price without doing any of the work. But, considering that you've decided to become cartographers, I'll trust you as my colleagues."

"And we're taking a risk with our skulls, trusting this map," the furball dug in. "If something happens to us, we won't even be able to ask anyone for help. Where's the Vespucci who drew this map, eh? He's not around! So let's just settle on 25 gold each and call it a deal. And keep in mind that we'll be marking the elevations as we chart the areas we travel through. Heck, if you give us the equipment, we'll even sound the depths of the bodies of water we come across!"

The cartographer scratched the bridge of his nose with a little doubt, weighing the pros and cons, then sighed and waved his hand.

"All right—twenty-five gold and not a copper more!"

"Agreed." Chip bared his fangs with satisfaction.

Quest available: *Update the Map of the Hidden Forest*. Description: The old cartographer hasn't left the Tree in a long time and his maps are out of date. Make at least 5% worth of improvements to the map and receive a reward from the cartographer. Quest type: Common. Limitation: Only for cartographers. Reward: Variable, depending on the degree of success. Penalty for failing/refusing the quest: None. Penalty for failing the quest: Pay 150 gold to the cartographer.

"We agree," I announced, prodding the pirc with my elbow and accepting the quest.

"Eh?" the pirc started. "Sorry, I got caught up—the game has offered me the bartering skill. Guess I'll take it. Should come in handy."

"Excellent!" Ignoring the pirc's remark about his new skills, the cartographer smiled and handed Chip the map of the Hidden Forest. "Come back to me when you reach Level 10 in your new profession!"

"Done and done," Chip accepted the scroll gingerly.

Despite his noticeable disdain for the local topographers, I noticed that he was pretty respectful towards the maps themselves. No doubt it was due to his profession, though who in our age looks at paper when there's a digital map on hand?

"Did they teach you to haggle in the army as well?" I inquired when we had left the cartographer's stall.

"Uh-huh," Chip nodded seriously. "Whether you're posted in the East or in Africa—if you go to the market, you better know how to haggle. Otherwise they won't understand you and decide that you're an uneducated oaf and won't take you seriously. They have a different mentality out there—it's like a pastime for them. You'll spend fifteen minutes haggling over some smoked piece of meat for fifteen minutes. The seller will provide all sorts of excuses—everything from his personal recipe for smoking it, to the illness that has recently afflicted his mother-in-law—yet when you mention that you're trying this snack for the first time, he'll give you three extra just so you can have a taste. The skill of haggling is part of the culture there and a pretty important one at that. But here, I sense that we've been conned, oh my sylvan bouquet. That soggy lettuce seemed only too happy to accept our deal."

Hearing such a poetic description, I guffawed and reckoned it impolite to remain in debt.

"Well, I don't know, oh my fanged ruffian, the map really does cost three hundred gold and we could easily do the quest in good faith but also make a copy and get it for half-price. My hunch though is that if we do this, the cartographer is going to charge us extra for any further instruction. Heck, he might even tell the other vendors to raise prices."

"The cartographer got a promotion back there. Say what you like, but when it comes to maps I know my business."

"We'll need to make two maps of the same locale and compare them. I don't know a thing about cartography, but according to the fora, I don't need to—the system does everything automatically. We can see how much difference it makes."

"Never trust stupid electronics," the pirc raised a claw to the sky. "Even the most cutting-edge device with the most elaborate software is but the work of a human. And humans are prone to error."

"That's what I'm saying—we can check. Meanwhile, let's find another player and try out our mettle hunting the local fauna."

Just in case, I re-read the descriptions of the quests I had and finding no mention of the Council's schism, nor the imminent visit of the Kartossian delegation, sent Chip the quest for exterminating the blighted beasts. I decided to keep the quest for destroying the source of the blight secret for the time being. Sometimes a player seems decent enough but changes entirely when the first difficulty arises. It'd be silly to share a rare quest with someone who was still a stranger after all.

"Here you go. We'll be able to grind our rep with the locals while we're at it."

"What's with reputation in this game?" grumbled Chip, accepting the quest. "This kind of thing was much simpler in Afghanistan.

"Huh? What are you talking about?"

"You never had to annihilate anything there— simply haul the chow and pass it out to the locals," Chip was happy to share his remembrances. "Blitz through a gorge, unload, have some tea with the locals and off you go back home to base. But the reputation, oh the reputation—in our unit, when Jake slipped on the ice and fell, why there was a line of well-wishers stretching around his tent."

"Why there're plenty of quests like that here in actual fact. I read that the majority of quests in Barliona are focused on the social component of the game. Help a grandmother cross the street, bring a kitten down from a tree, save the world. I grow my reputation whenever I play music to the biota. It just so happens that this quest we have is one of the 'search and destroy' types."

I was being a bit of a hypocrite here—the quest for finding the source of the blight was precisely one of those 'save the forest' kind of quests.

"I don't want to save the world here either," Chip waved. "Saving the world is my job as it is. I'm here playing so that others can save me for a change. *'But I guess that's my fate: Thirty years I've been flying in the mountains...'* Let's go do a bit of poaching, my lovely sundew."

"Let's, oh super nerd."

Seeing no point in running around the entire Tree in search of players and hesitant to ask in the public chat, I decided to use the game mail.

The mailbox was located in the local bank, which is where we went. While Chip spoke to his bank representative, figuring out the local system of deposits and bonuses, I quickly wrote a letter to Prickly Sloe, the necromancer I'd come across the Market Branch when I met Chip.

Hello Sloe!

We've already met. You told me about the social quests for preparing for the festival. My friend, a pirc warrior, and I have decided to descend from the Tree and level up a bit at the expense of the local critters.

Want to join us?
Lorelei

I sent the letter and decided to ask the banker about the bank's services. It turned out that I could acquire a special wallet which would immediately transfer any money I earned to the bank so that I wouldn't drop it if something happened to me. And yet simply hearing the price of this service forced me to say no to the idea: They wanted 2000 gold per year! Why I wouldn't even earn so much in a year! Hearing about the other services offered by the bank—such as the portable mailbox—I grew downright despondent. So many interesting goodies and all so expensive. Eh, I should've agreed to the beggar trait—I would've spent my days playing at some busy intersection, grinding my Fame and earning my money.

Chip managed to articulate my thoughts better than I could. Leaving his meeting, he broke into an expansive oration consisting of brief but very clear and vivid images. If I strip it down to its essence, the gist of what he was saying could be expressed with a simple sentiment: These people have lost their damn minds.

"Where's my red flag and cap?" Chip concluded his fiery monologue.

"Eh?" I asked, once again puzzled.

"I'll clench it in my fist, climb aboard my tank and lead the people to revolution," Chip clarified.

"Just like Lenin in October. You can be our *Aurora*, singing something revolutionary." He assumed a picturesque pose, tucking one paw behind his back and stretching the other one before him as if pointing to some distant point only he could discern. "And then, the oppressed masses of gamers, groaning beneath the yoke of the local plutocracy, shall burst their bonds of slavery and...Listen, do you think Communism is a viable ideology for Barliona?"

"Maybe, I guess. But I only really know how to play the *Marseillaise* from that, uh, genre," I warned just in case. "Although, I could always expand my repertoire if it's for a good cause."

Our nascent revolution was interrupted by a group of players who'd become excited at the sight of a pirc. Only it wasn't his heroic pose that drew their attention.

"Eh bro, you'd make fine tank, bro!" offered a shaman named Coleen the Acute. "The party's ready, you're the only one we're missing."

"Comrades!" the pirc exclaimed with fire. "I am pleased to see you among the ranks of defenders of the revolution! But I am not alone—my trusted commissar is with me." He nodded towards me. "You will have to forgive us—we haven't the means yet to supply you with Mausers and leather dusters."

The puzzled silence that came in response clearly indicated that none of the newcomers were much interested in history.

"I don't get it, are you gonna tank or not?" Coleen clarified just in case.

"We already have a party," I reminded Chip about our plans to invite an acquaintance. Traveling somewhere with a person with this kind of attitude...Sure I'm a snob but I can't do anything about it.

"I don't collaborate with bourgeois lapdogs who don't support the ideals of the proletarian struggle," the pirc quipped. "We work exclusively with the tried and tested comrades. So no, no business for you, bourgeois!"

He slid his handaxe from its sheath and began to pare his nails with it, making a show of ignoring our prospective employers.

"What a Spartacus!" Coleen remarked and moved onward with her gang.

Judging by the tone, this was supposed to be an insult, but it was a bit of an odd one. However, everything fell into place once I read the next system notification that popped up:

Attention! Your profanity filter is turned on. You may turn it off in the character settings (only for players aged 21 and older).

So that's what it was. This game is simply bristling with filters for all kinds of things. As I fiddled with the settings, I failed to notice Sloe approach the bank. But of course—how else would he read the letter? The necromancer had already managed to reach his third level. He sure wasn't losing time.

"Hey Sloe—wait up!" I barely managed to call my acquaintance before he entered the bank. "If you're here for the letter—it's from me."

"Yes? I'm listening."

"...Shush!" the pirc interrupted. He made a terrible face, brought his finger to his lips and in a theatrical whisper that was quiet enough for the groundhogs under the Tree to hear, said: "The sentries don't slumber, comrade! We are offering you a chance to join the Red Guard and fight for the proletariat with a rifle in your hands!"

Sloe's eyebrows hiked up, which, along with his branched hairdo gave him the resemblance of a surprised moose.

"I sort of always preferred the royalists," he finally replied to the pirc. "But if the quest is an interesting one, I am prepared to examine the options."

"That's precisely how the Communists recruited professional soldiers to their ranks," Chip announced in a normal voice. "Your turn, commissar," he jabbed me with an elbow and then froze, blinked several times in puzzlement and then broke into a grin.

"The system's offered me the Chatterbox trait," he reported. "Accepted. Revolution's definitely on now, boys!"

"What's the Chatterbox trait?" I inquired.

Sloe replied instead of Chip:

"A bonus stat like 'Elocution' or 'Charisma.' It enables you to increase your Attractiveness with NPCs by blathering and also gives you the option of talking an NPC's ears off until he falls asleep. Helps with crowds too. Like if you find yourself in a tight spot in some remote village where all the villagers are armed with pitchforks and torches and chasing you—with Chatterbox you'll have a chance to talk your way out. Not a bad trait for a pirc to have. So why'd you send me the letter?"

This Sloe is clearly an experienced player. He'll come in handy for a couple newbies like us.

"We have a quest to kill some forest critters and a big fat tank in our party."

"I ain't fat!" Chip took offense. "I'm fluffy!" As proof he tousled his nape fur. He had a point—he didn't much resemble a tank so much as a garrulous brush for washing bottles.

"Either way, let's go!" I concluded, ignoring the pirc.

"Why me?" the necromancer asked suspiciously.

"You helped me so now I'll help you," I replied honestly. "In addition, you gave me the impression of a reasonable person and an experienced player. Our little newb team could use a leader."

Sloe drummed on his belt buckle pensively, looked over Chip skeptically, then me, and finally made his decision.

"Send me the invite. I have to exit the game in a few hours anyway. If we get wiped it won't be a big deal."

I sent Sloe the party invite as well as the same quest I'd shared with Chip.

"We take precautions," Chip reassured him in the meantime. "Or what are you on about?"

"Oh, you're really newbs, huh?" the necromancer sighed and explained: "'Wipe' is when the entire raiding party dies. In our case, simply our party. Oh...Lorelei, what have you been doing this entire time?"

"Erm, playing," was my honest answer.

"So why's your Intellect still at two?"

"Well I only just leveled up, I still haven't allocated my stat points."

"What's wrong with you? Intellect for the biota grows automatically through casting. Heal me with all the mana you got."

Sensing that I had already made some mistake, I did as he requested.

Skill increase:

+50% to Intellect. Total: 100%. +1 to Intellect. Total: 3.

Attention! You have healed another player.

A new trait has become available to your character: Healer. The higher your level in Healer, the less mana you need for healing spells and the spells themselves become more powerful. There is a percentage chance for the spell to be cast again without costing any mana at all.

Do you accept? Attention! You will not be able to remove an accepted trait!

Damn...What a dummy I am. So this entire time, I could have been burning my mana to level my Intellect? I suppose my regret was writ large on my face because Sloe simply shook his head:

"Don't waste your unallocated stat points for now. Level your Intellect by means of spells any chance you get. All right. The tank's pretty fat indeed. He should be able to survive without needing to be healed—and my dps should be high enough."

I checked his general stats and whistled to myself. At only Level 3 he already had his Intellect up to 42. Yeah, this guy could one-shot a forest critter.

"All right. Let's go. Intellect comes with time, and your quest's a good one. Where'd you get it, by the way?"

"Talking to various NPCs about various topics."

"Yes? Will you tell me exactly how you received it?"

"Why not?"

By the time we descended from the Tree, I

managed to share my sad tale of my first venture into the greater world and my subsequent questions to Amaryllis about the blighted creatures. Sloe, in his turn, let me in on how I can activate my natural camouflage ability and when we landed, we were invisible (or so we hoped) to the local aggressive monsters.

My old acquaintance, the Blighted Lynx didn't keep us waiting: As soon as we stepped off the leaf, something...strange...attacked Chip. This member of the feline species was covered with thorns like a stegosaurus, only instead of bone, the thorns were clearly botanical in nature. The pirc swiped away the beast with his halberd, a clump of dark energy shot from Sloe's hands and the lynx vanished without a trace before I could even check its properties.

Experience gained: +80 XP. 37 remaining until next level.

Achievement unlocked: 'Bane of the Animal Kingdom Level 1' (19 animal kills until next level).

Achievement reward: +1% damage to Animals.

You can look at your list of achievements in your character settings.

"Grants less experience, but it's more reliable," Sloe nodded approvingly. "Last time I killed four, earned two levels and then ran into two mobs at once and had to beat it."

"I don't know about mobs," Chip poked his halberd at where the 'body' of the monster had dissolved, "but if a kitty like that jumped me somewhere out in reality, like in the Congo let's say, I'd lose it too. And I mean in my pants. Back in my younger days I dropped acid several times, but never did I see anything like that."

"Huh?! You're from Africa?" Sloe asked surprised. "What are you doing in Kartoss? You're supposed to start on a different continent."

"Shush!" the pirc hushed him once again, then straightened out, slapped himself on the chest and leaned against his halberd. "I'm undercover. I've been working for the Belgians in the Congo. But now they've sent me here. A new post, new responsibilities."

"You're one of those patients playing from a psychiatric capsule, aren't you?" Sloe asked surprised.

"Did you skip your history classes or something?" Chip replied in kind. "Damn kids these days. They see all the Africa stuff, but don't know their history enough to know where it all comes from. So where to, comrade commissar?"

"I'm no commissar, but I can answer your question," Sloe began to issue orders. "Lori and I camouflage ourselves and start running in circles slaughtering every forest critter that comes across our path."

In two hours we managed to complete and re-complete Amaryllis' quest, killing as many blighted creatures as got underfoot, and as a reward, I earned my fifth level, Chip his seventh, and Sloe his sixth. In the course of our adventure, my Intellect grew to eleven points and now I began to bitterly regret the days I'd wasted. On the other hand, I rummaged around the combat logs, disabling any superfluous notifications like the one about how much XP I had until my next level. I just didn't need useless numbers flying around me.

"All right, you newbies. I need to get some sleep. I have work in the morning. Kill me real quick and we'll see each other tomorrow," Sloe said in a business-like tone.

"Kill?" No doubt my eyes had grown as wide as Chip's saucers. "What's with you?"

"Are you guys not aware of the killing thing? Lemme explain. If a player attacks another player in Barliona, the system assigns him 'outlaw' status for eight hours. That entire time he earns no XP and other players can attack him without becoming outlaws themselves. There are other details but the main point is that towns will reward you for killing outlaws. Since I'm not planning to be in Barliona in the next 12 hours, I'll attack one of you, get the outlaw status and then you can kill me and earn 100 gold. When I come back, you slip me my cut. And you can do this any time a player is about to leave the game for more than 12 hours."

"Why does the corp permit this?" I asked surprised. "Isn't this an exploit?"

"The higher your level the more the 30% XP penalty hurts you. For higher-level players, a hundred gold is a drop in the ocean. It's not worth the bother. And farming is out of the question—if all you do is die at your buddies' hands for a month on end—you'll only earn about the cost of a monthly sub and the corp will break even. For minnows like us, it's a nice bonus and the taste of easy money."

"Will you just look at those corporate pigs," Chip even sounded pleased. "They've calculated all of it. But look, won't your being a party member affect us somehow? Like some extra fine or something?"

"You have to kick me from the party first. You won't hurt me otherwise. As for fines—that's only if you attack me in some sacred place, in the middle of a city or in front of a bunch of guards or even some location where that kind of stuff is explicitly prohibited. There's not much to it really. I've already checked it out. Say the word and I'll attack you."

"Erm...You won't slay us with a single spell, will you?" I asked cautiously, remembering the damage the necromancer did to the mobs.

"You, for sure. Chip, I'd have to see what his resistances are. But I'm just going to smack you with my staff, don't worry."

"Well in that case, *en garde!*" Chip removed Sloe from our party, stepped in front of me to shield me and saluted the necromancer with his halberd like a regular duelist.

"At least I'll get to see how much real damage I do with one blow," the necromancer smiled, raised his staff and brought it down as hard as he could on Chip's nose. Chip tossed his furry head and then performed some fancy flourish with his halberd and drove it straight into Sloe's stomach. Sloe doubled over from the force of the blow and dissolved into thin air, dropping some change which I instantly picked up. It was about three gold.

"I think it'll be fairer if we take thirty apiece and he gets forty." Chip rubbed his nose. The staff left a notable scratch on the pirc's nose and he now looked like he'd just been in a cat fight.

"He did sacrifice himself," the pirc explained his reasoning.

"Uh-huh. And we should remember to give him his change back."

"There it is!" Chip patted me on the shoulder. "That's your proletarian solidarity speaking! Well commissar, let's go claim our blood money and after that we can get back to cartography. Dang..." He suddenly smacked himself on the head. "The hell did we get into this for! This...topography!"

"What? Why?" I asked surprised.

"'Cause if there're any grunts playing this

game, all our labor will be in vain. While the enemy peers at maps, the ground infantry alters the landscape by hand and the enemy loses his way!" Chip winked to me. "Come on, let's go. You're just standing there, staring at me, scaring me."

"They haven't offered you the 'Comedian' trait yet, have they?"

"Is there one?" the pirc grew animated. "Oh boy, oh boy. Can't wait till I get it..."

"Come on you bard-wannabe," I barked. "You're just bursting with song..."

CHAPTER EIGHT

S NUG IN A SHACK IN THE BRANCH OF THE CRAFTSMEN, Chip and I began to chart our first maps. Having no idea how this was supposed to be done, I blindly followed the forum's instructions. I tried to recall the path we took that day as clearly as possible. And indeed: My hand twitched like a hand possessed and began to make confident strokes on the paper, which gradually rendered a map fragment of the location abutting the Root we had set out from. We hadn't really covered a lot of territory so my recollections only sufficed for about five minutes or so. But Chip went on drafting and drafting, piquing my envy and curiosity.

"Do you recall the name of that creek we waded across?" he asked, pausing and looking up.

"I don't believe the creek introduced itself," I grumbled, kicking myself in my head. I'd somehow forgotten all about that creek and now surreptitiously added it to my map. Something told me that its inky course deviated from that of the true thing. "Check the map that the cartographer gave us. The name should be there."

"Uh-huh." The pirc buried his snout in the scroll, pressed his ears to his head and growled unhappily.

"Nope, nothing. And the entire creek is misplaced. The topographer—may he take a spike in his beaver—is off by half a league. We'll just have to name it ourselves. We'll call it 'the Rude Creek,' After all, it didn't introduce itself, right?" The pirc went on scratching the parchment with his quill. "Now let's see, the fording depth was about..." He stared at me and wriggled his ears pensively. "...a meter thirty. Dang, and what if it's shallow at the moment? What season is it here anyway, eh?"

"I hadn't gotten around to inquiring. I'm not sure there're seasons here at all. I'll need to check the fora."

"You should...I'll indicate that the data requires clarification on seasonal precipitation," the pirc scratched with his quill. "Like that...And then there was marsh beyond the creek."

Once he'd completed his piece of the map, Chip decided to compare it to mine. Is it even worth mentioning that the comparison didn't go in my favor?

"A little off..." the pirc assessed my cartographic talents diplomatically. "Look, right here," he pointed at a glade in the forest that I had recalled and reproduced, "there's an elevation there. When you recall it as you're creating your map, remember its details: the height, the little features like the springs or the conspicuous tree with the symbol. By the way, we'll need to figure out what that symbol is. On your map, it's not clear whether it's a glade or a hillock or a ravine. And there's a little marsh here, but on your map it's all just one glade. Someone will go following it and sink to their ears in the muck. We don't want that. It's not that I care about the guy who gets stuck but if this happens, a spot will soil our little firm and that spot will be the dirt from his boot!"

I tried my hardest to recall all his important details but for an urban dweller who'd only travel out to the forest for picnics, all of these subtleties were like Greek. I never even noticed the little marsh. Maybe the grass was taller and denser, but in my mind it went down as a glade. It's not like I walked into the marsh or anything.

"Yes, we should definitely ask about the symbols. I asked Amaryllis about one I came across and received a class quest for finding similar ones all around the Tree."

I sketched an outline of the Tenth's sigil on the map's margin. Chip scratched his nose pensively, furrowed his brow and said uncertainly:

"I've seen this before somewhere...Either among the Buddhists or among the esoterics searching for Shamabala...Give me a sec." The pirc froze and his eyes went glassy for a few minutes.

"It's the flower of life," Chip announced upon

returning to the game. "An herbarium of sacred geometry. No one really knows what it means, so everyone kind of just runs with their own interpretation. We'll need to ask the locals about it. Maybe they have superstitions about it."

"Amaryllis would have mentioned them," I said dubiously. "It does make sense to check out the library though. We could research the one in the forest too. Could be another quest in it."

"Agreed," the pirc accepted the plan. "Now work on the map some more."

I looked with melancholy at the inaccuracies Chip had pointed out in my map.

"We really need to grow our respect with the biota so that we can record video. Everything'll be a lot easier then. We'll just watch the video and fill in the details. Or even simpler—I could just copy your maps," I drawled dreamily.

"It's better if you learn how to remember landmarks and measure distances accurately," Chip brought me back to, uh, virtual reality without any anger. "And so—we'll commence with lessons on topography," the pirc adjusted his imaginary glasses on his nose and switched to a mentorly tone. "As we may recall from our geography lessons in school..."

I wonder if this guy's ever serious. He seems to find a reason to goof around in everything he comes across. It's a good thing at least that he explains things so clearly to a dilettante like me—it's experience after all. Or perhaps a hidden talent for teaching. But one way or another, in a few hours I managed to get a grip on the art of the topographer, even though Chip kept referring to it as 'mere sketches,' 'botchery,' and 'invention.' He forced me to redraw the map several times until he was sure that I had gotten some knack for indicating distance and size relatively accurately. In the process, I leveled up my cartography skill to three and stopping only to dump my accumulated mana to heal Chip and level up my Intellect, sat down to the task of updating the map we'd received from the Cartographer. The updates we contributed didn't even add up to one percent so we could forget about completing this quest in the coming week.

"Right. I desperately need the 'Scroll Scribe' specialization. In addition to the +5% to Intellect, I'll be able to craft you more scrolls and you'll be able to heal yourself in combat. But to do this I need to level up my cartography to ten. One option is to explore every nook and cranny in this city and make a map of it. When are you going to sleep?"

"Not any time soon. Either way I have to..." Chip cut himself off mid-word. "I don't sleep much. Are you going to sleep already?"

"Not yet, I was just trying to figure out how much time we have. Wouldn't mind a chance to off you," I drawled dreamily. "Another hundred from the bush. But since you don't sleep a lot, you can do the honors when I go to bed."

"Really is a nice name you chose for yourself," hummed Chip. "You're bursting with humanism. All right, you bloodthirsty clump of violets, let's go put our plan in action. We'll start the first information booth in this place. Eh, there is much to be done in pursuit of the freedom of the proletariat..."

We decided to start our map of the Tree right from the place where we were—the Branch of the Craftsmen. I should mention that given the pirc's methodical approach, our task moved ahead at a snail's pace. He wanted the map to include every tiny trifle and depict the buildings' proportions accurately without limiting ourselves to schematic notes. He also insisted that we add descriptions to each building.

"This pace will send me back to the grave or the bulb or whatever," I objected after several hours, once the Branch of the Craftsmen with all its details was depicted on our map. The only consolation were the several sigils we'd found in the process. "On the other hand, my cartography skill is growing. I've reached six already. Let's go on. I have to get it to ten."

Raising my foot, I froze in mid-stride. An idea had bloomed in my green head. No, that's not even right. AN IDEA! I quickly relayed it to Chip who agreed and praised my intelligence, after which we reached the Market Branch and began to put our plan in motion.

First we marked all the buildings on the map

and then, rustling with parchment, burst into the nearest vendor stall.

"Good day," Chip began from the threshold. "We are representatives of the Red Guard and you, esteemed merchant, have been selected for an unheard of opportunity to participate in a historical event that could well revolutionize the merchandise industry. As you know, we are currently mapping the Tree with all its details and for a measly—and I want to emphasize *measly*—fifty gold, you my esteemed..." Chip paused for a second, checking the name of the stunned proprietor—"Orchidea, have the unique opportunity to memorialize you and your establishment for all posterity! For a mere fifty coins, all maps of the Tree will indicate your establishment with a description which you can choose yourself! Hurry—in two days, our promotional event will run its course and the price will grow to one hundred gold for future updates."

As Chip chattered, his Attractiveness with Orchidea grew by 1 point. On the whole, though, the NPC did not look very convinced.

"Everyone already knows where my store is located and if a traveler needs to find it, they can ask the guards and they'll tell them where to go," she said uncertainly. "And we don't get that many travelers anyway, just some odd pircs like you from the Lair."

Oh how I wish I could tell her about the coming changes, the alliance with Kartoss and the opening of the border. If I could do that, we could easily charge her five hundred gold instead of fifty. If it weren't for those meddling state secrets...

"And how will your guests even know that your store exists?" I came to my furry companion's aid. "Take me for example. I've been out of my bulb for two days now and it wasn't until this promotional event that I discovered that your wonderful establishment even existed. But with the service we're offering you, someone would just have to stop by the Cartographer's stall, buy a map and he'd see this business: 'The best household supplies store in the entire Tree!' And you get to choose this text yourself."

The NPC chewed her milk-white lip, which matched her hair for some reason, and then objected:

"But fifty gold...is a bit pricey."

"A bit pricey for a chance to become a part of history?!"

Chip really missed the mark with his meatspace profession. He'd do well in an ad agency. He'd do more than sell Australian sand to construction projects in the Sahara—he could sell sand dunes to the Bedouins for the price of a house!

"All the maps of the Tree will bear your name," the furry salesman went on chirping. "You'll be able to frame the map and hang it above your mantelpiece. You don't have a mantelpiece? Then hang it on a wall in your bedroom! And it won't be a mere map, but a..." the pirc paused for effect and then continued reverently: "an artifact of enormous historical value!"

For a moment a glowing aura surrounded Chip, indicating perhaps that his Chatterbox trait had grown. Although perhaps he improved his Bartering too...who knows?

"Are you offering the same thing to the others?" Orchidea was clearly on her last legs. Little-versed in the advertising business, she was already reckoning up the income from the influx of customers.

"Absolutely," I didn't bother to equivocate. "And try to imagine how much money will be lost by the vendors whose stores aren't described on the map with a recommendation. All the customers will go to the stores who're using our service!"

This finally convinced the poor NPC and she opened up her wallet, insisting only that we complete the map in the next two weeks and then sell her a commemorative version at a discount.

An agreement has been reached. You must complete the map of the Tree in the next 14 days and include a marker for Orchidea's store with the following text...

If you violate the terms of your agreement, your reputation with the Biota will decrease by 100.

"The store of the venerable Orchidea..." Chip muttered into his nose as he carefully drew in the new location. Feeling generous, he even drew a little five-pointed star and wrote: 'The first entrepreneur in the history of the Tree to be included in the register of entrepreneurs, businessmen and merchants, as compiled, maintained and certified by the Topographical Service of the Workers' and Peasants' Red Army (henceforth the Red Army)'

"Lordy, what a yarn I spin," he giggled. "But it's fun, isn't it?"

"Uh-huh," I nodded with satisfaction, examining the rows of stores and estimating how much gold we could shake from this one Branch. "I'm not so sure about the whole Red Army thing though. If they start asking us about armed militancy and our odd color, what are we going to tell them? Why don't we come up with some logo and name of our own? Something that stands out. So that everyone who sees it knows that they're looking at the best map in the world," I added modestly.

"The best map in the world? Bah!" The pirc began scratching the parchment with his quill enthusiastically.

"There!" he announced several minutes later, showing me his sketch.

It was vaguely familiar: A globe surrounded by a wreath of wheat that was wound with a red ribbon. It was topped with a red star with a sickle and hammer within it.

"All right, you history geek, why don't you drop

the sickle, eh? It's a bit passive aggressive for us plant people. But on the whole it's a curious idea. Give me your paw, pirc, for good fortune," I declaimed, offering Chip my hand. He shrugged his shoulders and reciprocated my gesture—only to have me pour ink on his paw and press against the reverse side of the map. The ensuing mark was something between an animal's paw and a human hand.

"Something's missing," I muttered pensively, snapped my fingers and drew a claw at each finger.

"Uh-huh, and below that write, '*Non plus ultra*, natch!'" quipped Chip. "Worthy of the Coat of Arms of the Duke of Alai..."

I guess my stupefaction was evident because the dock-tailed nerd sighed and explained:

"That's not from history. Well, not real history. It's from an ancient fantasy. There were these writers named the Strugatsky brothers. And one of their novels had a duke who had a similar coat of arms."

"In that case, let me add some distinguishing features," I promised taking the quill again. Nature hadn't granted me much drawing talent, but a stick figure lute isn't exactly The Last Supper. My final touch was a floral ornament which framed the lute against the paw print.

"Something like this, but with the paw in outline—otherwise the lute gets lost in it," I offered my sketch to the pirc.

"Excellent," he agreed. "But also let's add a

compass rose, since we're cartographers and all."

"Uh-huh," I redrew the logo, crowning it with the compass rose. "Now we need a name with a ring to it. What's a company without its brand? Red Army's already taken," I warned the pirc as he opened his mouth.

"What about the All-Union Communist Party of Bolsheviks?" He inquired carefully and receiving a nod and a fist with a grimace of 'I'll rip your tail off,' sighed deeply and went back to thinking.

"Oh!" He suddenly jerked up his head. "What about Allied Cartographic Society? We're from different races after all," Chip reasoned.

"Too long, too dull. Better something significant like 'Susanin & Co.' I guess the only problem was that Susanin had a knack for getting lost."

"Hmm...." Chip scratched his chin. "Well there are all sorts of great names to choose from: Captain Cook, Lapérouse...no, the hell with Lapérouse, he didn't end up so well...Krusenstern, Bellingshausen, Nansen...Nansen...listen, how about maybe just 'Mason & Dixon & Co.?'"

"How about something that a layperson will understand?" I offered. "Like 'The Explorers' or something? Or 'Hardcore Maps'... Hmm...How does 'Map Corps' sound to you?"

"Like the name of a porn site for cartographers," the pirc replied honestly.

"And 'The Map Gang?'" I tried again.

"It's better, but still, it evokes salacious associations in my ailed mind," Chip shrugged guiltily.

"All right, we'll come up with a worthy name later. Let's get back to our promotional activities in the meantime."

By the end of the promotional activities, Chip and I had amassed a fantastical sum of six hundred fifty gold coins, and that's not including the bounty we'd gotten for liquidating the dangerous outlaw Prickly Sloe. Only two vendors refused our promotional offer: An itinerant pirc merchant, whose tent was a temporary construction and a cantankerous old shrub who was the only jeweler in the entire Tree. Despite the high cost of his merchandise, this biota refused to pay even a single coin to the 'unknown pair of freeloaders.'

"That old root will regret scrimping his gold soon enough," I prophesied unkindly. "When he changes his mind, we'll shake no less than 300 out of him."

"Three hundred?" Chip jerked up his lip menacingly, displaying a fang as long as my finger. "For 300 we'll deign to hear his case..." He showed me the note to the jewelry store: '*Pierre's Jewels. A paltry selection of wares at inflated prices is unlikely to pique the interest of the Trees' residents and visitors.*'

"Maybe I should add something else?" he said pensively. "By the way. Why should he change his mind anyway? The moldy stump, I mean." The pirc waved his thumb over his shoulder.

"Can't say. Top Secret. Although...Give me your comm number out in reality. Confidentiality won't apply out there."

The pirc thought for a few seconds and then nodded a bit uncertainly.

"Only my camera's on the fizz at the moment," he warned. "I keep forgetting to fix it."

"The hell with the camera. We can email, if you prefer. It's just quicker by voice. You don't even have to get out of the capsule, merely leave full immersion mode."

Five minutes later I was relating to Chip the schism that had taken place among the biota elite and the imminent embassy with its logical consequence that the borders would be opened to players from different races.

"Interesting," Chip concluded when I had finished. His voice sounded a little strange. It had some light metallic timbre to it, as well as a tinge of...was it tension? As if Pavel, as Chip introduced himself, was worried about some catch or unpleasant question. As I suspected, he was simply trying to conceal his advanced age. Considering he'd mentioned being a pilot for thirty years, and some simple calculation that he couldn't have started any earlier than 18, my furry friend was probably over fifty. It's no surprise that he was trying to mask his voice a bit. Who wants to admit that he's started playing games at his respected age—and that he behaves in them like an ordinary teenager, even if a very well-read one. So he used a speech scrambler, judging by the metallic tone.

I have a lot of respect for the privacy of others. If Chip needs to guard a secret, that's his lawful right.

"You can't mention any of this in the game. I'm restricted from talking and if I spill any of this, I'll be fined heftily. But keep these future developments in mind. If we gain some reputation and get an invite to the palace, we'll have a chance of attaching ourselves to some embassy and traveling with them to the wider world."

"Don't worry, my field bouquet, if there's anything I have it's an understanding of confidentiality and secrecy," Chip assured me. "The only thing is that you shouldn't tell anyone else, since as the Arabic proverb has it, what two know the bulrushes know too."

"What about Sloe? He seems like an experienced player. He might have good advice for us."

"What guarantee do you have that he's not working for the local counterintel?" Chip objected. "If there is a secret, then there is someone charged with keeping it secret. I don't feel like tangling with spooks in a video game. So on the whole, you shouldn't. It's too early. Once we know who this Sloe is, we can think about it."

"You seem to be taking this game fairly seriously," I was flabbergasted by such a response, "but you're right, we have plenty of time to tell him. All right. Let's get back."

I have to admit that I was a bit apprehensive as I re-entered Barliona. I'd read on the fora some panicked threads about the system's capability to track what you said to people even outside of the game. As I should've expected, the rumors were just rumors. My reputation didn't change for the worse— nothing changed for the worse—except maybe the pirc's mug. He looked concentrated and consternated, as if he was trying to solve some kind of problem. As it turned out, I had guessed correctly. He barely laid eyes on me before beginning without introduction:

"Right. We need to solve the riddle of the seasons as well as learn about the local climate: when it rains here, when it snows and for how long."

"Why don't you take care of that?" I found an excuse to avoid wading deeper into various cartographic details that were clearly superfluous to the game. "I need to work on my class quest and go see the instructor to see if he has anything new for me. I have to research the other class's skills too, to see which ones I might take."

"That's right...by the way..." Chip recalled his to-do list. "I still have to try out the magic classes. Level 10 is around the corner and I need to decide soon. I won't get a chance to see what the magic stuff is all about later."

"In that case, here's the plan," I proposed. "We leave the money in the bank, fill in the rest of the map, remembering to mark Cypro's sigils, level up our cartography skills to ten, unlock the specializations— and then you kill me, I go out to reality and when I return, I'll complete my class quest. Meanwhile, you can try being a mage and learn all you can about the local climate. After that we'll pick up another couple quests for the festival. And when Sloe returns, we'll brainstorm further."

"Deal," the pirc nodded. We popped into the bank and returned to drafting the Tree's map.

Orphis, the cartography instructor was pleased with our progress on the map, and Chip managed to squeeze him for a small discount for unlocking the specialization. The golden glow that surrounded him, indicated that Chip would soon transform from a warrior to a merchant.

New cartographer specialization unlocked: 'Scroll Scribe.' This specialization allows you to enchant scrolls with spells of up to level 50 inclusive. Additionally, you may write down recipes for new items of up to level 50 inclusive. Bards unlock the ability to create their own songs.

'Scroll Scribe' specialization bonus: +5% to Intellect.

"Interesting," Chip muttered to himself, staring straight ahead. "The 'Eagle Eye' specialization increases your attentiveness. +5% chance of seeing creatures in stealth, secret items, areas and doors."

"Sounds legit. Let's go to some remote location so that you can bring me to justice. I want to go to sleep."

"Damn, I feel like some serial killer creep...going with a girl to some dark corner to kill her," the pirc joked. It didn't seem like he was pleased at having to kill me. Must be his conscience.

"Everything's worth trying once," I quipped a little glibly. "Never imagined that a military person would object to the PKing part of the game."

"It's not the kind of experience worth seeking," Chip replied and didn't say a word more.

We walked over to one of the quiet dead ends of the branch. I bet many generations of young biota came here to spend time alone concealed by the leafage. Well, and how am I worse after all?

"Why are you so grim?" I objected, noticing Chip's expression. "It's just a game. So you'll smack me a couple times and that's it. It'll be fun."

After my exchange with Sloe, I didn't forget to keep leveling my Intellect and now was worried about accidentally slaying our tank with a spell. The damage was high, after all, and we were in the forest, which granted a double bonus. It would be better to avoid magic altogether.

"Let's see now, what's that script again...? You good-for-nothing, deadbeat bastard! You've ruined my life! I've wasted my best years on you!" I launched into the most melodramatic, boilerplate argument I could think off and swung as hard as I could at the pirc. The attack didn't come off: Due to our difference in height, I had to stand on my tippy-toes and the blow glanced off his armor doing no damage.

"Damn it..."

"...and you thought you were marrying a future General of Aviation," Chip muttered barely audibly. And then added in a normal voice:

"You should try with your lute. With your body composition you're going to be hopping and swinging until the next carrot harvest. Try singing something."

"I don't sing so bad that they'll call me a murderer if I do. All right," I muttered getting a better grip on the lute. "Who told you that the guitar isn't capable of blunt force trauma?"

Swinging with all my vegetable might, I smashed the pirc in the face with the lute while screaming: "I've had it! I'm going to my mother's house!"

This time I managed to do some damage and the system instantly declared me a wanted outlaw.

"Sorry," Chip pressed his ears guiltily to his skull and took a grand swipe with his halberd.

A damage notification flashed past me and I instantly found myself looking at the game's splash screen. Well, let's hope that the cozy dead end works out better for future generations of young biota.

Despite my weariness, I just couldn't fall asleep: My thoughts kept coming back to the history of ancient battles and the schism of the Council. A motif for a future song kept spinning in my head, and as a result I sat embraced with my guitar synth until the middle of the night, trying to find the right words for the melody that was slowly coming through. Something told me that a new ballad would soon see the light of day.

I fell asleep around morning. In my dreams, I dreamed of the blighted creatures. Wave after wave of them rushed at the Tree, rising far above, each wave smashing against the bristling wedge of an allied Kartossian army.

CHAPTER NINE

I RETURNED TO BARLIONA well-rested and set on making the best of my time. In the coming days I would need to make decisions about my character's development, complete Coleus' quest and continue my training, solve the riddle of the Tenth's sigils, delve into the local library in search of the records of the past I was interested in, solve the secret of the blight that had afflicted the Hidden Forest, find my way into the high-level meeting and leverage that to find a way out of the starting location to meet with my friends. And that didn't include all the little quests I had taken on as well as my cartographic obligations to the merchants.

Stopping by the bank, I sent a letter to Chip, withdrew all the gold that had accumulated in there and went off to purchase supplies. I was planning on picking up gear and jewelry for Constitution. If every item would grant me +1 to Const, I could reckon on an extra 160–170 HP. I can't recall how many necklaces and bracelets I can wear here, but that doesn't matter. Either way, my survivability would shoot through the roof and I'll be able to start leveling up solo.

Unfortunately, my dreams were soon smashed upon the reefs of reality: A single trifle with stat bonuses cost no less than 30 gold. Even if I spend all my cash on hand, I won't have enough for a full set. On top of it all, the miserly Pierre, the jeweler, quoted me a price that was so inflated that I swore to myself I'd include him in one of my songs as a ghoul and use all the unflattering words I could think of to do so. The lack of competition has gone to his head, the damn vegetable-patch monopolist.

By the time the pirc and Sloe showed up, I was a hundred coins poorer. In exchange, I had a new cape and boots, and was 30 HP 'fatter.'

"Hello, Othello!" I greeted the pirc without looking up from my belt which increased my Constitution by almost two points. It was quite attractive from all angles, only it cost 55 gold. If things keep going this way, I'll spend my meager share of earnings in one day.

"Uh, which one of us is that directed at?" Chip inquired carefully, counting his share of my blood money. It really was a cute little scam we were running here.

"You're the one who killed me," I reminded him, deciding to pull the trigger on the belt purchase. Easy come easy go.

Unused to the interest of poor players, the

merchant became so ecstatic at the deal that you could think I'd bought not just a simple belt but had swept up all his wares from his shelves.

"By the way, when can we expect the completed map?" the merchant reminded delicately, looking from me to Chip and back.

"Soon!" I promised with some bluster. To my surprise, Chip went further, bluffing completely:

"It's half-done already, my esteemed friend."

The merchant beamed. I led the pirc aside and ignoring Sloe's puzzled look, whispered:

"What's with you? What half? We've barely done two branches."

"Well, while a certain someone was drooling onto her pillow," Chip replied with a note of self-satisfaction, "a certain hardworking someone was occupied with being productive. I've crawled all over this Tree and drawn most of it in. That's how we do it!" He stuck his elbows out, slid his hat over one ear and winked:

"Ain't I jive old pirc?"

"What?" I asked, simultaneously referencing the work he'd done and the meaning of the strange word.

"Could you let me in on the loop too? What are you talking about?" our horned friend reminded us of his presence.

"We're doing a cartography quest," the pirc smirked. "We've decided to become cartographers and we've been tasked with making a map of the Tree."

I didn't fail to notice that Chip hadn't mentioned our small but profitable side-venture.

"Well and while the decorative element of our collective was off resting," the pirc bowed to me clownishly, "I decided to make some extra progress. As for 'jive,' my young lady, that's a bit of ancient slang. I'm asking for your approval in a nutshell. A quote from the past, so to say."

"A real literary shmuck," Sloe hummed to this and deciding that the topic was closed, launched into the business at hand. "Anyway, here's the deal. We need to make our way out of this forest into the world at large. The guilds can help us level up out there, as well as supply us with gear and help us to our two feet in general. The only catch is we have to figure out how to get out of here."

"Well we already know that the critters don't pose much of a threat to us. We can head towards the border and cross it, the three of us," I offered.

"Uh-huh, on our own two feet...I thought the same, so I tried to sneak past the mobs while in camouflage. It turns out that the further you get from the Tree, the larger the monsters become. And some of them can detect you while you're camouflaged."

"As I understood it, you have friends in the world outside," Chip butted in. "Why don't you give them a whistle? Then they can come riding in to break us out of here. Like the cavalry in the ancient

Westerns." The pirc began to whoop like an Apache.

"They can't cross the Arras," I reminded. "Without a biota or a pirc with them, they simply won't be able to cross. And if someone leads them through, the penalty will be hatred status with the biota."

"Look at that," Sloe said, surprised. "I'll keep that in mind. In either case, good luck even reaching the Arras. I sent the guys my coordinates for a portal. Well, it sent them to the very border of the Arras— they ended up in a swamp full of a bunch of angry mobs. Those who got away, drowned later. Five people all together were sent to respawn. We tried shifting the coordinates a bit to avoid the swamp. But that time my friends emerged from the portal on the very edge of a precipice, surrounded by a bunch of aggressive undead: everything from phantoms to skeletons and zombies.

"The Stone Maw," I recalled the name of the crevice that the Tenth had created.

I suppose the fallen enemies of that ancient conflict never found their rest and turned into aggressive monsters doomed to continue their invasion and therefore defend the meagre borderlands afforded them. I wonder if the Sixth had had a vengeful hand in all this. She's a specialist in the dead and clearly wouldn't wish an easy death on her enemies.

"How do you know this?" Sloe asked, surprised

at my geographical knowledge.

"I had a vision about how there was a battle there once," I replied briefly. "So we have to reach the forest boundaries on foot. By the way, what guild are you from? Just so I know..."

"Day of Wrath," he spoke proudly, as if there was some sacred sense to the words. But, seeing Chip and my nonplussed faces, Sloe slumped a bit and waved his hand: "I keep forgetting that you two are newbs. It's one of the continent's leet hundred, number 43 in Kartoss."

"The continent's leet hundred?" the pirc echoed. "Sounds like the first cohort of a Roman legion or something. Is it like a military unit or what?"

"The leet hundred are simply the hundred most successful guilds in the game," I spoke up before Sloe could unleashed the tirade of gaming slang he'd readied. "Typically, it's a composite of multiple factors: The number of members, their levels, the level of their gear, their progress with dungeons and so on. The top ten are like corporations. The top 100 are large public companies with a decent income."

"Something like that," Sloe nodded, understanding the need to communicate with more everyday phrases.

"A guild? All these weird organizations are starting to confuse me—party, guild, hundred...What's the difference finally?" Chip made a bewildered face.

"It's simple. The top hundred is a simple rating, like the top wealthiest people of the planet," Sloe began to explain. "A party is simply several players who form a small team in order to do quests or dungeons, the way we're doing. A raiding party is theoretically the same group but with more members and assembled for a serious goal like the completion of a complicated dungeon or capturing a city. Although, technically, there's no difference between a party and a raid. A guild is more of a political or economic organization: It has a leader, a deputy, a treasurer, officers and rank and file members, such as raiders, craftsmen and gatherers. Each guild sets this up on their own, but in general the idea's the same. Guilds busy themselves with earning gaming cash or other boons. They protect their gatherers and craftsmen, negotiate trade deals, wage war with other guilds and launch sieges. They can also build their own castles. Large guilds pay salaries to their members. The more important officers earn as well or better as they would in real life."

"Bedlam," Chip concluded. "It's like people have nothing better to do. All right, we can babble in about this while we walk. What are our plans?"

"I propose we compare schedules and decide on a convenient time to stray further from the Tree. So that in case one of us has to respawn, everyone else will have something to do in reality and won't have to sit around for 12 hours stewing about the venture. I have two free evenings and then I go on a week-long business trip. After that it's vacation and I'd like to level up to the point that I can leave the biota location," Sloe expressed his desire.

"Well I'm basically on vacation for the next month, so any schedule will suit me," I announced carelessly. "But I need to do band practice three times a week and today I need to complete my class quest and finish the cartography one too."

We looked over at Chip without whom any attempt to break out of the forest would be doomed in advance.

"You two intend on spending your vacations in here?" The furball ogled us with amazement. "In the game? Seriously?"

He received no-less-amazed looks in return.

"Why? What's the big deal?" asked Sloe. "It's a lot cheaper than flying off to some Mediterranean island. And it's no less pretty—and life is a lot more fun and safer. If you like, go to the beach and get a tan. If you like, go to the dating house. If you like, go to the forest for a stroll and incinerate several monsters on your way. And if you die—no big deal, you'll respawn in 12 hours. It's all the same in reality, only more expensive, shabbier and there aren't any do-overs."

"On the other hand—and forgive my tautology—reality is full of the real," Chip didn't agree. "While here...it's just an artificial imitation, no more.

All of this is simply a bunch of ones and zeros and we are really interred in a cross of Snow White's sarcophagus and a medical capsule for transporting the critically-wounded. I don't know about you, but when I start walking again, I won't set foot in this place. One should live instead of engaging in self-deception. But whatever, it doesn't matter, it's your business. I'll accommodate my schedule to yours. Either way I'm sitting on my ass at home. The only problem is that I might be late at times, but I'll try to warn you all the same."

The necromancer's expression was as somber as mine. So our invaluable tank is simply whiling away his time in game as he convalesces. Stomping out my curiosity and at the same time wishing to avoid further discussion about the pros and cons of virtual life, I switched to a more constructive topic.

"In that case, today I'm going to finish my class quest. We'll wrap up the map of the Tree and tomorrow head out on our journey to the Arras. By the way, I should ask the locals roughly which direction we need to go in."

"I already did that. I'll show you the way," Sloe spoke up. "By the way, how much do you want for the city map?"

"We'll just make you a copy," I said with some surprise. "Aren't we all humans here after all? All the things you've told us have helped a lot."

"I won't refuse, but here's a bit of advice: Don't

pass up a chance to earn some cash. Rare cards, quests and information cost money."

"There's another minus," Chip began to moralize again. "Everything's calculated to manipulate the player into spending money and normal interpersonal relationships are turned into a zero-sum game."

"Everyone decides for himself here," Sloe remarked philosophically. "If you want to reach the game's peaks, you need money, connections and the ability to make the most of every opportunity. My intent is to hone this character properly and end up making money in-game. I'll quit my irl job and make more here. As for those who come here to relax—they don't need any of that. They're here to pass the time, like anywhere else."

"What's your job, if you don't mind me asking?" Chip inquired.

"Geologic surveying," Sloe replied without much enthusiasm. "Rumor has it that they're about to release an imitator that can do the work of an entire team. All you have to do is send any old high-school dropout to deliver the surveying tools to the right location and the imitator does the rest. And we professionals are out of a job. So on the whole, I'd rather try and make a living here in Barliona. It's more interesting here anyway."

"I've heard about the project you speak of. And I've seen the trials with the prototype," said Chip. "No one's going to replace living people, don't worry. It'll work as an auxiliary system—like our drones and remote scouts. I mean, judge for yourself: How could an imitator, even a very advanced imitator, replace a seasoned geologist? When we were stationed in Joburg, as few geological prospectors as we had, we'd still send them in to the field, and I will tell you this: Ain't no spintronic contraption can determine the strata and the gradients and mineral composition the way an experienced geologist does."

"From your lips to god's ears," the necromancer sighed. "Okay, since we're not going anywhere today, I'll go work on my trades. By the way, I suggest you buy as many recipes as you can. You won't find similar ones in other locations and you will be able to make some good money."

"Why that's an idea! The most commonplace junk costs insane sums of money here. Maybe it'd be cheaper to just craft it ourselves? We have the starting capital," I added, noticing Sloe's interested look, "thanks to our murder pact. I don't think that the starting ingredients are that expensive. We can craft ourselves some simple gear for Constitution and have an easier time of it in the forest."

"It's reasonable," Sloe nodded. "And we should put some points into gathering. Maybe we'll find something on our way through the forest. The initial training is cheap. We can more than afford it. And we should determine who does what. It's dumb to have everyone take jewelcrafting, for instance. It's much simpler if one person sews the clothes, another does the budgeting and the third specializes in herbs."

"I'm not a big fan of sewing," I warned.

"No big deal. Here's your chance," grinned Sloe. "All right, I'll sew the clothes for Lori and me, but I wouldn't count on me mastering jewelry or alchemy before my vacation if I were you. And it doesn't make any sense for me to forge the armor for our warrior."

"I'll figure that out on my own," Chip spoke up.

"In that case, alchemy and perhaps jewelry are on me," I went on. "I need to try them first to see what I like."

"To work then. We'll meet tomorrow at seven server time and we'll try for the Arras," Sloe concluded and thanking Chip for the copy of the map he'd sent him, headed towards the Branch of the Craftsmen.

"So what should we begin with?" The pirc inquired, staring at me expectantly.

"I need to run over to see my instructor and catch up. I also have to figure out what to borrow from the other classes. It'd be nice to complete my class quest too just to strike it off the list. Finally, I need to check out the crafting professions."

"Cool. In that case, I'll go on working on the map of the Tree to settle our obligations to the merchants. When you're free, you can run through all the sigils of the Tenth and then we can go work on the professions together."

I quickly agreed, pleased at the chance to shift the tedious composition of the map onto the pirc's mighty shoulders. To be fair, it was his own enthusiasm and attention to detail that had turned this simple gameplay mechanic into a complicated and subtle task that demanded contemplation and a ton of extra time. If he wants to create maps of such detail, let him do the work himself. If he settled for the ordinary ones, we'd have finished this quest a long time ago—and found all the sigils in the process. On the other hand, even if it was slow going, Chip was doing most of the work.

Having said farewell to the pirc, I could barely keep myself from sprinting to the Branch of Vocation. Although—why restrain myself? Why not sprint? Sprint, dash, run to discover the gaming possibilities of Barliona! The possibilities turned out to be far vaster than those irl: I could run faster and longer than I could back in meatspace and my Agility and even Constitution leveled up at the same time. The only thing was that my Stamina evaporated at a maddening rate, forcing me to keep taking sips from my flask. But I did reach the branch I needed on foot: As we were making our map, Chip and I discovered that besides leafevators there were pedestrian links between the different levels, integrated quite naturally into the entire colossal trunk. At the same time, we discovered the secret of the water supply. The local wizards used magic to pump water from the river through specially grown channels within the trunk. This magical water main passed though the majority of the branches and returned into the trunk, headed back to the river. We really should find out what it's called—'cause the Rude Creek is simply silly.

Along with the customary cacophony, a pretty cello part was emanating from the purple tent. It sounded like Coleus had encountered some promising students.

Overflowing with curiosity, I dove into the tent's dusk. Some Level 1 players without chosen classes looked at me askance with surprise and curiosity. Yeah. On the Tree, even my paltry Level 5 looked respectable.

The aforementioned cellist who was still at Level 1 and bore the name 'Reed' was a solar biota with golden markings. He flourished his bow forgetfully, ignoring entirely his audience as well as target. It looked like he simply enjoyed playing. But the most unusual thing was that the majority of players had sat down and were attentively listening to what he was playing—Bach's suite for cello, which was far from customary to the modern ear.

"I can see that things are going better..." I whispered into the ear of the enraptured Coleus. He glanced over at me and looked back at his new prodigy.

"You could say that again. He's been playing two hours now. Others show up and listen but no one dares interrupt with their clatter, or howling or the other infernal sounds they're wont to make."

I nodded with understanding. Reed was playing like a professional but he was also playing like an addict who had scored a hit after a long spell of cold turkey. There are true fans of music alongside whom even those like me seem like pathetic amateurs. And if I, like most of the players around me, was full of questions about how Reed would travel around Barliona schlepping the enormous instrument, then he was clearly unperturbed by such minor details.

I don't know how long I spent sitting there and listening but at one point I remembered the point of my visit.

"Coleus, I need to figure out my abilities and how to take them from the other classes, as well as how to change them," I whispered to my instructor. He swatted the air, as if he didn't wish to deal with my training at the moment, and then looked at me slyly.

"Did you complete my quest?"

"Not yet. I'd like to acquire some knowledge before I get to it. That's why I'm here."

"When you complete it, I'll continue our training," the Bard announced, satisfied with the excuse he'd come upon. I barely opened my mouth to protest when he added: "But you can also simply give up and I'll train you right this instant. However, you won't be able to restart the quest chain for another three months. Agreed?"

I shut my mouth and shook my head negatively. Yeah right. I'd rather go do the quest, I won't break. It's a social quest anyway, I'll survive without any extra skills. The important thing was to manage to grow my arsenal before tomorrow.

The further I got from the tent, the faster my decisiveness melted. What did I even have to do? I couldn't very well start accosting random NPCs, saying, 'Please wait while I play you something on my lute.' Lacking any idea how to solve this problem, I decided to visit all the sigils Chip had uncovered first. A half-hour jog increased my quest progress to 16/30 sigils located.

Distracted from the initial plan, I spent the next two hours crawling around the branches, charting what I found on the map and looking for more sigils. In the process I ran headfirst into Chip, listened to a brief but dense lecture on the topic of the proper division of labor and the virtue of sticking to the plan at hand, and was finally sent to complete Coleus' quest.

I didn't have a single idea about how to begin my instructor's quest and therefore decided to try and start with what I already knew—an improvised concert at the Market Branch.

Having filled my flask in the fountain, I took up my familiar place on the auction dais and began to contemplate what I should begin with. Joy, a light sorrow, love...No. I should start with something neutral. I need to amass an audience, grab their attention and only then roll out the heavy guns. The more people I gather, the higher the chance that someone will be struck by my playing, fulfilling the quest requirements.

No doubt, I was still under the impression Reed had made on me: When I took the lute in my hands, I felt the same sense of euphoria thanks to which I had once decided to become a musician. In moments such as this, it seems like there are angels dancing a jig with some demons on the guitar's headstock and the whole world shrinks to the point of the guitar pick.

I don't even recall what I played and for how long—I returned to consciousness only due to a sense of falling. And I don't mean some kind of moral fall, but an entirely physical one—my avatar collapsed onto the improvised stage and a system notification appeared and covered all the former ones about the stat increases that I had received.

You are so exhausted that you cannot move. Current level of Stamina: 0. In order to move, your Stamina must be at least 10.

So this is what it feels like to pass out in VR. A compassionate NPC biota approached me and poured a sour liquid into my mouth that reminded me of cranberry juice.

Current Stamina: 100. You have received the 'Tireless' buff (-50% Stamina used).

"You bards are always passing out," the NPC winked at me. "Either you drink too much and slump under the table or you don't drink enough..."

"Yes, I seem to have lost track of time, thank you," I replied automatically, making a mental note to study the Stamina mechanics a little more closely. I don't remember seeing a warning or anything. Instead, in addition to a notification that my Fame had reached 6, a further system message brought me some good news:

Attention! You have unlocked the 'Song of Inspiration' class ability. Your performance instills combat spirit and raises the stats of your allies. You may learn individual songs from songbooks or by composing your own.

It follows that I unlocked a way of buffing my party, but I still need to get my hands on the buff. I'll wager a tooth that the songbook Coleus had promised me, will teach me a basic party buff. As for composition, I'll need to figure that out on my own. I'd guess that I can write my own song and enchant it with some buff? I doubt the composition part would be difficult—I'm familiar with that—but how do I bind a spell to it? I really really need to pump my instructor for more information…

My audience, realizing that the improvised concert had ended, began to disperse. The 'Impressed' buff had increased their Attractiveness with me by 3 points. Does this mean that if I play here for a few more days, the locals will all love me? Seems suspiciously simple.

I was particularly pleased to see the little heap of money among which there were some silver coins. It was spare change compared to the gold I already had, but being able to hold 'material recognition' (as my first teacher had referred to it) in my hand was pleasant all the same.

Chip, by the way, could be seen nearby. Judging by his preoccupied mug and periodically glowing paws, he was coming to terms with the art of casting spells. Glancing at my party status screen, I praised my guesswork. The pirc had become a priest and, judging by his stats, was leveling up his Intellect as his mana regenerated. It was a useless stat for a Warrior, but his natural thriftiness kept Chip from passing up on it all the same.

"How'd it go?" he inquired when I approached.

"Devil knows," I admitted honestly. "The system granted me the opportunity to cast buffs, but didn't tell me what part of the quest has been completed. Non-linear quests are cool and all, but there should be a limit."

"In that case, you should continue. Listen, have

you tried to update your repertoire? I mean, classic rock is immortal and all, but still...For example, if you performed the old song about the wandering artists— why can't that be a bardic hymn?"

"What's that?"

Chip rolled up his eyes, chewed his lip trying to remember and then sighed:

"It's a song from the 20th century. I'd hear it here and there growing up—it's like a marching song. Listen."

The pirc coughed a bit and then began singing an old wandering musicians' song. He sang well but a bit tensely and without much soul. It seemed like he lacked a bubbly and clinking catalyzer as well as suitable company to spur him into unleashing his artistic talent fully. The joke here was 'No booze means no vocals.'

"I like your idea about the repertoire. I'll need to dig up some fantasy and folk songs. But this song instills neither love nor courage. The hell with it though. We'll take a break. Maybe something will occur to me while we're checking out the other trades."

"Wouldn't hurt to eat either," the pirc scratched his belly. "I feel like my intestine is crawling up to my brain to strangle it. I found out that here in Barliona there are only two races that feel hungry. Everyone else eats only for the sake of buffs. Gee, I really wish I had a nice stew about now."

"Well in that case we should begin with the culinary trade. Although, biota don't eat solid food and I doubt some juice will make you feel full. Pircs need their meat."

"Vegetarians," sighed Chip. "All right. Let's go and study. We'll see what there's to eat later."

"Nah. Vegans eat vegetables. We biota are vegetables ourselves. All we do is drink. By the way, it might even be possible that we drink blood too. And why not? It's a liquid. A vampiric potato, what do you think?"

"In Djibouti I saw an old movie about killer tomatoes," shrugged Chip. "You won't scare me with some moldy Idaho."

"If you ask me, since the invention of cinema, humanity has exhausted all the ways of scaring itself. Killer elevators, snowmen, condoms...They've done it all."

"A condom is a killer by function and designation," Chip proclaimed pedantically, sniffing the air, "of your future offspring and half the pleasure you get from the act. But hold, you vampiric tuber! I smell the smell of meat. Follow me!" And grabbing me by the hand, the furball rushed decisively into an alley from which the aroma he had sensed was emanating. It wasn't even finding cooked meat among the biota that surprised me, so much as that its smell was...unpleasant...revolting even. And I'm normally a big fan of barbecue, steaks and other meat dishes.

The mysterious smell was emanating from a small courtyard. A culinary instructor named Artichoke was puttering over an improvised grill. An NPC biota with bright yellow petals for hair was helping him. Her name fit her well—Mimosa.

"And how does one eat this?" Artichoke was frowning, smelling the barbecue with evident revulsion. "And, more importantly, how am I supposed to assess its taste if I can't eat?"

Chip froze without releasing my hand and suddenly exclaimed:

"What are you doing, you child of glucose?! Who taught you to cook like that, hellion?! Why you'll turn it all into ashes in a second! Step aside, greenhorn and let me work my magic!"

Saying this, he moved the vegetable chef unceremoniously from the grill and began to yank off the skewers, instructing in the meantime: "You can't just up and throw the meat on the fire. What's wrong with you? No, we need embers first...And who cuts meat into pieces like this? You could as well simply stick the entire cow onto the skewer, you weirdo." My companion looked around seriously and began to issue orders: "All right. Give me a sharp knife. The maestro is in the kitchen! What do you have for seasoning?"

The chef initially opened his mouth in outrage but then quickly realized that this furry ruffian could solve half her problems—if anything, in terms of tasting—so he turned around and began to relay Chip's demands to the assistants.

A copper pot of impressive size appeared from somewhere with a lid, as well as plates, platters, spoons, smaller pots and the work got underway. Half an hour later, the courtyard looked like a kitchen under the open sky at some historical reenactment festival: Stew bubbled in pots, meat sputtered on pans, fat sizzled dripping into the coals, small biota hands worked the dough, sliced toppings for pies, and above it all the pirc's deep bass resounded, teaching my cousins the secrets of 'food-magic.' Mmm...yeah. It looked like my friend hadn't wasted his time during all the vacations he'd taken. Not every autocook had as many recipes in its memory banks as Chip did in his head.

"Is there anything you don't know how to do?" I asked just in case, taking a plate of pies from Mimosa's hands. She had already dropped several platters and tipped several pots, so I tried to keep a close eye on her.

"Lots of stuff," Chip replied without looking up from his work. "For example, how to build. Or how to dance. The academy had a dance hall and a teacher, and one could study in one's spare time, but I preferred hand-to-hand combat and marksmanship and paid extra for them as well as for language classes."

"Oh! I did hand-to-hand combat too," I bragged,

keeping one eye on Mimosa. The girl looked so discomposed that everything was falling out of her hands.

"And, how'd it go?" the furball inquired. "Did you become the bully of your block?"

"No. I realized that if someone wanted it, they could drop me with one blow and so I switched to running," I confessed. "But I still go to training every once in a while. Just to stretch and hang out with my friends. Besides, nothing brings you back to reality like a blow you fail to block. Really makes you want to live…"

"Uh-huh, uh-huh," Chip nodded. "And after that to get back to your feet and let your opponent have it. No, but what is this disaster!" He yelled at the clumsy Mimosa who had yet again dropped a knife. "All right, lady, you really need a smoke break…or just a break. No objections!"

Instead of objecting, Mimosa broke down in tears and ran out of the courtyard.

"I guess she doesn't smoke," I remarked.

"Or she's made of tobacco," Chip proposed a reasonable alternative. "All right, my vegetable muse, go console her. Tell her that I don't smoke either."

"What am I, the local therapist? Go figure out what's wrong with her yourself. These kinds of situations aren't my forte. My typical response in these cases is, 'It's your own fault, dummy.' Never seems to go over well."

"I'm busy with this work, that's one. You're a fellow biota, that's two. And finally, which one of us has the consolation quest?" Chip summoned his best counterarguments.

"Fine," I had to admit, looking ruefully in the direction where the biota had fled.

The quest had to be completed one way or another. In the end of things, how bad could it be? Had she broken a nail? Had her petals faded since the day she'd emerged from her bulb? Had her boyfriend forgotten about their pet hamster's fifth birthday?

I almost guessed right. My trembling little Mimosa, it turned out, was the odd one out among her cohort of married friends. The NPC's imitator mind—designed to simulate a human one—instantly generalized the situation: 'No one loves me and no one wants to kiss me.' I sincerely tried to recall something uplifting and hopeful, a song about an epic love awaiting each lover in her due time, but for whatever reason, my head was spinning with other stuff.

"In the Twilight Dream I beheld the world beyond the Arras," I began tangentially in a fairy-tale tone. "And I heard a song of a human minstrel. It's a song of brides, love and fortune."

Mimosa sobbed and stared at me with her enormous, tearful eyes, as I in my turn drew the first harmonious chord from my lute. I don't know what spurred the author to write the song, but it had become my personal go-to on the topic of family life.

Little Adele came running to the glade
To tell the daisies of her sorrow...

I sang about how the young shepherd girl was torn because she had to choose among three handsome young men. Mimosa listened and sniffled, secretly envying the heroine's fortune. The song skipped ahead ten years. The narrator returned to the older shepherdess, wishing to find out what choice she had made and how her life had turned out. Unfortunately, Mimosa's curiosity would have to go unsatisfied—it was no longer possible to identify one of the handsome paramours in the bloated, red face of Adele's husband.

Three different paths
Will give you in the end
Just a red face and a belly...

The young biota hiccupped and looked up at me.

"Marriage is like a phone call in the night: first the ring, and then you wake up," I shared my bit of popular wisdom. "There's nothing for you to be upset about. Live and be happy and in several years your married friends will envy you."

"Really?" Mimosa smiled meekly.

"You bet!" I nodded confidently, secretly rejoicing that in several game years I wouldn't be around to find out. Who knows how this story would really turn out?

Attention! New bardic ability unlocked: 'Song of Consolation.' Dispel one or more negative status effects from the party. You may learn individual songs from songbooks or by composing your own.

Ah! It worked! In other words, consolation for us means the dispelling of debuffs. I wonder what 'awaking love' will unlock?

Stepping out on the street, I immediately stumbled onto the pirc's mocking look.

"And where were you when I got married?" he sighed with exaggeration. "I would have dodged so many problems...Try and stay nearby, will you? What if I get married again and get my head knocked off a second time?"

"Hah! In that case, you should memorize these verses!" I snorted happily and took ahold of my lute again.

My mood was excellent and only a human would understand this poem about lost love I had rattling around my head.

All in green went my love riding
on a great horse of gold
into the silver dawn.

Chip listened to the poem quietly and, contrary to my expectations, grew more and more somber as I sang. Once I'd finished he sighed:

"Ah...yes. And the Loveboat flounders against the bluffs of life..." He turned to the bustle behind him and began to bellow with exaggerated rancor: "What are you dumping all that salt into the ground beef for? You woeful leek, you vacuous onion!" And the pirc hurried to the site of the disaster as I read another system notification:

Attention! New bardic skill unlocked: 'Song of Woe.' Song of Woe causes negative status effects in your listeners. You may learn individual songs from songbooks or by composing your own.

Mmm. An odd outcome. It looks like I had accidentally rankled a sore wound in my furry friend. I don't remember anything about woe in Coleus' quest either. On the other hand, the option of dishing out debuffs could come in handy. Though it seems I'd managed to debuff Chip without any particular spells for the purpose.

I opened my quest journal and reread the description: Demonstrate that your performance can awaken courage and love, grant warmth and succor, instil joy and light sorrow. No mention of anything negative. A strange quest. But tomorrow is a new day and I can finish my class quest then. For now, it's time to cook.

It was clear enough that Chip—and I by extension—had received a new, rare quest that led to a chain of further quests associated with the preparations for the Festival. Formally speaking we had to prepare dishes for our guests from the Lair, but the pirc and I knew whom the hospitable biota were really planning on feeding. Guests from beyond the Arras. And seeing as I was nauseated by all the dishes I loved so much out in meatspace, this quest was undoable for a biota. How can you prepare a dish that revolts you? I suppose the quest had been planned for visiting pircs, but our biota friends had a role in it too: Drinks had to be prepared both for our guests and for other biota. Soon enough I learned what the difference was: Whereas visitors to the Tree were accustomed to drinking punches, juices and lemonades, biota beverages were a bit more elaborate. Would you care for a cocktail of spring water, mixed with copper dust and garnished with a pinch of earth from some special hill? Sounds awful, to put it mildly—and yet it tasted...Well, I don't even know what to compare it to. I suppose some kind of energy drink with a citrus taste. This drink was called 'Copper Water' and it granted +1 to Strength and Agility.

This is all to say that we wasted more time on the culinary chain than we expected, but in exchange leveled up our culinary stats a pretty bit, as well as our reputations. We also got a chance to buy a sheaf of various recipes, including several rare ones.

"So what's up? Where are we off to next? To the blacksmith? The alchemist? The jeweler?" Chip asked, scratching his belly contentedly. His mood had clearly improved and the number of buffs he'd received from eating exceeded a dozen.

"First let's go find the sigils that we're missing."

"Makes sense," Chip said happily. "We'll finish the map while we're at it. Let me see what you have so far..."

We copied each other's updates and decided who would focus on what sector. It was looking like we would complete our project by the end of today or tomorrow.

It was fun to look for sigils, but it was dull to draft a detailed map. Who needs all this topographical data, gradients, watercourses and other details? The map had to be drawn with multiple levels, keeping the various branches and their distances in mind. But Chip was unshakable and I had to go along with him. We'd started this together, so I had to work honestly. At least given the detail of the drafting, it wasn't hard to find the Tenth's sigils. At first glance, they were chaotically distributed, yet it seemed to me that as soon as we marked them all on the map, the pattern would jump out at me. We had only one more left to find...

"...there's a blank over there in the southwest

sector," a conversation between some passersby drew my attention. "There's an interesting place there but the mobs are strong and those damn thorns..."

"You think it's worth looking around there?"

"Without a doubt. I'll need to level up my camouflage a bit more but then I'll go check it out."

A group of incredibly high-level players walked past me, all of them Level 20–30. One of them noticed the map in my hands and stopped, curious:

"Hey kid, where'd you get that map? What's on it?"

The word 'kid' almost made me lose my temper but the custom of teaching etiquette to passing players is a long-lost art.

"I'm making a map of the tree. Learning cartography."

"Oh..." the player drawled, disappointed and losing all interest in me, ran to catch up with his party. "Such a newb thing. Wasting time on maps."

And like a mirage, the party of elites vanished around a corner.

"What a constructive and civil exchange..." I muttered perplexed and returned to the task at hand.

CHAPTER TEN

B Y THE TIME I CAUGHT UP ON MY SLEEP and re-entered the game, the pirc had managed to locate all the other sigils and was currently bouncing in front of me like a furry ball. A very large furry ball with long sharp claws and a loud toothy mouth.

"Do you even sleep?" I asked, yawning from inertia.

"We'll have time to sleep after Neo-Communism triumphs over Late Capitalism! Let's go, commissar, I've stumbled on Kolchak's stash of tsarist gold."

We ran past the sigils he'd found in just over an hour, but our final discovery didn't shed any further light on the puzzle.

Quest updated: *The Mysterious Sigil* (36 of 36 sigils located).

Achievement unlocked: 'She may be a big girl, but she still believes in fairy tales…'

Achievement reward: +1 Attractiveness with NPC children.

And that's it. No fanfare, no congratulations or rewards—unless you count this super-useful Achievement.

"Looks like I'm a little bird," I replied to Chip's unasked question.

"What?" he asked, stumped.

"The naïve little bird, ever heard of her? She nests in the eaves and makes friends with cormorants."

"Aww what the hell," the pirc said annoyed when I showed him the Achievement I'd unlocked. "In other words we just scoured the entire tree like a pair of lunatics strictly for the glee of the developers? There has to be some kind of system, some riddle..."

"There doesn't have to be anything," I grunted in reply, also irritated. "Do you have any idea how many empty social quests over nothing they have here?"

I opened my mouth to go on but immediately shut it. The quest! There had been no notification that I'd completed the 'Mysterious Sigil' quest. And this meant that there was more to do.

"Let's look for patterns," Chip went on after I'd shared my realization with him. "What do we have?"

"A bunch of dots on the map," I grunted, unfurling my parchment. "No detectable system. They're distributed wherever, without any regard for the branches."

"Let's see..." Chip settled down beside me,

unfurled a clean parchment and glancing over at mine began to sketch a strange figure. As I understood it, he was drawing lines between the points we'd found. Completing his work, he placed both scrolls beside each other and began to slide his fingers over their surfaces.

"Bunch of convoluted, Fustian nonsense..." he muttered and began to sketch a second shape. He repeated this process several times, with the only difference being that on his third pass, the pirc made no comment at all.

"Ah get outta here!" He slapped my knee, exasperated, once he'd completed his check. Was he really tracing this flower because he had nothing better to do?

Checking the map one more time, the pirc gave up and waved his paw:

"That's it. Abort. Return to base immediately. Tomorrow's another day."

"It's already morning," I reminded him.

"Don't be pedantic. We'll have to sleep on this."

"All right, we can crack our heads on it again later. Pretty soon we'll hit Level 10 and we still haven't dabbled in jewelcrafting."

"I have this one idea..." Chip said in a conspiratorial tone and waved me to follow him.

On the way to the master jeweler, Chip suddenly stopped, frowned as if he'd bitten into a lemon and blurted out:

"Hold up. There's a...this thing...I lost track of time. I need to pop out to reality for a half hour. Will you wait?"

"Not even a question. I'll check out the various ways of growing my character in the meantime."

Chip exited to meatspace. I sat down in the shade of a large flower and decided to spend my time with purpose: crawl around the fora and consider the build for my character.

So, what did I have? I could merge my build with one of the standard classes or create something new and unique by mixing various traits and abilities. This means that I'd have to familiarize myself with the diversity of the various class skills and roles in general terms and then delve further into the promising directions.

I discarded warrior abilities for melee combat right away. Biota didn't distinguish themselves either with physical strength or constitution so outright melee combat was out of the question for me. Neither did I feel drawn to fencing. Back when I was a kid, I spent a month going to lessons simulated in a VR capsule. I tried foil, epee, sabre and even some unarmored longsword—and exhausted my childish desire to wield a sword. Plus there was the professional phobia of injuring my fingers. The mere notion of steel whistling past them forced me to cringe nervously. No. I would never be a Boudica or a Joan of Arc.

A long and exhaustive study of the other classes didn't yield any clear result. Everything seemed interesting at once, but reaching the skills and spells that drew my attention required a huge amount of training points, so I doubt I'll end up as a necro-mage-spy-priest. The most attractive approach seemed merging with the druid, priest and necromancer classes, but here I needed to speak to former players instead of choosing haphazardly. I'll ask Straus about it. He might tell me something useful. And anyway, it's stupid to make plans until I know what skills and spells are available to the standard bard builds.

Per lamentable tradition, a search of the fora uncovered nothing useful. Instead of simply listing the basic bardic powers and their descriptions, the rabble affected secrecy and sought money. Bunch of kobolds. Wish some paladins would teach them some manners. A few posts weren't worth trusting whatsoever. I guess I simply don't trust OP when his post is full of grammatical mistakes and poor orthography. Several times I came across posts about NPC bards; however, they were mercenaries, quest companions or something like pets—no one knew. At least this record reminded me that the Tenth had summoned an army of phantoms to fight the ancient invaders. And something told me that an analogous summons would be somewhere in my skill tree. I'll need to ask Coleus about it, but I doubt he'll want to tell me before I complete my quest. May the FSM curse him with a case of colitis! But fine—there's also the library that simply must contain some mention of bards. We'll deal with the jewelry business, and then I'll dig around the library before completing my class quest and dumping all my questions onto my colic instructor.

I closed all the fora and returned to the game where Chip, as it turned out, was already waiting for me. It looks like I'd spent more than a half hour reading the fora.

"I'm afraid I've been pollinated by your biota brethren—I think I've sprouted a root waiting for you," the pirc grinned happily. "So what's up? Are you ready to fight the gemstone monopoly?"

"You bet!"

CHAPTER ELEVEN

THE FAÇADE OF THE JEWELRY WORKSHOP did not look any different from the Tree's other buildings. And yet inside...The eyes wandered from glinting heap to glinting heap of gems and jewels, while the various items encrusted, bordered, and embossed with the precious stones and metals stunned the imagination. The heck with the jewelry store and its cheap ornamental jewelry when this workshop had it all! There was a bit of everything here—from diamond cuff links to emerald pendants to little statuettes and even a luxurious replica of the Tree as tall as the pirc. A bright red biota named Hibiscus was fretting around it, polishing his reflection in the future masterpiece. One didn't need a crystal ball to know that this was one of the future gifts for the Kartossian embassy. I'd wager my tooth that if I asked Hibiscus the right questions, I'd come up with a quest for jeweler players, but neither Chip nor I were interested in delving that deeply into the jewelcrafting business. It's simply too costly a profession for our immense (in newb terms) capital.

Nor was there any desire to mess around with accessories. Whereas mapmaking encouraged adventures and travels, which was the reason I was playing to begin with, sitting at a polishing wheel like the other biota—an apprentice named Anturium—was doing, didn't spur my fantasy to compose so much as a limerick. The sour expression on the young apprentice's face only confirmed this further.

"What wondrous work," I remarked loudly, turning to the pirc, but ensuring that everyone else heard my words too. "The work of a great master, worthy of adorning any palace or even the chambers of some divinity."

Hearing these words, Hibiscus couldn't help but glow with pride and redouble his efforts, while Anturium glanced at his instructor, sighed sadly and turned back to the task of framing some ordinary-looking stone. It looked like a bit of malachite, but I wasn't sure, since my knowledge of geology wasn't exceptional.

"A reverie fit for a maharaja," Chip agreed, "a sultan even or a pasha! It would look right at home in the Taj Mahal."

"Taj Mahal?" The master jeweler looked simultaneously flattered and puzzled. "What is that?"

"One of the prettiest palaces of the world, far beyond the Arras," Chip explained. "Thousands upon thousands of creatures travel from all around the world to see it. It was built by one of the rulers of the past for his beloved wife."

The cheeky devil omitted the fact that it was really a mausoleum, preferring to pour flattery on the jeweler.

"Your creation, esteemed master," I intervened, "would do justice to its ensemble perfectly. Gold, gemstones, a stunning attention to detail—all of this would have eclipsed the other details of the interior."

Briefly put, our plan was as simple as a cow's moo. Unwilling to study jewelcrafting on our own or buy costume jewelry at threefold the price from that Pierre, the merchant who had refused our advertising offer, we decided to bluff our way into the industry. Everyone knows it's cheaper to source the goods from the manufacturer and so Chip and I decided to butter up the jeweler and get a nice discount later on.

"This piece isn't finished yet but I'll agree that it is a promising one," Hibiscus humblebragged.

"I shall be unable to drink or sleep if I don't purchase one of your creations for posterity," I announced mournfully, transparently hinting at a business relationship to come.

"Generally, I don't busy myself with the retail aspect—I'd need permission from the merchants' guild to do so. I'd have to register as a merchant, you see. It is a lot of work and I am more interested in the creative aspect of the business. But if you like, you may acquire my creations from the jewelry store of the esteemed Pierre."

This bit of news was, let's just say, dour. I suppose the corporation had closed off this simple workaround, safeguarding the supply chains of the NPC merchants. It's too bad, after all that damn Pierre had not only refused to advertise through our map but had also jacked his prices for Chip and I through the ceiling, the damn bush.

"I'm afraid that Pierre's prices are a bit too steep. He raises them so high that your masterpieces are consigned to gathering dust in his stall instead of adorning biota and the Tree's guests with their magnificence. Have you not considered dabbling in retail at all? We would be happy to help you receive the necessary permits."

"It's an interesting idea, naturally, but I haven't a merchant's bone in my body. In fact I have no bones whatsoever, hah! Nor do I have the time. I am an artisan. It is more important to me to create something lovely than to barter and haggle over prices."

"There you have it! A master through and through!" Chip exclaimed with feeling. "Unlike that Pierre. As one religion has it, may he burn in a fire after death, for he is afflicted with a mortal sin: greed. And greed without reason to boot! For he merely proffers that which is created by a master's loving hands, and then behaves himself as if he had created it himself! Were he a pirc, I swear, I would dunk his head into the Bog of Eternal Stench and no one would say a word, for he would get what was coming to him!" His eyes smoldering with wrath, the pirc raised his chin and thumped the floor with his halberd.

This terrible sight made the apprentice hiccup nervously and drop an unfinished piece of malachite. The piece fell on the table and then on the floor and began rolling toward Chip, at which point the pirc stopped it deftly with the toe of his boot.

"I am not familiar with the customs of the Lair, but in the Tree it is not customary to treat merchants this way," Hibiscus warned just in case, yet the words of the furry guest had clearly flattered him.

"Perhaps we will be able to find some talented biota with a merchant's bone and the understanding to do the job. And you, in your turn, will conduct your affairs through him instead of the greedy hands of Pierre?"

"It is not a bad idea, but my time is committed to working on the replica of the Tree, and I will be unable to supply stock for the new merchant."

"But you already have an apprentice who, even a dilettante like I, can see is excellent!" I reminded the jeweler of the bored Anturium.

Hearing this, the apprentice perked up visibly but Hibiscus clearly didn't share his enthusiasm.

"Forgive me, this is a very talented young man it is true, yet he is only beginning to discover the secrets of jewelcrafting and is barely beginning to work with silver. Currently, he is training his skills with simple copper and bronze creations. He does a decent job, but without the precious metals, the jewelry remains but a cheap imitation."

"But that's exactly what the free citizens want! Why they'll tear the cheap imitations, as you put it, straight out of your hands!" I assured the jewelers. "Simple and inexpensive items that raise their stats are exactly what they need. Even my companion and I wouldn't refuse them. It's foolish to risk expensive and beautiful accessories every time one goes into battle."

"Precisely," Chip nodded his head. "You can kill three birds with one stone: The master won't be distracted by trifles; that's one. The young Anturium will acquire invaluable experience; that's two. And the free citizens won't have to overpay and fill the coffers of a scoundrel merchant who has forgotten his place; that's three!"

Hibiscus looked over at Chip and then at me and finally at his apprentice pensively. The apprentice was looking at him so hopefully that I even felt sorry for him. No surprise there. He was clearly tired of working on the basics. Costume jewelry clearly wasn't in high demand here until players began appearing, and given Pierre's prices, there wouldn't be anyone willing to go bankrupt over some random ring.

"All right," Hibiscus decided at last. "If you manage to find a suitable candidate with permission to conduct commerce, I will send him all the creations of my apprentice. We'll see how things go then. And you will receive a lifelong discount on our goods as well."

New quest available: *Find a Vendor*. Description: Find an NPC with permission to sell goods and convince him to sell the jewelry of Master Hibiscus and his apprentice. Quest type: Unique. Restrictions: May not be shared with other players. Reward for completion: 30% discount on the jewelry of Master Hibiscus and his apprentice. Penalty for failure: None.

Attention! A new stat has become available to your character: Charisma. Charisma determines the strength of the character's personality, her appeal, her ability to convince and to lead, and also her physical attractiveness. Charisma also increases the chance of being issued unique quests.

Do you accept? Attention! You will not be able to remove an accepted stat later!

Ah! Here's a classic bard stat! I'll be taking this without a second thought, thank you.

A new stat has been unlocked for the character: Charisma. Current value: 1.

Attention! With every point of Charisma,

the bard will receive an extra training point.

Attention! The Charisma stat allows the bard to persuade members of another class to teach her their standard class skills.

Attention! The Charisma stat affects a series of bardic skills and spells. Please speak to the bard instructor for further information.

Attention! Charisma increases the chance of an NPC enjoying your performance.

Extra training points? Borrowing skills from beyond the standard skill set? I'll take two please! This changes my build strategy entirely! I need to wrap up these chores and grab Coleus by his gills. And if he resists, I'll ask Chip to apply his knowledge of interrogations to him. Even if he doesn't know anything about that, he'll be quick to improvise.

The NPC's expectant gaze, forced me to go on to my current quest.

"We will do our utmost to find a perfect candidate for this role!" I promised.

"We will select someone who conducts himself honorably and would never tarnish the good name of a great master!" Chip echoed majestically, fluttering his whiskers and bowing to Hibiscus.

Even though we left the workshop empty-handed, at least we'd received a discount on future jewelry. All we had to do was make good on the opportunity.

"Let's not reinvent the wheel. We'll simply talk one of the merchants into scratching our back," I suggested. "They already have the paperwork and the floorspace, all we have to do is get them to agree to cooperate."

Something told me that the long way around—finding some NPC dreaming of opening a store of his own and then petitioning the authorities on his behalf as well as all the other stuff that would follow—would ultimately reward us with some commercial quest chain and a much better final payoff. And yet I really didn't feel like delving too deeply into this problem. I'm not trying to become a local banker. I just need some Constitution so I can head into the forest and do the quest and check out that Arras. Even now my mind kept returning to class abilities and possible build orders for my bard.

"We just need to find some young scamp," nodded the pirc. "He won't be as greedy."

"Why do you say that?"

"When you're young, you haven't yet gotten a proper taste of money and the life that comes with it. You're cautious enough to understand that the slightest mistake will allow your competitors to eat you alive. When you're older, you know your business, its ins and outs, its squalls and doldrums. When you're older, you know when to fold and when to hold your cards."

"Makes sense. And as it happens we have a

complete list of all the Tree's merchants. Open the map and let's try and recall who was younger and more agreeable."

After some brief but heated debates, we decided on Orchidea—'The first entrepreneur in the history of the Tree to be included in the register of entrepreneurs, businessmen and merchants, as compiled, maintained and certified by the Topographical Service of the Workers' and Peasants' Red Army (henceforth the Red Army)' Our profitable venture had begun with her, so she should be lucky for us in other ways too. Only it didn't make sense to approach her with our proposal until our mapmaking quest was completed. We'll report on the progress of our work and before handing her the first copy, ask her whether she wants to expand her assortment of goods—since that'll be the last chance to update the map accordingly. If she declines, we can start going through the other merchants following the same scheme.

"What's the next plan?" the pirc asked enthusiastically. "Should we finish the map?"

It was a reasonable suggestion but I hadn't the appetite for another course on cartography from Chip. I kept thinking back to Coleus mentioning that the library should contain information about the various bardic abilities, and since I was currently obsessed with the skills I'd have to choose later on, I really wanted to look up that information as soon as possible. Plus there was the quest of the mysterious sigil and who knew what I could dig up on that.

"I'd like to stop by the library and see what it has about the Tenth and bards in general. Maybe we'll come across something unexpected."

"Good idea," Chip agreed. "Let's go see how well they take care of the public's informational needs around this place."

It was like the library had been copied from one of the fairy-tale holoflicks. No doubt these were among the reference materials for the location designers. There were endless rows of wooden shelves, filled with all sorts of paper books. Wandering amid the stacks, I sensed the romanticism of the place and reflected on the thought that all of this sheer, paper tonnage could fit onto a tiny microchip. It came as a shock to discover that the pages were filled with actual handwriting. No. I understood of course that I was looking at a bunch of exotic scripts, imitating handwriting, but still, I couldn't help feel stunned at the patience it would take to copy out a folio in calligraphy and then illuminate it with various engravings. This was far from your typical 'Ctrl+c, Ctrl+v' job.

I was surprised to find the library full of players, many of them above Level 3 which was rare around the Tree in general. Judging by the party of high-level players I crossed paths with earlier, the elites prefer to spend most of their time leveling up beyond the city-tree's limits.

After some asking around, I discovered that the players who had seriously committed to playing as biota spent their time learning the language of the Dark Empire of Kartoss so as to avoid the language barrier when they entered the larger world. To learn the language, you had to get a job in the library and work four hours a day for about a month. And it wasn't as dusty a job as it sounded: Replace the books in the stacks; retrieve books, folios and scrolls for library patrons; and do the bidding of the head librarian every once in a while. During your breaks, you could read or level up your profession, which is what most of the players were doing. The big fish could simply buy and install the language pack they needed, but those prices were outside my budget.

"We should learn the language too," I told Chip grimly. "Otherwise, there's no point breaching the Arras. We won't understand the locals on the other side."

"Uh-huh," my companion nodded. "We'll accidentally call them bad names in their language and cause a diplomatic incident that'll be followed by some armed conflict."

"In the hypothetical kingdom," I added, reminding the pirc to keep the info I told him confidential.

"Uh-huh," the pirc wrinkled his snout. "I hope there's nothing more complicated than Swahili here."

"Well, strictly speaking, you don't actually have to learn anything," I recalled the players' explanations. "You simply put in your hours and you'll start to understand the language of Kartoss."

"Topography is a higher priority for us," Chip reminded me. "If we waste time on the library too, we'll be here till the carrots come home to roost. But if we stay true to the idea of intelligent labor division, then you can pollinate in the library while I go finish the map. You'll be my personal interpreter later."

"I'd have to complete an advanced course if I want to have any hope of conveying your inconveyable wordplay."

"You'll need lots of military dictionaries too," giggled Chip. "Although, you won't be able to choose the right reference materials without my careful guidance. All right, let's go together. I'll see if there's anything interesting there."

My conversation with the head librarian brought good tidings: Players with 'Bardic Lore,' 'Wisdom,' and several other traits could learn languages faster than others as well as do it on their own, reading books in the foreign language or interacting with its speakers. I opened one of the Kartossian books before me and read aloud with much emotion: "*Chahbah urtik abrik tyuk-matyuk geem.*" I shut the book at this point: Nope. I'd rather run errands around a library then read about '*tyuk-matyuk.*' I signed up for community service (of which there was little, owing to the surplus of library volunteers seeking to learn the new language), received a brief tutorial and wandered into the stacks to seek information about the bards.

This turned out to be easier said than done. There were of course books about bards but...There were about thirty of them, no less, but instead of class information they were all about legends and stories featuring various bards. Sensing the pointlessness of this activity, I paged through several of them, chose one that mentioned the deeds of the Tenth and began to read.

Chip remained beside me. He was very busy being very sincerely and very eloquently outraged. It turned out that he could only turn to the first page of the book and couldn't go on to the next one until he'd read that first one all the way through. A player mage whittling a figurine at the library desk next to ours explained that this was the intended game mechanic. Books, with rare exceptions, had to be read sequentially from beginning to end. And only bards and players with special secondary traits could open a book to any page and flip through at will. This really got Chip's goat and he fumed and ranted for a short while. When he calmed down, he began to open the folios and scrolls one after the other and then toss them back to their spots on the shelves with contemptuous snorts. During the last half hour, he had opened several dozen of these texts and cursed every one. Only a single one, treating of local legends, earned his tentative sympathy and was placed aside in the 'to read' pile.

"There are certain authors who would do better to keep from ruining good paper with ink and limit themselves to toilet paper," Chip shook another book. I have to admit that the writing of most of the books had led me to a dead end too. Many of them were dull, composed in a plain language, and dealt with some incomprehensible trivia. At least reading them increased my Bardic Lore. A glance in the fora brought some clarity to the matter and I hurried to show off my erudition to my partner:

"Most of these books are required for various quests. They come down to 'read this unbearable gibberish from beginning to end, answer the comprehension questions and you'll get a reward from an NPC.' And they're written to waste the player's time as much as possible."

"Bastards," Chip rendered his verdict dumping a solid folio without much respect back onto its shelf. Next, he drew a scroll from its tube. Opening it, the pirc perused its verses and began to groan again:

"Do they even have anything to read here? Bunch of nonsense. The author clearly suffers from a truncated lexicon and there's even strikethroughs in places. He repeats himself every other line. 'The sun in the heavens is the mien of the Lord, a miracle that bore the family of planets. And the sun is a miracle of the Milky Way, granted by the Lord, a miracle, a miracle of the Lord...," he read and immediately interrupted himself: "Do you think the local astronomers know what a planet is? Or is it like in the olden days—a clockwork movement of concentric orbs and pinhole stars? Bunch of religious mumbo jumbo. Back in the Lair they tried telling me about the local brand of polytheism. I didn't really get it, but the text doesn't really jive with a pagan belief system. What are you staring at me like that for?" Chip asked surprised, noticing my expression.

"Let me see that scroll," I asked, without looking up from the holy parchment.

"Here," the pirc shrugged his mighty shoulders and handed me the sacred object.

I greedily read the text, took the tube from Chip's paws, examined it and began rummaging in my bag for the drafting kit. I could of course use the notepad in my interface but in these kinds of cases, I preferred to work the old-fashioned way—with paper and pen. The drafting set was typically used exclusively for scrolls and wasn't much good for writing (the corporation offered fairly expensive stationary for that) but I didn't need to take notes either. I'm a bard and bards can compose songs. This meant that we can write down musical notation. And what I was looking at was in fact musical notation.

"I'm afraid to ask what profound wisdom you found in there," Chip remarked, surprised by my odd activity.

"Check out the etching on the tube," I stuck the scroll's container under his nose.

"Ah the same babble here too." The pirc scratched at the flower of life etched in the leather. "You think that the Tenth marked this scroll with his sigil? Have you received a quest 'to incinerate the cursed text and spread its ashes to the winds?' Because this junk doesn't deserve anything better—even if it were autographed by all the local nobles."

"Have you heard of 'solmization' before?" I asked without glancing up.

"Unless it's to do with intestinal parasites...no," Chip gibed, dispelling my illusions about his erudition.

"Roughly speaking, solmization is a method of learning melodies by associating notes with syllables. It's called solfeggio too. Simply put, it's what you know as 'do-re-mi-fa-sol-la-si'—a way of naming notes."

"Got it," Chip nodded. "What's this garbage have to do with it?"

"In the Middle Ages, an Italian music theorist named Guido de Arrezo came up with the solfeggio system and the names of the notes as we use them. Instead of 'do' though, he used the syllable 'ut.' He took them from an acrostic of a hymn in honor of John the Baptist. In the 18th century, some of the European countries changed the 'ut' to 'do,' but that's not important. Over the intervening centuries, the acrostic was forgotten and the notes began to be interpreted differently: '*do*' for *Dominus* or 'Lord'; '*re*' for *rerum* or 'matter'; '*mi*' for *miraculum* or 'miracle'; '*fa*' for *familias planetarium* or 'family of planets' (or the seven planets, which is the solar system); '*sol*' for *solis* or 'the sun'; '*la*' for *lactea via* or 'the Milky Way'; and finally '*si*' for *siderae* or 'stars.' *Do-re-mi-fa-sol-la-si*...Got all that?"

"You trying to say that these are musical notes?" the pirc poked the parchment.

"A hidden melody. I still have to work out the articulation, dynamics, inversions and other issues, but all of this seems to be encoded in the rest of the text, the punctuation and, as you put it, the scratch marks."

"Say, how do you know all this?" the furball asked surprised. "My more musical buddies tend to limit themselves to power chords."

"I used to drink at this bar next to the conservatory. So tequila Thursday rolls around and I get blackout hammered. And the next morning I wake up with a killer hangover and perfect proficiency with musical notation. I still don't remember exactly what happened," I said sarcastically, getting Chip back for his earlier 'I only use my head to eat because I'm a dumb soldier' gibe.

"Touché," the pirc guffawed, comprehending. "The only thing I don't understand is what you need to decode this nonsense manuscript for."

"First of all, sheer curiosity. Second of all, I believe you've come across something pertaining to the bards. An encoded, rare songbook, the beginning of some quest or something else perhaps. Maybe I'll play some melody and figure out why the Tenth left his sigils all over the Tree. Or unlock some unearthly power. Or go straight to Level 100. Or get a mound of gold. Or an army of Shadow that will conquer Barliona. Who cares? Should be interesting."

The pirc nodded in agreement and examined the scroll with greater care.

"Judging by the situation, my sonorous Tinker Bell, you'll be here awhile. And in that case, I'm going to get on with our community initiative of mapping the Tree. But you owe me a recitation of this mysterious melody. I'd like to see what the hoopla is all about."

I spent no less than five hours trying to decode the scroll. Once the notes before my eyes began to dance their own jigs, I understood that it was time to give up on my musical inquiry for today. My head hummed, my eyes were beginning to stick together and I still needed to do some chores and rest before our party headed out to the Arras. There wasn't any point in looking for Chip, so I sent him a brief letter and exited to reality.

In my gig inbox I found an order from my lady goatherd, the one whose gentlemen suitors all invariably turned out to be goats or rams. It didn't do to neglect my freelance work, so I locked myself in my room, unpicked the most recent drama and quickly rattled off a juicy message with an acerbic contents: the kind of message that doesn't violate typical forum guidelines but at the same time really makes its recipient feel the sting of scorn. Someone would surely say 'ugh, how revolting,' but I don't share that opinion. People will always insult each other, so let this happen within the bounds of censorship and with a deal of creativity—call it what you will, but it's progress. And I'll earn my pennies for my contribution to Internet discourse. Something has to pay the rent after all.

Having sent the completed message, I set my alarm to give myself two hours of sleep. It would do good to clear my head before making a foray into unknown territory. And who knows how long we'll spend in VR today?

And I dreamed a dream of an old goat, mechanically chewing the scroll with the mysterious melody.

CHAPTER TWELVE

U PON RETURNING TO BARLIONA, I ran past the instructors for the various trades. The mining instructor looked at me with immense doubt but taught me the basics and at the same time sold me a basic pickaxe, forcing a smile from me. The guys in the band would have a nice laugh seeing me with a pickaxe in my hand. It's too bad that my reputation was too low to take a screenshot. But no big deal. I'll get a chance at my selfie later.

The herbalist doubled as the lumberjack instructor. At first the combination surprised me but the explanation wasn't long in coming. It turned out that the biota only had one way of gathering these resources. To pursue herbalism, a player of another race had to first study the rules of harvesting the given type of plant. Daisies, for instance, had to be cut right under the bulb, whereas blue bottles had to be cut at the lower third of the stalk. If you erred with the location of the cut, then instead of an alchemical ingredient, you'd end up with a snack for some cow.

As a result, players who occupied themselves with harvesting grasses and herbs, measured the plants with rulers repeatedly, made mental calculations, measured again and only then dared to snip the stalk with one quick pass of the knife. Just like carpenters in meatspace. Due to this mechanic, it was practically impossible to harvest an unfamiliar herb. The chance of harvesting it properly was close to zero. For biota, all of this was rather simpler. Being related to the vegetable world, we could simply see the right place to cut if we spent enough time looking. As the instructor explained, the higher the skill, the faster you'd see it. Accordingly, if you were trying to harvest high-level plants, the chance of finding this sweet spot was tiny, while the length of time it took to find the right plant was great. The upside was that I could harvest familiar herbs as I traveled without even pausing.

Besides this, during the gathering of herbs and the felling of lumber, biota could identify strawberries, onions, brood buds, shoots and other vegetative wisdoms. All of these things lent themselves to cultivation and growing. It's not that I was dreaming of starting a vegetable patch, but who knows, maybe, some greenthumbs would buy what I found from me. While I was at it, I got a quest for gathering local plant seeds—which was nice too.

Another nice bonus was that I unlocked the passive 'Nature Literate' trait, which helped me identify certain plants by looking at them, as well as see which factors affected their growth (both the negative and the positive) and determine the status and needs of my green cousins. In addition, this trait allowed me to determine soil conditions and other properties.

I could level up my Nature Literacy by gathering grasses and seeds, growing plants, as well as, to a lesser degree, traveling around the natural world. In general, if the opportunity presents itself, I'll be able to chat with country folk about the coming harvest and even perhaps advise them on the best type of manure to dump in their vegetable garden. Fantasy, what can you say.

The alchemist's store, in addition to furnaces, alembics, and vials was furnished with a rocking chair and a respectable fireplace. The fire in the fireplace was an unusual purple color and emitted a strange odor. A biota named Paun snoozed in the chair with a heavy tome still open in his lap. The folio teetered precariously and—at last—tumbled to the floor.

"Eh?! What?!" Paun woke and jumped from the abrupt clap.

"Pardon me, I didn't mean to disturb you. I was told that I could learn the basics of alchemy here."

"Yes, of course, of course." Stifling a yawn, the alchemist trudged over to one of his desks and produced a hefty-looking case. "It will be one gold for the alchemy set. You need that to prepare potions, elixirs and infusions. It will be another twenty silver to unlock your specialization. Recipe scrolls are ten silver apiece. At the first skill level, there are only five available to you."

"I'll take the lot." I didn't want to waste time and placed the money on the desk. The mysterious case, the alchemist's set, passed to my possession.

"Okay..." muttered Paun, patting around the folds of his cape, which had been singed in places by some chemicals. "Where are they then...? Just one minute..."

The alchemist left the room, leaving me at a loss.

For whatever reason it seemed to me that an alchemist should be more...collected? This one could easily confuse a mouse tail with a toad's paw and cook up something nightmarish.

The time ticked on but the scatterbrained alchemist remained absent, so I decided to examine the room around me. My wandering gaze alighted on the rocking chair.

Item: Rocking chair. Effect: +1 XP for every hour of rocking. Class: Unique.

I couldn't help but burst out laughing. The devs had a sense of humor after all.

"There," Paun returned at long last. "Five recipes as promised."

Recipes learned:

Small Mana Potion

Description: The weakest potion—restores 20 MP.

Crafting requirements: Alchemy Level 1.

Ingredients: 2 cornflower stalks.

Instruments: Alchemy set.

Small Health Potion

Description: The weakest potion—restores 20 HP.

Crafting requirements: Alchemy Level 1.

Ingredients: 2 daisy flowers.

Instruments: Alchemy set.

Small Stamina Elixir.

Description: The weakest elixir—reduces Stamina cost by 5% for one hour.

Crafting requirements: Alchemy Level 1.

Ingredients: 4 briar berries.

Instruments: Alchemy set.

Ore dust

Description: Ingredient required for certain alchemical and culinary recipes.

Crafting requirements: Depending on the Alchemy level, various types of ore may be processed.

Ingredients: 1 piece of ore.

Instruments: Alchemy set.

Soil Infusion

Description: An ingredient required for certain alchemical and culinary recipes.

Ingredients: 1 clod of soil.

Instruments: Alchemy set.

"Now I'll teach you the foundations of our arcane and vaunted science."

To my immense relief, the lecture was brief and informative. The instructor showed me how to use the alchemist's set and demonstrated how I could prepare a health potion. There didn't seem to be anything complicated about this so I didn't hang around to ask further questions—I had several other affairs to attend to. I didn't have the time to prepare the strategic reserve of potions I needed anyway, so I bought some flasks with the finished product from Paun directly.

Thankfully, this biota had no issue with selling his goods. I imagine that for low-level players, the price of five silver coins per potion would seem exorbitant, but the business Chip and I had launched allowed me to make this expenditure without much anxiety.

I had less than an hour left before our rendezvous and I decided to try my fortune with Coleus as well. It was true that I hadn't yet completed my class quest, but perhaps he'd answer some questions anyway?

The tent was once again reverberating with the cello. Reed was in his former spot as if he'd never left. And yet he was now at Level 4. I didn't see any prospective bards—either the virtuoso was making the other players shy or everyone had already tried this class and was now trying out the other options around the Tree.

"I can see that you have still not completed my quest—although you have made progress," Coleus remarked as soon as I sat down next to him on one of the benches.

"I'm not very good at awaking love," I sighed with mock exaggeration. "And what's the point of awaking it when I have no use for it?"

"Yes," agreed the malignant bard, "it's clear that you're much better at awaking sorrow."

"Happens to everyone..." I replied philosophically. "Not everyone can be a lover hero conquering hearts and minds. Maybe I'm dreaming of becoming a barbarian with a huge club—a drummer who drums on the skulls of her enemies instilling fear and loathing?"

Coleus laughed to himself and bowed his head in a gesture of agreement.

"You're right. Every bard seeks her own way. Music is omnipotent and capable of instilling joy and loathing, kindling love and hate, inspiring and sapping strength. What your music brings depends on you alone. I am glad that you have understood this."

Quest completed: *A Bard's Calling. Step 2.*

+100 Reputation with the Biota. Current status: Friendly.

Experience gained: +120 XP.

+5 gold.

Attention! Class stat unlocked: 'Introspection.'

The bard's knowledge of herself allows her to unlock various skills and spells without resorting to an instructor or a songbook.

As I ogled the system notification and tried to understand how I'd managed to complete the quest, Coleus produced several scrolls and arranged them in front of him.

"I promised you one of my songbooks. Choose whichever suits you best."

Songbook. Songbook class: Common. Contains 'Song of Weakness.' Once you use the songbook, the songbook will vanish and the Song of Weakness will be added to your spellbook. When you perform the Song of Weakness: -1% to target Strength.

Songbook. Songbook class: Common. Contains 'Song of Cleansing.' Once you use the songbook, the songbook will vanish and the Song of Cleansing will be added to your spellbook. When you perform the Song of

Cleansing: remove one negative, magical effect from target.

Songbook. Songbook class: Common. Contains 'Song of Encouragement.' Once you use the songbook, the songbook will vanish and the Song of Encouragement will be added to your spellbook. When you perform the Song of Encouragement: +1% magic damage for party members for one hour.

At first glance, the choice was obvious: Currently, the battles happened so quickly that weakening the enemy would do little good. Meanwhile, our stats were too low for percentage boosts to have any noticeable effect. The ability to remove negative status effects was much more useful, but...In the long term, buffing my entire raid party was much more important, and weakening a dungeon boss by 1% was even necessary. On the other other hand...What's the long term matter to me? I'm still paying a subscription fee that's much too high for my budget and the largess of our sponsors was unlikely to hold out for longer than several months.

Nevertheless, I refused to rush my choice.

"First of all, explain to me how I'm going to learn new skills and spells? I can borrow some things from the other classes and there are other things that I can learn from the songbooks. But that can't be everything."

"You're both right and wrong at the same time. Reflect on what the essence of being a bard is."

"Music," the answer popped up on its own, but I thought a little more and couldn't help generalize it a bit. "Creation. Art."

"That's right. For you, it's music, for someone else, it's dance, for another, it's a recitation, and yet another might create her own unique activity. But the essence remains: Our life is creation. Bards are creatures that live their emotions, expressing them to the outer world. We dedicate our entire lives to the search of inspiration. Some seek novelty, some to the opposite, pursue the unplumbed depths of things long known. Some look outwards, others never leave themselves. But all of us can unlock something within ourselves that will help us on our way. Until you learn this, the only thing you can do is learn from other songbooks and study the abilities of the other classes."

"Does this mean that if I find my own way, I will be able to teach myself?"

"Not exactly. You will merely unlock what is within you already. Only you will determine what new opportunities you will unlock for your talent and how finely you shall polish it."

Coleus' words were odd. Without directly studying skills and spells, an intelligent build for my character will be all but impossible. And yet, on the other hand...Did it matter? After all, had I come to

Barliona to earn in-game achievements or to find inspiration? If the latter still held, I should simply go where the game takes me—with eyes wide open.

"I think I understand you."

Coleus gave me a curious look.

"A fairly rare quality for a free citizen. The majority of you prefer to cause trouble and demand to be taught the skills and spells their levels have qualified them for."

"My kind are a pretty strange crowd in general," Reed suddenly joined our conversation. "You shouldn't pay us too much attention."

Engrossed in our conversation, I hadn't noticed him place his bow aside and start following what we were saying.

"I was getting accustomed to you," Coleus laughed. "You contribute a certain playful dissonance to life's customary harmony."

"Your play is lovely," I used the opportunity to praise the cellist. "Many years of stubborn practice?"

A smile that was at once embarrassed and flattered appeared on Reed's face.

"You could say that again. I fell in love with the instrument when I was a child. I fell out with my parents over it and went to the conservatory. Couldn't find work after that. Who needs a cellist in our day and age?"

"Sounds familiar," I nodded. "It's a well-worn story. I had many a friend who struggled to find his place in the sun and ended up discarding music for more earthly, in-demand employment. Where are you from? I have an acquaintance who's a talent agent. He's a real toad but he should be able to send some gigs your way—for a fee as steep as highway robbery, of course. It might only be once a month but it's something."

Reed hummed oddly and shook his head.

"Thank you, of course, but it's no longer necessary. A while ago, I got myself involved in a very unpleasant affair...And, well, they broke my fingers. Out there, when I hold my bow I may as well be a crab trying to eat with chopsticks. I thought I was done for. But my brother saved me. He gave me a capsule and sent me into Barliona. If I find work playing music again, this will be the only place. I don't know if I'll find it, but the chance to play again..."

Reed trailed off, smothering his roiling feelings beneath an expression of outward calm. Even I had a lump in my throat. I could only imagine what it was like: First no one has any need for you and your life's dream and later even that dream is taken from you. From a musicians' perspective, Reed was a person of disability out in meatspace.

I recalled the passion and hunger with which he played the first time I'd encountered him. It had reminded me of the way a drowning man gulps air, trying to satiate his lungs. You can't force that kind of thing, nor fake it. This was why I believed Reed's story instantly and without a shadow of doubt.

"Listen, I'm planning on heading out with my party later. We're going to leave the Tree and check out the surroundings," I said once I'd calmed the emotions that had filled me. "If they're okay with it, maybe you'll join us?"

Neither Chip nor Sloe seemed like soulless bastards who'd simply take this person's story in stride. A trifle like another party member and therefore a diminished share of the overall experience wouldn't bother them.

"Well I seem to be progressing all right here in the city, but it would be interesting to leave its limits," Reed agreed politely. "But you should first ask your party. What if they don't like the idea?"

Here I recalled Reed's mysterious fourth level and couldn't help but ask:

"How did you manage to level up? I saw you a few days ago and you were still at Level 1."

"I'll tell you something more," Coleus popped into our conversation. "He's basically been in here the entire time. He's progressed much further than you along the bard quest chain and did so without budging from his spot."

I looked at Reed with bafflement but he just shrugged his shoulders.

"To be honest, I didn't even give it any thought. I was so happy that I could play again that at first I simply played. I remember there were messages about new abilities, spells, traits...Coleus handed me several rewards, experience, songbooks..."

Seeing my scandalized face, the bard instructor simply spread his arms helplessly:

"It's not my fault he has a keener sense of his calling than you. There's a story of an unparalleled flautist who once lived in a village. He was a shepherd who took care of the village sheep from the day he was old enough to walk to the day he was too old to walk. He earned worldwide renown. Kings and emperors who wished to hear him play were forced to travel to a little Sylvyn-forsaken hamlet because the bard simply refused to leave it. And it should be mentioned that this village never experienced a war because all the neighboring kingdoms declared themselves the protectors of the legendary flautist and his village. If the current situation keeps up, Reed here will turn our Tree into the center of Barliona."

"In that case, perhaps it's a mistake to draw you into our dubious venture?" I glanced at Reed askance.

"It's time to test his mettle," Coleus announced dogmatically. "Even the flautist of yore would leave his village to reach the pastures."

"Let's not confuse the forest around the Tree for pastures," I grinned. "By the way, on the topic of leaving the Tree. Coleus, are you aware of the strange happenings in the forest? Some mysterious blight has affected the creatures. They've begun to attack whomever they come across, ambushing peaceful travelers."

"I have heard," the bard nodded with an odd indifference.

"Well in the meantime, my companions and I are risking our lives to go down there and figure out what's happened to the animals! To try to cure them of the mysterious plague or at least kill them to keep the Tree's residents safe. Alas!" I injected a dose of pathos into my voice, "Perhaps you're seeing me for the last time and before the sun sets today, I will be lying fallen and torn by the merciless claws of the rabid beasts. Or perhaps we will discover the source of all evils and save the forest after a heroic battle. Then I shall pen a ballad of our deeds and relate in it how you, instead of properly preparing your student for the dangerous trial, offered her one of three COMMON songbooks. In the great myths and legends, teachers impart great wisdom to their students and equip them with legendary weapons like the Vorpal blade or some other magical weapon. But you've decided to discharge your duty with a tattered songbook containing a weak spell! The memory of your parsimony shall live for all eternity, mark my words..."

You have increased your Charisma stat. Total: 2.

You have received another training point.

Unallocated training points: 3.

At the end of my blistering speech, Coleus burst into raucous laughter and raised his hand:

"Enough, enough, I see the full breadth of my failure. You took it a little too far with the part about seeing you for the last time. Free citizens have the enviable blessing of being able to return from the Gray Lands, and yet there is truth in your words. You really are on your way to accomplish a vital deed and it would be dishonorable not to help you."

Items acquired:
'Song of Weakness' Songbook
'Song of Cleansing' Songbook
'Song of Encouragement' Songbook.

"This is more like it! Worthy gear for a great battle!" I said happily, activating one songbook after the other.

You have learned 'Song of Weakness.'

Attention. Because you have the Charisma and Fame stats, this spell has been altered.

Song of Weakness: -(1 + Charisma + Fame)% to all enemies that hear your performance, not to exceed -50%. Effect duration: Intellect × 5 seconds. Casting time: 4 seconds. Cost of performance: Character Level × 10 MP. Range: 30 meters.

You have learned 'Song of Cleansing.'

Attention. Because you have the Charisma and stat, this spell has been altered.

Song of Cleansing: Your performance removes 1 + Charisma negative magical effects. In addition to the song's target, you may choose extra targets for your song, whose number is equivalent to your Charisma. Casting time: 2 seconds. Cost of performance: Character Level × 2 MP for each target of the spell. Range: 30 meters.

You have learned 'Song of Encouragement.'

Attention. Because you have the Charisma and Fame stats, this spell has been altered.

Song of Encouragement: Your performance increases the physical and magical damage of all party members by (1 + Charisma + Fame)%, not to exceed +100%. Effect duration: (1 + Charisma + Fame) hours, not to exceed 48 hours. Casting time: 1 minute. Cost of performance: Character Level × 7 MP. Range: Charisma + 20 meters.

Reading these updated descriptions for my new spells, I all but jumped from excitement. Now this I could understand: My secondary stats affect my spells! With buffs like this, I'd actually have a tangible impact on my party.

"In addition to this trifle," Coleus interrupted my silent exaltation, "I can teach you an unusual spell that I learned in my travels. However, in order to learn it you will need to spend one training point."

"What spell is it?" I inquired.

"'Canopy of Silence.' You saw me use it on that noisy free citizen with the tympani. It may help you travel through and perform in a dangerous territory without attracting the attention of nearby enemies."

"Actually, I was quite worried about just that," I admitted.

Coleus has offered to teach you 'Canopy of Silence.' If you agree, you will expend 1 training point on learning this spell. Do you wish to learn the new spell?

Of course I do.

You have learned 'Canopy of Silence.'

Canopy of Silence: At your performance, a canopy descends on the target area or creature, absorbing all sounds emanating from the area within the canopy. The canopy's Area of Effect may be chosen at will, but may not exceed (Intellect) meters in diameter. Casting time: The canopy is conjured as soon as your performance begins. This spell is channeled, though you may perform other songs during the channeling of this one. Mana cost: (Canopy AoE × 2) MP. Range: (Intellect) meters. Mana cost for maintaining the

spell: (Canopy AoE) MP per second.

Unallocated training points: 2.

Achievement unlocked: 'Student Level 1.' +1% chance to persuade an NPC to teach you a non-standard skill or spell. Learn 19 non-standard skills or spells to reach the next level.

"The canopy is cast as soon as your performance begins. As a result, you won't divulge your location. The canopy traps all sounds within it, meaning that if you are inside, you will still be able to hear sounds produced outside of it as well as inside of it."

And so the issue of extra noise has been solved and all I need is enough MP to channel the spell.

"Thank you! I am certain that this will be a great aid in our journey."

"Just be so kind as to present me in a positive light in that ballad of yours," the instructor winked happily. "And since you're on your way to a dangerous part of the forest, you should stop by Master Pirus' place. He was just recently complaining to me that he's run out of the wood he needs to make his instruments."

"I'll be sure to stop by right away," I promised. A companion quest is just what the doctor ordered. "Let me ask you one more question. I'm a cartographer and a scroll writer, which means I can create my own songbooks. Does this mean that I can compose songbooks only for the spells I already know?"

"No—songbook composition works a little differently. You may fill songbooks only with music you have created."

"And what does that grant me?"

"You will be able to pass it on to any other bard, teaching him the spell you have created."

"Are you saying I can create my own spells?"

"At the moment, no. But I am certain that one day you will learn how to. Now it's time you go and save the world."

"Can you teach me Canopy of Silence too?" Reed asked. "I'm going to save the world too."

"No. You do not yet have the required qualities. Besides, you don't have a single training point yet."

"That's true," Reed nodded in mild perplexity. It suddenly dawned on me that I hadn't the slightest idea what this person, whom I'd just invited to my party, was capable of. Sloe would definitely want to know what this bush in a bag was all about.

"Listen, what do you know how to do in general?"

"What do you mean?" Reed replied.

"Well, like spells, skills...that kind of thing."

"Ah, that's what you mean. Let me check..."

I sighed to myself and began to sort through the arguments I'd have to use to convince Sloe to allow yet another newbie into the party. The most convincing line that popped into my head ran something like: 'One newb more or one newb less, what's the difference?' But something told me that the necromancer wouldn't be very receptive to this.

"Magic Missile and Song of Healing," Reed reported predictably. However, contrary to my expectations, the list did not end here. "Song of Demolition, Charming Song, Stunning Song, Heroic Song. I think that's about it."

"All that at Level 4? How?"

Reed shrugged as usual.

"I was playing."

"I heard gunfire..." I muttered a well-known phrase from an ancient movie. I suppose Reed really had completed a part of his class chain without leaving the tent and progressing further than me. In this manner he had unlocked different songs, which would help the party a great deal. The two bards wouldn't be singing over each other. "All right, Sayid, what do all these songs do?"

"Sayid?" Reed echoed, puzzled. "Who's Sayid?"

"It's a long story. Just watch *White Sun of the Desert* sometime. It's a good flick. We're about to head out and I still need to stop by Pirus' place."

"Song of Demolition allows me to clear obstacles like fallen trees, flimsy walls and so on. As my stats grow, the spell gets stronger. The Charming Song causes the enemy to stop and listen. It lasts as long as my performance lasts or until the target takes damage. The Stunning Song stuns enemies for five seconds. The Heroic Song removes fear, suppression and similar negative effects from the party, and makes them immune to further negative effects during its performance."

"Sounds absolutely perfect! Do you need to do anything before we set out?"

"No, I'm free whenever."

"In that case, let's run to Master Pirus. We'll take his quest and then hurry to the Market Branch."

We almost made it to our rendezvous in time— Chip and Sloe were deep in conversation and greeted our appearance with an expected question:

"Hello, oh my mellifluous Tinker Bell. I see you've brought me a new shrubbery. Who's he?"

"This is a prospective member of our crusade into the dark and scary wood," I introduced Reed. "If you're not opposed, I would like to invite him to our party."

Sloe and Chip stared at Reed who tried to melt into the background.

"He has some nice crowd control spells," I played my trump without further delay.

The pirc's face took on a stumped expression:

"Sorry...is mounted police a class in this game?"

"Sort of. He'll come in handy if we encounter a mob of angry mobs," Sloe assured him and then turned to me. "I don't understand: You're both bards and his level is lower than yours, but at the same time he has AoE spells and you don't? What's the deal?"

"I don't really understand it myself, but it looks like every bard develops along her own plan. Unlike him, I have various buffs and debuffs in my arsenal.

"That's better," Sloe perked up. "Tell me what spells you have and let's brainstorm some battle tactics before we descend..."

CHAPTER THIRTEEN

"**E**VERYONE REMEMBER EVERYTHING?" Sloe asked sternly after we had unanimously reelected him our party's leader.

"What's there to remember?" Chip asked surprised. "It's not exactly the *Iliad*. Shouldn't be hard to memorize."

"Good. Let's go then."

Reed, Sloe and I activated our natural camouflage, while Chip (who had switched back to warrior after all) tossed his halberd over his shoulder and stepped off the leafevator with a carefree whistle. Just like last time, a few seconds passed before the blighted lynx came flying out of the foliage right at the pirc's face and was warmly welcomed by the halberd's edge and our necromancer's spell. I quickly healed Chip and camouflaged again, out of sight of any aggroing mobs. Reed remained hidden the entire time, nurturing his low HP pool.

"As we get further from the Tree, make sure to only play music when a canopy's cast," Sloe reminded us. "We don't know whether the noise aggros monsters, but we can experiment with that before leaving the game when dying won't be a problem."

"Roger that, cap," I replied.

Meanwhile, Chip picked up the loot that the lynx had dropped.

"What a bunch of junk," he remarked, dumping it into his backpack.

We had agreed to entrust Chip with the goodies. No one wanted to waste time and effort on picking up the dropped items, opening us up to potential attacks, and no one had any doubts about the honesty of our tank. In fact, as we were discussing how to divvy up our profits, the pirc announced that none of this interested him and he was willing to forgo his share.

In the end, we decided to distribute our winnings on a 'per need' principle and later split the proceeds from whatever we sold. There really wasn't much to divide up though: The blighted beasts didn't so much as drop useful items, to say nothing of treasures.

"Halt! There's some flowers up ahead." The necromancer halted us and squatting down beside a blue bonnet among the grass, began to examine it carefully from various angles. Chip watched Sloe's movements with curiosity and then coughed politely:

"What's up? Have you encountered a butterfly cousin of yours?"

"I'm trying to identify the place where I should

cut the stalk, my uneducated friend. What are you waiting for, Lori? Don't you want to level up your gathering skill?"

"Of course I do!"

"In that case, have a squat. You should gain some XP just for identifying the place of the cut, let alone gathering."

Feeling a bit stupid, I squatted down beside our fearless leader and looked as intelligently as I could at the flower. It looked a bit worried by such unwarranted attention. But nothing happened and recalling my PE classes in school, I began to waddle about like a clumsy duck trying to see the flower from all angles.

"Bunch of vegetable voyeurs," the pirc remarked and turned to Reed who was standing to the side a bit shocked. "Don't you want to take part in this fetish? It seems that this is a hobby for you green folk."

"No," Reed hastily declined to participate in such a strange activity. "I'd rather hang back and cheer them on."

As he said this, he somehow produced his enormous cello from thin air and began to play some ditty in a major key, perfectly suited to the scene unfolding before him.

I was about to remind him that making music in these parts without a canopy was a bit risky, when a system notification appeared before me:

Buff received (*Song of Creation*): +4% to skill growth.

"Whoa!" You didn't tell us you had that buff," Sloe said, surprised. "I've never even heard of this."

"I didn't know it before," Reed seemed no less surprised. As soon as his bow stopped, the buff vanished. "I simply figured that this tune was a fitting tune and ended up accidentally unlocking a new song."

"Song and dance helps us build and live," Chip mimicked the Soviet slogans of yore. "What about you, commissar? Can you do the same?"

"Noodle knows," I admitted honestly. "Yesterday I couldn't, maybe today's different. I finished a class quest, so maybe something's different now."

"Well, we can experiment later. Let's harvest this flower and move on toward the Arras."

I'm not sure what the reason was—Sloe's words or Reed's musical accompaniment—but a short while later, I noticed a barely shimmering section of the blue bonnet's stalk.

Skill increase:
+11% to herbal gathering.
+4% to One with Nature.

"Got it," I told the necromancer.

"Excellent," Sloe gingerly cut the flower and placed it in his inventory, after which he picked off a piece of the turf and coddled it in his hands pensively.

The pirc's face expressed a barely restrained desire to make some comment, but I had figured out what Sloe was doing and picked up some earth in my hand to examine it more closely as well:

Humus. Rich in minerals, salts and organic matter. Good for the majority of plants.

And that's it? I went on examining the clod of earth.

You have learned the properties of the Hidden Forest humus.
Rich in minerals, salts and organic matter. Good for the majority of plants. This ingredient increases the rate at which plants grow as well as the rate at which biota gain experience.
Skill increase:
+15% to One with Nature.

"Cool," muttered the necromancer, who I guess had increased his trait too. "I see no practical use for it, but it's cool nonetheless."

I suppose that since he had no culinary or alchemical skills, he'd only been able to see the general description.

"Biota use humus in their cooking and alchemy," I shared my knowledge, placing the humus in my flask. "It's worth it to gather several clumps. It'll come in handy."

"So it's like that? I'll need to study that," Sloe grew animated. He produced several flasks and began filling them. "All right, let's move on. We need to try and reach the border of the Arras."

The further we strayed from the Tree, the higher the monsters' levels grew. I was beginning to heal regularly during the random encounters—Chip's health decreased noticeably after each attack. As luck would have it, my current Intellect sufficed: I had enough to maintain a small canopy for Reed and me as well as to heal. Sloe's Intellect allowed him to slay any mob with two spells at most and once I'd buffed him with my *Song of Encouragement*, he became the scariest monster in the forest.

"Oh look, the poor thing lost its claws from fright," said Chip, picking up yet another bit of loot. "We can use them to make bracers."

I was about to congratulate the pirc on his newest acquisition, when a sharp though mild pain struck me in my shoulder and knocked me flat down:

Damage taken. -76 HP: 87 (damage from Blighted Wolf) - 11 (physical damage resistance). HP Remaining: 14 / 90.

At the same time, the Stun debuff appeared on my character.

While Chip examined my suddenly empty health bar in the party interface, a bluish-black orb began to grow in Sloe's hands. I looked helplessly at the monster looming over me. Unlike the wolves I'd seen before, this specimen bore a striking resemblance to a biota. Its fur was made of stiff-looking, little leaves, while his fangs looked quite ordinary and very sharp. Like the rest of the blighted beasts, this one did not look like he was in very good health. Various thorns grew out of his body and he was enveloped in a shadowy fog.

The apparition was so terrifying, shocking and hypnotizing that I forgot about my party, the goal of our mission and even that I was in a game. It was more like I was in a dream and the sensation of the unreal remained in the background—at once keeping me from panicking and at the same time making me live every terrifying second to the utmost.

In the moment when the monster's fangs were almost upon me, I caught its maddened eyes and plunged headfirst into the series of visions that I was already growing accustomed to...

Drawn by an untamable will, the animal stopped at the border separating the green grass from the black stretch of blighted earth slowly creeping in all directions. The animal senses the danger, but the call is stronger than instinct and the paws carry the wolf forward against his will. Each step gives rise to a change in the creature. The body grows, thorns pierce the hide, the color darkens until it is indistinguishable from the coal black grass underfoot. Suddenly I realized that I was seeing all of this through someone's eyes: A hand reached out and scratched the blighted animal's scruff. The hand belonged to a biota, but was covered with the same thorns. The fingers seeped a dark fog.

The vision ended. The wolf was shaking his head in puzzlement over me, while a melody from the cello wound its way through the forest. In the next moment, a blue-black orb of magic smashed into the wolf turning him into a quickly evaporating wisp of smoke.

As soon as the battle ended, Sloe camouflaged from any potential reinforcements.

"Excellent work, Reed," he praised the bard. "You stunned him just in time. Camouflage right away or the next mob will make mincemeat of you. Lori, what are you resting for? Heal up and camouflage too. That wolf knocked off your canopy. Half the forest heard Reed's ditty. Pay more attention, Chip."

"Sorry, I blinked," the tank muttered in a guilty voice, offering me a paw to help me up.

"It's okay. It happens," I replied a little absentmindedly. I was still distracted by my most recent vision.

Bardic Lore isn't quite so helpful when the

information comes pouring out in the middle of an encounter. Or does that happen when I don't have control over my avatar? I quickly grabbed my lute and recast the canopy. Then I healed up, took a swig from my flask, camouflaged and sat down on the grass to give my mana time to regenerate. Reed sat down beside me. Even though he had managed to level up to Level 5 during our trip, his Intellect was still low and every spell he cast would drain his mana pool.

"Hey there, guppers." A voice sounded from nowhere, making us jump from surprise. "Whatcha up to?"

"Well, personally, I am considering the voice in my head and how that affects my further notion of my mental health and self," Chip admitted sincerely, looking in the direction where the voice was coming from.

"We're grinding," Sloe replied with a note of tension in his voice.

"Seen anything interesting?" the voice went on.

"Blue bonnets and daisies," I joined the conversation.

"You should move on," the stranger advised. "It's a bit dangerous here for you rugrats. The mobs up ahead are tougher. Why a party of guppers like you lot will get your bones picked clean."

"Well, we'll give it a shot at least. It's interesting after all," I objected.

"Don't even try it. I promise you, you won't get

out alive," the voice warned a little ambiguously.

"Where do you suggest we go grind in that case?" Sloe inquired with unexpected accommodation.

"At the Tree. And to the south. That's right. South of the tree, there're some nice places to stroll. A kilometer and a half, no more. Everything after that is perilous."

"Thanks. We'll head back," the necromancer promised to everyone's surprise.

"Very good. See you around then."

The voice didn't say anything else and we looked inquiringly at Sloe.

"What are we waiting for? Let's go head back to the Tree. Lori, cast the canopy so that the nearby monsters don't hear us."

"Whatever you say," I muttered and began to play a soft melody, creating a canopy four meters in diameter. I had enough mana to sustain it for just a few minutes, yet Sloe wouldn't have issued the order without having some reason for it. And really—no sooner had our party set out on the return journey, than the necromancer began to gesticulate at some random branch without slowing his pace and said:

"Make a show of heading back and looking for resources along the way. Those were cutthroats back there. They won't let us onto their territory."

"What cutthroats? And what's so scary about them that they even have their own territory?" Chip became indignant. As he did so, he pointed at the trunk of a far-off tree.

"The kind who cut throats. This is a new location so there must be some new dungeon here. Some of the guilds have hired biota and pirc players to form scouting parties. They helped them level up and sent them into the forest to look for any dungeon entrances. A part of these scouting parties are kill groups, charged with eliminating any potential competition. If you stray into their search quadrants, they'll cut you down. We are potential competition after all."

We had walked up to the tree Chip had indicated and he now produced his handaxe. Squinting at the tree, I saw that it was an ash. Just the kind of wood that Master Pirus had asked for.

"And if we kill him?" I floated the most obvious way out of our predicament.

"I doubt we could so much as lay our eyes on him," Sloe shook his head. "Imagine a biota rogue with insane agility and a dozen levels on us. He'd wipe us in one fell swoop. He should easily be at Level 20."

"Level 32 actually," the pirc suddenly announced. "His name's 'Otolaryngologist.' My dictionary informs me that this is a surgeon who specializes in throats and ears, but if you ask me, I think that plant's got his tongue planted firmly in his cheek."

"How'd you see him?" Reed asked with surprise.

"As an experienced cartographer, I am blessed with a keen eye and a sharp mind," Chip replied modestly. "Also I hate it when people tell me what to do. I vote we kill him."

"We don't have any options," Sloe shook his head. "He'll eat us alive. It'll be like Garfield and his lasagna. And that's not mentioning that the rest of his party is lurking around here somewhere. The best option is to double back, level up, do some quests related to seeds and herbs and then go back to the Tree. We'll craft some gear, build up our strength and head out again tomorrow. There's a chance that by then they will have scoured their quadrant and moved on. Then we can go through unimpeded. In the meantime, Reed will get a chance to increase his Intellect and Lori will pick up some extra spells."

"All right," Chip agreed unwillingly and something in his expression told me that he wouldn't forget Otolaryngologist or his insult.

We spent the next three hours circling around the Tree, doing our best to not stray too far from it and complete the quests we had. I should say that neither mining nor woodcutting were my forte. I waved the axe around for half an hour and gave up. I ended up asking Chip to chop me enough ash to complete Master Pirus' quest. Chip let fly several quips about murderers who would slay their own kind and then quickly and stylishly chipped up the lumber I needed. Meanwhile, Sloe and I went crawling on our knees (to the amusement of whoever happened by) in search of herbs and other alchemical ingredients. The sun smiled on our little, green meadow and Reed played on, so basically the entire thing looked like a *Teletubbies* episode. The only consolation was that no one around us had the reputation to record video for posterity.

After all was said and done, I reached Level 7, Chip and Sloe reached Level 10 and Reed reached Level 6. Here and there we'd encounter player parties. Two of them even contained huge and mighty pircs.

"I see your brethren are drawn to the Tree," the necromancer remarked.

"I wager caravans have arrived in time for the festival and the pircs arrived with them as their guards," I guessed.

"In any event, soon it'll be harder to level up," Sloe warned. "They'll clear all the mobs at the Roots of the Tree, while the higher-level parties might not let us stray further afield. That's to say nothing of the PKers."

"Placekickers? Penalty kills? Penalty kickers?" Chip ventured.

"'PKer' means 'player killer,'" the necromancer explained. "They're humans who like to hunt other humans but in VR."

"Well just let them try," Chip shifted his halberd in his hands like he was expecting a PKer to pop out at any moment.

"They don't like to take risks," Sloe hurried to disappoint him. "Typically they choose the rogue class, but since biota have natural stealth and gain combat bonuses in the forest, there should be several magic classes that would fit the role too. They'll follow you around while camouflaged until you don't have much health left and that's when they'll gank you. With their bonuses to agility and intellect, they'll finish you in one hit or spell. Or maybe they'll team up and fall on you in a mob. That's pretty common too. Our best option is to reach the Arras tomorrow and meet my friends there so we can gear up and get some funds too. We'll need to figure out the local bureaucracy to allow them to cross the border. How much reputation do we need to gain permission? Or is there some quest chain we have to do?"

"We'll try to figure it out," I agreed. The plan sounded reasonable to me.

"In that case, let's finish up with our quests and meet up again tomorrow at the same time. Whoever plans on exiting for a while, send me a letter. We'll arrange for some bounty money when you get back. And, just in case, let's exchange comm numbers. Who knows what might happen?"

Once we'd exchanged contacts, Sloe and Reed went about their business and Chip reminded me with the implacability of a cliff face that it was time to finish our mapping of the Tree. Sighing, I said adieu to my desire to burrow into the Tenth's scroll and plodded after the furry sadist. At least, half an hour later, we were the proud owners of a complete and extremely detailed map of the Tree.

"There you have it! And you were worried..." Chip muttered with satisfaction, smoothening the final product.

"There's one last 'i' to dot," I reminded him. "We need to figure out who our jewelry outlet will be."

"That's right! Let's go see Orchidea!"

Persuading the merchant to offer a wider range of goods turned out to be a fairly simple matter. What merchant would refuse extra profits, especially when they simply come knocking?

"Of course. Tell Master Hibiscus that I would deem it an honor to sell his wares. There's only one problem. I won't have the floor space to show the new goods."

"You are mistaken, my dear. This is no problem at all," Chip immediately objected. "Maybe I'm a novice carpenter but I'd be happy to whip up a new and elegant display case for you."

"Oh, I simply cannot imagine how I can thank you!" Orchidea grew emotional. "You have already earned a discount on my wares..."

"Why don't you simply say a kind word about us to your fellow entrepreneurs," Chip offered graciously. "Then if they need something, they can come and speak with us."

"Indubitably!" Orchidea was pleased to hear

this response. "And of course I shall pay for your work."

We triumphantly handed Orchidea the first edition of our map. She lovingly read the advertisement of her store and bestowed on us a lifelong 30% discount on her wares.

"We should hit the others up for a discount too," Chip offered, rubbing his paws.

"Uh-huh," I nodded. "When'd you become a carpenter?"

"Well you see, I went to the local blacksmith and it turns out instead of forging armor out of steel he uses locally sourced wood. It's pretty malleable when you work with it, but after you soak it in some special resin, it turns tougher than steel and yet is pretty light too. However, to learn how to craft this armor, I have to learn both smithing and carpentry."

"Cool. What class is the armor for?"

"Erm...I don't understand the question..."

"For instance, mages can't wear armor at all. They incur some kind of penalties on their spells from wearing armor. That's why they go around in capes and cloaks. Rogues wear light armor, typically of leather. Hunters wear chainmail, warriors wear plate. If you look at the recipe, it should say what type of armor it is."

"Hang on...Uh-huh. There's heavy, which I have to hammer for a good while, there's medium and then there's light which I can ornament and adorn with wood."

"Theoretically, you should be able to use the wood to reinforce armor of any kind."

"By the way, what do bards wear?" Chip livened up. "Maybe I can forge you an armored bra or something?"

"You better check your privilege, pirc," I brandished a fist at the shaggy joker. "Although, it's not a bad idea. If a bard can become a hybrid of any class, then I should be able to wear whatever armor I like. I'll ask my instructor."

"First let's hand out our map and discharge our contractual obligations."

This took about an hour, during which the cunning pirc managed to get a discount from every merchant we visited. The final 't' to cross was completing the jeweler's quest, thanks to which we earned four chains and seven rings granting +2 to Constitution each. While we were at it, we submitted an order for a further fifteen. If we're going to band together into a party we need to increase our survivability.

"Goodbye, my svelte figure," I muttered happily as I put on the chain and eight rings one after the other.

"What's your svelte figure have to do with it?" Chip asked surprised.

"In gaming slang, the more HP you have, the 'fatter' you are. You are a fat tank. And I'm about to become a fat biota."

And yet, the notification that appeared shattered my dreams:

Due to the racial penalty to the Constitution stat, the maximum bonus to this stat derived from items can only be (Character Level) + (base Constitution).

Your current maximum Constitution with item bonuses is 10.

"Damn it...What a flop! I can only buff my Constitution to ten with items. Racial penalty."

"And there's no workaround?" Chip asked surprised.

"Either I increase the level or I increase my base Constitution. And the latter option costs four stat points or a ton of time and energy spent on leveling up."

"It's too bad," the pirc sympathized. "As soon as you increase your level, you can slip on more rings."

"All right. At least we'll have some jewelry for Sloe and Reed. They have racial penalties too. They won't be able to wear too much of it."

"Still, it's better than it was," Chip consoled me. "All right, I need to start working on those display cases. Until tomorrow then."

"Aight. I'm going to spend another hour or two on the scroll and then head to bed...".

CHAPTER FOURTEEN

I T WAS MORNING IN NAME ONLY—the sun had long since risen over the horizon and was already nearing its zenith—when I decided to get out of bed. Never a fan of starting my day with discipline, I had completely let myself go with all these daily gaming sessions. Pretty soon I'll start waking up in the evening and staying up all night like the aristocrats of the past.

A cold shower didn't do much to wake me up and I trudged over to my kitchen to seek succor from my autocook. While the imitator made coffee, I assembled a sandwich and sat down to read the gaming news. Someone was waging war against someone else, someone was building a guild castle, Anastaria had accomplished some great feat...All the names and titles were foreign to me and didn't stir my interest. Thus, when I came across a mention of the Day of Wrath guild, I was as happy as if I'd encountered some old friend. Sloe's guildmates had completed some kind of complicated dungeon, raising their rating by several points. I bet the necromancer will be pleased.

I sighed and closed the forum. Boring, boring, boring...

A fine drizzle began coming down outside my window, joining with the sunlight to form a quick rainbow. I wanted to take a walk, but my capsule glowed reproachfully in its corner. I bet Chip's already waiting for me. And that scroll's waiting too. And Toad, may he croak, is expecting his in-game hit.

I stepped out on my balcony, leaned against the railing and took my time drinking my coffee, savoring the view. I should take a break and go to the forest with the guys for some barbecue.

I entered the capsule in a good mood. I had managed to meditate with the rainbow.

"Right then, let's go submit our work to the cartographer," Chip proposed as soon as we met. "Last night, in our excitement we stopped by everyone but him."

"Hang on," I muttered. "Let me copy the last part from your version. He may check to see that we both did the work."

"I'm starting to feel like the class geek who has his homework copied by the cool girl," the pirc giggled, unfolding his completed map of the tree before me. "A girl who is both cool and a future dropout," he added in a grumble looking at my map.

"Why a future dropout?" I was even slightly offended.

"Because you have as little sense of scale and accuracy as I have rhythm and pitch!" he grumbled, tapping both maps with his claw. "This branch is much too high over here—and over there it looks like it has come apart from the trunk and is hanging in midair on its own! Unattached! And that's not mentioning how you've proportioned the elevations! This is pure chaos!"

"What are you getting on my case for?" I bristled. "The built-in cartography mechanic drew them this way! Who needs these details anyway? Every branch is drawn in detail."

"Right, and the tree in 3D looks more like a Rorschach test than a tree," Chip continued to critique me mercilessly. "Adjust this right here, shift this over, rearrange the levels one over the other and check to make sure that they fit the trunk regularly. To do that, you'll need to select all the levels and drag them over to be around the trunk. Like so..."

"Like so..." I echoed in shock, staring at the result. The different levels of the Tree had evened out along the trunk and the sigils of the Tenth, which had earlier been scattered chaotically around the entire map now arranged themselves into seven straight lines of various lengths, forming in their totality a simple and utterly proportional hexagon.

"Like I said: A future dropout!" The pirc reached into his bag for his own map. "And I'm a dummy too—I should've figured out earlier that you are a hardened and unrepentant abstractionist. A real Salvador Dali when it comes to botany...We should have used my map as a reference instead of yours..."

"Yeah," I agreed, copying his map and connecting the dots I had missed. The hexagon that emerged did not tell me anything new. "Something's not right...This is something else...Something familiar..."

Scratching the back of my head and then my nose magically stimulated my thinking process. I made a new copy and having no compass on hand, began to draw the surroundings to scale.

"Look," I demonstrated the result. The familiar drawing of the flower of life emerged at the intersections of the lines. "All that's missing is the central point. There was no sigil there."

"Thus we may conclude that there is something there," Chip completed my thought. "I can sense it in my tail: If we go there, we'll make off like villains. So...well, let's go and see what we can dig up."

"Should we tell Sloe and Reed?"

Chip thought for a little and then shook his head negatively.

"Let's go take a look first to see what's going on. It'd be dumb to call the guys if there's nothing there. So let's swing by there quietly, look around and if there's something of value—then we can assemble the brigade. No—we simply mark them on the map and the autochthons will scatter of their own volition."

He straightened out to his full height and began to twirl his halberd happily.

"Autochthons?"

"Aborigines," the pirc explained. "Natives, indigenes...The original inhabitants of this place basically. Damn it all. When I level up a bit, I'll buy myself a helmet of cork and a red uniform like a colonial sahib." Chip glanced me over, stepped behind me for some reason and then summarized sadly: "It's a shame you won't make much of an elephant."

"That's okay. I can fan you with palm fronds."

"Why you're already your own fan! Or a prize banner from some colonial foray." Straightening his shoulders, the pirc placed his halberd on one shoulder, picked me up underarm and set off bellowing with all his might: "We have tarried here overlong, oh brothers!"

The chant that followed was rhythmic and not so bad on the whole, but the pirc hollered like he wanted the very moon to hear him.

"Put me down where I grew!" I demanded from the manic Chip. "I'm not your hand baggage!"

"You are a recon drone!" The hairy bastard replied and tossed me up in the air. "A multi-functional drone with an advanced Imitative Intelligence!"

"You should make up your mind whether I'm a future dropout, a palm frond fan, a colonial trophy or a highly advanced Imitative Intelligence. This kind of talk is enough to give a girl a mean case of DID."

"When it comes to cartography, you're a dropout. When it comes to being a drone, you're highly advanced," Chip clarified without, however, placing me down on the ground (or rather branch).

I wonder whether he is like this in real life too...I suspect so. And the boot up his ass that he carries back from boot camp is his main piston on his life's journey, metaphorically speaking. My gran told me about his kind—one like him won't die his own death, but break his neck in some remote place.

The point on the map we sought turned out to be a notable part of the trunk near where the Branch of Oblivion began. I walked around it several times but didn't find any additional markers, explanations or hints.

"Are you sure we're where we're supposed to be?" I asked Chip. "Check your map. Maybe I've messed up something with the scale again?"

The furball unfurled his scroll and after careful scrutiny nodded.

"Here."

Putting away his map, the helicopter pilot also looked around but failed to find anything—except for a large turquoise bug who had settled on the pirc's pink nose.

"Scram," Chip snorted, chasing away the upstart insect. "Found yourself a landing pad.

The bug flew off to another airport, while we

settled down next to each other and got down to a difficult task: Thinking.

"Maybe you have to play or sing something here too?" Chip proposed uncertainly.

"Makes sense in theory," I agreed, picking up my lute. "This is a bard quest after all. Any requests?"

"Something laid back. Otherwise, we might wake someone and then get embroiled in some new quest."

"Laid back..." I repeated pensively and after a few moments the strings began to sing beneath my fingers.

Well we know where we're going
But we don't know where we've been...

The classic poured forth like a warm spring rain, washing away the weariness of mind and soul. For some reason, it seemed to me that the song about the wanderers would please the Tenth. Why him? I don't know, but I wasn't singing for the pirc as much as for the ancient bard who had brought us to this place.

I'm not sure whether the pirc heard me either: While I played, he turned his ears here and there like a cat and carefully looked around himself, waiting for something to happen. And so he was the first to see the fruits of my efforts.

"There," he said quietly, pointing at the trunk

of the Tree beside us.

The outline of a passage began to shimmer in the bark, and in its center, I could make out the flower of life glowing dimly. Beneath it, some notes glimmered.

"Looks like we need to enter a musical password," I concluded, playing the musical phrase.

The outline of the passage flared up and faded, while the passage itself turned into the shimmering ring of a portal.

Quest completed: *Mysterious Sigil.*
Reward: +200 Reputation with the Biota.
Quest chain available: *Road to Nowhere.*

Quest available: *Road to Nowhere.*
Description: Following the sigils of the Tenth, you have opened a portal leading to an unknown destination. Do you dare discover what lies on the other side and solve the riddle of the Tenth?

Quest type: Rare chain. Reward: Variable. Penalty for failing/refusing the quest: None.
Do you wish to accept this mission?

"Speak, friend, and enter," muttered Chip, adjusting his grip on his halberd. "A quest's been offered. Shall we take it?"

"Of course we take it!"

"Done."

Stepping up to the opened portal, he sniffed it, twitched his ears, listened and then stepped decisively into the portal.

"Bad idea," I said too late and stepped in after him.

On the other side of the portal, I immediately slammed into my partner's furry side. He was standing stock-still staring at the fairly odd location we had been transported to. We were standing...on a white marble floor, in the middle of an enormous hall, with a vaulted ceiling that had been painted to look like the night sky.

"Where are we?"

The question was a rhetorical one—we were nowhere on the world map. Neither in the Hidden Forest, nor in the areas we had explored. It was like we had stepped out of Barliona altogether.

Chip approached a window pane that bore the emblem of the flower of life and began to study its sash. Locating the latch, the pirc carefully opened the window and stuck out his curious nose.

"Nowhere," he voiced his observations right away with resignation. Squirming under the pirc's paw, I caught sight of clouds of gray fog. And that's it.

"Up and down, it's all the same," the pirc stepped away from the window. "It's like we're suspended in a cloud. Like we took a wrong turn in a hot air balloon."

"Strange place..." I said, looking around. There was neither an entrance nor an exit. The tables, ledges, shelves and walls bristled with a myriad of diverse items, whose purpose could only be guessed. Priceless cups, weapons, paintings, alchemical alembics, vials containing mystery liquids, jewelry decorations, costumes and suits of armor...

"Maybe the Tenth is a hoarder?" I ventured, pulling up the properties of the nearest item. They were hidden. Who could've guessed?

"Uh-huh, this must be his attic," the pirc agreed.

Looking around, he picked up a golden ring from the shelf beside him. It was plain, without gems or ornament and the pirc twirled it in his fingers and then stuck it in his pocket.

"I'll fence it with the jeweler," he explained his looting. "Wouldn't do to leave here empty-handed, I mean, really..."

But before he could finish his thought, Chip vanished in a wisp of smoke and a short puff—while the ring fell to the floor and rolled under a tattered ottoman.

Your party has been disbanded.

"Great..." I muttered to myself. I left full-immersion mode and made a call to Chip's communicator.

"Hey," he replied almost immediately. "Can you imagine—I got kicked out for theft, the jerks. The message said that 'only a bard can earn something in that location.' Listen—what if that was the One Ring? You should look around and see if there's a skinny bare-assed halfling running around there, hissing 'my preciousss, my preciousss...'"

"The last thing I need in my life is a bare-assed halfling. Where'd you get kicked to?"

"The entrance, where we started. I got a debuff too—I can't enter the Tenth's portal for the next twelve hours. Bunch of asshole tightwads—all of that over a tiny ring. The hell do they even want from us?"

"If I only knew...All right, I'm going back in. I'll try to get to the bottom of it."

Nothing had changed during the few minutes that I'd been absent. The cursed ring was lying in the same place and there were no scantily-clad riddlers lurking about. In fact, there was no one at all to tell me what to do next.

"Hey!" I called for the sake of decorum. "Is there anybody out there?"

There was no reply. Not a word, not a sound, not the slightest system notification. Not wishing to overthink things, I tried the tested method of unlocking stuff—first I played a song on my lute (without effect) and then played the melody that had opened the portal to begin with.

Nothing.

All right, I guess I'll try and think this through logically. This is a quest for bards and its author is the first biota bard. This means that I have to figure out how this location is related to my class. Another visual inspection didn't make anything clearer. No entrance, no exit, no hints. Given all this, it looked like the items in the room were the key to the puzzle. Although, why should they be a key? Maybe this is the end of the quest? Choose your prize for solving the pattern of the sigils and be on your way. Maybe, but this seemed a little...well...boring? I'd expect more from the top biota bard. All right, in any case, I should select an item and see what happens.

I stayed away from the valuables: a classic greed check in every story ever told—as evidenced by Chip. Armor...A couple of sets looked pretty attractive, but the opportunity to get my hands on a bunch of high-level equipment evoked nothing but a healthy dose of skepticism. Either it'll turn out to be cursed and I won't be able to remove it—or I'll get kicked for greed again. Weapons weren't really bardic things.

Regrettably, I found no music instruments in the hall—and I definitely wouldn't mind getting my hands on an instrument of the legendary bard this early in the game. On the other hand, I stumbled upon a table with three books that really interested me. Every one could be a songbook or contain some information about this location. Or it could be yet another compendium of drivel from the local library.

But the books seemed like the most reliable option. All I had to do was select one of them.

The first folio made me anxious. Enormous with gilded edges, wrought-iron corners and clearly decorated by some master craftsman—it was clearly destined for the study of some king or mighty mage. The small book next to it—with a modest, worn binding—looked pathetic and insignificant. Soiled with dirt in places and with a torn corner, it was like a pitiful beggar lying at the feet of an illustrious nobleman.

The third book lay a bit to the side, its lock glinting. The black leather cover revealed a barely noticeable, embossed inscription either in runes or symbols of some unknown tongue—perhaps even magical signs. A matching key was nowhere to be seen.

My initial urge was to take the third book. Secrets, mysteries...they are always alluring. They promise something valuable. And yet this choice seemed as obvious and attractive as the one offered by the luxurious folio. In this company, the tattered little book seemed quite out of place. Why would the Tenth hold onto something like this? There's only one conclusion—whatever's inside is something worthy of attention.

Weighing the pros and cons one last time, I picked up the worn book from the table and immediately received a system notification:

Selection made.

Item acquired: Cypro's Notes.

You have foregone the power of wealth and knowledge and confirmed your title as a bard. The way is open.

Quest updated: *Road to Nowhere* (One trial completed).

A flash and a new portal opened before me.

I stepped forward.

Twilight, the smell of moisture and mold. The deathly-pale light of the lichen plastered along the walls of the cave. And a mirror. A large mirror that was one-and-a-half times my height, its frame a verdigrised bronze, enclosing the dim light of the glass.

It was so very cold. Vapor billowed from my mouth. I wanted to sit by a fire and warm my chilled fingers. Unfortunately, there wasn't anything to make a fire out of around here.

I approached the mirror and glanced at my reflection. Instead of myself, I saw a ghostly silhouette, barely discernible in the lichen's pale glow. Without night vision, I'd probably not have seen anything at all.

"Who are you?" I asked and my words formed a small cloud of vapor.

"I am the guardian of the path," sounded an

otherworldly, terrifying voice. "You wish to continue your journey?"

The voice acquired a deep chill that pierced me to my bones, my very soul. I wanted to flee—away to the bright, warm sun, to the hot fire, to the living. But there was nowhere to run.

"I do," I exhaled and, as I did so, it felt like my body lost its last vestiges of warmth.

"Death lies in wait for all travelers, always," the voice of the creature in the mirror rustled with snowdrifts. "To continue on your way, appease death. Take another's life to save your own and continue your journey."

"There is no one here whose life I may take," I replied, rejoicing to myself that Chip had been expelled earlier. "Is there some other way for me to continue my journey?"

"No," rustled the inhabitant of the hall. "Go back to your world and find the toll. When you are ready, merely say 'I have brought the toll,' and your sacrifice and you shall be brought here."

Quest updated: *Road to Nowhere*.
Find a sacrifice whose life you are willing to give to appease death and continue on your way.

The world grew dim for a moment and then I found myself in the same place where Chip and I had begun our adventure.

"D'you make it very far?" the furball inquired. Chip was lazing in the shade, with one leg over the other, watching me from under the brim of his hat, shoved down low onto his forehead. He looked revoltingly at ease.

"I needed to make a sacrifice and there was no one around," I grumbled, basking in the warm sun. The chill that had invaded my body was slowly retreating from its light.

"Will I do?" Chip stretched and yawned deeply, showing off his picket of teeth and curling his red tongue.

"There weren't any particular limitations, so I suppose you would. Then you can off me when you reach the same step."

"Well I can off you whenever," Chip joked darkly, standing up. "Let's go, oh my predatory queen of the flowers. We'll play out our little melodrama about the unhappy couple again."

"Here's the invite."

Once the pirc accepted the invitation, I announced triumphantly:

"I have brought the toll!"

A member of your party is prohibited from traveling to this location for the next 11 hours and 19 minutes.

"What a flop!"

"So we'll wait," Chip concluded philosophically and lay down in the shade again.

"We shall meet the Swede on the field of battle!" he declaimed dramatically and pulled his hat lower over his nose. "Eh, it's a sin to lie around the shade without a beer in this type of weather."

"You're planning on lying here for the next eleven hours?" I asked surprised and sat down nearby—at the very edge of the shadow where I could still bask in the sun's hot rays. After the freezing, humid cave with the mirror, shade was the last thing I wanted.

"Why not? I have a nice thing going here," Chip rejoined. "Listen, my little corncob, isn't it time we invite a couple soloists to our ensemble? I mean, Reed and Sloe."

"Yeah, we can invite them. Theoretically, they should complete this quest faster than us—especially if they don't start stealing stuff. I definitely won't share the chain after its beginning, but they can get it themselves. They can ask Amaryllis about the sigils, run past them following our map and continue from there. By the way! I acquired Cypro's notebook in the first room. Maybe they'll contain some clues?"

"And you waited to tell me?" The pirc perked up. His laziness vanished in an instant. "Let's see it!" he demanded, wiggling his pink button nose.

Unfortunately, we were in for a disappointment. The pages of the book (or was it a journal?) were blank. Not virginally blank, since they were pretty ragged—but it seemed that someone had enchanted the ink and turned it invisible.

"Why does this bard make everything so complicated?" Annoyed, I slammed the book shut. "The scroll's encoded and the notes are invisible."

"Your Cyprus or whatever his name is, is a bard too, correct?" Chip asked.

"Cypro," I corrected him automatically. "Yeah, he's a bard. The first bard of the biota."

"Uh-huh…" the pirc riffled through the journal one more time and returned it to me. "So then the key to the cypher has some musical aspect to it. Let's do some thinking: If you are a musician, how would you go about making a cypher? Would you use some kind of notes? Or would you scramble the words into a song?"

"If only…These pages are simply blank."

I opened the book one more time and held it up to the pirc, demonstrating the utter lack of symbols to decipher.

"I'd guess there's some kind of magic or alchemy at play. Either I need to sprinkle, rub or slather something on it, or utter some kind of magic words that will make the text appear. That, or play the right tune. Could even be the same one I found in that library scroll, by the way."

"Well what are you sitting there for? Play on," Chip commanded. He even adjusted himself to be more comfortable, placing his palms on his knees.

"Come on now," he hurried me.

I didn't object and simply placed the prize book of the Tenth before me, took my lute and commenced with my concert. I tried it all: instrumental pieces, a cappella, and even a duet with Chip—all without effect. The pages remained bare.

"That's it. I'm done," I gave up after an hour and a half. "There're two possibilities remaining: Either the text is revealed further on in the quest chain or the scroll holds the key."

"Well let's try the scroll then," the pirc suggested. "It's right here after all and we still have a good long while before I'm allowed back in."

"All right. In that case, I'm going to head back to the library. You can get in touch with Sloe and Reed and tell them where they can get the quest and how they can activate the portal."

"Aye aye, sir," the pirc saluted comically, jumped up to his feet and hurried off to do his errands.

CHAPTER FIFTEEN

EITHER I HAD CHOSEN a bad time or by mere coincidence, the library was impossible to get into. As per usual, everyone in the city was occupied with their quests, crafting and leveling-up, while here the public was openly bored. Those wishing to learn Kartossian instantly announced their readiness to work in the library, and yet there was only enough actual work for a single player. And supplying this huge mass of people with work turned out to be a difficult task, so the majority of players were simply wandering from place to place. Many people were reading—some for pleasure, others to level up their skills—a few were occupied with their professions, but the majority were simply trying to find a way to kill the time.

The librarian had given up on herding this mass into some semblance of order and locked himself into a utility closet, leaving one of the language students in charge. This player was now utterly at a loss for what to do and a little shell-shocked by his abrupt promotion. Unlike the librarian, he didn't even try to shush the talkers and limited himself to fulfilling the few requests that were coming in. I knew where my scroll was kept and didn't bother bothering anyone. I took my musical riddle and sat down at one of the unoccupied desks.

As history would have it, ladies on their lonesome attract more attention in games than in real life. In part this is because in VR, in their gaming persona, people find it easier to interact with one another. A degree of anonymity goes a long way in this sense. At times it also goes too far.

The absence of private chat in Barliona was at once an inconvenience and a blessing. The inconvenience were evident to everyone: To speak to someone, you have to get your hands on a fairly pricey amulet that allows you a one-on-one connection with that person. Or you can write them a letter. The mailing option isn't particularly fast: You have to go to the mailbox, write the letter and then wait for the recipient to read it...Once you acquire a portable mailbox, this problem is partially ameliorated, and yet this is a steep expense for most newbies. The budget option is the general guild chat, but you can forget about privacy here and you can only communicate with others in your guild.

The good thing about Barliona's lack of private chat was evident to the female portion of the playerbase. In other games, the private chat would instantly flood with messages like 'Ey gurl lets get to no each other!1!!' or even outright disgusting (and anatomically unsound) propositions. I'm not entirely sure what the point of such missives is, given the availability of virtual imitators for every possible taste, but I guess, some people simply enjoy accosting strangers of the opposite gender with inappropriate offers.

In Barliona, the issue of unwanted attention was much more innocuous. Either you had to become an epistolary stylist and hope that the recipient wouldn't dump your letter into the trash bin on sight, or you'd have to approach face-to-face and speak all the revolting things you had creeping around your head. There was practically no one who was willing to do this eye-to-eye, so male attention as a rule remained within the bounds of decorum.

Another reason for heightened interest toward female persons was the notable gender gap among the playerbase. Even though virtual worlds drew members from all genders, ages and social layers, player preference remained differentiated. And even though Barliona's appearance had closed this gender gap a great deal, there were still significantly less female gamers here than male ones. Some linked this fact to deep-seated psychological differences, some with a maternal instinct spurring women to give birth and care for their children out in meatspace, but I personally suspect that everything came down to high-quality story simulators that had become quite popular in recent years. If earlier women of all age groups dreamed of great, true and at the same time fairy-tale love—as they held a novel in their hand— then now there were custom-made game worlds like *Fifty Shades of Twilight*.

When you create a character in a game like that, you have a thousand and one appearance settings to choose from, special characteristics as well as other stuff, while the plot revolves around a romantic relationship with a partner that the gamer finds most attractive. And if in Barliona for instance, it was practically impossible to become a princess or a courageous corsair, then in the game-novel you could simply start right with that. And no one was bothered that every other player was of royal blood or the Chosen One. This contradiction was explained by the intersection of a thousand worlds in each of which lived the girl of everyone's dreams. You could stay in your own world or step out to the Middle World, interact with other players, compare your outfits, coolness, number of suitors, sumptuousness of jewelry, et cetera et cetera.

The gameplay and mechanics were typically superfluous. The heroine could scatter a wall of foes with the wave of her hand or allow her army of lovers to take care of the problem. And yet these simple mechanics seemed to appeal to the playerbase. After all anyone who wanted to grind levels and contemplate battle tactics had Barliona and similar worlds. In the VRomances meanwhile, the players spent their time worrying about which suitor to choose—the dangerous but sensuous vampire, the decisive werewolf or the wealthy nobleman with a dark history and terrible skeletons in his closets. Accordingly, the characters' skills revolved around these kinds of quandaries and had relevant names: Seduction, polyandry, racial attractiveness...

How did I know all this? I played a free trial one time. I rolled a beggarwoman for curiosity's sake and was promptly propositioned by two princess on my first day—as well as four barons. I also received an invitation to a ball and some gaudy fripperies, a magical pet and countless compliments. I managed to save my native village from an ancient evil and discovered that the blood of the local divinities flows through my veins (I had chosen the *Mysterious Ancestors* perk when rolling my avatar) and that I'm destined to accomplish great deeds. All in all, I didn't hang around much longer than the first day— uninstalled the nonsense and deleted my account. I mean, it's nice and all to feel like a great hero, but it should require at least some effort, brainpower and perseverance. All that game was missing was a 'Defeat Everyone' button, though maybe I didn't play long enough to earn it.

One way or another, there was a gender imbalance in Barliona which at times engendered inappropriate scenes around members of the female gender. The girls sitting at their books—a priest and a bard—simply clapped their hands over their ears in an attempt to concentrate on their reading. And despite this obvious sign that they weren't in the mood to talk to anyone, they were periodically approached by the bored, idle players. I was not spared this sad fate either. As soon as I sat down and unfurl my scroll, an attention-starved mage named Lapushock sat down beside me.

"Hey. What's up?"

I sighed to myself, regretting that Chip wasn't beside me. His mere presence was enough to ward off any creeps. On top of this, the sight of a potential tank for one's party typically diverted any public attention from me anyway.

More than anything, I wanted to lock myself away somewhere near the librarian and calmly decipher the scroll, yet a promise I had made to myself long ago forbade me from sending him straight to the pircs. The thing was that most of my friendships had been with men and so I knew how difficult it was for them sometimes to collect their spirits and approach a girl they liked. And recalling the agonies of my friends in this matter, I promised myself to respond with as much friendliness as possible to such attempts in order to lower the number of insecure people in this world. A minute of conversation wouldn't hurt me and my 'suitor' wouldn't perceive the encounter as some kind of epic battle with a dragon.

"I'm working on a class quest," I lied amicably. Best intentions are best intentions but I'd like to complete the quest on my own. "I've been tasked with copying the scroll and that's what I'm doing."

"Uh..." Lapushock drawled eloquently. "How're you doin' anyway?"

This question stumped me harder than the scroll had.

"Fine." My reply was as meaningless as the question.

"What, do you, like, play or something?" the mage asked nodding at my lute.

"Yeah. I'm a bard."

"Can you play something?"

Some other time I may have even indulged him, but I was way too interested in the riddle of the scroll and if I actually started to play in this place, all the other players would flood me with requests.

"How about another time? The quest has a time limit. I have to finish it. I'm here every day anyway. I'll play something another time."

"Sounds good, sounds good," Lapushock agreed and to my relief moved on to jabber with some other group.

Hardly had he stepped away when another took his place. The conversation was just as dull and devoid of substance, so when the seat next to me freed up again, I quickly waved at a hunter named

Tell sitting at the neighboring desk.

"Listen, can I sit down with you by any chance? I won't bug you or anything. You can read in peace," I begged in a whisper.

"Why?" He didn't understand.

"So the guys don't distract me from my quest."

"All right, why not," he agreed and I quickly sat down next to him.

"I owe you. When it's time for you to go, let me know and I'll give you a buff."

"Cool," Tell instantly perked up.

My new company practically eliminated any further attempts by randoms to get to know me and I finally got down to the work of decoding the scroll. The general hullabaloo in the library continued to interfere, making me sorry that the canopy of silence didn't work in the contrary direction—blocking all the sounds from outside of it.

My unhappy musings were interrupted by the appearance of a new character. In a lovely whirlwind, a biota with notable physical characteristics burst into the library: A perfectly-shaped face, enormous, green eyes, legs that sprouted straight out of her ears and a chest that would have made Toad kick me out of the band and take her instead. This beautiful creature had a strange name—Annastarriia—and she immediately became the star of the place. The attention of the various wandering players immediately zeroed in on her, and since the young maiden clearly welcomed such attention, everyone forgot about me and the other readers. In exchange for this, however, I had to now listen to the babble of the beautiful fairy, but this was the lesser of two evils. And when I finally figured out the principle behind the scroll's encryption, I stopped noticing the background noise entirely. Soon enough I'll be able to play the mysterious melody and figure out what's concealed in it.

My work went in starts and fits, but then suddenly it was like I'd been walloped in the head with a dusty bag. A terribly false plinking invaded my mind, accompanied by a tone-deaf singing that was closer to bleating than singing. This aural nightmare was supposed to be a serenade that one of the courters had dedicated to the biota of his dreams, who in turn was listening with evident pleasure.

Maybe my own voice isn't unimpeachable, but my ear is perfect! It was completely impossible to listen to this. Sparing a kind word for Coleus, I took up my lute and began to play quietly. A canopy of silence descended on the noisy revelers. Several readers whom the cacophony had distracted, broke into smiles, while a bard with the clever name 'Brouhaha' gave me a thumbs up. Meanwhile, the players inside the canopy's shimmering dome began to take notice of it. While the majority stared at the mysterious phenomenon, one of the mages crossed the boundary of the canopy, assessed its effect and returning to his companions began to explain with much gesticulating what the canopy did. This gave rise to mass migrations in and out of the shimmering film, exclamations of wonder and astonishment. Someone started an argument about the purpose of such a spell and someone else began to experiment on the very edge of the canopy.

The reaction of the quarantined bard and the biota babe, however, was far from enthusiastic. The bard stopped strumming his instrument and said something with a hurt look; however, due to the canopy, we could only assume that this was something along the lines of 'don't shoot the pianist if he doesn't know how to play.' The vibrant beauty, in turn, was clearly offended. Leaving the canopy that I had cast over the bard, she set upon me:

"Who do you think you are? You think you're smart or something? Why don't you just admit that you're jealous? You didn't get any songs and now you're salty!"

To be honest, I've never known what to say in this situation. To argue with a dummy, you have to descend to her level. And how am I so confident she was a dummy? Well, intelligent people wouldn't start pointless arguments. I had to resort to a tried and tested way of yanking the rug from under my assailant's feet. Agree with her.

"Yes, I'm envious," I replied with all the sincerity I could muster. "No one has dedicated any songs to me and I'm very hurt. You shouldn't flaunt your success in front of others. Find yourself an out of the way place and coo and caw there to your hearts' content."

The girl, who had been ready to challenge any word I spoke, momentarily lost her gift of speech. There was nothing to argue with after all. Still, the fire of outrage continued to roil in her ample chest and she managed to find another issue to take offense at.

"You've got a guitar yourself, but you have no respect for others! The boy was playing and you interrupted him! How about you wait your turn?"

I have a lot of patience for all kinds of things, but when a vain bimbo orders me around... well...I find that vexing.

"Got it," I acquiesced. "Is it my turn now? I want to sing you a song too."

This sudden turn knocked the feet from under Annastarriia, but gathering her thoughts, she nodded magnanimously.

"All right—let's hear it."

I began to pluck the strings of my lute with a very serious look on my face, recalling a bit of Scottish-American alt rock:

> *You pretend you're high*
> *Pretend you're bored*
> *Pretend you're anything*
> *Just to be adored*

And what you need
Is what you get...

Quiet snickering sounded around us and grew steadily to uproarious laughter as Annastarriia's face paled with rage.

Attention! You have unlocked a new ability: 'Taunt.'

Your performance can anger an enemy, goading her to act carelessly. The number of targets you may Taunt at once is equal to your Charisma. Enemies affected by Taunt, rush in your direction, wishing to crush their offender. Targets suffer +10% incoming damage, -20% to defense and -50% chance to identify traps. Your Attractiveness is decreased with the target by a variable amount.

Effect duration: (Fame) seconds. Casting time: Variable. Cost of performance: None. Range: Variable. The target must be able to hear your performance.

Ah! New abilities! It's too bad this one's fairly useless—I won't ever be a tank in my wildest dreams so drawing aggro isn't something I'll need to do. But it's nice all the same. Now I can acquire new abilities from thin air, as they say. I wonder how many hidden abilities there are to unlock and how much time unlocking them will take...

Meanwhile, Annastarriia did not share my elation. An odd mixture of outrage, anger and hurt appeared on her face.

"You...! Why you...!" her voice broke off, her eyes glinted suspiciously, and she exited the game without having properly unburdened her chest.

I guess I'm a bad person to make a girl cry and rage quit. But I've always suffered from bad manners, what can you do?

"And why did you do that?" Brouhaha inquired sourly from the neighboring table. "She was like a lightning rod, a real life-saver."

"My bad. I simply found her much too irresistible," I confessed. "I confess my guilt: its breadth, depth and degree. And I humbly request that you send me to fight in the nearest war. And if there's no war on hand, I'll accept anything else: exile, a chain gang, incarceration! But please in the summer months and preferably somewhere that gets a lot of sun and has nice beaches."

Brouhaha burst into contagious laughter and waved her hand:

"All right, all right. Your crime wasn't that great. By the way, where'd you get that spell? I'm a bard too, but I haven't encountered anything like that yet."

I looked her over with interest. She was Level 11 but I hadn't noticed an instrument on her.

"I persuaded my instructor to teach me—Coleus."

"Ah...I should give that a shot. I'm not studying with him."

"Hmm...Isn't he the instructor for all the bards?"

"I'm studying to be a circus dancer, so I have a different NPC as my instructor."

"Circus dancer? And what do you do?"

"Whatever. Dances, tricks, a little gymnastics. I studied in circus school several years when I was a child, so I decided to give it another go now. It's a lot of fun!"

I tried to imagine the specialization of circus dancers and, honestly, found myself at a loss.

"Listen, can I look at your training sometime?" I asked, holding my breath.

"Why not? I'll ask Daisy whether it's okay with her. She's already retired, but I convinced her to take me on, so our lessons are held in her home. As you can imagine, I can't just invite someone without asking permission first. I'll finish my reading here and go ask her. Then I'll send you a letter."

"Can I bring friends too?" I asked. "No more than three. We'll bring something—just tell me what Daisy likes."

"Not even a question. I'll find out for you. But you owe me a demonstration of your own in return."

"Deal!"

I didn't get a chance to return to my study of the scroll. Stripped of the lovely Annastarriia, the would-be courters surrounded me. Some of them wanted to know about the canopy, some of them wanted me to 'play something,' and on the whole I wasn't able to concentrate on my deciphering of the musical mystery. To be perfectly honest, I was even considering simply running away when an interesting idea occurred to me. Grabbing the scroll, I quickly dashed behind some shelves and as the curious gaggle was coming up behind me, activated my natural camouflage. It worked! I suppose the system considers the Tree and all its buildings a natural environment.

"Hey, so what's the deal with that spell?" A particularly prying mage asked one more time, entering my little hiding hole.

"What the hell? Where'd she go?" asked a priest following on his heels.

"Looks like she exited the game. I guess it's too much to ask her to answer a couple simple questions..." the mage said bitterly, and the two friends returned to the rest of their ilk, bemoaning cold human nature.

Once they were gone, I stole my way to the quietest corner I could find among the various stacks and tomes, unfurled my scroll and continued my painstaking investigation.

After three more hours, I froze in anticipation.

All that was left was to inscribe one last note on the parchment and then who knew what Barliona would open for me? The most powerful spell in the world? A unique quest? The ability to read the Tenth's notes? I'm about to find out! The note took its rightful place and...Nothing happened.

I frowned, trying to understand what the matter was. I thought I'd done everything right. The melody was clear in my mind, even if it sounded a little incomplete. Maybe that was the problem? The melody is unfinished and I have to come up with the coda? I peered into the scroll and noticed that its bottom edge wasn't even—as if someone had cut off a piece of it there in a confident but not entirely accurate motion of a knife. It looks like I only have a part of the composition in my hands.

I didn't have anything left to do in the library, so I returned the scroll to its place and quietly slunk in the direction of the exit. There were a lot less players doing nothing now, but there were still plenty. In the city, the guards I came across followed me with suspicious gazes. No wonder. A citizen who is hiding (even if poorly) from strangers' eyes, evokes suspicions about her motives. All the same, they didn't bother stopping me and asking questions. I suppose, my friendly status and lack of a criminal record played their parts. Then again, it's possible that creeping around like this wasn't even an issue and this was merely the product of my fevered imagination.

As promised, the pirc was laboring with a plane in his hands, fashioning the display cases for Orchidea's shop.

"Something tells me that carpentry is viewed a little suspiciously around these parts," I remarked.

The pirc jerked up his mug, turned it in the direction of the voice, squinted and bared his fangs in a friendly smile:

"Ah! Our secret geek has returned."

"Why secret? Why geek?" I asked, baffled.

"Because you were in the library geeking out and because you're in stealth mode," the pirc snickered with pleasure.

"There's something to that," I was forced to admit, leaving my natural camouflage.

"Well? Any luck?" Chip asked, returning to his work.

"Hmm, how can I put it...It's like I solved the riddle but now I don't know what to do with the solution."

"Let me hear it. I'd love to hear it! Get that journal out too while you're at it. Maybe we'll see some change."

"That's why I came here," I nodded, taking out the score and arranging it on the display case. It's no music stand, but it'll do. I placed Cypro's notes beside it, opened to a random page. What if the text begins to appear as I play?

The lute's strings sounded, arranging a pretty melody out of separate sounds. Unhurried and soft, it was better suited for a harp but sounded good all the same. Chip had even begun to hum to the tune— when suddenly the melody stopped, leaving behind only the sensation of something unfinished.

"And that's it?" the pirc asked with surprise, but I wasn't listening. A system notification had appeared before my eyes:

You have found the first fragment of Cypro's Songbook.

Quest available: *Restore the Songbook.* **Description: Once upon a time, Cypro, the Tenth member of the Council, decided to share one of his songbooks with all the bards who liked solving mysteries. An avid reader of myths and legends, Cypro enciphered a song and hid it amid the library's thousands of histories. Only the most well-read bards, whose tenacious minds could decipher the script, would receive Cypro's gift. Alas, it was not to be. A fragment of the scroll was lost and no one knows who could have snatched Cypro's inheritance. Find a way to recover the lost melody or locate the villain who dared violate Cypro's will—and restore the complete scroll. Quest type: Class-based unique. Restrictions: This quest may not be shared with another player. To recover a song from Cypro's songbook, the player**

must possess a musical instrument that is at least rare. Quest type: Class Chain. Reward: Cypro's songbook. +500 Reputation with the Biota, +40 Attractiveness with the Tree Librarian, +10 to Fame, +300 gold.

"Oh come on," Chip remarked to my prolonged silence. "Don't lose hope. It'll be interesting all the same. It's too bad all your work didn't help."

"I got a new quest!" I bragged. "I need to find the missing scroll fragment and recover the complete melody."

"Oh! The corncobs are on the case?" The pirc giggled. "You, uh...If some cabbage gives you attitude—let me know and I'll help!"

He brandished the plane in his hands:

"I'll peel it in a blink."

"If my charisma doesn't bear fruits, we'll try your way," I promised, putting the notes back in my bag. "What do you say? Shall we take a break in meatspace and get back to our sacrifices tomorrow?"

"I don't want to save the world here either," Chip waved. "I'll get back to my Mister Geppetto roleplay. Look! Here comes our thorny friend."

A pleased-looking Sloe walked up to us:

"Cool quest you sent us, thanks! I got a dagger and plus two to Int and Const."

He proudly brandished an ugly looking knife of the type typically used in evil sacrifices.

"You guys finished the entire quest chain?" I asked, astounded.

"Not really much of a chain, not many links to it..." Sloe shrugged. "Soon as I snuffed out Reed, the mirror whisked me off to a dungeon and offered me a reward. It's not amazing but for our levels, it's nothing to sneeze at either. When Reed respawns tomorrow, we'll do it again."

I must say I was a bit disappointed. I had expected a new quest from the Tenth...Something more.

"Did you manage to decipher the notes?" I asked, not counting on anything.

"There weren't any," the necromancer surprised me. "Nothing like the book you showed me."

"Say what? But what did Reed choose?"

"A music stand."

"A music stand?" I echoed. "There wasn't a music stand there last time."

"And there wasn't a book there this time," Sloe spread his arms. "Not a one. I think they generate a new set of items every time someone new goes to that location."

"Listen," the pirc perked up, "maybe we should place our notebook on your music stand and then the notes will appear?"

"Might work. We'll need to wait for Reed though."

"All right. In that case, I'm going to go and

grind my profession some more." Sloe waved goodbye and went whistling on his way.

"It's time I got down to business too—I need to farm me a new instrument..."

The luthier's shop was among our cartographic clients and thanks to Chip's incessant chatter, Master Pirus had already promised us discounts. However, whereas for the pirc, musical instruments were little more than a kindling substitute, for me, they were an unavoidable expenditure. The only thing was that the prices weren't just steep, they were prohibitive. Rare instruments started at 1.5 million gold, while the cheapest stringed instrument cost two thousand. We wouldn't have close to enough even if we pooled all our resources, so I had to reject the idea of buying one. There are always other ways.

"Ah! Lorelei!" Master Pirus greeted me enthusiastically. "What brings you here?"

As a result of doing the quest and my modest level of Charisma, my Attractiveness with Pirus was at 37. This was what I wanted to exploit.

"I dream of nothing more than acquiring an instrument of your craftsmanship," I announced, injecting a note of flattery into my voice. "But having never held the instrument in my hands, having never tried it out, how could I possibly make such a weighty decision? Who understands what an instrument means to a bard better than you? Like a sword to a knight, a wand to a mage, a dagger to a rogue—an instrument is the conduit of the bard's powers. When the music plays, it's not I but you who creates the magic with your unparalleled masterpieces! Without your genius, my creative path cannot set off on a good start."

Listening to my speech, Pirus proudly spread his shoulders and nodded approvingly. Encouraged by this mimed support, I went on:

"Even the most wonderful ballad shall lose its glamor if the instrument in the musician's hands is no good—if it does not suit her. Even the most heroic march will fail to inspire the army unless its sound is deep and powerful. It is the talent of masters like you that forms the bedrock of any bard's fame."

You have increased your Charisma. Total: 3.
You have received another training point. Unallocated training points: 3.

I suppressed the grin of satisfaction from my face. Any minor detail could deflate the heightened atmosphere I had created.

"I am happy to hear that my work is highly prized," the NPC replied, flattered. "The work of a luthier involves many nuances and each one has an effect on the final product. Shaping ordinary lumber with a palette of techniques allows me to create surprising results. Here, have a look!"

He gingerly removed a domra from a velvet

cushion and held it out to me.

"Listen to its sound, mark the intonation of this beauty."

I received the instrument as reverently as I could and ran my fingers across its strings. The sound was stunning—as for the instrument's properties...

Rosewood Domra of Joy. Two-handed item. Durability: Unbreakable. Description: Used by Bard for Performance. Item class: Rare. -30% to casting time for Bard Spells when equipped by a bard. +15% to encouragement spells.

"Now come here and see what I achieved by slightly altering the process of wood drying."

The second domra seemed like a twin sister of the one in my hands, but its properties turned out to be different:

Rosewood Domra of Melancholy. Two-handed item. Durability: Unbreakable. Description: Used by Bard for Performance. Item class: Rare. -30% to casting time for Bard Spells when equipped by a bard. +15% to weakening spells.

"Yes, this is quite stunning," I played into Pirus' excitement.

I had rather more ordinary materials in mind

for my own axe. It looks like different instruments have different effects on spell classes. I'll need to have a careful look around and choose something that fits. It'd be ideal of course to have an instrument for every occasion, but that would take an unimaginable heap of money.

"How much would I give for a chance to play each one of these wondrous instruments," I drawled and shook my head as if a light bulb had gone off in my head. "Master—I can help you with your business!"

"Yes?" Pirus asked surprised. "Have you thought of something else to add to your map?"

"No, Master. As long as these amazing instruments remain on their rack, their myriad virtues are lost on the world. However, if a capable bard plays them, everyone who hears him will learn of your shop. Moreover, the bard is sure to tell his friends and acquaintances—among whom there will be some who will want to purchase an instrument of their own."

The weakest part of the plan was that Pirus' store was the only place you could by an instrument on the Tree.

"It's not a bad idea," Pirus muttered doubtfully, "I could even trust you, Lorelei, with one of my creations. But what will I owe you?"

This was the strong part of my plan.

"The opportunity to use your masterpieces in

my work will be the greatest honor, Master Luthier," I assured him boisterously.

Who'd say no to such a deal?

"It's decided then! Come by any time my store is open and choose any instrument you like. Just make sure to stay close to the store when you have it."

"I wouldn't think of wandering away," I reassured Pirus.

You may play any instrument you like inside the store of Luthier Prius. Attention! If you leave the area beside the store with an instrument that doesn't belong to you, its entire price shall be withdrawn from your account.

"If I may, Master Luthier, I'd like to begin right away."

Receiving permission, I selected one of the rare lutes—one that would increase my Attractiveness if I played it well—sat down at the entrance to the shop and began to play. The secret trick in my plan was that I played not for prospective instrument buyers, but for Pirus himself. Four points of Fame would result in +1 Attractiveness with Pirus, and by praising his instrument, I raised that stat even higher. Since the shop was on the Market Branch, listeners should show up and my Fame will grow little by little as a result. And in several days, if I don't screw it up, I'll be able to raise my Attractiveness with the luthier, raise several other stats, find the instrument I want and come up with a way to acquire it while I'm at it. Under the incessant influence of my music, Pirus may issue me a fitting quest or tell me something interesting. Who better to know about bards than the maker of their weapons?

I didn't hurry to ask him questions, focusing instead on the advertisement of his goods I had promised him. If you give a client time to 'ripen,' the payoff will be much larger. Accordingly, I didn't strike up any new conversations that evening and, having returned the instrument, said goodbye to Pirus and exited the game.

My inbox had a new order from my longtime client, who this time around wished to trounce another woman who had interfered in her romantic relationships. Relishing the chance to work on something entirely different, I whipped up an excoriating and scorching tirade that was sure to reduce its target to tears. I wouldn't be going without a bite to eat thanks to this hyper-romantic lady. And even if the bite will be scant, it won't be unwelcome.

I sent off the completed order and collapsed in my bed. Tomorrow was band practice.

CHAPTER SIXTEEN

THE GUYS AND I spent band practice trying out some of the new songs and catching up on our exploits in Barliona.

"Beast, have you reached Level 5 yet?" Straus ribbed the bassist.

Edilberto grimaced and shook his head.

"So what are you doing?" My astonishment knew no bounds. "Even I'm at seven already—and leveling up among the biota isn't exactly easy."

"He's our very own serial killer," Straus guffawed. "Check it out—soon as he rolled his character, he attacked another player. So the guards threw him in the slammer."

"The hell did you decide to PK for?"

"I didn't decide a goddamn thing!" grunted Edilberto unhappily. "While I was getting my bearings, this dimwit shows up and starts cussing at me and calling me a newb. Well so I let him have it."

Everyone burst out laughing, while Beast asked with puzzlement:

"What was I supposed to do? He was talking

shit! Am I supposed to give him a hug?"

"What happened next?" Hal asked through his laughter.

"What do you think?" Straus gibed as Edilberto gave him an unhappy look. "He respawned and tried again. Did some basic quests, gained a couple levels and then ran smack-dab into the same troll. One thing led to another...The troll started trolling him again and good old Beast let him have it again."

Overhead, the garage's only light bulb swayed from our laughter.

"Don't stop!" Charsky begged, once he'd regained enough composure to say something.

"So he killed the troll—and his friends. Our Beast is a warrior now. He's got a zweihänder and all. I sent him some gear when he started. But it was supposed to help him! Instead, he decided that the trolls must die and became a murderer. He didn't bother going back to his town and began wandering the countryside. Tormented by his guilty conscience, Edilberto sentenced himself to penal service in the mines..."

"You can take your guilty conscience and shove it," Beast took offense at this retelling of his story. "Outlaws can't earn XP and there's nothing else to do. So I went to work in the mines."

"The hell for?" I managed with difficulty, restraining another fit of laughter.

"I want to become a blacksmith. I always

dreamed about forging iron back when I was a kid."

"Your dreams are becoming reality then!" Charsky congratulated him. "You're already hammering iron, albeit in a different form!"

"The hell with you guys," the odd bassist said sadly, while Straus went on:

"That's not all. Briefly put, Beast waved his pickaxe around, earned some ore, leveled up his strength and when his outlaw status expired, returned to the town. At the blacksmith's some dude told him he sucked at forging or something, so Bang! Bang! Beast's iron hammer came down upon his head."

"He killed him?" Hal managed through the tears in his eyes.

"He would have, except the turkey was over level fifty," Beast muttered unhappily.

"Anyway, the turkey sent Beast to respawn," Straus continued his tale of his friend's incarcerations. "And then sent him back after he'd returned. And as if this wasn't enough, a red orc NPC walked up to him and started making fun of him. Obviously Edilberto won't stand for something like that and tried to take out the NPC. That didn't work, but the NPC declared that Beast has a mighty, proud and savage spirit, and told him that he'd be happy to take him on as a student. As a result, Beast landed himself into the rare specialization of berserker."

"Oh! A noble line of work!"

"You the man, Beast!"

"Way to kill 'em, Beast!"

The others couldn't match such adventures. Hal had chosen the way of the frock and became a priest of Vlast, tending and ministering to the various rites of this deity. And since being drunk wasn't a feature of Barliona, sober Hal had already reached Level 27. Charsky had rolled a bard like me and was already traveling around with some necromancers, on his way to becoming a Singer of Death. This was the draft title of the song he played for us. And we spent the next hour or two working on its various parts, brainstorming lyrics, editing them, jamming, arguing and jamming some more.

* * *

Hanging out with my buddies, I barely noticed the time fly by and I ended up reentering the game fairly late. Chip and Reed were already waiting for me, lazing around the drinking fountain. As I understood, these fountains were like free cafeterias for the biota. They were sprinkled generously around the Tree. Reed was playing a quiet melody, while the pirc lay beside him, ignoring the passersby that periodically tripped over his feet.

"Ah here comes our party's decoration. Lori, we did some talking here and decided to try and assemble a unified party. Since we're at the same stage of the quest, maybe one sacrifice will suffice to open the portal," Chip announced as soon as he laid eyes on me.

"Hello," Reed greeted me, staring at the toes of his shoes. "Do you guys mind if I join you?"

"I'm all for it!" I assured my colleague. "Will you let me borrow your music stand for a moment? I want to see whether I'll be able to read my book on it."

"Here you go," Reed replied, pulling a hefty music stand from his modest bag. It looked a bit like a magic trick—only instead of a rabbit the magician had pulled a giraffe out of his bag.

I quickly placed Cypro's notes on the music stand and stared greedily at its pages. No changes.

"Dang nab it," sighed Chip. "I was hoping we'd guessed right that time."

"Unfortunately not," I sighed in turn, returning the difficult little journal to my inventory. "All right, let's form a party and finish up with the quest chain. Ready?"

"I'm always ready!" Chip saluted and yawned deeply. "It's sleepy-time."

"I'm ready too," Reed added, replacing his music stand trophy in his bag.

"I have brought the toll!"

Our teleportation was instantaneous. A second ago we were standing beneath Barliona's bright sun and already the stilted cold was creeping through our clothes, under our skin, to our very hearts.

"Christ, it is freezing in here," Chip shuddered. "Did they send us to the local Antarctica or something?"

"Do you wish to continue your journey?" The voice in the mirror sent chills down my spine.

"Y-yes." My teeth were chattering as if I'd dived into an ice hole. "But I have a question first. Do you know how to read this book?"

The creature in the mirror made a strange, terrifying sound and I couldn't help but start when I realized that this sound was supposed to be laughter.

"These writings are open only to the dead. And since we're speaking about the dead, which life shall you gift me? Whom shall you sacrifice to continue your journey?"

"I'm always ready to submit my belly to the sacrificial altar for the good of the proletariat!" Chip announced dramatically and sneezed.

I looked at the pirc and then at Reed who had wrapped himself in his cape—then I looked back at the mirror. Why had the Tenth decided to deal with such a revolting creature? What was the lesson here? What does the vocation of a bard have in common with my willingness to sacrifice my companions and tread over their corpses on my 'journey?' I guess I'll never know...

"I have decided that I do not wish to continue this journey," I sighed and the words, frozen, fell at my feet. "Another dead end is cheaper than the price you ask. Chip, how about we smash this evil glass?"

"With pleasure!" the pirc smirked maliciously and without waiting stuck his halberd into the center of the mirror. The sound of shattered glass failed to smother the scream of wrath emanating from the empty frame.

Selection made.

You have refused to sacrifice your companions for the sake of personal gain thereby proving that friendship and faithfulness is no empty noise for you. The way lies open.

Quest updated: *Road to Nowhere* (Two trials completed).

A shimmering portal opened in the center of the room and I could feel the heat radiating from it.

"Curious," Reed muttered and stepped into the portal without further ado.

"Haven't you heard the proverb about the cat and its curiosity?" The pirc rejoined. "I'd rather not reaffirm it with my personal example."

Nonetheless, he stepped in right after Reed without further vacillation.

Contrary to my reservations, the other side of the portal did not contain the room of rewards Sloe had described. There wasn't a room there at all in fact. We stood in the middle of a mountain canyon. The vertical slopes on either side and the impassable mass of rubble behind us indicated that there was only one direction to go.

"Where are we?" Reed asked what everyone was wondering.

"Somewhere in Barliona," I announced after checking my map. This time around, our location lay somewhere north of the Hidden Forest, amid unexplored territory.

"Somewhere close to the rear end of this world," the pirc explained further. "You could say we're in the ante-anus."

At first we were forced to walk in a file one after the other—the width of the fissure didn't allow anything more. After that, the walls began to spread bit by bit and we finally emerged into a wide clearing that reminded me somewhat of an ancient coliseum. The skeletons of various creatures clad in rusted armor and tattered, faded clothing only intensified this resemblance.

"Looks like a real melee took place here," Chip whistled, carefully stepping over a crested helm of bronze with an orc's skull still in it.

"We have company," Reed distracted me from my examination of these ancient artifacts.

Looking in the indicated direction, I saw a ghostly figure standing over one of the skeletons. The mighty warrior was about the size of the pirc. He was leaning against a battle axe and looking in the distance, paying us absolutely no attention.

Ghost of a Fallen Warrior. Level 40.

The inscription was red.

"Is it time to brawl?" Chip asked with some doubt in his voice and shifted the halberd in his paws.

"Doubt it. There should be another way."

"Scaling the canyon is a waste of time," the pirc announced with finality. "We'd need gear to do that."

"This is strange…" I looked around in hopes of finding a clue. "A quest issued by a bard for bards or parties that have a bard. And then suddenly a trial by combat. Is the moral supposed to be that 'in the end, the sword decides?'"

"A dead man," Reed reminded. "We are looking at a dead man. Maybe he is the one who can read the book?"

"Reed, you're a genius! I'll try it out right away."

"Eh, not so fast," Chip restrained me. "Let me go first: If he strikes me down, it won't be a great loss."

"It's only a game, Pavel. If he clocks me, we'll at least gauge his damage and aggro-radius."

"All right," the pirc agreed with a sour look.

I pulled out the mysterious journal from my bag, opened it to the first page and holding it a bit like a shield walked toward the ghost.

"Excuse me," I called when there were ten meters between us. "Are you familiar with the name

Cypro? Do you know what this says here?"

The ghost looked in my direction, studied me through his helm's eye slits and then slowly and even a bit leisurely brought down his axe...

Attention! Respawn Penalty: -30% XP.

Quest updated: *Road to Nowhere* **(Third trial failed). Two attempts remaining. To try the third trial one more time, speak the words: 'I want to try again.'**

You have died. Enter Barliona again in 12 hours.

"Good talk, good talk," I muttered, climbing out of my cocoon.

The guys would call me in ten minutes.

"Briefly put, we tried our best," Pavel reported in his strange voice. "You should've seen it! Our little Reed grabbed his music stand and tried to bash the ghost with it."

"How'd it go?"

"Predictably," Pavel sighed, "and fatally."

"The music stand is made of iron," Reed explained shyly, "and legend has it that ghosts are afraid of iron."

"This one turned out pretty unafraid." I could tell that Pavel was yawning. "Or perhaps he hasn't read the legends."

"How did you die?"

"I tried to run up to the stiff that the ghost gladiator was standing over and chop the bones in half."

"Did you make it?"

"Uh-huh. While our fearless leek brandished his music stand, I hammered the dusty bones. I'm not sure whether the ghost was insulted by such sacrilege or whether the bones weren't even his, but he wiped me out with a single blow. Didn't even have the courtesy to break a sweat..."

"Damn it...Any other options?"

"Tomorrow is another day," Pavel yawned again. "We can chew it over then. I'm going to take counsel from my pillow."

"We need to tell Sloe that we have to reschedule our raid," Reed reminded. "We won't have time to respawn."

"Send him a message," I asked. "I'll go for a walk and clear my mind. Maybe, I'll hang out with the guys and they'll slip me some idea."

"Cool. Until tomorrow, everyone."

When I returned to the game, I made a beeline for the library. First of all, I had just remembered that I owed Tell the buff I'd promised. Secondly, I had promised Lapushock and some rogue named Blades_of_Grass that I'd play something for them in the same library. It's not that I really wanted to go there, but the promise I made weighed on me and it was easier to do it and strike it off my list than deal with the guilt. Sending Chip, Reed and Sloe letters, I headed to the library. There, I encountered Tell, Lapushock and a few dozen others. Some were practicing their crafts, but many were languishing aimlessly as yesterday.

"Hey," I greeted Tell. "I had to go yesterday and forgot to give you the buff I promised. I've returned to pay my debt."

"Ah. That's cool of you," he said. "Does the buff last long?"

"Let me see here..." I froze for a bit, pulling up the buff description and making some educated guesstimates. Charisma 3, Fame 3, plus one..."Seven hours."

"Not bad," Tell approved. "Buff away."

"A sec."

I invited him to my party and then did the same for Lapushock and Blades_of_Grass.

"You requested a song yesterday, correct?"

"I thought you forgot," Lapushock replied with surprise.

"Debts must be paid."

When the party was complete, I thought for a little about what I should sing. For some reason, I recalled the ballad of a bard who lived in the twentieth century. Maybe it was all the books around us, or maybe it was the game itself.

Amid the melted candles and vespers,
The wartime prizes and the peacetime fires,
Bookish youth lived without knowledge of
battles,
Languishing in their juvenile desires...

The players around us stopped staring off into nothing and began to listen. For most of them, the song was unfamiliar: Despite the undoubted talent of the bard, his voice wasn't well-suited to singing and his songs were about serious matters that kept them out of the mass media which the subsequent generations had grown up on. It was a ballad of bookish children who only knew the history someone else had made. Over a century had elapsed since it had been written, and yet even now every listener recognized herself in its verses. And even though our generation had spent its childhood in virtual reality, each verse penetrated right into our souls.

And even though my voice was very different from the original's and the lute didn't quite fit the song, my cover struck home for the players. Everyone came away satisfied. And no one wanted to argue. They listened to the ballad in silence and even the NPC librarian peeked out of his hermitage. The last words were sung but no one wanted to break the silence and one girl was even wiping away a tear.

A new system notification popped up but I swiped it away. I didn't feel like reading anything about more skills just right now.

"Powerful stuff," one of the players said at last. "Is it yours?"

"Nah. It's a translation of a Vysotsky song."

"I'm gonna go download it," muttered a player and his avatar dissolved into thin air. Another six or so followed on his heels. The radio DJs don't play the right stuff—the people want something real and profound...

"Sing us something else, will you?" the impressionable girl asked.

"After that ballad, it's better to stay in silence," I warned and someone nodded their head in agreement. There's not much that can rival the power of Vysotsky's songs—perhaps only Dylan and Gardel. "If you want to listen some more, I'm going to play every day on the Market Branch, around 3 p.m. server time. Come on by."

No one else bothered me, so I disbanded the party, left the library and spent some time wandering around the Tree city, trying to understand what it was that the long-departed bard had added to his song that to this day managed to move minds and hearts.

The system notification twinkling at the edge of my vision finally drew my attention.

You have increased your Fame stat. Total: 4.

Attention! You have unlocked a new ability:

'Inspiration.'

Your performance inspires your audience, increasing the chance of crafting a more valuable item by (0.2 × Fame)%, not to exceed 30%. You may simultaneously target (Charisma) targets with Inspiration. The effect's duration is equal to the duration of the performance. Cost of performance: None. Range: Variable. The target must be able to hear the performance.

Heck of an inspiration this...I'm not sure about the whole skill growth thing, but at the moment what I wanted was to create something as real as Vystosky's songs. Without a further thought, I turned onto the Market Branch, reached the store of Master Pirus, greeted him curtly, grabbed an instrument from the rack without looking, sat right down on the floor and went on working on the melody that had practically formed itself in my mind. Pirus didn't bother me, listening pensively as the new music was born from my fingers.

The guys came by an hour and a half later. We decided to level up first and only then attempt the Tenth's trial.

"We'll follow the earlier plan," Sloe assumed his accepted leadership role. Chip unfurled a map that glowed with white spots and began to confer with the necromancer about where the enemy might be. "Last time, we encountered the recon party here—in the northwest. They told us that the south was safe which means that they had already combed that quadrant."

The pirc nodded and made a mark on his map.

"We can assume that they are moving in the standard way, in an expanding spiral. In that case they've managed to pass here and here and should move eastward from where we met them. We'll head further west and theoretically slip through to the Arras."

"And we'll be able to chart a new area while we're at it," Chip added, pleased. He gingerly rolled his map up again.

"Uh-huh, and then we can sell it for some extra cash out in the larger world," I agreed, having already gotten used to the relatively easy income in Barliona.

"We have to first reach that larger world," the necromancer sighed.

"We'll reach it," the pirc waved his paw. "By the way, we've wrangled up some supplies for the trip here..." he announced and produced the rings of Constitution we had acquired earlier.

"Oh! Now that's useful!" Sloe said happily, one by one slipping the rings on his fingers. "Hmm..." He coughed, staring nowhere in particular. "So that's how it is...What a crappy penalty. I figured that once I gear up, I'll be a bit fatter...Eh, I guess we'll have to grind Constitution. What do I owe you for the rings?"

"You don't owe anything," Chip was even taken aback by the offer. "Accept them as a gift from a brother in arms."

A simple smile appeared on Reed's expressive and honest face and he briefly thanked the pirc, while Sloe frowned:

"Well, I didn't come here empty-handed either."

Saying this, he produced three capes from his inventory in the manner of a magician. They looked like local ware: improbable constructions of large oblong leaves, attached to one another in some mysterious manner.

"Yeah—they have their own sewing technique here," the necromancer confirmed, intercepting my look. "The only thing is that I didn't consider the penalties and crafted them to boost Const as much as possible."

"No big deal," I shrugged, putting on the cape. "Once we level up, the Constitution we get from the gear will go up too."

"I look like a cotton bud," Chip complained. The new cape really did bear a resemblance here: something white and puffy, sticking out from between the leaves.

"It's okay. At least you're a fat cotton bud," Sloe cheered him up.

"That's right...Fluffy," I added wryly, recalling all the vivid monikers that the chattering pirc had bestowed upon me.

"Who asked you, Arugula?" the pirc gibed without any ill feeling and, concluding our traditional repartee, we headed out onto our journey.

This time around, the trip was easier: The tactics were all worked out more or less, the Intellect was a smidge higher (and in Reed's case more than a smidge), and thanks to his carpentry, the pirc's Strength and Constitution were higher as well. On top of this, there were less aggressive monsters around the Tree: The other players were slowly becoming accustomed to leveling up in adverse conditions and the pirc tanks trickling in to the Tree were making this task easier.

Heading more west than last time, we traveled the same distance as yesterday without much problem. We were more cautious this time too. We tried to make less noise and spoke in a whisper. Either we were sufficiently careful or the search party had headed further east as we had assumed, but we didn't end up meeting a single player along our way. Instead, we discovered something interesting.

"What is this? The barrens?" Chip asked quietly, standing at the edge of a blighted portion of the forest. Right at his boots the green grass became dark and bristled with thorns amid which clumps of dark fog curled. The trees changed here too, causing the blighted area to look dour and foreboding. Here and there, hedges of deformed thorn bushes formed a kind of maze.

"Looks like a quest," Sloe voiced the logical conclusion. "Too bad we don't have it in our logs."

"Actually..." I said, opened my quest journal and shared Eben's quest with the rest of the party.

"Will you look at that!" the necromancer muttered, having read the quest description. "Where'd you manage to come up with a rare scenario with a scaling item as a reward?"

"And while you're at it, tell us what a scaling item is," the pirc added. "Do they scale to my body type or something? I'm not into fashion that much. I'll be happy if it's ugly too."

"Being a bard, I received additional information, started asking the NPCs about it and ended up receiving this quest. A scaling item, as I understood from the fora, is when an item's stats increase with each level the character gains and you don't have to change items as you level up—the item grows with you..."

"Cool," nodded Chip.

"It isn't simply cool. It's straight up awesome. Items like that cost tens if not hundreds of thousands of gold, and that's if you have good reputation with the Thricinians."

"Thricinians? What are they, like the local equivalent of leprechauns?" the pirc asked.

"It's a faction that sells these kinds of items. All right, what are we going to do?"

Reed, who had been silent this entire time, shrugged and suggested: "Go on?"

"Eh, no. Not right away," Chip stopped him.

Looking around, he picked up a large stone and hurled it into the midst of the brambles. Nothing visible happened and in reply to our inquiring looks, the pirc explained:

"What if there's some kind of minefield around here?"

He snapped off a branch from a nearby tree and prodded the blighted ground with it. The leaves on the branch immediately curled up and died.

"I don't know what's up, but I'm not really raring to get in there..." Sloe muttered pensively.

"Oh come on!" I protested. "This is a game. Onwards to adventure!"

Before anyone could stop me with some intelligent or reasoned argument, I stepped forward. And why not? You only live as many times as you respawn in this place. Dying ain't that scary.

You have entered the blighted part of the forest. -50% to all stats. +50% to strength of all blighted creatures. -1% to max HP for every minute you spend on blighted ground.

"And where are you going against good advice?" Chip, who had stepped after me, grumbled.

"I told you—onwards to adventure! Our motto is stupidity and courage!" I replied glibly and for the sake of curiosity returned to the green grass. The debuff instantly vanished and my max HP returned to its previous value, though my current HP remained diminished.

"What's over there?" the necromancer interrupted Chip who had begun to read the debuff description.

"A debuff," I replied laconically. "It cuts stats by half and buffs blighted beasts."

"Sucks," Sloe summarized, also crossing the border. "Now any mob will take us out with one hit, even with our new gear."

"You all maybe. Me—good luck," our tank objected bravely. "With the new gear, I'm still fatter than yesterday, so I'll be all right. And our dear little bit of chlorophyll slipped me some healing potions. I won't die."

"By the way, that's right!" I remembered and pulled out the potions I had bought. "I forgot to hand out the medkits."

"I feel myself utterly indebted to you," Reed muttered with embarrassment.

"Don't stress it. When you become the greatest musician of Barliona, you'll remember us with a kind word," I assured him. "Plus we have this bloody little business going here in which we regularly kill each other, so there aren't any particular problems with money."

"Huh?" Reed asked, baffled.

"I'll explain later," Sloe promised. "Right. We don't have a lot of time on research. First of all, the debuff is having its effect. Second of all we need to reach the Arras to get the money and equipment from my guildmates. We can deal with the quest afterwards. I propose that we look around quickly to see what's what here and then head onward toward the Arras."

"I second the speaker before me," Chip agreed with this option.

There weren't any objections and we began to march among the grass submerged in the grim fog.

Razor-sharp thorns rip your footwear. -2 durability to shoes. Current durability: 78 / 80.

"Damn," Sloe voiced what everyone was thinking. "To complete the quest, someone will have to learn how to repair gear. Otherwise we'll be left first without footwear and later without feet."

"I'll take care of that easy," Chip perked up. "Anyone that needs maintenance can ask me—I'll take care of it without a problem. It'll be better than new."

"Hold your horses," the necromancer checked his outpouring of enthusiasm. "As I recall, you can only learn to repair one type of armor at a time. It makes most sense for you to deal with plate armor, while I deal with textiles."

"And I'll have to check what bards wear," I added.

"Maybe I should do something too?" Reed

asked with such a note of sadness in his voice that I even felt a little embarrassed. It was true—we hardly left him a chance to do anything and feel like he was useful to the party.

"We'll head back to the city and think about it together," Sloe promised.

"Thanks," Reed replied with relief.

"I have a sudden hankering for rabbit meat," Chip licked his lips and pointed at a pair of ears sticking out of the grass ahead. The rest of the creature didn't look particularly appetizing: The fur had grown dark, the body bristled with thorns, the eyes were glowing red and the front teeth looked quite a bit like fangs.

"I don't know what it is, but I don't like the look of that bunny," the necromancer remarked, forming a ball of dark energy in his hands.

I took my lute too, ready to blast the bunny with a magic missile. If you factor in our recent debuff and the monster's buff, Sloe's spell might not be enough. But in the next moment, the rabbit—who had been about twenty meters away from us—performed an unbelievable leap and in a blur traversed the distance to the 'charging' necromancer. I don't know whether he had managed to cast his spell or not, but if it weren't for Chip's halberd that literally cleaved the rabbit in half in midflight, Sloe may have been done for.

"A crit, a very palpable crit!" the pirc who was

coming to terms with the gaming slang, roared triumphantly.

"If I weren't a plant, I'd have a seat." The necromancer camouflaged instantly. "If they have these assault bunnies here, then what about the wolves or bears? I suspect that we need to get out of this deadly place and move on around it. We'll reach the Arras, get some guild help and then return well-armed to look for the source of the blight."

Everyone nodded with agreement. This quest clearly demanded some preparations. As it turned out, though, we didn't have enough time to leave.

"I see dead people..." someone said in a sinister voice and in the next instant a biota with the memorable name Otolaryngologist appeared behind Reed's back. A flash of the dagger and the bard turned into a heap of falling coins.

"What the hell?" barked the pirc, swinging his halberd, but the assassin wasn't where he had been. With incredible agility, he rolled up next to me. I felt a fairly painful prick in my throat and...

Attention! Respawn Penalty: -30% XP.

Hello launch screen and hello 12 hour countdown timer...I mean, this is unbelievable!

Unprintable words danced on the tip of my tongue. He came, he saw, he wiped us. Judging by the damage I had taken, the rest of my party was gone too by now. I climbed out of my capsule, picked up my comm and called Chip, Sloe and Reed in turn, bringing everyone in on conference.

"Goddamn son of a two-bit, one-legged, six-toed..." Sloe was mid-oath when he picked up. "Oh, sorry, Lori."

"Don't worry about it—I feel roughly the same."

"We need to off that bastard," Chip announced flatly. His voice sounded distorted, but no one was paying attention to that anymore. "Divide him by zero."

"What was that?" haplessly asked Reed, connecting last.

"A future dead man, that's who," Chip prophesied gloomily, still fuming. "I'll bite his ear off and cut his throat for good measure, the tumbleweed."

"That's a good pirc," Sloe quipped. "You should first worry about leveling up and then think about what you'll do to him. As it happens, you'll have a week to do just that. While the countdown timer is doing its thing, I'll have to go on my trip."

"Eh, damn it, what a trip to the Arras...Well, maybe Chip, Reed and I will make it while you're gone. Can you send us some contact info for your guild? Maybe we'll make it across the border."

"Why that would be perfect," Sloe agreed. "If you do that, we won't have to worry about any local PKers. The guild will locate the dungeon a lot faster too."

"In that case, it's agreed," I concluded. "Reed, what are your plans in the game?"

"Let's try to complete the Tenth's quest chain. I don't have other plans beyond that. I'll read around the forums and try to choose some useful professions to master. I need to learn how to make money in this game, after all."

"Choose sewing—you won't regret it" Sloe recommended. "The gear here looks pretty unique. You'll be able to sell it in the larger world sheerly due to how it looks. And you should master embroidery while you're at it. It's pretty handy."

"Perfect. Thank you."

"Okay. Then until tomorrow, everyone. And until we meet again, Sloe," I said. "If anything, I'll be online."

CHAPTER SEVENTEEN

ESPITE MY IN-GAME DEMISE, my mood was excellent. I had a myriad impressions from the game and each day the mystery of the blighted forest seemed more interesting to me. Solving the Tenth's riddle loomed on the horizon along with the arrival of the Kartossian embassy (by the way, I need to expend more effort on social quests for the festival's preparation). Meanwhile, the lyrics to the new song had formed themselves in my head. If I grind my reputation some more, I'll be able to record some fitting footage and edit it into a free and very pretty video. All of Barliona was curious about the new biota location, so my video should garner plenty of views. The thought of it alone drove me to jig with impatience and yet the countdown timer implacably told me that there were still eleven hours and change to go. As a result, I channeled all of my impatience into my guitar synth. This piece of cutting-edge tech allowed me to imitate most stringed instruments and I spent a good deal of time fiddling with the settings to find the right sound. If only I could play heavy metal on that lute of mine in Barliona. By the way, I'll need to ask Pirus if there's some kind of analog for my trusty synth. It's a magical world, after all.

As always, after the respawn time elapsed, I came back on the Branch of Oblivion. This time, it wasn't empty. A mournful procession was carrying four leaf-litters bearing deceased biota. I was struck by the withered pallor of their bodies, reminded instantly of the blight in the forest. It looked like the passive blight was gradually entering an active phase.

A beautiful cello part began to sound all of a sudden and I wasn't surprised when I noticed Reed. Like me, he had respawned in one of the buds and was now watching the passing procession with sincere compassion on his face. The bow in his hands slid smoothly across the strings, making the cello weep and grieve for the dead. Following his example, I took my lute in hand and cautiously wove its voice into the resounding melody. The NPCs glanced over at us and I thought I discerned gratitude in their looks.

Just like in my vision, the corpses were placed atop blooming flowers whose petals slowly closed over the dead, returning their corpses to the Tree. Their lives and memories would become the fragments of someone's dreams, the visions, and their bodies a part of the world we lived in. A beautiful, if odd, ceremony. As far as I know, in the rest of Barliona, the bodies of NPCs who aren't part of some quest simply disappear. I guess the location designers wanted to inject a little more symbolism in this natural cycle...

The conclusion of the ceremony was marked by the appearance of a new system notification:

Your music helped relieve the pain in the hearts of your audience and transformed their oppressive sorrow into a light sadness.
+100 Reputation with the Biota.
Current status: Friendly.

Contrary to my expectations, the sudden increase in reputation didn't bring me much joy. My condition was sad and serene and numbers were the least interesting thing to me at the moment.

"Shall we go?" I quietly offered to the silent Reed.

"Yes, it's time," he agreed and we headed out to meet Chip.

The pirc was sitting on a river's bank, trying to fish with a homemade pole. However, either the fish didn't frequent these waters or the bait didn't please them, or even—and more likely, the pirc's fishing skill was too low—but whatever the reason, the pirc couldn't boast of a single catch.

"We need to die less," the pirc announced, changing the tackle. "I almost died from boredom waiting out that damn timer. If you were to tell me a month ago that I would miss this high-tech casket—

I'd never believe you."

"Are you telling me that the idea of spending your vacation in VR doesn't seem that barbaric to you anymore?" I nudged him.

"It's pure savagery!" Chip doubled down on his earlier verdict. "If I weren't stuck between four walls, you couldn't force me in here for the life of you."

"All right, all right. Let's party up and try that canyon again. By the way, does anyone have any new ideas?"

"How about we trigger a rockslide?" Chip offered. "Maybe it would open a cave or a passage overhead."

"We'd be more likely to perish in it," I demurred. "Reed?"

"Remember the funeral," he replied. "Music can confer peace. Maybe that's what that ghost needs?"

Chip and I exchanged glances and I spoke the pass phrase:

"I want to try again!"

A flash—and we were in the canyon again—the silhouette of the ghost warrior standing sentry in the distance.

"Okay my vegetable duet, let's hear your best requiem," said Chip and sat down beside a large boulder.

"Shall I lead?" Reed asked shyly and once I'd assented, produced his cello out of thin air like a magician. Looking around, he found a suitable boulder, sat down on it and began to play.

Good Noodle up in the Heavens, how well did Reed play! The bow in his hand seemed alive gushing with its harmony of sounds. The lute's voice blended with that of the cello, birthing a special and unseen magic. The music filled the canyon with itself, flooding it, submerging the listeners. Even Chip lowered his halberd and listened with a strange expression on his face—as if he was regretting something or remembering someone.

The ghost also began to listen, turning his head in his hefty helm. After a bit, he sat down on the stone beside him but continued to watch us, and later still, his battle axe dropped to the earth and the warrior froze completely, his chin rested on his fist. The inscription over his head faded, blinked and then filled with a neutral yellow color.

"It looks like it worked," Chip's voice was deafening amid the silence that followed the music. "Let me check."

He heaved his halberd over his shoulder and began to walk. Trying to look as non-threatening as possible (although, if you ask me, the very look of this beast, striding toward you with a giant piece of steel on his shoulder would be cause enough for anxious thoughts), the pirc approached the quiescent ghost. The warrior glanced up at the pirc and then went back to his contemplation.

Reed and I exchanged glances and carefully

followed in Chip's wake. The canyon narrowed yet again and ended at another portal.

Quest updated: *Road to Nowhere* (Three trials completed).

"Same thing all over again," the pirc sighed. "Isn't there some directory service here or something? An operator? A guide? The service in this place is just atrocious..."

"You're blocking the way," I complained, trying to squeeze past the giant.

"Don't crawl across pappy to throw yourself into the oven," Chip slid me back behind his back and dived into the magical ring.

As soon as I realized where we were, I gripped the pirc's paw with a death grip. The stone floor beneath our feet collapsed to...nowhere. The inky darkness winked with a myriad of stars. And all that supported us over this abyss was a slab about two meters in diameter.

"This isn't real, this isn't real," I repeated until my head stopped spinning from a mere glance at the abyss.

"This is like Kon-Tiki but in space or something," the pirc sighed ecstatically. Embracing my shoulder, he added: "Easy there, Lori. I have you."

"What majesty!" Reed wasn't on the same page as me either. "Look! They move! The constellations!

It's as if they're alive!"

Without moving a millimeter from Chip, who had become my symbolical anchor, I glanced in the direction Reed had indicated. I glanced and remained staring with bulging eyes and a daft smile on my face. The stars lived their own fairytale lives here, possible only in childhood fantasies. A stellar fish fanned its tail and dived into the Milky Way; nearby, a dragon flew alongside a Pegasus. A colossal warrior raised his sword in a salute and turned back to his combat with a titanic hydra.

"Like in that ancient cartoon about Sinbad the Sailor," Chip turned his head back and forth, examining the animated constellations.

Quest completed: *Road to Nowhere.*
Receive your reward from Cypro.

"Cypro?" Reed said, shocked. "Didn't you say that he disappeared?"

"That is not quite accurate," replied a stranger's voice.

Before us stood a biota stitched from starlight. I recognized the Tenth from my visions. The First Bard of my race was looking at us with happy curiosity.

Chip instantly bristled the fur on his nape and just in case shielded me behind himself, the overcautious furball. After that, glancing warily at the new ghost, he reached for his map. As I suspected, this location wasn't on the map either.

"Check that out—the road really did bring us to nowhere," the pirc remarked. "Doesn't look too shabby..."

And yet he didn't drop his guard for a second, drilling Cypro's ghost with a menacing stare.

"Not quite accurate?" Reed echoed the stranger.

"Not quite Cypro," the Tenth clarified. "I am a recollection. Something akin to an agglomerate of the individual I was. So basically I am at once Cypro and not Cypro."

"Don't you get bored of living for eons?" My acrophobia temporarily abated from the uncommon sight. Woven of light, the figure spread its arms as if trying to embrace this strange world.

"Time passes differently here," he said. "Only a few hours have elapsed for me—and you are the fourth set of visitors I've received since my creation."

"And who was here before us?" I couldn't help but indulge my curiosity.

"Too much knowledge," Cypro said, winking, "makes a good bard. Still, I will keep their names secret. I'll say only that they reached this place following a different path from you."

"Are there other paths?" Reed asked with surprise.

"Multitudes. Long and short, complicated and simple. Each choice you make generates a different path and a different reward. First I shall reward your companion."

His bodiless arm touched Chip's brow and the pirc started.

"Without true companions, many roads are closed to the bards. Remember their worth and help them on their way."

The pirc's face took on a surprised expression.

"Well...Thank you...I guess..." he muttered. "I'm always ready to work and defend the fatherland."

"Now you," the recollection turned to Reed. "You do not seek adventure. Music is your entire world, full of mysterious riddles and stunning discoveries. This shall help you find new sounds."

"Thank you," Reed broke into a smile and gingerly accepted an ordinary-looking bow.

"And you—you are possessed by the spirit of adventure." These words were for me and I finally squeezed between Chip and Reed. "I am confident that with time you will find a way to read my notes and set forth on wondrous travels."

"Maybe you could give me a hint about how I can do this?" I asked without much hopes of success.

"That would be too easy," Cypro shook his head. "I'll say only that the notes are a magic copy. Every time I add a new note, it appears in your journal too. I imagine that you and I shall meet again in the real world. The spirit of wandering lives within you—you seek stories. This shall help you on your journey."

The stellar ghost offered me a strange object: a small piece of stained glass depicting the flower of life in a carved wooden frame.

Item acquired: Mirror of Wisdom.

Requirement: Bardic Lore 100 required to access the properties of this item.

Requirement: Bardic Lore 100+ required to use this item.

"What is this?" I asked, turning the strange object in my hands.

"You shall understand in due time," the recollection promised. "And now it's time you go. Do not try to return—this road is forever closed to you."

"But I have a million questions..." I blurted out and discovered that instead of the star-studded abyss, I was surrounded by the already-familiar Tree.

Chip was the first to come to his senses. Smoothing his fur, he looked around, stuck his nose into the map for some reason, lowered his ears with disappointment and said:

"Can you believe it? What a generous ghost we have on our communal farm. He gave me a lordly present: I get +10% to my stats from your labors now."

"Solid," Reed and I approved and then stared at my prize.

"I'll speak for everyone: What does this little flower do?" Chip asked rhetorically.

"I wish I knew," I sighed, placing the present in my inventory. "I'll only find out when my Bardic Lore reaches one hundred. Reed, what did you get?"

"This bow allows me to alter the register and tonality..." He broke off, seeing Chip's stumped expression. "I can change the sound of the cello. In theory, I should be able to mimic a violin or even a double bass. But we'll see in practice."

"Cool," I said with admiration. "Once you master it, let me know."

"Uh-huh," Reed nodded happily.

"Why you're already an ace when you face the bass," Pavel examined the bow skeptically. "You're so good without any bells or whistles that your music gets me right through to my toes. Although, nothing is wasted in a master's arsenal."

"Thanks," Reed blushed. "What will you do now?"

"I don't know about you, but I need to process what just happened," I announced. "I'm going to exit to meatspace and practice a bit."

"And I'm going to work on the map." Chip was clearly still fixated on marking all the locations we had visited during this adventure on his map. "If you like, you can come with. You can try out your new wonder bow on the natives while you're at it."

"No, thank you. I'm going to play for a bit..."

I didn't hear the rest of their exchange—waving my hand in farewell, I exited to reality. I wanted to create something...

My guitar synth and I sat together late into the night. What I had seen in the game transformed note by note into a melody—drop by drop draining my roiling emotions. It was only when the notes began to breakdance before my eyes that I managed to place my instrument aside. And several minutes later my head touched the pillow, plunging me into a deep, dreamless sleep.

CHAPTER EIGHTEEN

I SLEPT IN UNTIL LUNCHTIME and then spent a while on chores, hesitant to return to Barliona. After my recent experience, it seemed strange to have to farm XP, gold, stats all over again—meaningless quests and dull everyday errands. I wanted fairy tales. Shocking, impossible ones. Unfortunately, even in VR, miracles don't happen that often.

Therefore, I prescribed myself a treatment of mundane chores, canceled my daily deliveries and went to the supermarket on my own, stopped by the garage and found a very hungover Beast, had some coffee and sandwiches with him, exchanged news and gossip and only after all that felt ready to return to my in-game life.

Master Pirus' store was as empty and quiet as ever. The master himself was working on the body of a future violin and responded to my entrance with a curt, welcoming nod. I didn't want to distract him, so I chose one of the guitars, sat down in my favorite place at the entrance, chose Pirus as my target and activated my 'Inspiration' ability. The master merely hummed approvingly and went on with his work.

Bit by bit, people began to gather around me. A seamstress peeked out of the neighboring workshop, tarried a little, then pulled her chair out to the street and resumed her work to my accompaniment. I had enough Charisma for two more targets and the mana cost wasn't an issue, so I expanded my inspiration buff to her too. After her a player priest appeared. Judging by the strange textile, which resembled flower petals, in his hands, he was trying to master the tailor's craft. He too settled nearby, becoming the last target of my spell.

"Whoa! Cool beans!" the priest exclaimed when he saw the buff. "Does it last long?"

"Long as I'm playing. Savor the moment!"

"Got it!"

We spent three hours like this, no less. Every once in a while, more NPCs and player craftsmen came by, but my Charisma wasn't enough to buff more targets so the newcomers didn't get anything but the music. Then again, this was good enough too—the public had more fun working, my Fame grew to 8 and my Reputation went up by another 64 points. Yet another bonus was the Attractiveness which increased with everyone around me, in particular with the seamstress, whose embroidery gained a new additional effect thanks to my buff. I wish I could have been so lucky when it came to Pirus. And yet, even without that, the work went well:

The master luthier now looked at me with more approval than before and even mentioned that my talent deserved a better instrument. I thanked him for his praise modestly but didn't start developing the topic further. There will be time enough for that later. I'll level up my Fame, increase my Attractiveness some more, and then we'll have a more substantial chat.

Chip was nowhere to be seen. In any case, he didn't answer my letter and I got his voicemail when I called his comm in meatworld. As a result, I headed out to see Amaryllis on my own. Catching sight of the NPC, who was chatting with a merchant, I didn't bother catching her attention and starting a conversation. Instead, I placed the trusty flower that was my change mug before me and began to improvise. As expected, the NPC I needed grew curious and joined my growing audience. Several songs later I had earned six silver pieces and eight points of Attractiveness with Amaryllis.

"I always enjoyed bardic performances," she smiled when I had finished my mini-concert and approached her. "I like it when there's music playing around the Tree."

"I am happy to do something for the community," I immediately agreed. "But I would like to do more to earn the respect of my fellow biota."

"That is an admirable goal," Amaryllis approved. "As it happens, I have several tasks I need done. Come with me. I'll tell you about them."

If you ask me, she could just as well have told me right then and there, but why argue?

"As you know, the Kartossian embassy will arrive soon," said Amaryllis when we were left one on one. "They do not speak our language, so we will have to furnish interpreters for our guests. If you master the language of the Dark Empire, you will be able to accompany one of our guests during the length of the visit."

Quest available: *The Tongue that Takes You to Kartoss*.

Description: The guests from the Dark Empire do not speak the tongue of the Hidden Forest. Class: Rare Scenario. Reward for completion: +1000 Reputation with the Biota, +50 gold, the right to accompany one of the members of the Kartossian delegation throughout the entire duration of the embassy. Penalty for failure: -500 Reputation with the Biota.

"I will be happy to help you in this matter," I replied, accepting the quest.

Just what I need: a hike to my reputation and access to a historical meeting. And as it happens, I'm already learning the language in question through another quest.

"I have a friend, a pirc. He too is trying to learn

the language of Kartoss and could help," I offered.

"If he masters the language, he can become one of the interpreters as well," Amaryllis agreed. "As soon as the delegation's arrival is announced publicly, we will begin selecting interpreters."

"We will have to take breaks to clear our minds from all the language lessons. Do you perchance have other assignments you need done?"

Amaryllis immediately dumped a bunch of small quests on me—of the 'polish, decorate, prepare' type. Nothing epic but I needed the reputation and sooner than later.

"And one more question," I remembered. "Let's say that I head out on an adventure that takes me beyond the Arras and I make some friends out there. What do I have to do to invite them back to the Hidden Forest?"

"A guarantee from an esteemed biota. Her reputation will be a guarantee that the guest shall not violate our laws. Any misdeed by the guest shall cast a shadow on her who vouched for him."

In other words, a reputation status no lower than 'Esteem.' Damn. I don't even know what's easier—to grind reputation and invite Sloe's guild to help, or to level up on my own and deal with my enemies autonomously. Then again, to summon them I'll need to reach that Arras thing first...

My cogitations were interrupted by a new mail alert. It turned out that I had two pieces of new mail—

from Chip and Brouhaha. I had quickly forgotten about my meeting with the latter and now I had to write a reply full of apologies and request to arrange a new meeting with Daisy. I was still curious to see a bard tumbler in action. And she might know something about Cypro and his songbook so it wasn't worth it to pass up this chance.

The second letter was from Chip. The pirc showed up not just anywhere but on the warrior's training grounds. It turned out that he had run into Otolaryngologist again and had only just respawned. His desire to get at this 'future compost' had only grown during his 12 hour timeout and the pirc was now actively embroiled in what he termed 'T&ST'—or, 'tactical and special training.'

"I'll raise my stats, check out the other classes, and then get down to leveling up in earnest. I'm going to bury that biota."

And yet he was enthusiastic enough when I told him my idea about learning Kartossian and increasing his reputation with the biota.

"We've already completed the mapping of the Tree and it's pretty dull in here when I'm on my own," Chip explained with a bit of embarrassment.

Just then, a female voice full of rage sounded behind my back:

"You think you're so smart, don't you?"

Turning, I had the dubious honor of encountering none other than Annastarriia, pouting her doll's face in anger. To be honest, my first thought was about an attempted PK, but instead of a hail of blows, the beauty burst into a well-practiced tirade that, with each word, caused my face to grow longer and longer. Once she had concluded, I buried my face in my hands, turned around and shook my shoulders in a mute weeping. Chip, who like most men didn't interfere in arguments between women, stared at me with astonishment.

"Hey...What's with you?" he asked carefully.

I couldn't answer—I was shaking and I simply fled from any strangers' eyes. And it was only once I had been left alone on my own that I burst out laughing as loudly as I could. No—coincidences like this weren't possible. It's a small world of course but it couldn't be that small...

Chip caught up with me and froze with an expression of utter bafflement on his face.

"What the hell was that? What's the matter with you? I thought that that shrew had gotten to you and here you are enjoying yourself."

"Oh," I finally finished laughing and shook my head, coming to. "That flowery monologue that she prepared for me. I wrote that."

"What?" Chip asked, stumped even more.

"Remember I told you that I write various letters for people—from confessions of love to tirades and rants? And I have this one old client. Well, I whipped up that very tirade only several days ago."

It was Chip's turn to laugh now.

"No way! So it turns out that you insulted your own self? Oh what a lark...Why'd you flee then?"

"I mean, if I had laughed right then and there, I doubt I'd get another order from her...This way, she's sure to be back for more."

"That's cold," the pirc approved. "Okay, what are our plans?"

"Find some zombie and hand him Cypro's notes to read. Is he dead? If yes, let him do the reading."

"Where are we going to find a zombie?" Chip sighed.

"Either among Sloe's friends or among the Kartossian embassy. Which means we need to find a way into those talks. We'll start by working at the library. I'm going to try and find out more about the songbook while we're at it. We'll see what to do once we're there."

"If it must be the library, the library it shall be," the pirc agreed easily. "I'll relive my high school years...Eh, how many sweet dreams I dreamed in that place..." he winked to me and laughed uproariously.

"It might be a little too loud in there to sleep," I warned my naïve companion.

Despite my apprehensions, this time the library was quieter. Either it wasn't the season, or the bored-out-of-their-minds players had finally thought of mastering some useful professions and were now occupied with crafting various items. Chip received the quest to help out at the library without any trouble. The reasonable thing to do for the NPCs was to send him packing—there were too much volunteers here as it stood—but it seemed that the devs wanted to make sure that the players could learn the new languages and didn't want to institute limitations on this mechanic.

"For some reason I was certain that you wouldn't pass up a chance to do some reading," I remarked to the pirc who was pretending to be asleep.

"What's there to read here?" the pirc started. "You couldn't even call this Pabulum. A cheap parody of a pathetic misconception, written in a touching attempt to imitate the style of *Song of Roland*."

"I'm not sure whether you've checked out the local legends—they're not bad at all. It's not Shakespeare, of course, but it's still interesting."

"*De gustibus non est disputandum*," Chip concluded diplomatically, "—that is, there is no disputing against hobby horses; and, for my part, I seldom do. What's next in our plan?"

"We need to ask the librarian about the songbook. Maybe he knows something..."

"Well he's about to tell us!" the pirc scowled happily. "I've got some good grub stashed away here. It'll loosen his tongue, it will."

"Eh...Whoa there! What's this bloody scene your imagination's painting? We're not trying to extract top secret info from an enemy spy here. We just want to ask an esteemed biota academic about one of the scrolls stored in his library."

"And have breakfast while we're at it," nodded the pirc and produced from his bag a beef steak and a bundle of leeks.

"For war may be war but dinner comes every night at seven," announced the furball and bit off half the steak, stuck the bundle of leeks in his maw and began chewing loudly, purring with pleasure.

Having roused the NPC librarian, who had secreted himself in the utility closet, I introduced myself and asked:

"Pardon the bother, esteemed sir, but could we speak alone?" I nodded my head at the players eavesdropping nearby.

"As long as you ask your friend not to treat the library like a cafeteria," the librarian pointed with irritation at the loudly-smacking pirc.

Chip made an innocent face and spread his paws, as if to say, 'Wha...?' then swallowed his mouthful and folded his arms across his chest seriously. The librarian simply shook his head and stepped back into his utility closet, inviting us in after him.

In the company of the broad-shouldered pirc, the small room instantly became so cramped that I never even noticed its furnishings if there were any.

"What did you want to speak to me about?"

"I discovered a songbook among the stacks. It

was authored by Cypro sometime long ago, but it also turned out to be incomplete. Someone stole a part of the scroll and I would very much like to locate the lost fragment and the culprit. Do you know anything about this?"

The bored expression on the librarian's face instantly gave way to embarrassment.

"I'm afraid this is an oversight of mine," he confessed. "Literally two months ago, the songbook was in one piece and one of your bard colleagues would spend evenings with it. Later I discovered that a part of the scroll is missing."

"Which bard?" I immediately perked up.

"One of those who set out to become a Singer of the Blade. Oh what was his name..." the old man furrowed his brow, trying to remember, "...Vex, I believe. I even tried to find him to ask what had happened but Vex has not been seen since. The guards say that he descended from the Tree into the forest and never returned. As of late, there are many who do not return."

"Maybe the forest denizens didn't take to his vocal stylings?" the pirc joked clumsily.

"You free citizens of Barliona have the wondrous gift of being able to return from the Gray Lands. Perhaps this is why you jest so lightly of such matters," the librarian responded dryly.

"One can survive for days without food, longer even, but there are times in war when it is impossible to survive without a simple byword, a basic joke." Unexpectedly seriously, Chip quoted some poet I didn't know. "Forgive me, esteemed librarian, at times my wit is so subtle that no one but I can see it."

The NPC's face warmed a little and he nodded in a conciliatory manner.

"Each creature suffers in its own way. But if you wish to discover what happened to Cypro's songbook, you should ask Vex about it. If, of course, you manage to find him."

Quest updated: *Restore the Songbook*. A bard named Vex was the last to study Cypro's songbook. He has vanished in the Hidden Forest. Locate Vex and find out what happened to the songbook.

"Thank you very much. We will try and locate this bard and restore the songbook. You don't happen to know one of Vex's friends, do you? Perhaps he mentioned where he was going?"

The biota scratched his bushy beard.

"Try to track down his friend, Tauvolga. If Vex told anyone where he was going, it would be her."

"We will make sure to ask her," I promised.

"And do so thoroughly," Chip slipped in his meow and earned a sharp elbow to the ribs.

"All the best," I quickly said my farewells and began pushing the woolly troll out of the closet.

"They haven't offered you the 'Terrorist' trait yet, have they?"

"Actually, that was a recent offer I received," Chip deadpanned, "but I was at the airport at the time and it didn't seem an appropriate occasion to accept something like that."

"Well, you'd make a good one," I couldn't help imagining the terror of the NPC biotas facing Chip's angry mug.

Having completed our shift at the library, we tracked down Tauvolga without much difficulty. She related a sad story about the disappearance of her beloved. According to her, Vex headed north in an attempt to find the source of the blight that had afflicted the Hidden Forest. Obviously, the brave young man didn't return and we took up the quest to find him again.

"It's looking like we'll have to delve deep into these blighted areas," I said to my partner once we'd left Tauvolga. "A whole bunch of our quests are all coming down to one thing."

"It would all be so much easier if we had a chopper," sighed Chip. "We'd fly a spiral pattern, comb the entire area, rescue the boy and return back to base. All in time for lunch."

"Well, since we don't have one, we'll have to do it on our two feet."

A new letter appeared in my mailbox. Brouhaha announced that in half an hour her lessons would begin in Daisy's house and I could come by if I wished.

"Listen, Chip, is it true that those who serve in the army never laugh in the circus?"

"Verily, so it is!" the pirc replied hotly. "Why?"

"I just wanted to go take a look how the local circus folk study here and also check out the accuracy of this bit of wisdom. Will you come with?"

"*Pourquoi pas, ma chère laitue?*" No, one day I'm definitely going to kill this polyglot. In the best of traditions, I'll grab my lute and craaa-ack-ack-ack on the back of his stupid skull. Loud enough that Mars hears about it...

"Come again?" I asked just in case, without really expecting a useful translation.

"'Why not, my dear lettuce?'" Chip translated. "Picked it up from the recce squad—they'd sing this song. It's from an ancient movie about some musketeers."

"I'm getting the impression that all our glorious army does is watch old movies and read books."

"Why what else would we do?" Chip sighed sadly. "It's boring as hay in there. A dull routine. Anyway, let's go see what our local competitors can show us."

Mentally promising to myself that I would figure out how much communication amulets cost, I sent an invitation to Reed and headed to the tavern in order to purchase some home-warming gift for the kind Daisy. My culinary skills allowed me to prepare simple and healthy beverages, but I wanted to make the best impression possible on this potential source of knowledge and spells—and this meant that the drinks I brought would have to be good. A bottle of water from some inaccessible mineral spring ended up costing me twenty gold, but I really hoped that my investment would pay off. Who knows, maybe I'll learn something useful?

Reed caught up with us at the last moment, practically right at Daisy's doorstep.

"I just got the letter," he shyly accounted for his disheveled look. "I was in a crazy hurry."

"A crazy hurry, my young friend," Chip said in an admonitory voice, "is necessary in three cases: When you have fleas, when your stomach is upset and when you're sleeping with someone else's wife. And the lasts one is only the case if her husband is busting down the door."

"Didn't he just come in a great hurry? How do you know where he came from?" I added, and Reed blushed a deep crimson from our combined laughter.

"Ah forget you guys," he waved and quickly knocked on the door to preclude any further speculation about his private life.

Brouhaha opened the door.

"Whoa," she blinked with surprise upon seeing the pirc. "You got a heck of a phiz on you."

Chip started as if someone had smacked him in

the phiz.

"Is this a face check?" He asked coldly, pressing his ears to his head in a gesture I already recognized as irritation. "I think I'll wait outside after all."

"Nah," the circus performer waved her hand guilelessly. "I've simply never seen your race before. You're a scary looking lot. What are your people called?"

"The Stephen King It Squad," barked the pirc. He placed his paws on our shoulders and went on, "All right, guys. I think I'll go see what the local Radagasts are up to."

Chip nodded to Brouhaha and left. It was the first time I'd seen the furball slump his shoulders and hunch his spine—it seemed that the dancer's words really had stung him.

"What's with him?" Brouhaha asked, surprised, following Chip with her gaze.

"I have no idea," I admitted sincerely. "I'll go find out."

"Hang on," Brouhaha grabbed me by the sleeve. "Since you're here, step in for a bit and say hello to Daisy. If you want to learn something later, it'll be easier."

I looked askance at Reed who was shifting from foot to foot and nodded unwillingly. Ten minutes wouldn't change anything.

But then again, ten minutes wasn't enough

either: After the gift of mineral water—which was accepted like some rare wine of a venerable vintage—I couldn't help but chat for a bit and play a couple songs. My thoughts returned to Chip again and again and the conversation didn't flow freely, so in the end, I praised Reed's talents and once he'd engrossed his audience with his cello, quietly snuck out.

I found the pirc at the Branch of Vocation. He was in a trance, hammering a training dummy that wasn't guilty of anything with his halberd. All you could hear were the cracks from his halberd and all you could see was the straw flying every which way.

"And why did you leave?" I asked, sitting down nearby.

"You think there's something I haven't seen in that circus?" he replied, sitting down beside me. "All I need is some trouble with a bunch of clowns. What if they decide that I've come to take their bread? Do you have any idea how powerful their union is? Tangle with those guys and you'll be turning tail before you know it..." He scanned our surroundings cautiously from the shadow of his paw.

The excuse was a fairly tepid one, but it was clear that he didn't want to continue talking about it, so I simply decided to play his game.

"I don't know about you but if I were in their place I'd be the worried one. You're like a circus tent on two legs and if I play accompaniment for you, why we'll steal their entire audience easy."

"It's not a bad idea," the pirc grew pensive. "By the way, I switched to a druid," he announced. "It turns out that they get a bonus to healing when healing pircs and biota. Looks like it's because we're so closely linked to nature. Maybe we should find some sensible druid for our party? He can heal while we let that putative medical student have it."

"We could try it," I approved the plan. "Especially if we find one with bonuses to healing."

"Healing," Chip sighed a little wearily. "If there's anything that's good here in Barliona it's the healing. Kazaam!" A mysterious green glow appeared in his paws and after several seconds the system notification announced that the healing spell had been cast on me, "...and that's it! No catheters, sensors, syringes, needles, therapy, bed rest, regenerative devices, tissue compatibility checks and recovery periods. Abracadabra and you're good to go."

"Are you really tired of your convalescence?" I asked cautiously.

"It's been worse," the pirc waved with exaggerated bravado and quickly changed topics. "What do you have to do? Have you composed your hit of the century yet?"

"Actually, yes," I admitted, happy to somehow cheer up my companion. "Whether it's a hit or not isn't up to me but I do have something. Would you like to hear it?"

"Like you need to ask! Come on, my Celery

Dion, belt it like you mean it!"

"It's all keks for you, isn't it? Let's go find a quiet corner where no one will bother us."

Following our cartographic activities, finding a quiet corner on the Tree was not a problem so we headed to the nearest one and I placed the lute on my knees and with some anxiety played my new composition for someone for the first time. The lyrics were still a bit rough, yet the ballad ended up being pretty. It told of the Sixth and her fate. Naturally, the main part of the ballad dealt with the death of her beloved, her transformation into a vengeful necromancer and the battle I saw between the allied armies of the eight races. And the ending was a wistful one—consumed by her thirst for revenge, the Sixth abandoned her home and friends, with whom she had spent the last hundred years, and set off into the dark and the unknown.

A glow appeared before me—within it, a scroll roiled with a pearly, silver light.

Attention! A new stat has become available to your character: 'Composition.' Composition influences the bard's ability to combine the effects of several songs into one and lowers the penalty for such a combination. Composition also affects a series of other abilities and enables you to create unique spells by composing new songs. The effect of the created spell consists of many factors,

including the content that the bard invests in her new creation.

Do you accept? Attention! You will not be able to remove an accepted stat!

I accepted the new stat without further thought and glanced through the rest of the notification. I'll read it more carefully later. At the moment I'm more curious about Chip's opinion of my ballad.

A new stat has been unlocked for the character: 'Composition.' Currently: 1.

You have created a new Song: 'Vengeful Flame.'

Vengeance is one of the most destructive feelings in the world. Vengeance knows neither mercy nor friendship, vengeance destroys indiscriminately. And the first thing vengeance consumes is the one who pursues it.

The Vengeful Flame incinerates everything around the vengeful bard, without distinction for friend or foe. Casting time: This spell is channeled. Cost of performance: 1% of max HP per second. Damage: 1% of target's max HP per second. Area of effect: (Fame + Composition) meters. Cooldown: 24 hours.

Achievement unlocked: 'Unique Repertoire

Level 1' (19 compositions remaining until next level).

Achievement reward: +1% to efficiency of created unique spells.

I took the shimmering scroll in my hands and glanced at its properties.

Lorelei's Songbook. Songbook class: Unique. Contains Vengeful Flame. Once you use the songbook, the songbook will vanish and the Vengeful Flame spell will be added to your spellbook.

Attention! Your spellbook already contains Vengeful Flame.

Attention! This songbook may not be copied.

Attention! This songbook may not be traded.

"Astounding." There was so much sincere admiration in Chip's voice that I couldn't help but break into a wide smile. It's always nice to know that your creation has appealed to the listener.

All of a sudden, a portal fizzed to existence before me and none other than Eben himself stepped out of it and up to me.

"Yes," the Seventh said pensively. "It is indeed a lovely ballad, Lorelei. It's too bad that bards are incapable of biting their tongues in their music."

You have broken the promise you made to Eben!

-1000 Reputation with the Biota. Current status: Friendly.

It's true when they say, 'one born a fool, shall die a fool.' Art is art, but the ballad did mention the Schism which I swore to stay silent about. And what would it have cost me to leave the game, call up Chip on the comm and play him my new song irl? FSM, why didn't you bless me with a brain?

"I got carried away...Forgive me."

What else can I say in this situation? I'm a fool who forgot that within the context of the game, this was a grave secret. At least Chip had something to say, as per usual. The pirc bristled his fur, stuck his hands in his sides and fixed Eben with an unfriendly stare.

"Look here, you fossil, you're not lost in time, are you? It's not that I mind, but this is a private affair and you weren't on the guest list if you catch my continental drift."

"Chip, this is Eben—the seventh member of the biota council," I hurried to check my simmering companion. If he borks my rep right now, I'll have only myself to blame.

"He could be a knight of the Round Table for all I care," the pirc replied utterly unfazed. "I'll say it again: No one invited you, Eben. And that means by implication that you're free to go."

I opened my mouth to try and reason with my white knight—when Eben stopped me with a weighty gesture.

"It's all right, Lorelei. I have known pircs for a long time. Our friends are renowned for their unbridled, unchecked temper as well as their devotion so I would expect nothing else. And yet we are at an impasse. You did not keep your word and the news of the Council's schism could spread. My job is to ensure the security of the coming embassy and secrecy is its guarantee. It is not your fault that you became involved in this affair. And, moreover, it is not this pirc's fault that he is now involved in it either. However, I must prevent these rumors from spreading further. Does either one of you have any solution to my problem?"

Well, I could tear my unruly tongue out—there's one solution. But then I'd still have my hands to write with so only a good ol' fashioned quartering would do. Chip, however, turned out to be much more quick-witted.

"So you decided to send us to the brig? Well I don't hail from your herbarium. I have my own staff headquarters I report to."

"I'm not entirely sure what a brig even is," the Seventh said with a tinge of surprise, "but you are correct in that I have decided to send you away...for some time. And yes, you are entirely correct, Chip—I cannot order you to obey me directly, but I can ask you to meet me halfway. I shall send you both to a closed training ground where several of my pupils are pursuing their studies. It is well-hidden from prying eyes and you won't be able to leave it without external help. At the same time, there are many training opportunities there and your time there ought not be a waste. You will be able to increase your stats and perhaps even acquire certain new skills. Then, on the day the embassy is scheduled to arrive, I shall return you back to the Tree."

I started to think. On the one hand, it didn't sound so bad. We were clearly going to be sent to a special location with the opportunity to level up and return in time for the most interesting part. On the other hand...We'd spend almost two weeks FSM-knows-where. No quests to complete, no reputation to increase, no profits, no class instructor near at hand...

"And what will happen if we refuse your generous offer?" Chip crossed his arms over his chest and stared at Eben defiantly.

"I shall be compelled to exile you from the Hidden Forest," the Seventh said ruefully. "You shall leave me no choice."

Chip and I exchanged glances. In theory, it wasn't a bad option for quickly reaching the wider world and yet exile...Exile means that we wouldn't be able to return, complete our affairs and quests and explore the Hidden Forest...

"I am partial to being isolated at the training ground."

"Well I'm partial to sending him somewhere dank and dark where he won't stand out so much," barked Chip. "Who do you think you are to be dictating terms to me? Since you're so smart—why aren't you marching lockstep and singing songs, eh? Why don't you account yourself per the regs—to Lori and I, that is—and explain what the carrot you're sending us to basic like a bunch of bolos for?"

The imitator's eyes clouded over for a moment. It was clearly trying to digest, Chip's jargon-rich speech. At last Eben replied:

"Everything is very simple. Your friend was unfortunate enough to see things she wasn't supposed to in her Twilight Dream. She promised to stay quiet about it but she did not keep her promise, leaving me a very poor choice. Either I isolate you, furnishing you with enough chances to develop, or I exile you. And whereas when it comes to Lorelei, this is fairly straightforward—in your case, I will need to discuss the matter with the pirc ambassador. However, something tells me that he will suggest exactly the same solution to our problem. So, what shall it be?"

Attention! For breaking your promise you shall be exiled from the Hidden Forest and suffer a

penalty to your reputation with the Biota that shall reduce your status to Suspicion—or you shall be isolated at a training ground until the Kartossian embassy arrives. If you choose the latter option, you will be allowed to continue developing your skills during your in-game imprisonment.

"I choose the training ground," I decided. We had too much unfinished business in the Hidden Forest to accept the exile.

"A wise decision," nodded the spymaster.

"In that case, I choose the same," Chip squinted unkindly and added: "But I shall return and you will rue the day you escaped the local natural history museum. Do I make myself clear, fossil?"

This threat didn't make much of an impression on the Seventh, though perhaps the imitator simply didn't think of anything to reply to this strange and esoteric speech. Instead, he uttered dryly:

"Do you have any requests before I send you to the training ground?"

"Bash your head against the nearest wall?" Chip ventured.

"An enticing proposition, but no," Eben refused such a generous offer. "And you, Lorelei, do you have any requests?"

"Yes. I would like to take several books from the library with me."

"This may be arranged. Which ones do you need?"

"Any that treat of the history of the Hidden Forest, the biota, the pircs, Cypro and bards. And one more in Kartossian."

"Very well."

In the next instant, Eben opened a portal and made a welcoming gesture with his hand:

"It is time."

"Tea time?" asked the pirc. Receiving no response whatsoever, Chip regarded the biota as if he wished to remember him better, spun his halberd and said: "Let's go, Lori. We shall try out the chow they serve at the training ground's mess."

CHAPTER NINETEEN

T
HERE WERE NO shimmering portals this time around. The picture simply changed and, in a blink, instead of the Tree, I found myself somewhere in the Hidden Forest. How did I know this? Well, there were buildings made of plants and trees, silhouettes of enormous plants, and also the maps indicated that we were somewhere in the northwestern part of the forest, in the middle of one of the white spots.

Unlike back on the Tree, there was a certain utility to observe here: less decoration, more functionality. A squat, elongated building that resembled a barracks for several dozen, an immense training area filled with various contraptions and an obstacle course, a small forge and several buildings whose purpose I could only guess at. All of this was surrounded by a living stockade of tall, impassable thorny brambles getting through, over or under which seemed entirely unfeasible. I was happy to see some ore lodes, useful plants and trees that would be good for lumber. It looked like the developers wanted to furnish the imprisoned players with everything they needed to pass their time productively.

"You think they train ninjas or like super-duper-Spetsnaz here?" Chip drawled, examining the obstacle course. "Hell, we should record this and show it to the recce squad—they won't believe it otherwise."

I was in agreement with the pirc here—I'd encountered things like this only in far-fetched action flicks about commandos—or in fantastical books. Pendulums, balls with spikes on ropes, some kind of toothed contraptions sawing in and out of stretches of bog punctuated by mounds of earth, between which something more dangerous than toads and frogs lurked in the muddy sludge...

"Well, we won't be bored here," the pirc took heart. "Want to bet who'll complete this mess first?"

I didn't share his enthusiasm. Not because the obstacle course scared me, but because I was haunted by my sense of guilt. It was my stupid oversight that landed Chip in this pen.

"Forgive me for putting you in a tough spot. I messed up and you're paying for it," I drooped my head and prodded a fresh molehill with the toe of my shoe.

"Come on now," Chip nudged me with his elbow. "Found something to be upset over. This is a game, buddy! We'll level up here for a bit. I don't see anything catastrophic in this. I'll relive my days as a snot-nosed recruit when I would go AWOL for any dumb reason. What a time it was..." the pirc squinted in reminiscence. "This place—why it may as well be a resort. There's nature, warm weather and a charming lady for company...This is a recruit's fantasy!"

"Charming as in she'll charm you, lead you into a bog and then drown you?"

Chip's levity caused me to cheer up. If he didn't mind losing several weeks of freedom, then maybe things weren't so bad. After all was said and done, I can read about the local stories in the books and maybe slap together another song or two. And after that, there'd be the embassy, the new alliance and, I can bet, an easing of the border security. While I'm here, I'll see what it's like to learn a new language by reading. And I'll level up my Bardic Lore. I can't wait to reach 100 and discover the properties of Cypro's gift.

"Everyone knows you can't drown a pirc in a bog!" Chip proclaimed dramatically. "Right, oh my intrepid lily of the valley, let's check out what there is to do here."

"I think, officially, the options are leveling up and geeking out. When the books arrive, I'll research the local legends and gather some material for our album. I could also raise my stats or mine some ore and chop some lumber. When it comes to unofficial ways of spending time, there's no dating house here, so the options are rather limited. I don't know the prices they charge there, but I doubt we'd afford it anyway."

"The dating house is like Barliona's version of a whorehouse, right?" Chip asked. "No thanks. That kind of thing doesn't draw me in the least. To be honest, I've never been able to understand the pleasure of tumbling with a bunch of numbers and letters."

"I think the point is that full VR immersion simulates real-life sensations..." I objected. "Plus, you're not likely to find an elf, a gnome or some orc maiden out in meatspace. It's exoticism! Or, you could even order yourself a copy of Anastaria. Half of Barliona has lost its mind over her."

"I think I belong to the other half," Chip waved his paw dismissively. "I saw her a couple times before I ended up in the hospital bed. They showed her on the news. I wonder how she lives out in meatspace, as you call it, knowing that there're hordes of nerds in here ordering copies of her at the Dating House all night and day."

"To be honest, I can't imagine either. It's hard to fathom why someone would give permission for their likeness to be used in a VR bordello. Maybe in extremely dire circumstances, but I doubt that the face of the largest guild of her continent needs money that badly. Maybe I'm old-fashioned, but in my view, it's not that different from prostitution. Even if she doesn't personally service the johns, how must her husband feel when his buddies tell him that 'I ordered your wife in Barliona the other day; she's a hell of a ride.' That's beyond my understanding. Am I bigot?"

"If you are, so am I," Chip voiced his solidarity. "But...another's soul is not for us to know. Then again, there are peoples who exchange wives as gifts, as a show of respect."

The very thought of it made me start.

"More like, there are men who exchange wives as gifts as a show of respect," I objected. "Ain't no peoples who exchange husbands as gifts as a show of respect. All right, let's look around and figure out how to use that obstacle course. Hell, we might die in a flash and respawn in a cemetery outside of this reservation."

A quick examination of the training ground didn't add much to my initial impression. It was the size of a football field and offered a fairly exotic inventory of exercise equipment. There were the ordinary dummies as well as complex, anthropomorphic ones, created it seems for special rogue training. I was also pleased to see dummies in clothes hung with bells. As Chip the know-it-all explained, thieves would use these back in the Middle Ages, the objective being to steal something from the dummy without ringing a single bell.

The obstacle course turned out to be much more complicated than it looked. Almost right away I understood why in army jargon (again according to

Chip), these were called 'death valleys.' Except you couldn't die here—my Hit Points would simply drop to 1 HP and then I was sent back to the beginning—but sometimes I wished I could. And also I wished I could kill a certain two-meter tall ball of fur, whose extremely long tongue never missed a chance to let the 'vegetable brats' have it. I swear—by the end of the day, Chip was alive only because I didn't have the strength to smack him on the head, or the mental energy to kill him with my spells. But at least I managed to increase my Constitution by two whole points! Against the backdrop of this achievement, a respectable increase in my agility seemed like a fairly insignificant development.

The books arrived by courier—a taciturn and serious biota whom I recalled from one of my visions. He was one of Eben's apprentices. And he showed up the same way—through a portal—which suggested that there weren't any other exits. He refused to make small talk, ignored all of Chip's quips and, dropping off the books, re-entered his portal without a word.

"Good chat," I muttered, assiduously arranging my personal prison library in my bag. Who knows how realistic things are here? Maybe it'll start raining and the books will get wet and fall apart, and later I'll be responsible for them. Or not, but either way, I wouldn't have anything to read.

"What's there to chat with him about anyway?" Chip plunked down on the ground and stretched loudly, then threw one leg over the other and dreamily stared at a convoy of clouds plowing through the heavens.

"Eh, when I get better, it'll be straight up into the sky in my bird for me," he shared his reveries.

"What's with you anyway?" I asked carefully, sitting down nearby. I hadn't the strength left for anything but conversation and as it happened, our circumstances welcomed an open and heartfelt exchange.

"Uhh...A stupid turn of events, let's say," Chip sighed. "I was coming in for a landing. We were picking up some infantry. A rebel launched an RPG from the jungle. Hit my right engine. I ordered the navigator and my snipers to bail, and then tried to save the bird...Didn't make it. My bird crashed and I got crushed in the cabin. There was a fuel leak...and, well..."

For a few moments, I stared at him blankly, trying to comprehend what he'd told me. Either I didn't understand something or Chip crashed in his helicopter, the fuel leaked and he...

"Did you get burned?" I asked the dumbest question in the world.

"That too," nodded Chip. "Fractured my spine when I fell, broke my legs and some debris cut up my face. I lost an eye and a part of my lower jaw. If it weren't for the grunts, I'd be done for. One broiled pilot *au jus*. The boys pulled me out as the bird burned. They laid some fire down on the rebels and rescued me before I could cook in my flight suit."

Chip fell silent and I simply looked at his furry face at a loss for what to say, all the right words escaping me. What could I say here? That I'm sorry? A stupid and meaningless phrase. What kind of words of consolation were available here? And does he even need that from a person he barely knows? Should I cheer him up? How can you cheer someone up in this situation? Or maybe I should stay silent? That's even worse...

"What do the doctors say?" I asked directly.

Since I struck up this awkward conversation, I should at least go through with it until I have a complete idea of Chip's condition—maybe I won't say something wrong later. Maybe he'll only be able to walk in-game now. Although, no, hadn't he mentioned being 'out of bed' repeatedly? Either way, knowing for certain won't hurt here.

"They're promising an almost complete recovery," came the reply. "Paid for by the ministry of defense, naturally. At the moment, I'm limping around the apartment like some kind of cyborg—decked out in all kinds of equipment. The only awful thing is that I can't eat properly—all the grub at the moment is liquid and tubed in down the old gullet."

"And how is that they released you from the hospital in this condition?" I wondered at the carelessness of the army doctors.

In my imagination, traumas of this level required lots of rest in a regenerative capsule. Although, I have to admit that my medical knowledge was limited to cold remedies, dealing with alcohol poisoning and providing first aid to various non-serious traumas.

"I asked them myself," Chip confessed. "They monitor me around the clock and the doctor comes by daily. In the hospital...I just can't. It's horrible there. Burn-victims all around me—and above us, patients with abdominal wounds. And sometimes..." he fell silent, staring at the grass. "Well...when the morphine wears out, they start screaming..." the pirc added, when I already thought that he wouldn't be saying anything further. "And that's...horrible to hear."

I had been lucky enough that I'd never even heard of these kinds of things and had difficulty imagining what it was like. But I had enough imagination to cringe. Yeah. When you have neighbors like that, I would prefer to hobble around my house too, even if I had to crawl, as long as I wasn't in the hospital.

"Does someone stay with you in your apartment? To help out, bring food, wash the dishes or do laundry?"

"Well, like I said, the doctor comes by," Chip faltered. "As for the rest of it...It's not a big deal. I can always just order what I need on the web."

"And where do you live?" I asked,

contemplating an idea.

"In the Russian sector," Chip replied a little taken aback. "In Pyatigorsk, if you've ever heard of it. A resort region. The so-called Caucasian Mineral Waters."

"Why we're practically neighbors! I'm in Russia too, near Voronezh. It's all forest, mountains and barbecue here."

"Pff, please!" Chip snorted playfully. "What could you know about barbecue, oh child of the northern forests? Why, you people still use vinegar as marinade."

"To each her own. But in general, here's your chance to teach the savages how to make proper barbecue. I'll come by for a visit, help you around the house, take care of you a bit and then you'll return the favor by making me some barbecue, southern style. How do you like the idea?"

"Are you serious?" Chip didn't believe me.

"Uh-huh," I nodded. "I have a friend who works for the Kislovodsk monorail. I'll catch a ride with him in the service car right to your area. I'll borrow a good holoprojector from Straus, so there won't be a problem with band practice, and other than that, I'm as free as the wind in the steppe. I have no work, and I've amassed plenty of material for the album, I can compose wherever I am, and as it happens, Barliona's offering a promo in which they lend out their newest capsules for a month. All you'll have to do is hobble to your front door to let me in."

And here a miracle took place! Chip, the long-tongued, was stumped. I swear—if we'd been in reality—he would've blushed as red as a tomato. In Barliona, however, he expressed his embarrassment by pressing his ears to his head and kicking the earth with his paw.

"That really would be very wonderful," he managed at last. "But...don't be scared, okay? I don't look so good these days—I could play a villain in an action movie."

"Have you seen yourself in the game? A pirc doesn't even fit the edict that 'a man should be a bit better-looking than a monkey,' so I doubt that you'll outdo your alter ego in meatspace."

"And, what, you're not afraid to up and go visit some man you don't know?" the pirc asked, surprised.

"I trust my sense of people—and it's not like you're the one beckoning me into a dark lair," I laughed. "Again, if your jaw is in place and you have your Sauce-given two eyes, I'll turn right around and head on back. And if you're hobbling like a zombie, then I'll manage one way or another. I'll make sure to leave the address with my friends."

"And how is your boyfriend going to react? He won't turn into an Othello and make a scene, by any chance?"

"The last Tarzan already had his scene and the

curtain dropped a good while ago. But even if he were around, I doubt that in your condition, you're a victim of whatever romantic impulses you may have."

"You can say that again," Chip scratched his head. "To be honest, my only true impulse is to gobble up a normal piece of steak."

"Just promise me that I won't be said steak, so I can come visit you without any reservations."

"You're not meat. You're salad. So come on by with peace of mind," Chip joked. "The most you have to worry about is me yanking out a few bundles from your mop—for garnish, you see."

"I happen to identify as a poisonous plant," I warned him for good measure.

"In that case, I'll whip up my fugu soup. When are you coming?" the pirc asked, smiling. "I'll prepare a room for you. And I'll ask a friend to drop off a capsule—he's off on vacation and won't need it for three months."

"When it comes to the capsule—great! But as for the room...You're barely walking and have a fractured spine and you want to prepare something or other?" I asked. "Sit and chill. I'll figure it out on my own. If something, I'll toss a sleeping bag on the floor—I'll sleep perfectly fine on it. As for the rest of it—I'll call Frost and find out when the monorail leaves and whether I can catch a ride on it."

"I have enough strength to order some fresh sheets and order that lazy robot to prepare your room," Chip assured me.

"In that case, tell me your address and I'll find out when I can be there."

CHAPTER TWENTY

I CLIMBED OUT OF THE CAPSULE in that rare careless-impatient attitude that takes over when an adventure looms on the horizon. And even if it was merely an unplanned trip to an unknown city to visit a person I didn't really know, it's moments like this that cause the heart to beat a little faster. Someone might think it flippant, but I always thought that these were the moments that made life worth living, when the sensation that what you are doing is right empowers you to disregard your reservations.

It took me a half hour to pack and I limited myself to a large backpack. This was joined by a hardcase with my guitar synth and—aside from the issue of the holoprojector—I was ready to set out.

The boys reacted to my announcement with understanding—the only catch was that Edilberto announced implacably:

"I'll come along with you to see this goon with my own eyes. When it comes to what he says maybe he's barely walking but then it turns out he's some sort of prevert. If everything's fine, I'll roll on back with Frost. And if not, I'll smack him in the gob and we'll come back together."

It was pointless to object and useless too, so I called Chip and informed him that I wouldn't be coming alone. He assured me that he didn't have any problems with this and it seemed to me like he was only happier that I'd bring more company. I guess he was sick and tired of sitting around on his own.

"Just don't say anything to Toad or he'll pitch a fit," Charsky counseled. "If a concert comes around, we'll warn you ASAP so you have time to return. It's only five hours on the mono so there shouldn't be any issues."

"Listen Kiera, leave me the keys to your place, what do you say?" Straus popped up. "It's all the same to you and I'll be able to get away from my parents for a bit."

"Make sure you don't become a parent in the process," giggled Charsky. "The breath of liberty could make you lose your mind at the worst moment."

Straus waved his fist at him but Yuri didn't seem particularly afraid.

"Here," I handed Straus my keys. "Rent's on you while I'm gone. And when I come back, I better not hear any complaints from my neighbors about things that go bang in the night. If you go through my drawers, I'll kill you."

Once Straus had done giving me his oaths and assurances, I grabbed the holoprojector and headed to the station with Beast. Edilberto brought a bottle of cognac with him—a perk for Frost for his understanding and support.

"At least I'll be able to get some fresh air," he explained the grin on his face. "There're also nice places to visit out there. I'll head out to the mountains for a day or two. Sit around a fire. Think about my thoughts."

This explained the hiking backpack and sleeping bag on his back.

"If something happens, the city's right at the foot of the mountains. I'll come running as soon as I get your call," he added.

"Don't worry," I smiled hearing the concern in his voice. "You know firsthand that I'm smart when it comes to people. Everything will be fine."

"What I like about you, Kiera, is your healthy faith in other people," Beast laughed. "You're always ready to help and you never forget to bring your taser with you."

"You get a lot more from a kind word and a taser than from a kind word alone," I rephrased a famous saying of an ancient gangster.

The approaching train interrupted our conversations. Frost popped out to the platform and our evening of reminiscences began with the uncorking of the bottle of cognac. In the meantime, while my friends recalled their school years, I came to grips with the work of a conductor—handing out bedclothes and vintage tea glasses with glass holders (as was traditional in the Russian sector) to the passengers. Frost only bothered to get up when his alarm announced that the train was about to make another stop. I don't know what he sees in this career, but Frost enjoyed these kind of travels. Over about six years he had managed to travel all over the Russian sector and a lot of it wasn't even on the clock—he'd simply catch rides with other conductors he knew, following some line that had caught his eye.

We reached Pyatigorsk early in the morning and, declining the services of cloying taxi drivers (ordinary people who operated classic automobiles with actual internal combustion engines and without a single chip or other trappings of modern technology), entered the city. Walking along an old-fashioned city, a part of which was built in the days of Lermontov and Pushkin was a sheer pleasure, and Beast and I wasted an hour on simply getting lost and exploring. The city had been built on the slope of Mount Mashuk, which meant that we were constantly going uphill or downhill. Locals would pass us at a tranquil pace, an old-fashioned tram would creak through the intersections and dozens of flowerbeds exhaled a pleasant aroma.

Chip lived in a neighborhood with the funny and memorable name White Daisy in a typical apartment building, not unlike all the others I'd seen in the various cities I'd visited. The building elevator wasn't in service (as per tradition) and though we didn't have much trouble climbing to the fourth floor, I considered what Chip would do in the event of an emergency.

The door swung open, revealing the pirc in his human form. Naturally, Meatspace Chip was no shorter than his virtual avatar. It was clear at a glance that he was over two meters and that his shoulders barely fit through his own doorway. A chiseled face, a square chin, deep-set blue eyes...err...eye. The other eye-socket boasted an implant. A long, hunched nose, a high forehead and dirty blond hair which in places had been cut to a standard-issue buzz cut and in other places was absent due to the fire. Beside this fellow, Beast—who had long since left his adolescent years behind— looked like a feeble toddler.

Chip was wearing green Bermuda shorts and a baggy orange T-shirt, which formed a lump around where he carried his regenerative device. Other regen devices were attached to the patient's face and legs, really giving him the resemblance of the evil cyborgs from various space operas. The eye implant, which burned with a sinister dark-green light in the left socket only added to this impression, as did the bio-plasters stuck here and there where the burns had been most severe. I should also add that he looked younger than I had expected. Due to his injuries, I couldn't be certain, but there was no way he was over forty.

"Hello!" he boomed in the same metallic timbre I had heard on the phone. Only now did I notice the cause of this distortion: One more tissue regenerator blinked on his throat. Clumsily shuffling his feet, he hobbled closer and offered a shovel-sized hand, which Beast immediately shook.

"I'm Pavel, but you can go ahead and call me Pasha," Chip introduced himself. "I didn't think you'd have the same voluminous mop in real life...just like Kisya Vorobyev's."

My haircut still caused my grandfather to call me 'Parakeet' and my grandmother to sigh and lament the extravagant sensibilities of the youth. If you ask me, bright blue hair with several dyed braids was entirely appropriate and even a conservative choice, especially if you compare it to what the majority of my friends tended to sport.

"Edilberto," the bassist introduced himself and added, "What's a Kisya?"

"A fictional human," Pasha corrected him. "One of the main characters of a book called *The Twelve Chairs*. All right, come on in. The food's getting cold. What did you, take the long way over Mount Mashuk?"

Beast and I entered the apartment and looked around. It smelled like a hospital. If you ignored the African masks on the walls, mixed with various military gear and a large number of framed photos (I think I even noticed a couple 2D black and white ones), the place was entirely ordinary. Almost. Two of the walls in the living room were taken up with an old-fashioned library consisting of real, paper books.

"We took a walk," I plunked my bag on the floor and carefully leaned my guitar synth against the wall. "By the way, I always imagined that you were about fifty. And a good bit shorter."

"What gave you that impression?" asked Pasha and slowly, clearly struggling to move his feet, walked to the kitchen. "I'm only 36, so please don't consign me to the dustbins of history just yet. Okay, let's not clutter up the hallway either—there's the table. My robo-sponge already has everything ready. At least we'll get some use from these digital dimwits..."

As frequently happens, our friendship grew further at the table and by dessert, the thin ice of our first minutes of meeting each other had shattered. In person, Chip was much the same as in Barliona. The only inconvenience was his eye implant: I kept catching myself staring at it and each time felt very awkward. Pasha's sad look as he consumed a liquefied mass through a tube also caused me some embarrassment at my own ability to eat normally. Beast, on the other hand, was entirely nonplussed: He gulped down the offered breakfast without a shadow of shame. I suppose the cognac in the train played its part, but Beast wasn't very perceptive in general, so I couldn't say for sure.

Barliona quickly became the topic of conversation, logically enough since that is what all of us had in common.

"I'm still going to find that radish-head and consume him—without butter," Pasha shared his dreams of finding the much-hated Otolaryngologist.

"I'm with you there," Edilberto nodded in solidarity. "If you act like that, you deserve to have your face plastered to your heels."

"Two legendary warriors speak—without having reached Level 10," I giggled at this conversation.

"And so what? I have a bro who can crush those PKers without any levels at all. It's like watching a pastry chef make frosting," Pasha objected. "He doesn't even know what to do with all the orders flooding him."

"How's that?" A glint flared to life in Beast's eye. Despite his brief time in Barliona, he already had a long list of enemies.

"He simply applies what he learned in real life to the game," Pasha was happy to explain. "Various traps. He baits them in and wham—the bully's cooked."

"No way!" Edilberto exclaimed. "Can he teach me?"

"Sure thing," Pasha assured. "He's about to drop by with Kiera's capsule."

"Beast," I intervened, "let's be honest: You and baited traps are miles apart. You don't have the patience to hear the punch line to a 'yo momma' joke, whereas traps take time and preparation. You'll just end up in the slammer again."

"Maybe so, maybe so," Beast didn't bother arguing, "but it's worth a shot. I had enough patience to learn to play bass; maybe here I'll have enough too."

"You and the bass have a tender love affair," I objected and instantly cut myself short. "Although...Maybe you have a love affair with the trolls too. It might not be so delicate, maybe it's a bit singular and even a little violent..."

"On the topic of my love affairs, I'm really close to letting the back of your head have it," Beast joked grimly. The idea of mastering the dark art of traps clearly appealed to him.

"Now now. No violence in the kitchen, please. You two are like a pair of greenhorns...Although, I guess you're kids after all."

"Keep your counsel, old man," I snorted in reply. "You told me in Barliona that you've been flying in the mountains for thirty years, so I had good reason to figure you over fifty."

"Me?" Chip asked, surprised, then thought a bit and began to laugh.

"That's a line from a song," he explained. "Monologue of a chopper. Here," Pasha snapped his fingers, issuing a command to the imitator. "Play 'I've returned (Mi-8),'" he ordered.

Judging by its sound, the song was an ancient one, recorded on imperfect equipment. Its narrative, as I understood it, was told from the perspective of a helicopter. And one of the lines really was the one that had confused me about Chip.

"Whoops, I messed up," I confessed when the song ended. "The hell with it then, your age. As my granny liked to say, 'I'm not fixing to make a soup out of you, so who cares how old your bones are.'"

"Like you know how to make soup," Edilberto guffawed, missing the point as usual.

"Why would I need to if I have an autocook?" I protested.

"Those autocooks are nothing but heaps of junk," Chip the Luddite immediately got on his soapbox. "Not even the most advanced autocook in the world will ever be able to prepare a dish as well as a human. If these pieces of plastic could match a living cook—why the restaurants wouldn't employ anyone but. But as you can see, a living mind always triumphs over witless silicon. For this heap of junk simply can't follow the principle of 'a pinch of this and a half-dash of that!'"

"That may be, but for the time being, this witless silicon manages better than I do in the kitchen," I spoke up in defense of the maligned appliance.

"No big deal. If you can't—we'll teach you. And if you don't want to—we'll compel you," Pasha 'reassured' me to Beast's supportive laughter. These two were certainly getting along...

The capsule was delivered a few hours later, accompanied by a jovial soldier in green fatigues that were littered with a constellation of strange patches and emblems. The newcomer gingerly embraced Pasha, gave Beast and I a suspicious look and then announced indignantly:

"Can you believe it, Pasha? The street bums have lost their marbles completely: They tried to start something with me!"

"And how'd it turn out?" Pasha asked lazily.

Judging by his reaction, or rather lack thereof, this type of situation was commonplace for this *homo militaris*. And this would have been entirely understandable, were this new character of the same dimensions as Pasha—but he wasn't. He looked completely ordinary, neither particularly tall, nor well-built, nor especially fit. He was of average height, a bit thin, long-nosed and he looked more like an actor playing the role of one of the musketeers in the latest film version of Dumas' novel—if it weren't for his eyes. Even when the soldier smiled or grimaced, the look in his eyes remained weighty and unkind as if he wasn't looking at me so much as *aiming* at me.

"They ended up helping my imitator clean my place!" shrugged the warrior who'd brought the capsule.

"You're always picking on the little guys,"

sighed Pasha. "Want some chow?"

"Sure. I wouldn't say no to a glass or two of the fire water either!" His buddy didn't tarry with formalities. "Who are these guys?" he nodded in our direction. "The Junior Helicopter Club?"

"This is Kiera and Edilberto," Pasha announced weightily, "so leave your tough guy act at the door. Everyone's friends here. Don't be upset with him, guys," he turned to us. "He's recon—a ranger. They're not like other human beings."

"Hold your tongue, Iron Angel!" smiled the man. "And be envious in silence. I'm Alex," the warrior introduced himself at last, "but you can call me Sasha. Together, we're Sasha and Pasha!"

Despite this glib introduction, Alex didn't offer his hand and I could pick up a politely-concealed resentment lurking somewhere in his eyes.

"Edilberto," Beast introduced himself without particular need, and I could tell by his squinting eyes that the bassist had entered that dangerous state of mind where he was considering whether there was some slight or insult directed at his person. Beast didn't know how to forgive a slight and our new acquaintanceship was already verging on a fight, so I quickly changed the topic of conversation.

"So do you play Barliona as well?"

"I used to," Alex explained, heading to the kitchen. "I dicked around and had enough. There's no point in wasting life in a capsule," he added, plunging himself into the refrigerator up to his waist. Judging by the way he and Pasha spoke to each other, they had been friends for more than a year or two—in fact, it could have easily been longer than Frost, Beast and I had even lived in this world.

"Hey look! Salami!" sounded from the depths of the refrigerator and was followed by a contented smacking. "And vodka! Who'll be my company? Buster's out—liquor makes him touchy."

"I'm about to bust someone's tongue against his ass!" Pasha barked jokingly.

The fridge snorted contemptuously.

"Bring the vodka," Beast livened up, finding common ground with Alex.

"Buster?" I asked, looking at Pasha.

"It's 'cause I'm big," he explained a bit bashfully and followed his buddy with an envious look as the latter proceeded triumphantly to the table bearing a bottle of vodka and a salami in his hands.

"I don't get it," Beast confessed, gingerly taking the bottle and pouring its contents into the glasses that Alex had fished out of the kitchen cupboards.

"It's my childhood nickname," Pasha sat down beside me, still transfixing the bottle with his eyes. "This goof off," the pilot nodded at the ranger slicing up the salami, "is the one who came up with it. I used to threaten to bust the kids that made fun of me."

Noticing the suffering look of our patient, I found several wine glasses, filled them with apple juice, tossed in a straw and completed the arrangement with a slice of lemon.

"Here," I slid the glass to Pasha. "Just imagine that you and I are drinking cocktails like refined people, while these two slobs swill their grain alcohol. If you do it right, you'll even feel a light buzz—just like in *Peter Pan*."

"Really works," Beast agreed. "I don't know how but Kiera manages to keep a good conversation going in boozing company even without drinking herself."

"Well someone has to be around to tell you what you did last night," I replied philosophically, sucking the juice through my straw. Pasha followed my example, yet it didn't seem like the placebo helped him much.

"Oh we've acquired a court scribe!" Alex proclaimed and clinked glasses with us. "Well, let's drink to your chronicle then!"

By the end of the first bottle, the danger had passed: Beast and Sasha had become good friends and by the evening, when we finally decided to part ways, they were the best of buddies. During this time, the technicians from the local Barliona branch had come and gone, connected and tested the capsule. No one wanted to go back into the game much, so as it so frequently happens, we ended up chatting late into the night. Or, that is, Pasha and I were chatting, while Beast had already shuffled over to the couch and passed out in his clothes, muttering, "May the blessings of heavy metal be upon you."

"Mmm, yeah. Young people don't know how to drink these days," Pasha quipped looking at him. "And this one's one of the better ones I've seen...You, uh, don't be upset with Alex. He's wary of freaks, even though we were freaks too at one point."

"I'm not having children with him," I shrugged, "so he can be wary of whoever he likes. What's it to me?"

"You never know," winked Pasha. "Who knows how life will turn out? He's single, so..." He trailed off ambiguously.

If my grandmother heard him right now, she'd kiss him all over, my still-kicking grandfather notwithstanding. If there's anyone who likes to start these types of conversations and insist on matching me with 'good boys,' it's her.

"Why don't you just admit it already? After you turn thirty, a wedding-industry lobbyist shows up and instills in you the need to marry anyone around you who's still single?" I demanded.

"Has nothing to do with age," Pasha retorted. "I got married at twenty. Sasha was my best man."

"So you suffered from your own mistake and now you feel obliged to visit your experience on others?" I couldn't help but ask.

"Yeah, I was impressed into the marriage," Pasha 'confessed,' pressing his hand to his chest.

"Listen, why doesn't your buddy like musicians

anyway? Well, until he kills a bottle with them, I mean," I asked, recalling how much better everything went after the vodka had been consumed.

"I told you, we're from the same circles," Pasha said. "It's just that...Well, freaks don't frequently like other freaks. Do you understand? You and Edilberto are freaks and Sasha and I were lucky enough to make it out of the freak circles. The ones that are still full of people who are mentally about 16 (the ones that didn't die from drugs or booze) and who to this day want only to jangle on their guitars for enough change to buy a few bottles of rum and then pontificate on the 'way of the freak, man.' I bet you've run into plenty of them yourself."

"There's degenerates everywhere you look," I said.

"Precisely. But since we clambered out of that bog, Alex's reflexive reaction to anyone from those circles is to judge them on their appearance. He comes around to their minds a little later," Pasha drained his weak tea.

"No wonder he and Beast chummed up so quickly," I couldn't help pointing at the couch where Beast was snoring with all his bellows.

Pasha followed my finger and sighed:

"Almost. He and I started drinking...later. When we were first sent to Africa. Ever heard of the Great Duchy of Imbanga-Le?"

"Can you figure it out on your own, or do you

want me to flap my eyelids in wonderment?"

"Well...There were these activists there who were trying to resurrect their, let's say, cultural traditions. Sasha learned his craft there. And also...we learned to drink vodka there too. By the way, you don't drink? How come? Not that I have anything against it: It's simply a little odd for a rocker."

"I never enjoyed alcohol that much. I tried it back when I was a teenager but didn't really feel much of an effect. It was all the same baggage as when I'm sober, only with dizziness and nausea. After that I saw plenty of my buddies drinking," I nodded at Beast, "and kind of developed a steadfast dislike for premeditated self-stupefaction. As Pythagoras used to say, drunkenness is an exercise in madness."

"Indeed—life is unpredictable. I never imagined that I would meet a sober rocker," Pasha drawled with surprise, propping up his chin with his fist and staring blankly at the wall.

"Nothing is impossible," I winked at Chip and yawned widely.

"Okay, why don't we start heading to bed bit by bit? They'll come by in the morning to change my cartridges, and I doubt *Herr Doktor* and his retinue will allow you to get much sleep. We just need to prod the Beast there—what is he sleeping in his clothes for?"

"Forget it," I shrugged. "When he sleeps it off,

he'll wash up and change. He's not a kid. All right. Good night to you."

* * *

In the morning, Edilberto cleaned up and set out to the mountain with his new drinking buddy. I really hoped that they would continue their celebration of nature and avoid getting into a fight—the two were ornery enough. The doctor showed up a little later and, learning of my wish to help out, instantly put me in charge of changing the cartridges in the regenerative devices, paying no attention to Pasha's protests. Pasha was immobilized during the procedure and I should say, it was quite the sight. Even the time we had to call an ambulance for Beast, his crumpled face bore no resemblance to the sorry condition of the mutilated body. To be perfectly honest, at one point I felt nauseous from the sight and the smell and had to make an effort to control myself.

Aside from the nauseating sight of the mutilated flesh, servicing the regenerative devices was simple enough. Having made sure that I knew how to swap the cartridges and deposit the used ones into a special container, the doctor made some note on his tablet and left, leaving us alone.

"Sorry," panted Pasha, struggling to get up from his bed. "I didn't want you to see that..."

"Come on now. Found yourself a muslin lady,"

My voice was so unnaturally glib that I didn't believe myself too much. "Shall we enter Barliona? I wanted to read the local legends. Maybe I'll find something for my new song."

Pasha nodded gloomily and we went to our rooms where the capsules had been installed.

CHAPTER TWENTY-ONE

NOTHING HAD CHANGED IN BARLIONA: The training ground which had become our prison stood empty as before. This time around I decided to forgo any further torments in the obstacle course.

"I'd rather read some books and gather some material than jump around that devil's playground."

"Well I'm going to stretch and warm up," said Chip and hurried to the obstacle course almost skipping from joy. No wonder that, considering the trouble he had moving out in meatspace.

The book I picked up was full of tedious prose, so I didn't last too long.

"Come on and take a break. Let's explore the training ground!"

Chip responded enthusiastically to my offer and we spent the next several hours exploring. Contrary to our hopes, we found neither a secret passage nor any secret areas in our new location. Maybe we had to be rogues to do so or have the relevant skills—or maybe they simply didn't exist. But at least we discovered a spring, some patches of plants and four more ore lodes. Chip tried out the forge and the carpenter's workbench and I tried my mettle at mining one more time.

"What...sadist...came...up...with...this...profess ion?" I wondered amid swings of my pickaxe. "And...what...kind...of...masochists...choose...it?"

"Oh come off it!" Chip guffawed and moving me aside, let the lode have it with the pickaxe. With his strength, the lode yielded its fruits much faster. "Just imagine yourself as a character in a Jack London novel—a prospector during the gold rush. We're just like Smoke and Junior, don't you think?"

"I'm feeling more and more like a convict, to be honest," I shared my impression and took a swig from a bottle of water. My depleted Stamina instantly surged back to its maximum level. "I'm better off providing you with musical accompaniment."

The soundtrack made his work go faster, though it wasn't really my talent so much as a new spell that did the trick:

You have unlocked a new ability: 'Support.'

Your performance supports your companions, increasing the speed at which they harvest resources by (Fame + 0.5)%, but no more than (30 + Composition)%. Chance of finding a rare ingredient increased by (Composition)%. You may simultaneously target (Charisma) targets with

Support. The effect duration is equal to the duration of the performance. Cost of performance: None. Range: Variable. The target must be able to hear your performance.

For the sake of curiosity, I riffled through my book of skills and discovered that Composition influenced a variety of spells I had.

Because you have unlocked the Composition stat, the Magic Missile spell has been altered and changed to the Magic Missiles spell.

Magic Missiles: Using performance, you cast a barrage of magic missiles at your enemy: Each missile has its own type of damage that is different from the preceding one.

Quantity of missiles available: (Composition +1) missiles.

The damage done depends on your Intellect stat. Time to cast: (Composition + 3) seconds. The first missile is cast three seconds after the performance begins. Subsequent missiles are cast every second thereafter. Cost: (Character Level × 4) + Composition MP. Damage: (Intellect × 3). Range: Fame + 20 meters.

Because you have the Charisma stat and Song of Healing, this spell has been altered.

Song of Healing: Your Performance heals the chosen target as long as your Performance lasts. You may target (Charisma) targets. HP healed depends on your Intellect stat. This spell is channeled. Cost: (Character Level × 2) MP per second. Healing rate: (Intellect × 2) HP per second.

Song of Weakness: -(1 + Charisma + Fame)% to all enemies that hear your performance, not to exceed (Composition + 50)%. Effect duration: (Intellect × 5) seconds. Casting time: 4 seconds. Cost of performance: (Character Level × 10) MP. Range: 30 meters.

Song of Courage: Your performance increases the physical and magical damage of all party members by (1 + Charisma + Fame)%, not to exceed (100 + Composition)%. Effect duration: (1 + Charisma + Fame) hours, not to exceed (48 + Composition) hours. Casting time: One minute. Cost of performance: (Character Level × 7) MP. Range: (20 + Charisma meters).

Inspiration: Your performance inspires your audience, increasing the chance of crafting a more valuable item by (0.2 × Fame)%, not to exceed (30 + Composition)%. You may simultaneously target (Charisma) targets with Inspiration. The effect duration is equal to the duration of the performance. Cost of performance: None. Range: Variable. The target must be able to hear your performance.

The rest of the spells remained the same, but

even this was enough. It looked like, when it came to Barliona, Composition really expanded my horizons as it were. It seemed to affect the status effects inflicted by my spells, as well as crafting coefficients. I was very happy to discover that I now had more missiles available to me and I quickly tried out the spell on a nearby target.

"Check it out, I'm like a machine gun. I can shoot full-auto," I told Chip, selected a training dummy and played a classic Hendrix lick:

Machine gun
Tearing my body all apart
Machine gun
Tearing my body all apart...

Three seconds later, instead of a rainbow arrow, my lute emitted a bolt of lightning and then a fireball. Seeing the fire, Chip jerked noticeably. Damn...Using fire magic around him might not be the best idea. I should check whether I can control the missiles' elementals...

"That's more like burst," the pirc replied, smiling nervously.

"I'm still working on it," I muttered, riffling through the various game guides.

I found nothing intelligible and was forced to leave full-immersion and start combing the fora. I posed my search query one way and another, but could find nothing substantial among the faqs, guides and ads. All I could glean from a heated exchange that at times devolved to outright flaming, was that the sequence of elementals cast by the improved magic missile spell was random and could not be controlled by the bards. The most curious thing was that the discussion utterly ignored questions by other players about how they could acquire this strengthened spell. It seemed that no one wanted to share any in-game secrets. Everyone wanted to be special and secretive.

Chip took another crack at the obstacle course. With every attempt he looked more and more like some dirty, furry hedgehog. His very appearance inspired me to do something as far removed from physical activity as possible, so I returned to my exploration of my updated arsenal. A little experimentation verified the fora's information. Each magic missile had a different, random type of damage and the sequence had no determined order whatsoever. In addition to the basic elementals, I also noticed the bursts of dark energy that the necromancers would cast, as well as the priestly glow of holiness, the druidic green shimmering and even another type of magic I had never seen before. According to the detailed combat logs, the magic missiles did shadow, holy, elemental, chaos and even blood magic damage. The last was probably wielded by some particularly evil sub-classes of necromancers or NPCs such as vampires.

The next puzzle turned out to be how to combine the effects of several songs into one. Simply playing and activating two spells at once didn't work. Activating them one after the other didn't do anything either. And, to be honest, at this point my imagination was at a loss. The option of composing a new song every time to combine effects was unrealistic—there were too many possible permutations and doing this would be too complicated. There had to be something simpler, something fairly obvious...

The most obvious solution was to ask Coleus about it, but for several reasons my instructor was unavailable and I was forced to leave full immersion, call up Reed and Charsky and ask them to ask their instructors about it. They promised to do so, and I calmly tossed this issue out of my mind.

In general, our imprisonment was going by with tangible effect: Under the pirc's careful and at times outright sadistic guidance, I managed to increase my Constitution by 4 points, my Agility by an entire 10 and my Strength by another 3. Members of other races might scoff at such paltry progress, but to me, the increase seemed epic. At least I didn't have any complaints about my Intellect. Even though with every new point this stat grew slower and slower, the grinding process was incredibly simple: Simply spend all your mana again and again and enjoy watching your Intellect counter tick up.

Chip was in the exact opposite situation: His Strength, Constitution and Agility grew with barely any effort, while his Intellect hardly budged at all. The upside was that Pasha had been sent to the training ground still in his druid class, which allowed him to grind this stat in the same way as I did—the problem was that he hardly had any mana. He literally had enough for two spells, and given the glacial pace at which his mana regenerated, he could barely earn one point a day.

"Listen, why are you even bothering with Intellect?" I asked at one point.

"Everything can come in handy," Chip replied enigmatically, casting another healing spell on himself and going back to his mining.

He had also fashioned some of the ore we'd gotten into, well...I have no idea what the things were called, but now my shoes were protected by iron pieces on their soles, toes and heels. In addition to feeling like a horseshod mare, walking and running now cost me twice as much Stamina.

"At least it'll protect you from the thorns," Chip explained, trying to justify the new difficulty I had walking. There was nowhere to buy new shoes and neither of us knew how to craft them from scratch, so all I could do was hope that these little tanks would encounter no problem in the blighted part of the forest.

Back in reality, life settled into a well-worn

groove as well. In the mornings I would change Pasha's cartridges (the doctor was happy to charge me with this task, leaving only monitoring to himself), after that we ate breakfast, then, if the elevator worked, Chip would get in his wheelchair and I would wheel him out for a stroll. Sometimes Alex would join us, turning our stroll into traveling show—he hadn't a mote of seriousness about him. I couldn't even believe that this comedian actually served in the rangers and two decades at that. Although, maybe, he would simply infiltrate the enemy camp in the guise of a clown? This was the most believable theory in my opinion.

After the stroll, as a rule, we would have a cup of tea at Chip's place and then climb into our capsules. Or, rather, Chip and I would climb into our capsules, while Sasha (if he was around) would head off on his business. As I understood it, one of his and Chip's friends was about to get married and Sasha was helping arrange the event. I hoped that the young people knew what they were doing—if I were them, I wouldn't trust this goofball with his dark humor to arrange my dishes, let alone my wedding. He was the kind who would plant some surprise 'just for shits and giggles.'

"So why did you drop the curtain on your last Othello?" Pasha asked an entirely expected question as we were drinking tea. We had just begun talking about various family matters.

"How come you think that I dumped him instead of him me?" I asked, surprised by such confidence.

"What? Am I wrong?" The two defenders of the fatherland exclaimed in unison.

I shrugged my shoulders, grabbed another cookie and bit off a sizable piece. It was my first time baking cookies on my own—under Pavel's close and strict supervision and without any autocooks whatsoever. They really did come out better than when the robots made them. Or did I simply imagine this?

"You know, I have difficulties saying one way or another myself. He went to the capital to do his postdoc and started going out with a classmate out there—which I heard about through the grapevine. I asked Simon whether it was true but he denied it. So I called the classmate. She was taken aback at first but then she reexamined her relationship with Simon and broke down in tears. It turned out that her boyfriend had left her that same day. He had been courting another girl for a long time and stringing her along as a backup. And here she suddenly realized that she was in the same exact situation but with the roles reversed. So we had a chat, commiserated and both decided to send him to the pasta devil. So, technically, I dumped him...but in actual fact..."

I spread my arms akimbo.

"What a cretin," Pasha concluded.

"Why'd you get a divorce?" I asked, returning the favor and watching Sasha assemble another 'Bunker Buster' sandwich.

"Ah," Pasha smiled unhappily. "I was away on assignment. The dame was at home where her parents were more than happy to chatter on about how poor of a choice she had made. I was pretty unpalatable to them—they had hoped for a prince on a herd of white horses. So they kept harping on how I'd eventually bite the dust in my line of work—and she'd be left a widow. And what the hell did she want with a glorified taxi driver anyway? So she left. I come home one day—and home's empty...Not an uncommon story, really."

"Buncha crap," Sasha grinned crookedly. "Everyone wants a general. But could you handle that kind of life? To see your husband once every three months and jump every time someone rings the doorbell?"

I sipped my tepid tea and considered it:

"Who the hell knows...You can praise swan-like fidelity as much as you like, but I personally have had it with long-distance relationships. Although, if my career works out the way I want it, I'll be touring for months at a time myself. And then there'll be all kinds of jealous scenes..."

"Well, it's a bit easier for you guys," Pasha didn't agree. "Just look up how many rockers tour with their entire families. Like Ozzy—his wife was beside him all the way."

"Sure," I nodded. "There's a metric million of guys who are ready to abandon their jobs and vocations and spend their lives touring with their wives. What the hell do I need a woodpecker like that for anyway?"

"That depends on the woodpecker in question," Sasha cast a predatory glance over the table looking for the next sacrifice to his gastronomic altar. "If he's got brains, he'll take over the business. He'll become your manager or whatever it is musicians have. Artists are by and large all the same anyway—they all want nothing short of empyrean heights. Oh and where have you been hiding, my lovely piece of cheese?"

"You're not going to burst and bespatter us with your viscera, are you?" Pasha asked cautiously.

"I can't hear you. Lean a little closer, dearie," the other rejoined, placing the cheese on the salami and crowning his construction with a slice of tomato.

"So you're suggesting I court our Toad?" I managed to ask before this Edible Tower of Pisa busted Sasha's bunker.

"Well..." he pretended to think. "It's a worthy idea: The guys's clearly a crafty fellow, brings his work home again and again, and as for his appearance—you wouldn't exactly put him on the podium. So what's the big deal, just give it a good thought." He giggled revoltingly and ducked the hand towel I launched at him.

"Also you should bear in mind that a kiss of love turns the toad into a handsome prince," Pasha added weightily and received a look of immolation in return.

"I don't hit persons of disability," I decided and raised my cup of tea. "A toast! To the life of the bachelorette!"

"*Dreimal hoch heil!*" Sasha saluted.

Three tea cups clinked triumphantly over the table as though placing a period to this discussion.

"So what? Did you manage to make a super ninja out of old Beast?" I brought up the topic everyone was curious about.

"Nah," Alex shook his head. "Soon as he laid eyes on the sapper's shovel he recalled that he's a musician and he has to watch his hands. Like that cat that couldn't do anything because he had paws. And when I showed him how a 'Vietnamese music box' works, he went green all over and went back to cooking. After all, Barliona isn't real life—in there, everything is soft and polished."

"Have you lost the plot?" Pasha roared. "What the hell are you showing off your stupid toys for, you idiot?"

"He wanted to know how it worked," Sasha replied calmly, but his eyes turned to ice for a second, "so I showed him. He didn't take a liking to it, it happens.

And the ranger turned back to his sandwich.

"You psycho," sighed Pasha but let the matter drop.

I didn't risk getting involved in this exchange. Something told me that in the best case scenario, I would encounter only apish mockery interwoven with the same weighty stare that was starting to make me feel like I was an extra in this company. At times, there was something in these people beyond my comprehension. And it wasn't a matter of my dullness so much as too great of a difference in the worlds we had seen.

In the end, I used my first opportunity to say goodbye to the ranger and dived into my capsule, leaving the friends to their own devices.

CHAPTER TWENTY-TWO

THE GAME GREETED ME with unexpected changes: The inapproachable stockade around the training compound had turned black, deformed and gaps appeared in the even weave of its branches. Gaps large enough to admit two waltzing elephants. Through the hole closest to me, I could make out the already familiar, terrifying landscape of blight, seeping with a viscous dark fog and slowly spreading and consuming more and more of the forest and the training ground.

"Would you look at that..." I muttered to myself.

It's well-known that when an exit magically appears in a location that has no exit or entrance, it's not just for nothing. Had the quest's critical moment arrived or had one of the players launched some scenario? Who knows? But I had to make up my mind about what to do. Should I head over there and see what's going on? But then, technically, I'm leaving my place of imprisonment on my own and might really get it in the neck. Should I stay here and wait for the

Seventh or one of his apprentices? But then I'll miss out if there's something interesting going on there. If you ask me, it's better to get it in the neck than spend the rest of my life wondering what could have been.

Having arrived at this uncomplicated decision, I bravely set forth for the implacably-growing spot of heightened thorniness.

You have stepped onto a blighted part of the forest. -50% to all stats. +50% to strength of all blighted creatures. -1% to max HP for every minute you spend on blighted ground.

The shoes that the pirc had reinforced for me, no longer deteriorated as I walked and I confidently crushed the thorns under my iron-shod boots. And I couldn't care less that they weren't actually boots: It sounds better and you can't tell a good story without telling a pretty lie.

The clods of dark fog floated exotically from place to place which, in the general perspective, looked incredibly sinister. As luck would have it, this time I was spared the blighted bunnies. In exchange, I was blessed with a different crew. Having walked about a hundred meters, I came upon a strange biota whose left hand seeped that very same terrifying fog. On top of this, this distant cousin of mine looked quite unique: His body was covered with sharp thorns, giving him the appearance of a porcupine, and his eyes glowed with a strange green light. At least the name of this NPC was perfectly familiar to me: It was none other than the missing Vex in person. Bending one knee, he plunged his left hand into a small crevice in the ground and when he straightened out, his fingers no longer seeped the odd fog. It was now seeping from the ground.

You have discovered that the source of the mysterious blight afflicting the forest are the renegade biota. Report your finding to Eben.

You have located the missing Vex. Report your finding to Tauvolga.

So that's it? It's that simple? I came, I saw, I reported? I suppose Eben will forgive my prior transgression in exchange for this information. Hell, he might even send me on another quest chain. It's not bad in theory, but...It's boring! Where's the catch?

"Hey Vex!" I hailed the local renegade.

The biota turned his head lazily in my direction, as if sensing no threat to himself. He examined me and frowned, evidently not recognizing me.

"Who are you, what are you doing and how do you know me?" he asked demandingly, lazily twirling a dagger that had appeared from nowhere in his hand.

"It just so happened that wherever I went, fate kept leading me toward you. First of all, I came upon an encrypted songbook of Cypro's and I've been looking for you in order to ask why it's damaged. Second of all, I met your friend, Tauvolga. She's worried about you and asked me to find you."

As soon as he heard the name of his friend, Vex relaxed noticeably and the dagger ceased moving in his hand.

"How is she?" my thorny acquaintance wondered unexpectedly.

"She misses you," I replied curtly. "I imagine she would be happy to see you."

"That's not possible," Vex replied quietly. "At the moment, it's not possible..."

"You better be on your way, radish-head," barked the pirc, struggling through the stockade's remnants.

Weird. I thought that Sasha was going to hang out for another few hours. What prompted Chip to get in his capsule?

"And keep your rakes where I can see them or you'll be sorry that you left Granny Lemon's Cabbage Patch," the pirc warned, eloquently brandishing his trusty halberd. A change of class is a change of class, but he had taken a liking to this weapon.

The events that followed took up several seconds: Vex darted at Chip, whipping out a second dagger in mid-stride. The pirc took a better hold of his halberd, while I grabbed my lute and cast magic missiles. The renegade had only several steps left before he'd lock with Chip, but by this point my spell was ready. Two magic missiles cut Chip's HP in half and Vex took off the rest of the health with one blow. The pirc's silhouette dissolved in the fog leaving behind some orphaned coins—half of what Chip carried with him for daily expenditures. I'd give them back to him later.

"As I understood it, that's a friend of yours," the renegade squinted menacingly. He looked like he had decided to send all unwanted guests to the Gray Lands and be done with it.

"He was," I explained quickly. "As you can see, we don't see eye to eye anymore."

Vex clearly didn't like my response very much. The renegade smirked and began to slowly walk in my direction.

"Real good friend you are if you're prepared to kill your friend over a disagreement."

I wouldn't rustle about friends, blighter of the forest! Take a look at yourself first!

"My friend is a free citizen. He'll return from the Gray Lands and we'll resolve our disagreement. If he had killed you, I wouldn't be able to talk to you."

"We have something to talk about?" Vex asked with surprise, continuing his unhurried, calm and therefore quite scary approach.

"Yes. As I already told you, fate has brought us

together. I emerged from the bud very recently. In my Twilight Dream, I saw the Sixth, the Schism and Geranika."

Strictly speaking, I lied a bit here—I had only heard of Geranika, but this was enough for Vex anyway. He stopped and peered into my face.

"And what do you think about all this?" The question was clearly an important one for this strange biota.

"I think you're right. All of you—including the Sixth and the Second. We must accept Geranika's assistance and once and for all smash the other races' will to interfere in our lives. I wanted to tell the others the same, but I only managed to tell about the Schism to my friend, whom you just saw. He had his doubts and while we were arguing, Eben somehow found out and imprisoned us here, further from the Tree. If it weren't for you, we'd still be penned in there, locked in until the alliance was announced. It is dishonorable to make an important decision without considering the will of the people, all the biota and all the pircs!"

You have increased your Charisma. Total: 4.
You have received another training point. Unallocated training points: 4.

Attention! A new stat has become available to your character: Deceit. The true art of deceit is

available only to those whose charm and eloquence are capable of assuaging others. Deceit affects your chance of misleading NPCs, to the point that you can receive rewards for uncompleted or failed quests. Deceit allows you to display false stats to those around you, as well as use a false name temporarily.

Do you accept? Attention! You will not be able to remove an accepted stat!

The temptation to accept the stat and thereby increase my chances of befuddling Vex was very great, but I swiped the notification away. At the moment, I was more curious about the change that had taken place on the renegade biota's face.

"And so what do you want, Lorelei?" asked Vex after a long pause.

"I want to join the Sixth and help her make our people secure for centuries to come," I lied without blushing.

"Big words. But are you prepared to prove them with deeds?"

"Try me and you will find out."

"For the sake of our people, we voluntarily accept Shadow, allowing it to alter us," Vex held up his thorny arm. "Are you ready to sacrifice yourself and your nature for others? Are you ready for everyone to turn their backs on you, including the Guardian of our forest and even Sylvyn himself?"

Quest available: *Shoots of Shadow.*
**Description: In pursuit of the power that could
forever protect the biota and the pircs from the
aggression of other races, the renegades have
accepted Shadow and changed their essences.
Demonstrate your readiness to follow the way of
the renegades by accepting a particle of Shadow
and changing your own essence. Quest type:
Scenario. Reward: Friendship status with the
Renegades of the Hidden Forest, Suspicion status
with Shadow creatures, Hatred status with all
other factions of the Hidden Forest, the Empire of
Malabar and the Dark Empire of Kartoss. Race
change to Blighted Biota. Penalty for declining the
quest: Hatred status with the Renegades of the
Hidden Forest.**

**Attention! You may change your race in this
scenario. If you undergo the change, your pain
filters will be temporarily disabled.**

On top of it all, a supplemental agreement
popped up, according to which I absolved the
corporation of any liability for my physical and
psychological state in the course of this scenario. I
should mention that I was a little terrified. It's one
thing to change one's race to FSM-knows-what and
crash my rep with both empires. It's something else
entirely when the corp also forces me to sign a

document which amounts to 'we wash our hands of the consequences.' On the other hand, they covered themselves exactly the same way when I did my sensory filter adjustment. No doubt, this was simply another requirement of their legal department. Why would they start torturing and killing their users over nothing? Or would they...?

I didn't spend a long time thinking about it. After all is said and done, we only live once and it's worth trying everything. Declining the dubious Deceit stat (I don't like to lie and something told me that in this scenario I could end up acquiring a more interesting stat), I pushed the scenario's Accept button.

"I'm ready!"

Was it me or did a shadow of surprise slip across Vex's face?

"This is a serious step, but if you are resolute, follow me."

The way was quite long and not very direct. I don't know what the matter is, but Vex outright refused to stray from the blighted ground, so we meandered and snaked along a winding path of fog and thorns. Very large thorns. A veritable labyrinth of thorny bushes. As soon as we entered further into the blighted areas, I lost my sense of direction entirely. The endless turns gave me the impression that we were going in circles. Maybe that's the way it was. For the life of me, I wouldn't be able to recreate our path on a map.

The lengthy walk was less than average when it came to enjoyment. It didn't matter much to Vex, he just trudged along his way. However, I had to heal up again and again to account for my falling HP. It's a good thing that my shoes held fast because otherwise there'd be nothing but my ears left by the time we made it. Thinking about the shoes made me think about their cobbler. I wonder whether Pasha was annoyed by my attack or whether Sasha and he were currently laughing their heads off, discussing the latest turn of events. The latter was more likely— otherwise, I'd be seeing a notification about an imminent disconnect from my capsule. I'll complete the quest, climb out and explain myself.

When Vex and I were approaching the boundaries of the blighted ground, I kept noticing strange creatures that resembled living trees on the other side. They looked more like gorillas that moved on very long legs than Tolkien's ents. Large, no shorter than six meters tall, they followed along the boundary of the blight with a fairly aggressive posture until we disappeared from view, plunging into the thorny labyrinth.

"What are those?" I broke our silence for the first time.

"The sentries of the Forest," Vex replied with a little surprise. "It's odd you didn't see them in your dreams. The First may summon them in times of trouble to guard the borders or—as now—to eliminate a threat to the forest."

"Are we the threat?"

"At the moment, it's just me. The sentries sense Shadow but cannot do anything as long as I remain on blighted ground. Shadow interferes with their link with Sylvyn and, separated from his will, the sentries turn back into trees. So they're patrolling the borders, watching, looking out."

He smiled wistfully. This seemed like a painful topic for him. His entire bunch made for strange sorts of villains. They didn't draw much dislike from me. I felt sympathy and curiosity but no negative feelings. A big thanks to the devs for avoiding cardboard cut-out idiots who spilled their plans the first chance they got and periodically burst into bombastic laughter. The formula of 'kill the bad guy and ride your white horse into the sunset' had put more than a few generations of players to bored sleep.

"Why did you join the Sixth?" I asked Vex, trudging morosely beside me.

"Like you, I beheld many things I would prefer to forget in my dreams. I saw battles, I saw the foreigners who brought war to our forest. It is time we end this."

"How?"

"You shall see," Vex replied enigmatically and fell silent again.

I realized that we were getting close to the

renegades' camp on my own: We began encountering blighted biota and pircs more and more frequently. And I should mention that the latter were quite the sight: The same dark fog coiled around their fur, their eyes glowed with the same green flame, and their fangs and claws had grown several-fold. The renegades regarded me with suspicion but without any particular enmity.

Blighted wolves, lynxes, bears, hawks, foxes and hares—as well as creatures that didn't exist irl— lurked all around us. Some of the members of this menagerie began to show glimmers of appetite regarding my person, but as soon as Vex recited some verses, the same dark fog would appear beside me, I would receive the 'Shadow Protection' buff and the beasts' aggression would evaporate. It was like they had ceased noticing me entirely.

I should say that being able to cast a spell with nothing but a recitation was more impressive to me than the ensuing spell. It's such an obvious form of performance and I'd never even thought about it before! At least now it's clear how this guy manages to wield two daggers and at the same time use his bardic powers. You don't need free hands for recitation at all.

"We need to see Astilba," Vex interrupted my reveries of poetic evenings.

He was addressing a very imposing-looking pirc who guarded a passage into a dense hillock of brambles. The pirc didn't bother with politesse and simply stepped aside, letting us enter. Either Vex was in good standing or the pirc was here to guard against external threats rather than bureaucratic ones. Through the bramble patch we came upon a familiar vista: A blighted meadow, turfed with thorny grass, shreds of fog drifting among it, and gnarled trees that looked more like bushes. One of them, the largest one, served as Astilba's throne. The Sixth in person sat in a niche formed among the trees' branches. Just like everyone else, Astilba had transformed: Her torso had darkened and become covered with thorns. The same thorns lengthened her fingers, crowning them with nails that were so long that I unwittingly assumed they were extra phalanges.

"Greetings, oh Sixth," Vex bowed his head in a simple, respectful bow.

"Vex," Astilba nodded in response.

Her face was cold and majestic at the same time and her eyes glowed with an even green flame. Beholding such majestic repose, I couldn't help but repeat Vex's gesture, bowing my head before the Sixth. I had never seen someone like this in real life: Our epoch of democracy and avowed equality had practically eliminated majesty, substituting it with haughtiness, arrogance and self-indulgence. It was left to the games to recreate true majesty, the kind incident only to hereditary rulers and creatures ancient and mighty.

"I imagine there is a reason you have brought

me one of our sisters, Vex," Astilba said with regal calm.

"Yes, oh Sixth," Vex met her eyes, but in a manner that was more of an unspoken addition to the conversation than an expression of opposition. "This is Lorelei. She saw you, the Schism and Geranika in her Twilight Dreams. She wishes to join our struggle and is prepared to pay the price to do so."

"Is this so, my dear?" Astilba's eyes alighted on me. I don't know how the devs managed this effect, but I felt goosebumps pop up all over me. There was no menace in the Sixth's look—only a silent question adulterated with inexpressible bitterness. And beyond that festering wound, I sensed a vacuum and something terrible striving to fill it.

Once again the sequence from the Twilight Dream flashed before my eyes. I could see through the Sixth's eyes. A series of failed rituals, the summoning of the mightiest demons, the search for ancient manuscripts with long-forgotten spells...All in vain. The dead have no place in the world of the living. All she managed to achieve was to keep the soulless vessel from rotting. The thirst for vengeance filled the abyss in her soul day after inexorable day and was strengthened by her determination to spare her kind the same fate. I saw Geranika, presenting her with a source of immense power that could forever protect the Hidden Forest from dangerous incursions. I sensed Shadow, softly creeping to fill the hollow in her heart.

Attention! Through Bardic Lore you have recovered lost information about the Sixth.

"Y-yes," I managed. The vision refused to relinquish their grip on my mind.

Damn. I'm going to end up with a dour diagnosis from a shrink when all of this is over.

"Do you understand that both races of both empires will turn their backs on you? You shall become their eternal foe," Astilba's voice rang like an alarm bell in my head.

"I understand."

"Do you understand that Sylvyn shall turn his back on you as soon as you adopt Shadow? Are you prepared to be separated from the Forest Father?"

"I have seen much through your eyes in my dreams, oh Sixth. I am prepared to pay this price."

For an instant, bitterness and...compassion?...flashed across Astilba's face.

"I am sorry," she said quietly looking me in the eyes. And in the next instant, the Sixth's face took on an aloof expression and her voice grew in volume. "Geranika! Heed my summons!"

Tongues of fog twirled upward spinning in a whirlwind, and several moments later, a tall dark-haired man with a jovial face and smug smile appeared in its midst.

"Oh, am I to understand that one of the free has decided to join our ranks?" he asked in a business-like tone.

Unlike the Sixth, Geranika reminded me of someone from my own time: He was quick, to the point, full of self-indulgence and overflowing energy.

"Grant her the strength, Geranika," Astilba asked, calmly and evenly.

"Are you prepared to accept Shadow into yourself, Lorelei?" Geranika asked in the voice of a kindly wizard and with the smile of a serial killer. In his clenched hand I noticed a tiny fragment oozing the same old dark fog.

Attention! If you agree, your pain filters will be deactivated and your race will be changed to 'Blighted Biota.' Your reputation with the Empire of Malabar, the Dark Empire of Kartoss, the Biota and the Pircs shall be changed to Hatred status.

A chill coursed down my spine, but its cause wasn't so much the in-game penalties as Geranika's stare. There was some kind of malicious anticipation in it.

"I am ready," I managed all the same.

In the next instant, a dagger appeared in Geranika's right hand and with one swoop he cleft my breast-cage open. I don't know how this might feel in real life, but here, a hellish pain pierced me.

I screamed as loudly as I could, my legs wavered, but Geranika had grabbed my shoulder with an iron grip (the dagger vanishing, mysteriously, from his hand) and made sure I remained standing. I have no idea whether biota have bones but something inside of me cracked perceptibly.

Geranika paid it no attention. He stuck the tiny fragment into my cleft torso and unclenched his grip. I collapsed to the grass, ignoring the sharp thorns that pierced my body.

These scratches were nothing in comparison to the pain that had pierced my essence. Hundreds of thorns tore their way from within me, rending my body and piercing my skin.

It seemed like my agony lasted many hours and when the pain at last abated, the in-game clock suggested that only a minute had gone by. But I didn't care. A euphoria enveloped me. What's the old expression? To do someone good, you first have to hurt them and then return them to their prior condition. The pain departed and I felt happy.

Quest completed: *Shoots of Shadow*.

Your reputation with the Renegades of the Dark Forest has grown.
Current status: Friendly.
Your race has changed. Current race: Blighted Biota.

You acquired a passive ability — Sharp Thorns: Counter any close-range attack with 5% damage.

You acquired a passive ability — Ironwood: +(Character Level × 2)Armor. Thorns, brambles and needles and similar, pointy objects cannot pierce your epidermis.

New ability acquired — Shadow Film: Target area is covered with a film of impenetrable Shadow in which only creatures who are aligned with Shadow can see.

New ability acquired — Shadow Protection: The fog of Shadow envelops the target, keeping other Shadow creatures from attacking it.

Achievement unlocked: 'Shadow Spellcaster Level 1.' +1% to Shadow spells. Learn 19 Shadow spells to reach the next level. This achievement is available only to players with Shadow alignment.

Your reputation with the Malabar Empire has decreased.
Current status: Hatred.

Your reputation with the Dark Empire of Kartoss has decreased.

Current status: Hatred.

Your reputation with the Pircs had decreased.
Current status: Hatred.

Your reputation with the Biota has decreased.
Current status: Hatred.

Due to the current scenario, you may record video in this location.

"Now you are a part of Shadow, Lorelei," Geranika announced with a satisfied smile. It was the last thing I saw as I exited the game.

CHAPTER TWENTY-THREE

I SPENT SEVERAL MINUTES in my capsule, stilling my thumping heart. What kind of monster made the race change mechanic so painful? What idiot even had the idea of forcing others to suffer such torment? Maybe convicts had earned what was coming to them, but normal players? What for?

I could hear a hushed conversation in the neighboring room. Pasha...I need to get out, eat dinner and explain myself. And also I have band practice coming up...Unlike normally, the thought of this did not improve my mood. I clambered out of my capsule with a little difficulty, my trembling hands located my clothes, I managed to get dressed somehow and opened the door.

I was met with friendly laughter: Pasha and Sasha were slamming tea in the kitchen, exchanging jokes. Seeing me, Pasha greeted me with his paw:

"Why hello there, oh Brutus! Would you like some tea?"

"Uh-huh, and let's have it—who were the other senators that were in on the plot," Sasha joined him, getting a cup for me from the cupboard.

"Why are you so pale?" Pasha asked, noticing my condition.

Hearing this, Sasha squinted, examining me and then, with a care I had never seen from him before, helped me to a seat.

"Hey...What's with you?" he asked without a trace of his former mirth.

"I overplayed it..."

Judging by their faces, my explanation didn't make anything clearer. The half-full mug of tea, shamelessly appropriated from Sasha, returned me to life and I briefly summarized my last hour in Barliona.

"What are you, Mata Hari?" Having made sure that I was okay, Sasha returned to his earlier sarcastic disposition. "You have nothing better to do, or what? At least set your filters so that when it hurts, it hurts less, you salad-head. Or are you one of those who like the sting of the whip on their bottoms?" He squinted suspiciously.

"Really, Kiera, you need to be more careful," Pasha echoed him.

"How's it my fault?" I objected. "My pain filters are at 90%. Ordinary death hurts as much as sparrow's sneeze. In this case, it's the devs who cooked up this torture—may heartburn keep them awake all night. First they warned me that in this scenario the filters might be disabled and then they forced me to sign a release that it's my fault if I get hurt, and finally, well, I got it with a whip to my bottom. I never imagined that these damn marquises de Sade would arrange that execution. It's supposed to be a family-friendly game after all: humanism, socialization, all that."

"Sure, it's super-duper friendly," Sasha grinned maliciously. "It just oozes friendliness from all its nooks and crannies. The same friendly guys who own it were betting on whether I'd make it when they sent me behind enemy lines."

"The game's friendly enough, it's the humans who are jerks," I quoted Straus.

"Check out this philosopher," Pasha scoffed. "Why don't you tell me this: What are you planning on doing next?"

The question was an interesting one. Very much so.

"First I'm going to find out what I can about the renegades, Geranika and everything related. This is pretty incredible material, after all! I can already see the album title: *The Lord of Shadow*. Doesn't it have a nice ring to it?"

"Uh-huh," my companion nodded. "Just like the nickname of the scariest baboon in the zoo. Ow!" The juice bottle lid bounced off Sasha's forehead. Pasha, who had thrown it, rubbed his chin and nodded:

"As a draft title, it'll do. Only, it's a bit banal, don't you think?"

"Outside of Barliona, it is," I agreed, "but among the fan base, it'll strike a chord! Who knows anything about Geranika? The latest update is obviously about him, so everyone wants to know something."

"Listen, you macabre minstrel, what's drawing you to the Dark Side anyway?" Pasha asked.

"Cookies, booze and babes," Sasha replied in my place. "So you may as well start calling her Darth Lori, my young Padawan!"

I did my best imitation of Vader's hiss, but it didn't come out too convincing.

"I'm curious," I replied seriously. "I have a pretty good idea of what a young Jedi Knight would find there: We will struggle against evil, overcome it in honest battle and receive a medals for our efforts."

These last words prompted uproarious laughter from the soldiers and I continued my thought:

"And when it comes to the villains, things aren't so simple. This Vex fellow isn't some Hannibal Lector, and Astilba ain't Sauron. I'm not so sure about Geranika though. This isn't looking like your run-of-the-mill battle between absolute good and abominable evil. The vibes here are a bit more tragic. The renegades are clearly convinced that they are doing the right thing. And their goal is to protect their people."

"Experience shows that this is seldom the full truth," Alex objected. "If the claim is that this game is as realistic as possible, then the villains are unlikely to be the idealists you make them out to be and are probably just looking out for their own hides."

"Same crap. I just want to see this story from the other side," I dismissed the generally-reasonable explanation.

"Well take a look, take a look," Sasha began munching a cookie, while Pasha took over the questions:

"And then? What are you going to do later when your reputation is in the dumps with everyone?"

"My rep is already in the dumps," I corrected. "I don't know. Maybe I'll become one of Geranika's palace minstrels? And why not? He seems like an ambitious fellow. Before you know it, he'll get his own empire—blackjack, hookers and all. And if not, I could always delete my character and start over. I'm not trying to be the top player in the game. I'm just looking for inspiration. Plus, there're always the Free Lands. I don't think that my rep with the empires matters at all out there. Though, what am I going to do out there at my newb level?"

"It's okay. I'll adopt you," Sasha consoled me and laughed.

"Uh-huh, to work as bait in your traps?" I asked suspiciously.

"Nah, I'll give you work as a DDD," the ranger shook his head. "As it happens, I have a vacancy I need filled."

"What's a DDD?" I asked, against my darkest suspicions. And the camouflaged bastard instantly replied, happily explaining the acronym:

"A disposable, demining device."

"Idiot," Pasha summarized with a sigh. "Can't you at least make up some new jokes?"

"A joke told twice is twice as funny!" Sasha brandished a finger with a smart look on his face.

"Strictly speaking, this joke is quite new to me," I remarked for fairness' sake. "And I'd never refuse such an enticing offer. Plus, in Barliona I'd hardly be disposable. By the way, Pasha, why did you get into the capsule to begin with? If you hadn't popped up, spewing threats, I wouldn't have had to kill you."

"I'll remember that," Pasha waved a fist jokingly. "But to answer your question, I got tired of sitting around and decided to go for a walk. I wanted to invite you along but when I entered the game, I came upon that evil cactus..."

"Isn't there like some button on the capsule...?" I recalled the instructions that the technicians had read us when they installed the device. "You push it and the player in the capsule receives a notification that someone wants to talk to them out in meatspace."

"Really?" Pasha asked surprised. "I had no idea."

"Band practice is in an hour and a half, so if the building elevator is working today, we can go for a walk," I took up the reasonable offer. It wouldn't hurt to get some fresh air.

"I'm with you guys," Sasha announced calmly. "We'll come back. Kiera will have her music date and then we can eat."

"Sounds good," I nodded. "And then I'll dive in one more time to see what they turned me into."

* * *

The summer stroll through Pyatigorsk was a sheer pleasure. The city roiled with green, the leaves languishing in the day's heat, and by afternoon, the weather made us wish we'd headed to the mountains of which there were no less than ten nearby, forgetting all about apartments, VR capsules and other miracles of technology.

"Listen, is it true that you have mineral water that comes bubbling up from the ground and you can drink it for free whenever you like?" I recalled a far-fetched legend.

"Yeah," replied Pasha, skirting in his wheelchair a puddle that a street-cleaning car had left. "But I'll tell you right away—it's an acquired taste. Each spring has its own taste, smell and mineral composition. Some of them are pretty good, but others stink like rotten eggs."

A flock of students passing us stared at him like he was an alien. Pasha blushed deeply and pushed the accelerator, forcing us to catch up to him.

"They got to me," he muttered, once Sasha and I were finally beside him again.

"Forget it," Sasha waved. "Civilians, what do you want? They probably don't even know that there's a war on in far-off Africa."

He had a point here: The media rarely reported on the insurgencies and other conflicts of the continent, preferring to broadcast news about celebrities' weddings and happenings in Barliona. Armed conflicts made the news only when people's attention had to be distracted from economic troubles or political scandals.

"Well," I tried to comfort my friend after the unpleasant encounter, "at least they're not taking selfies with you. When the guys and I dress up and go to concerts, every drunk mug tries to take a photo with us for posterity. And they always have to hug you and breathe booze breath all over you."

"You don't like sweaty guys and warm vodka? You should vacation in the winter," Sasha quipped. "Okay, so what were we talking about? That's right, the mineral water...If you ask me, most of them don't taste so great. But if you like, we can swing by a well-room and you can try it yourself."

"Swing by what?" I asked suspiciously. "It sounds like a place Edilberto goes after he's lost his mind on booze."

"Oh you dim northerners," Sasha scolded me.

"A well-room is something constructed over a mineral water source. Sometimes it's no more than a gazebo, other times a large facility—a tasting room where you can try different types of mineral water. As for Edilberto, well, that's his punishment for gluttony. He drinks so much that even I'm worried about him. Like last time—he simply slams one shot after the other like a seagull slams fish. You uh...well, you should tell him to slow down. After all, health isn't exactly made from composite armor."

"When'd you become such a straight-shooter?" Pasha even sounded little taken aback. "You haven't overheated a little, have you Sasha?"

"No brother," the other replied. "I was simply watching that moose down booze and I started thinking that I wouldn't like to see him become as decrepit and defunct by the age of 35 as I am."

I couldn't help but look at Sasha askance. He didn't look quite decrepit or defunct, but didn't seem in the best of health either. A guy like any other— you'd walk past without noticing him, unless you encountered his eyes.

"I'm not his momma. I told him once and he heard me. He can decide for himself. Although, I do have one evil idea..." I lowered my voice conspiratorially. "One time when he gets really drunk, I'll set up a scenario for him so that when he wakes up, he'll freak out and quit drinking for good."

"Go on, go on," the ranger replied with

curiosity.

"Come on, Kiera," Pasha prompted me, doing his best to ignore the stares of passersby.

"I'm still considering the details, but the general idea is as follows: I'm going to make a deal with the owner of a gay club, take Edilberto's drunkbody over there, take off his clothes, put a g-string on him and stuff it with cash. After that, the fellows there will advise me on where to go next. When he starts coming to, I'll slap him awake, yell at him a bit and start pleading with him to get out of there before his new friends come back to continue their little party. Something like that."

The response was another uproarious fit of laugher, which would have done justice to any stable. Sasha even squatted down right there on the sidewalk and began slapping his knees.

"Oh, Kiera..." he managed somehow. "Is this the effect we're having on you or were you always so cruel?"

"The plan occurred to me a while ago, but since I'm switching to the Dark Side, I guess it's time to put my evil machinations into motion."

"See?" Sasha said to Pasha proudly. "My young and talented student is already making progress! Onward, Darth Lori. A well-room awaits, full of pungent mineral water!"

Given that Sasha dressed up in imitation of Fievel from the eponymous cartoon, his appearance was quite...singular. For whatever reason, his red shit and yellow neckerchief didn't evoke a Sith Lord, and the ten-gallon hat didn't give him more gravitas.

Ironically or coincidentally (depending on which you prefer), the well-room turned out to be a venerable building of white stone, stone columns and tables outfitted with the strangest taps I'd ever seen. There were no sensors here, no motion sensors—a simple old-fashioned button which you pressed to get the water to come out. And the water looked just like the one from the tap in the kitchen, but its scent was quite different. Looking around, I saw a vending machine full of glasses—from disposable ones that cost a penny to oddly-shaped ones with spouts like the ancient teapots I'd seen in the movies.

"What's this mug with a trunk?" I asked surprised.

"That's for drinking mineral water, Kiera. You pour the water in the top and drink from the spout. The idea is that you can drink this way while lying on your back without spilling anything on yourself."

"All right you gourmands. Try everything out, enjoy yourselves," Sasha interrupted, scrunching his long (or 'aristocratic,' as he had characterized this facial misunderstanding) nose in disgust. "Meanwhile, I, as a person who is sick and tired of Narzan, will wait for you outside."

He produced a spintronic cigarette from his pocket—the descendant of the e-cigarettes invented at the beginning of the century for those who wanted to quit smoking—stuck it in his mouth and headed for the exit, having pushed his hat back onto the back of his head.

"What a fopling," Pasha muttered gently in his wake. "So what should we begin with?"

"Let's buy a mug that I can drink from lying down," I announced decisively and stuck my card into the machine.

Drinking from the newly-acquired vessel was fun and pretty convenient, once I got used to it. It was like a stationary straw. The mineral water, on the other hand, I had mixed feelings about. This well-room had three different types: Two taps poured water from hot springs and one from a cold spring. The hottest, which was about 40 degrees, was utterly revolting to both taste and smell. The warm one turned out to be pretty tolerable, and the cold one was almost like the kind you'd buy in the store, only a bit carbonated and entirely free.

"No way!" I shared my impressions. "A question—why aren't there lines of mineral-water-nerds here with cisterns on their shoulders?"

"Why who the hell needs this stuff?" Pasha asked, astounded. "After an hour and a half the springs are exhausted and you get ordinary smelly water, like from a puddle that's been filtered," he glanced up behind me and yelled: "Cut it out! Sasha! Kiera, stop him!"

'Him' was Alex who had begun a conversation with two representatives of the local street-life, bums who were wearing their customary T-shirts with holo-images of expensive cars, bright gym pants and high-tops festooned with several expensive brand labels at once.

I did not understand who had to be stopped and why: The conversation seemed peaceful enough and had clearly not transitioned from 'Hey, buy us a beer,' to a more critical phase. It'd be nice to call local law enforcement so that they could get here before this critical phase began, but why Pasha was demanding that I stop his friend remained a mystery...which was solved less than a second later when Sasha took off his hat and then...I didn't see the blow. The bum was simply standing there and suddenly he threw up his arms and flopped down on his ass. His companion turned out to be a bit more intelligent—as soon as Sasha dropped his friend, the other bum turned and ran, yelling, "I'll find you, you fuck!"

"You already found me!" Sasha yelled in reply. "Come back and pick up this trash you left here!"

Oddly this generous offer received no response. Hearing it, the bum hunched his shoulders around his head and pumped his feet with redoubled effort. Sasha whistled in his wake but didn't continue the chase, preferring to return to us. Seeing this, the 'casualty' stopped shaking his head, got to his feet and stole away limping.

"Does this happen frequently with him?" I asked Pasha. I had seen my share of fights but I'd never seen one end so quickly.

"He's a pain in the neck!" Pasha fumed, guiding his chair to the exit. "Not a day goes by without some adventure...What the hell is wrong with you, Sasha?"

Sasha looked down guiltily and admitted unwillingly:

"I wigged out. They say, let them have it in the teeth so hard that their heads start to smoke. Well, so I let them have it..."

Pasha drilled his friend with his stare and then waved his hand:

"It's easier to put you down than retrain you. When are you going to stop swinging your fists around? You could have simply explained things to them..."

"They wouldn't understand. They're bums," sighed Sasha. "Kiera, you uh, well, forgive me."

"I've been friends with Beast since childhood," I shrugged. "I'm used to it. Only difference is, it typically starts with, 'Hey, Kiera, hold my axe.'"

Judging by Sasha's face, this wasn't much consolation.

"It's always this way with him," Pasha explained. "First his reflexes kick in and later his brains. All right, you C-list last action hero, what's for dinner?"

"I have baked a fish," reported Sasha. "In aluminum foil. Oh Kiera, I forgot to ask, do you eat fish?"

"I'll try it and find out. Let's head home. All this mineral water has got me starving like a beast."

As it turned out, there was no band practice as such. As soon as the guys heard about my joining the side of Shadow, they placed the instruments to the side and began to discuss the news.

"Get out!" Straus said for the millionth time. "This is the hot thing! After that video Anastaria uploaded, everyone wants to know about Geranika and what he's up to."

"What video?" Charsky and I asked in unison.

"Are you two not aware of the latest and greatest?" Straus stared at us, clearly struck by the depths of our ignorance.

"No, why?" Hal said what everyone was thinking.

"To understand what's going on in the world, you newbs!" Straus replied admonishingly, reaching for his tablet. "Hang on, I'll show you. It's all about joining the Dark Side."

We stared at the keyboardist with interest as he looked up the video.

"Here. The video was edited together from footage recorded in different capsules: Anastaria's, Plinto's and some other players'."

The video really was pretty interesting.

Extremely so, actually. A certain player named Mahan, who played as a shaman, agreed to become Geranika's student, wiped out a metric mob of players in a scenario, underwent a series of trials, earned a new spell for the entire class and at the last moment, rejected his apprenticeship and impaled Geranika on a unicorn's horn. As a result of these epic events, shamans, warriors, rogues, paladins and druids from all over the continent unlocked new abilities that would help them fight the creatures of Shadow.

"Damn, that's cool," Beast summed up everyone's opinion after the video had ended. "So Kiera was supposed to figure a way out and unlock new spells for the bards, and instead she just ended up a renegade?"

"Looks like it," Straus tossed his tablet on the ancient sofa and pensively played the familiar chords from the Doors' classic on his keyboard. "This is the end, beautiful friend. This is the end, my only friend, the end..."

"Screw all that," I waved them away. "At least now I have access to the renegades and perhaps even Geranika. I can record any new happenings. Imagine how they'll spread across the webz...We need to hurry and record something that fits. If we work it out, everyone will hear it when they watch the video."

"I uphold this motion," Charsky nodded his shaggy head. "Kiera, your task is to get into every nook and cranny of the renegades' camp and shake everyone down for info, so we can get as much material as possible. To hell with rep, penalties and the ruin of your character. The most important thing is the video and the content. Everyone else gets to work on suitable music. We'll meet once a day and each person will present what they have. This doesn't extend to you Kiera—you're working on the Geranika thing. You can join us whenever you die."

"I can think of some tunes in-game too. I'll send you the video and you can edit it yourselves," I proposed.

"Uh-huh, let's do it that way," Beast hummed approvingly. "Just try and send us any interesting footage you get. We'll be working on it as it comes in. And now, turn the holoprojector off and get in that capsule. Oh and say hi to Pasha and Sasha."

"Will do."

The indicated individuals were waiting for me at a decked-out table and welcomed the new plan with measured skepticism and immeasurable appetite.

"Ah' you shure...you...wont..." Sasha said with a stuffed mouth, for which he earned an unkind look from Chip. Getting the hint, he swallowed his mouthful and went on with his question: "...get sick of marinating in the capsule for days on end?"

"Well if I manage to avoid dying, then I'll marinate as long as I can. I think the embassy should be arriving soon and that means that things will come to a head. I need to make it in time for that momentous occasion."

"And what am I supposed to do all alone?" Chip asked pitifully. "Killing bunnies on my lonesome is pretty boring. Maybe I should join the schismatics too?"

"They're renegades, not schismatics," I corrected Pasha proudly. "I don't know...Maybe let's play it differently? When you respawn, ask for a meeting with Eben and tell him that I joined the renegades as a double agent and that I'll be sending him information through you. In this manner, you'll get embroiled in the conflict, but on the other side, which will help us see the full picture a lot better."

Pasha thought a bit, twirled his juice straw in his fingers and replied:

"Yeah, we could do it this way. There's even a chance that they'll forgive you in exchange for your work, but...I'm not Austin Powers or James Bond. I'm not sure I'm much of a spy at all, in fact."

"There is time for us to consider what to do," I sighed. Meanwhile, Sasha had perked up.

"Heed me, oh Darth Lori, now you can cross the Arras without any trouble, so you can pick me up and then take me with you on your way back. You've already borked your reputation and I couldn't care what those triffids think."

"Didn't you tell me that you were sick of the game?" I asked with surprise.

"I mean, it's not like I'll have anything to do anyway if you two are stuck in your glorified jars day and night. Lena's wedding's over, the barbecue's eaten, the vodka's drunk and now there's nothing to do. And here's a chance to become a Sith Lord."

He made a grimace worthy of an epic hero of antiquity caught in the loo—his best imitation of Darth Maul.

"And how will you get through half a continent's worth of raging mobs?" I asked, genuinely curious.

"By means of shuttle diplomacy," Sasha replied enigmatically. "You just make sure to make it through to the Arras. I'll hash out the details once you're there. And while you're at it, you should map the blighted part of the forest along the way."

"Deal!" I raised the wine glass full of juice and triumphantly announced: "To the Dark Side of the Force!"

Three glasses clinked against each other, welcoming the arrival of a new life in Barliona.

"To the Shadow Bard."

END OF BOOK ONE

FROM THE AUTHORS

Dear Readers,

We are very pleased that you have read our work. For both authors this was the first time writing collaboratively: The work was very arduous and we constantly had to argue with one another, defending our points of view. We hope that the outcome was successful and you enjoyed it. If not, we will continue to work in order to make the next books better and more interesting. Please leave your comments about the work. It's important for us to receive feedback from our readers.

We have a nice surprise for all of our readers! A story we wrote which we wish to give you for free. Go to **www.Mako-books.com**, register and receive an extra story for free. Over the next year, I — Vasiliy Mahanenko — will publish one new, previously-unpublished story to every one of my novels, including those published on Amazon, for free. All new books that are published under my name will also feature free stories, published on this site.

Share the news with your friends and make them happy. Pleasant reading!

Want to be the first to know about our latest LitRPG, sci fi and fantasy titles from your favorite authors?

Subscribe to our **NEW RELEASES** newsletter:
http://eepurl.com/b7niIL

Thank you for reading *The Renegades!*

If you like what you've read, check out other LitRPG novels published by Magic Dome Books:

An NPC's Path LitRPG series by Pavel Kornev:
The Dead Rogue

Level Up series by Dan Sugralinov:
Re-Start

**The Way of the Shaman LitRPG series
by Vasily Mahanenko:**
Survival Quest
The Kartoss Gambit
The Secret of the Dark Forest
The Phantom Castle
The Karmadont Chess Set
Shaman's Revenge
Clans War

Dark Paladin LitRPG series by Vasily Mahanenko:
The Beginning
The Quest
Restart

Galactogon LitRPG series by Vasily Mahanenko:
Start the Game!

The Neuro LitRPG series by Andrei Livadny:
The Crystal Sphere
The Curse of Rion Castle
The Reapers

Phantom Server LitRPG series by Andrei Livadny:
Edge of Reality
The Outlaw
Black Sun

The Sublime Electricity series by Pavel Kornev
The Illustrious
The Heartless
The Fallen
The Dormant

You're in Game!
(LitRPG Stories from Bestselling Authors)

You're in Game-2!
(More LitRPG stories set in your favorite worlds)

The Game Master series by A. Bobl and A. Levitsky:
The Lag

The Naked Demon by Sherrie L.
(a paranormal romance)

More books and series are coming out soon!

In order to have new books of the series translated faster, we need your help and support! Please consider leaving a review or spread the word by recommending *The Renegades* to your friends and posting the link on social media. The more people buy the book, the sooner we'll be able to make new translations available. Thank you!

Till next time!